# AT AGINCOURT

A Tale Of The White Hoods Of Paris

By

## G. A. Henty

# About G. A. Henty

George Alfred Hent was born in Trumpington, near Cambridge but spent some of his childhood in Canterbury. He was a sickly child who had to spend long periods in bed. During his frequent illnesses he became an avid reader and developed a wide range of interests which he carried into adulthood. He attended Westminster School, London, as a half-boarder when he was fourteen, :2 and later Gonville and Caius College, Cambridge, where he was a keen sportsman.

He left the university early without completing his degree to volunteer for the (Army) Hospital Commissariat of the Purveyors Department when the Crimean War began. He was sent to the Crimea and while there he witnessed the appalling conditions under which the British soldier had to fight. His letters home were filled with vivid descriptions of what he saw. His father was impressed by his letters and sent them to the Morning Advertiser newspaper which printed them. This initial writing success was a factor in Henty's later decision to accept the offer to become a special correspondent, the early name for journalists now better known as war correspondents.

# At Agincourt

Shortly before resigning from the army as a captain in 1859 he married Elizabeth Finucane. The couple had four children. Elizabeth died in 1865 after a long illness and shortly after her death Henty began writing articles for the Standard newspaper. In 1866 the newspaper sent him as their special correspondent to report on the Austro-Italian War where he met Giuseppe Garibaldi. He went on to cover the 1868 British punitive expedition to Abyssinia, the Franco-Prussian War, the Ashanti War, the Carlist Rebellion in Spain and the Turco-Serbian War. He also witnessed the opening of the Suez Canal and travelled to Palestine, Russia and India.

Henty was a strong supporter of the British Empire all his life; according to literary critic Kathryn Castle: "Henty ... exemplified the ethos of the [British Empire], and glorified in its successes". Henty's ideas about politics were influenced by writers such as Sir Charles Dilke and Thomas Carlyle.

Henty once related in an interview how his storytelling skills grew out of tales told after dinner to his children. He wrote his first children's book, Out on the Pampas in 1868, naming the book's main characters after his children. The book was published by Griffith and Farran in November 1870 with a title page date of 1871. While most of the 122 books he wrote were for children and published by Blackie and Son of London, he also wrote adult novels, non-fiction such as The March to Magdala and Those Other Animals, short stories for the likes of The Boy's Own Paper and edited the Union Jack, a weekly boy's magazine.

Henty was "the most popular Boy's author of his day." Blackie, who published his children's fiction in the UK, and W. G. Blackie estimated in February 1952 that they were producing about 150,000 Henty books a year at the height of his popularity, and stated that their records showed they had produced over three and a half million Henty books. He further estimated that considering the US and other overseas authorised and pirated editions, a total of 25 million was not impossible. Arnold notes this estimate and that there have been further editions since that estimate was made.

His children's novels typically revolved around a boy or young man living in troubled times. These ranged from the Punic War to more recent conflicts such as the Napoleonic Wars or the American Civil War. Henty's heroes – which occasionally included young ladies – are uniformly intelligent, courageous, honest and resourceful with plenty of 'pluck' yet are also modest. These themes have made Henty's novels popular today among many conservative Christians and homeschoolers.

Henty usually researched his novels by ordering several books on the subject he was writing on from libraries, and consulting them before beginning writing. Some of his books were written about events (such as the Crimean War) that he witnessed himself; hence, these books are written with greater detail as Henty drew upon his first-hand experiences of people, places, and events.

On 16 November 1902, Henty died aboard his yacht in Weymouth Harbour, Dorset, leaving unfinished his last novel, By Conduct and Courage, which was completed by his son Captain C.G. Henty.

Henty is buried in Brompton Cemetery, London.

Henty wrote 122 works of historical fiction and all first editions had the date printed at the foot of the title page.[15] Several short stories published in book form are included in this total, with the stories taken from previously published full-length novels. The dates given below are those printed at the foot of the title page of the very first editions in the United Kingdom. It is a common misconception that American Henty titles were published before those of the UK. All Henty titles bar one were published in the UK before those of America.

The simple explanation for this error of judgement is that Charles Scribner's Sons of New York dated their Henty first editions for the current year. The first UK editions published by Blackie were always dated for the coming year, to have them looking fresh for Christmas. The only Henty title published in book form in America before the UK book was In the Hands of the Cave-Dwellers dated 1900 and published by Harper of New York. This title was published in book form in the UK in 1903, although the story itself had already been published in England prior to the first American edition, in The Boy's Own Annual.

# LITERARY CRITIQUES

George Alfred Henty (1832–1902) was a British novelist and writer known for his historical adventure stories for children and young adults. His works often combined fictional characters with real historical events, aiming to educate young readers about history while also providing entertaining narratives. Henty's writing style and themes have been the subject of various literary critiques over the years. Here are some common points made by critics:

**Formulaic Structure:** One common critique of Henty's works is that they tend to follow a formulaic structure. Many of his novels share similar plotlines, where a young British protagonist overcomes challenges, exhibits moral values, and plays a significant role in historical events. Critics argue that this predictable structure might make his stories less engaging for older or more experienced readers.

**Simplistic Characterization:** Some critics have noted that Henty's characters can be rather one-dimensional, often falling into stereotypical roles. The heroes are typically brave, resourceful, and morally upright, while the villains are often portrayed as scheming and unscrupulous. This lack of complexity in character development can limit the emotional depth of the stories.

**Colonial and Imperialist Views:** Henty's works are reflective of the time period in which he lived, which saw the height of the British Empire's power and influence. Some critics argue that his novels promote colonial and imperialist viewpoints, as they often depict British characters as heroic figures bringing civilization to "uncivilized" regions. This portrayal can be seen as ethnocentric and insensitive to the experiences and perspectives of other cultures.

**Educational Value:** Henty's novels have been praised for their educational value, as they introduce readers to historical events and periods that might not be covered in traditional history textbooks. However, critics have pointed out that his narratives sometimes prioritize historical accuracy at the expense of engaging storytelling, resulting in passages that read more like history lessons than compelling fiction.

**Language and Style:** Henty's writing style can be considered somewhat dated by modern standards. His prose tends to be formal and descriptive, which might not resonate with contemporary readers, especially younger ones. Some critics argue that the language could create a barrier for readers seeking fast-paced and accessible narratives.

**Relevance to Modern Readers:** Another point of critique is the relevance of Henty's works to modern readers. While his stories offer insights into historical contexts, some critics question whether his themes and values align with contemporary sensibilities and whether young readers today would find his narratives engaging.

**Limited Diversity:** Henty's works often lack diverse representation, both in terms of characters and perspectives. Critics have noted that his novels predominantly focus on white, male British protagonists, which can limit the inclusivity and relatability of his stories for a broader readership.

In summary, while George Alfred Henty's historical adventure novels have been cherished by many readers over the years for their educational content and engaging narratives, they have also faced criticism for their formulaic structure, simplistic characterization, colonial viewpoints, and limited relevance to modern audiences. It's important to approach his works with an understanding of the historical context in which they were written and to consider these critiques alongside their literary merits.

# CONTENTS

# PREFACE

The long and bloody feud between the houses of Orleans and Burgundy —which for many years devastated France, caused a prodigious destruction of life and property, and was not even relaxed in the presence of a common enemy—is very fully recorded in the pages of Monstrelet and other contemporary historians. I have here only attempted to relate the events of the early portion of the struggle—from its commencement up to the astonishing victory of Agincourt, won by a handful of Englishmen over the chivalry of France. Here the two factions, with the exception of the Duke of Burgundy himself, laid aside their differences for the moment, only to renew them while France still lay prostrate at the feet of the English conqueror.

At this distance of time, even with all the records at one's disposal, it is difficult to say which party was most to blame in this disastrous civil war, a war which did more to cripple the power of France than was ever accomplished by English arms. Unquestionably Burgundy was the first to enter upon the struggle, but the terrible vengeance taken by the Armagnacs, —as the Orleanists came to be called,—for the murders committed by the mob of Paris in alliance with him, was of almost unexampled atrocity in civil war, and was mainly responsible for the terrible acts of cruelty afterwards perpetrated upon each other by both parties. I hope some day to devote another volume to the story of this desperate and unnatural struggle.

**G. A. HENTY.**

"GUY AYLMER SAVES THE KING'S LIFE AT THE BATTLE OF AGINCOURT."

# CHAPTER I — A FEUDAL CASTLE

"And is it true that our lord and lady sail next week for their estate in France?"

"Ay, it is true enough, and more is the pity; it was a sad day for us all when the king gave the hand of his ward, our lady, to this baron of Artois."

"They say she was willing enough, Peter."

"Ay, ay, all say she loved him, and, being a favourite with the queen, she got her to ask the king to accede to the knight's suit; and no wonder, he is as proper a man as eyes can want to look on—tall and stately, and they say brave. His father and grandfather both were Edward's men, and held their castle for us; his father was a great friend of the Black Prince, and he, too, took a wife from England. Since then things have not gone well with us in France, and they say that our lord has had difficulty in keeping clear of the quarrels that are always going on out there between the great French lords; and, seeing that we have but little power in Artois, he has to hold himself discreetly, and to keep aloof as far as he can from the strife there, and bide his time until the king sends an army to win back his own again. But I doubt not that, although our lady's wishes and the queen's favour may have gone some way with him, the king thought more of the advantage of keeping this French noble,—whose fathers have always been faithful vassals of the crown, and who was himself English on his mother's side,— faithful to us, ready for the time when the royal banner will flutter in the wind again, and blood will flow as it did at Cressy and Poitiers."

"The example of a good knight like Sir Eustace taking the field for us with his retainers might lead others to follow his example; besides, there were several suitors for our lady's hand, and, by giving her to this French baron, there would be less offence and heart-burning than if he had chosen one among her English suitors. And, indeed, I know not that we have suffered much from its being so; it is true that our lord and lady live much on their estates abroad, but at least they are here part of their time, and their castellan does not press us more heavily during their absence than does our lord when at home."

# At Agincourt

"He is a goodly knight, is Sir Aylmer, a just man and kindly, and, being a cousin of our lady's, they do wisely and well in placing all things in his hands during their absence."

"Ay, we have nought to grumble at, for we might have done worse if we had had an English lord for our master, who might have called us into the field when he chose, and have pressed us to the utmost of his rights whenever he needed money."

The speakers were a man and woman, who were standing looking on at a party of men practising at the butts on the village green at Summerley, one of the hamlets on the estates of Sir Eustace de Villeroy, in Hampshire.

"Well shot!" the man exclaimed, as an archer pierced a white wand at a distance of eighty yards. "They are good shots all, and if our lord and lady have fears of troubles in France, they do right well in taking a band of rare archers with them. There are but five-and-twenty of them, but they are all of the best. When they offered prizes here a month since for the bowmen of Hants and Sussex and Dorset, methought they had some good reason why they should give such high prizes as to bring hither the best men from all three counties, and we were all proud that four of our own men should have held their own so well in such company, and especially that Tom, the miller's son, should have beaten the best of them. He is captain of the band, you know, but almost all the others shoot nigh as well; there is not one of them who cannot send an arrow straight into the face of a foe at a hundred and twenty yards. There were some others as good who would fain have been of the party, but our lady said she would take no married men, and she was right. They go for five years certain, and methinks a man fights all the better when he knows there is no one in England praying for his return, and that if he falls, there is no widow or children to bewail his loss. There are as many stout men-at-arms going too; so the Castle of Villeroy will be a hard nut for anyone to crack, for I hear they can put a hundred and fifty of their vassals there in the field."

"We shall miss Sir Aylmer's son Guy," the woman said; "he is ever down at the village green when there are sports going on. There is not one of his age who can send an arrow so straight to the mark, and not many of the men; and he can hold his own with a quarter-staff too."

"Ay, dame; he is a stout lad, and a hearty one. They say that at the castle he is ever practising with arms, and that though scarce sixteen he can wield a sword and heavy battle-axe as well as any man-at-arms there."

"He is gentle too," the woman said. "Since his mother's death he often comes down with wine and other goodies if anyone is ill, and he speaks as softly as a girl. There is not one on the estate but has a good word for him, nor doubts that he will grow up as worthy a knight as his father, though gentler perhaps in his manner, and less grave in face, for he was ever a merry lad. Since the death of his lady mother two years ago he has gone about sadly, still of late he has gotten over his loss somewhat, and he can laugh heartily again. I wonder his father can bear to part with him."

"Sir Eustace knows well enough that he cannot always keep the boy by his side, dame; and that if a falcon is to soar well, he must try his wings early. He goes as page, does he not?"

"Ay, but more, methinks, as companion to young Henry, who has, they say, been sickly from a child, and, though better now, has scarce the making of a stalwart knight in him. His young brother Charles is a sturdy little chap, and bids fair to take after his father; and little Lady Agnes, who comes between them, is full of fire and spirit.

"Yes; methinks Guy will have a pleasant time of it out there; that is, if there are no fresh troubles. I doubt not that in two or three years he will be one of our lord's esquires, and if he has a chance of displaying his courage and skill, may be back among us a dubbed knight before many years have passed over our heads. France is a rare place for gaining honours, and so it may well be, for I see not that we gain much else by our king's possessions there."

"There was plenty of spoil brought over, dame, after Cressy and Poitiers."

"Ay, but it soon goes; easy come, easy go, you know; and though they say that each man that fought there brought home a goodly share of spoil, I will warrant me the best part went down their throats ere many months had passed."

"'Tis ever so, dame; but I agree with you, and deem that it would be better for England if we did not hold a foot of ground in France, and if English kings and nobles were content to live quietly among their people. We have spent more money than ever we made in these wars, and even were our kings to become indeed, as they claim, kings of France as well as England, the ill would be much greater, as far as I can see, for us all. Still there may be things, dame, that we country folks don't understand, and I suppose that it must be so, else Parliament would not be so willing to vote money always when the kings want it for wars with France. The wars in France don't affect us as much as those with Scotland and Wales. When our kings go to France to fight they take with them only such as are willing to go, men-at-arms and archers; but when we have troubles such as took place but five or six years ago, when Douglas and Percy and the Welsh all joined against us, then the lords call out their vassals and the sheriffs the militia of the county, and we have to go to fight willy-nilly. Our lord had a hundred of us with him to fight for the king at Shrewsbury. Nigh thirty never came back again. That is worse than the French wars, dame."

"Don't I know it, for wasn't my second boy one of those who never came back. Ay, ay, they had better be fighting in France, perhaps, for that lets out the hot blood that might otherwise bring on fighting at home."

"That is so, dame, things are all for the best, though one does not always see it."

A week later all the tenantry gathered in front of the castle to wish God-speed to their lord and lady, and to watch the following by which they were accompanied. First there passed half a dozen mounted men-at-arms, who were to accompany the party but half a day's march and then to return with Sir Aylmer. Next to these rode Sir Eustace and Lady Margaret, still a beautiful woman, a worthy mate of her noble-looking husband. On her other side rode Sir Aylmer; then came John Harpen, Sir Eustace's esquire; beside whom trotted Agnes, a bright, merry-faced girl of twelve. Guy rode with the two boys; then came twenty-four men-at-arms, many of whom had fought well and stoutly at Shrewsbury; while Tom, the miller's son, or, as he was generally called, Long Tom, strode along at the head of twenty-four bowmen, each of whom carried the long English bow and quiver full of cloth-yard arrows, and, in addition, a heavy axe at his leathern girdle.

Behind these were some servitors leading horses carrying provisions for the journey, and valises with the clothes of Sir Eustace, his wife, and children, and a heavy cart drawn by four strong horses with the bundles of extra garments for the men-at-arms and archers, and several large sheaves of spare arrows. The men-at-arms wore iron caps, as also breast and back pieces. On the shoulders and arms of their leathern jerkins iron rings were sewn thickly, forming a sort of chain armour, while permitting perfect freedom of the limbs. The archers also wore steel caps, which, like those of the men-at-arms, came low down on the neck and temples. They had on tough leathern frocks, girded in at the waist, and falling to the knee; some of them had also iron rings sewn on the shoulders. English archers were often clad in green cloth, but Sir Eustace had furnished the garments, and had chosen leather, both as being far more durable, and as offering a certain amount of defence.

The frocks were sleeveless, and each man wore cloth sleeves of a colour according to his fancy. The band was in all respects a well-appointed one. As Sir Eustace wished to avoid exciting comment among his neighbours, he had abstained from taking a larger body of men; and it was partly for this reason that he had decided not to dress the archers in green. But every man had been carefully picked; the men-at-arms were all powerful fellows who had seen service; the archers were little inferior in physique, for strength as well as skill was required in archery, and in choosing the men Sir Eustace had, when there was no great difference in point of skill, selected the most powerful among those who were willing to take service with him.

Guy enjoyed the two days' ride to Southampton greatly. It was the first time that he had been away from home, and his spirits were high at thus starting on a career that would, he hoped, bring him fame and honour. Henry and his brother and sister were also in good glee, although the journey was no novelty to them, for they had made it twice previously. Beyond liking change, as was natural at their age, they cared not whether they were at their English or at their French home, as they spoke both languages with equal fluency, and their life at one castle differed but little from that at the other.

Embarking at Portsmouth in a ship that was carrying military stores to Calais, they coasted along the shores of Sussex and of Kent as far as Dungeness, and then made across to Calais. It was early in April, the weather was exceptionally favourable, and they encountered no rough seas whatever. On the way Sir Eustace related to Guy and his sons the events that had taken place in France, and had led up to the civil war that was raging so furiously there.

"In 1392, the King of France being seized with madness, the Dukes of Burgundy and Orleans in a very short time wrested the power of the state from the hands of his faithful councillors, the Constable de Clisson, La Riviere, and others. De Clisson retired to his estate and castle at Montelhery, the two others were seized and thrown into prison. De Clisson was prosecuted before Parliament as a false and wicked traitor; but the king, acting on the advice of Orleans, who had not then broken with the Dukes of Burgundy and Berri, had, after La Riviere and another had been in prison for a year, stopped the prosecution, and restored their estates to them. Until 1402 the Dukes of Burgundy and Berri were all-powerful, and in 1396 a great number of knights and nobles, led by John, Count of Nevers, the eldest son of the Duke of Burgundy, went to the assistance of the King of Hungary, which country was being invaded by the Turks. They were, however, on the 28th of September, utterly defeated. The greater portion of them were killed; Nevers and the rest were ransomed and brought home.

"In 1402 the king, influenced by his wife, Isobel, and his brother, the Duke of Orleans, who were on terms of the closest alliance, placed the entire government in the hands of the latter, who at once began to abuse it to such an extent, by imposing enormous taxes upon the clergy and the people, that he paved the way for the return of his uncle of Burgundy to power. On the 27th of April, 1404, Philip the Bold of Burgundy died. He was undoubtedly ambitious, but he was also valiant and able, and he had the good of France at heart. He was succeeded by his son John, called the Fearless, from the bravery that he had displayed in the unfortunate Hungarian campaign. The change was disastrous for France. John was violent and utterly unscrupulous, and capable of any deed to gratify either his passions, jealousies, or hatreds. At first he cloaked his designs against Orleans by an appearance of friendship, paid him a visit at his castle near Vincennes, where he was at the time lying ill. When he recovered, the two princes went to mass together, dined at their uncle's, the Duke of Berri, and together entered Paris; and the Parisians fondly hoped that there was an end of the rivalry that had done so much harm. It was, however, but a very short time afterwards that, on the 23d of November, 1407, as the Duke of Orleans was returning from having dined with the queen, and was riding with only two esquires and four or five men on foot carrying torches, twenty armed men sprang out from behind a house and rushed upon him.

"'I am the Duke of Orleans,' the prince cried; but they hurled him from his mule, and as he tried to rise to his feet one blow struck off the hand he raised to protect his head, other blows rained down upon him from axe and sword, and in less than a minute the duke lay dead. The Duke of Burgundy at first affected grief and indignation, but at the council the next day he boldly avowed that Orleans had been killed by his orders. He at once took horse and rode to the frontier of Flanders, which he reached safely, though hotly chased by a party of the Duke of Orleans' knights. The duke's widow, who was in the country at the time, hastened up to Paris with her children, and appealed for justice to the king, who declared that he regarded the deed done to his brother as done to himself. The Dukes of Berri and Bourbon, the Constable and Chancellor, all assured her that she should have justice; but there was no force that could hope to cope with that which Burgundy could bring into the field, and when, two months later, Burgundy entered Paris at the head of a thousand men-at-arms, no attempt was made at resistance, and the murderer was received with acclamations by the fickle populace.

"The king at the time was suffering from one of his terrible fits of insanity, but a great assembly was held, at which princes, councillors, lords, doctors of law, and prominent citizens were present. A monk of the Cordeliers, named John Petit, then spoke for five hours in justification of the duke, and the result was that the poor insane king was induced to sign letters cancelling the penalty of the crime. For four months the duke remained absolute master of Paris, disposing of all posts and honours, and sparing no efforts to render himself popular with the burghers. A serious rebellion breaking out at Liege, and the troops sent against the town being repulsed, he was obliged to leave Paris to put down the revolt. As soon as he had left, the queen and the partisans of Orleans prepared to take advantage of his absence, and two months later Queen Isobel marched with the dauphin, now some thirteen years old, from Melun with three thousand men.

"The Parisians received her with applause, and as soon as she had taken up her quarters at the Louvre, the Dukes of Berri, Bourbon, and Brittany, the Constable, and all the great officers of the court rallied round her. Two days later the Duchess of Orleans arrived with a long train of mourning coaches. A great assembly was held, and the king's advocate announced to them the intention of the king to confer the government upon the queen during his illness, and produced a document signed by the king to that effect. The Duchess of Orleans then came forward, and kneeling before the dauphin, begged for justice for the death of her husband, and that she might be granted an opportunity of refuting the calumnies that John Petit had heaped on the memory of her husband. A week later another great assembly was held, and the justification of the duke was read, refuting all these imputations, and the duchess's advocate demanded that the duke should be forced to make public reparation, and then to be exiled for twenty years. The dauphin replied that he and all the princes of blood royal present held that the charges against the Duke of Orleans had been amply refuted, and that the demands with reference to the Duke of Burgundy should be provided for in course of justice.

"Scarcely had the assembly broken up when it became known that Burgundy and his army was on the way back to Paris. Resistance was out of the question; therefore, taking the young dauphin with her, and accompanied by all the members of the royal family, the queen retired to Tours. Burgundy, unscrupulous as he was, finding that although he might remain master of Paris, he could not hope to rule France, except when acting under the pretence of the king's authority, soon sent an embassy to Tours to endeavour to arrange matters. He was able to effect this with the less difficulty, that the Duchess of Orleans had just died from grief at her husband's death, and at the hopelessness of obtaining vengeance on his murderer. The queen was won to the cause of Burgundy by secret proposals submitted to her for a close league between them, and in March a treaty was concluded, and a meeting took place at Chartres, at which the duke, the king, the queen, the royal princes, and the young Duke of Orleans and his adherents were present.

"The king declared that he pardoned the duke, and the princes of Orleans consented to obey his orders and to lay aside all hatred and thoughts of vengeance, and shortly afterwards Paris welcomed with shouts of joy the return of the king and queen and the apparent reconciliation of all parties. But the truce was a brief one; for the princes and adherents of Orleans might bend before circumstances at the moment, but their feelings were unchanged.

# At Agincourt

"A head of the party was needed, and the young duke married the daughter of Count Bernard d'Armagnac, one of the most powerful and ambitious nobles of the south of France, who at once,—in concert with the Dukes of Berri and Brittany and other lords,—put himself at the head of the Orleans party. On the 10th of July, 1411, the three princes of Orleans sent a long letter to the king, complaining that no reparation whatever had been made for the murder of their father, and begging him that, as what was done at Chartres was contrary to every principle of law, equity, reason, and justice, the case should be reopened again. They also made complaints against the Duke of Burgundy for his conduct and abuse of power.

"As the king was surrounded by Burgundy's creatures no favourable reply was returned, and a formal challenge or declaration of war was, on the 18th of July, sent by the princes to the Duke of Burgundy, and both parties began at once to make preparation for war.

"Now for my own view of this quarrel. King Henry sent for me a year since, and asked for whom I should hold my castle if Orleans and Burgundy came to blows, adding that Burgundy would be viewed by him with most favour.

"'My father and grandfather ever fought faithfully in the service of England,' I said; 'but for years past now, the line betwixt your majesty's possessions and those of France has been drawn in, and my estates and Castle of Villeroy now lie beyond the line, and I am therefore a vassal of France as well as of your majesty. It being known to all men that even before I became Lord of Summerley, on my marriage with your majesty's ward, Mistress Margaret, I, like my father, held myself to be the liege man of the King of England. I am therefore viewed with much hostility by my neighbours, and right gladly would they seize upon any excuse to lay complaint against me before the king, in order that I might be deprived of my fief and castle.

"'This I would fain hold always for your majesty; and, seeing how it is situated but a few miles across the frontier, it is, I would humbly submit to you, of importance to your majesty that it should be held by one faithful to you—since its possession in the hands of an enemy would greatly hinder any English army marching out from Calais to the invasion of France. It is a place of some strength now; but were it in French hands it might be made very much stronger, and would cost much time and loss of men to besiege. At present your majesty is in alliance with Burgundy, but none can say how the war will go, or what changes will take place; and should the Orleanists gain the upper hand, they will be quick to take advantage of my having fought for Burgundy, and would confiscate my estates and hand them over to one who might be hostile to England, and pledged to make the castle a stronghold that would greatly hinder and bar the advance of an English army upon Paris. Therefore, Sire, I would, not for my own sake but for the sake of your majesty's self and your successors, pray you to let me for a while remain quietly at Summerley until the course of events in France is determined.'

"The king was pleased to see the force of what I urged. As far as I had inclinations in the case, they were towards the cause, not of Burgundy himself, whose murder of Orleans was alike treacherous and indefensible, but of his cause, seeing that Flanders is wholly under his authority, and that in Artois he is well-nigh paramount at present. On the other hand, Amiens and Ponthieu, which lie but a short distance to the south of me, are strongly Orleanist, and I have therefore every motive for standing aloof. So far the fortune of war has been so changeable that one cannot say that the chances incline towards one faction more than the other. Even the Church has failed to bring about the end of the troubles. The Orleanists have been formally placed under interdicts, and cursed by book, bell, and candle. The king's commands have been laid upon all to put aside their quarrels, but both the ban of the Church and the king's commands have been ineffectual. I am as anxious as ever to abstain from taking any part in the trouble, the more so as the alliance between our king and Burgundy has cooled somewhat. But I have received such urgent prayers from my vassals at Villeroy to come among them, since they are now being plundered by both parties, that I feel it is time for me to take up my abode there. When the king stayed at Winchester, a month since, I laid the matter before him. He was pleased to say that what I had urged a year ago had turned out to be as I foretold, and that he would give me leave to go over and establish myself at Villeroy, and to hold myself aloof from both parties until the matter should further ripen. What will come of it I cannot say. The English king seemed to me to be ailing, and I fear that it may not be long before young Henry comes to the throne. He is a wild young prince, but has already shown himself in the Northern war to be full of spirit and courage, and methinks that when he comes to the throne he will not long observe the peaceful policy of his father, but that we shall see the royal standard once again spread to the winds of France."

"But, Sir Eustace," Guy said, when he had concluded, "how do these matters affect you? I thought that by the treaty the west part of Artois was English."

"Ay, lad, it was so settled; but at that time the strength of France had been broken at Poitiers, and the Black Prince and his army were so feared that his terms were willingly accepted in order to secure peace. Much has happened since then: war has been constantly going on, sometimes hotly, sometimes sluggishly; France has had her own troubles, and as the English kings have been more pacific, and England has become weary of bearing the heavy expenses of the war, the treaty has become a dead letter. Gascony, in which province Armagnac is the greatest lord, is altogether lost to England, as is the greater part of Guienne. A great proportion of the people there were always bitterly opposed to the change, and, as you know, even in the time of the Black Prince himself there were great rebellions and troubles; since then town after town and castle after castle has declared for France, and no real efforts have ever been made by the English to win them back again. I, who in England am an English baron, and—so long as things go on as at present—a French noble while in France, am in a perilous position between my two Suzerains. Were an English army to land, I should join them, for I still hold myself to be a vassal of the king of England, as we have been for three generations. As to the French disputes, I fear that sooner or later I shall have to declare in favour of one party or the other, for it will be difficult to stand altogether aloof from these conflicts, because all men, at least all men of condition, are well-nigh forced to take one side or the other. The plea that I am a baron of England will be of no avail, for both sides would turn against me and be glad of an excuse for pillaging and confiscating my estate. At present, then, I must regard myself solely as a French noble, for Villeroy has passed into the hands of France, just as for a while it passed into the hands of England, and if this war goes on we shall have to take a side."

"And to which side do your thoughts incline, Sir Eustace, if I may ask you?"

"I love not either side, Guy, and would fain, if it could be so, that my sword should remain in its sheath. I fear that I shall have to go with Burgundy, for he is all-powerful in Artois; but had I been altogether free to choose, I should have sided with Orleans. In the first place, it is certain that the last duke was foully murdered by Burgundy, who thereby laid the foundation for the present troubles. There were jealousies before, as there have always been between the great nobles, but that act forced almost all to take sides. The Dukes of Berri and Brittany, who had been of the party of the late Duke of Burgundy, were driven by this foul act of his son to range themselves with Orleans. Armagnac is very powerful in the south, Berri's dukedom is in the north, that of Orleans to the north-east. Burgundy's strength lies in his own dukedom,—which has ever been all but independent of France,—in Flanders, in Artois, and in Paris; thus, generally, it is the north and east of France against the south and west. This is broadly the case, but in a civil war provinces and countships, neighbours, ay, and families, become split up into factions, as interest, or family ties, or the desire to increase an estate by annexing another next to it, may influence the minds of men.

"So long as it is but a war between the great dukes and princes of France we smaller men may hope to hold aloof, but, as it goes on, and evil deeds are done on both sides, men's passions become heated, the spirit spreads until every man's hand is against his neighbour, and he who joins not against one or the other finds both ready to oppress and rob him. I should not have cared to bring out an English following with me had we been forced to march any distance through France; but as Villeroy is but a few miles from the frontier, and of that distance well-nigh half is through my own estates, we can reach the castle almost unnoticed. Once there, the fact that I have strengthened my garrison will keep me from attack, for either party would be chary in attacking one who can defend himself stoutly. I was minded to leave your lady and the two younger children in England, but in truth she begged so hard to accompany me that I could not say her nay."

The Castle of Villeroy was somewhat larger than the one in which Guy had been born and brought up. The plan, however, was very similar: there was the central keep, but, whereas at home this was the dwelling-house of the family, it was here used as a storehouse, and the apartments of the count and countess were in the range of buildings that formed an inner court round the keep. In point of luxury the French were in advance of the English, and they had already begun to combine comfort with strength in their buildings. The apartments struck Guy as being wonderfully spacious in comparison to those with which he was accustomed. On the ground floor of one side of the square was the banqueting-hall. Its walls were decorated with arms and armour, the joists that supported the floor above were carved, the windows large and spacious, for, looking as they did into the inner court, there was no occasion for their being mere loopholes. Above the banqueting-hall was a room where Lady Margaret sat with her maids engaged in working at tapestry; here the priest gave such slight instruction as was then considered necessary to Agnes and Charles; Henry had already passed out of his hands.

Next to this room was the knight's sleeping apartment, or closet as it was then called, a room which would now be considered of ridiculously straitened dimensions; and close to it were the still smaller closets of the children. Beyond were a series of guest-chambers. Another side of the court-yard contained the apartments of the castellan, Jean Bouvard, a sturdy soldier of long experience, and those of the other officers of the household; the other two sides were occupied by the chapel, the kitchens, and the offices of the servants and retainers. All these rooms were loopholed on the side looking into the outer court. This was considerably wider and more extensive than the one surrounding the keep. Here were the stables, storehouses for grain and forage, and a building, just erected, for the lodging of the English garrison. All these buildings stood against the outer wall, so that they would afford no shelter to an enemy who had obtained possession of the first defences and was making an attack against the second line. The outer wall was twelve feet in thickness, and thirty feet above the court; outside the height was considerably greater, as there was a moat faced with stone fifteen feet deep entirely surrounding it, and containing seven or eight feet of water.

Walls ran half across the outer court, and, from the end of these, light wooden bridges formed a communication with the wall of the inner court, so that in the event of the outer wall being stormed or the gates being carried by assault, the defenders could retire to the inner defences. the ends of these bridges rested upon irons projecting from the wall, and so arranged that they could be instantly withdrawn when the last of the defenders had crossed over, when the bridges would at once fall into the court-yard below. The inner wall was twelve feet higher than the outer one, and, like it, was provided with a crenellated battlement four feet high; there were projecting turrets at each corner, and one in the middle of each side.

The keep rose twenty feet higher than the wall of the inner court. The lower portions of the cross walls of the outer court were carried on as far as the inner wall, thereby dividing the space into four; strong gates gave communication from one to the other. Into these could be driven the cattle of the tenantry, and one of them contained a number of huts in which the tenants themselves would be lodged. The court-yard facing the entrance was the largest of the areas into which the space between the outer and inner walls was divided, extending the whole width between the outer walls. Here the military exercises were carried on. Along the wall, at each side of the gate, were a range of stables for the use of the horses of guests, with rooms over them for the use of their retainers. There was a strong exterior work defending the approach to the drawbridge on the other side of the moat, and in all respects the castle was well appointed, and to Guy it seemed almost impossible that it could be carried by assault, however numerous the foe.

# CHAPTER II — TROUBLES IN FRANCE

As soon as it was heard that the lord and lady had returned, the vassals of Villeroy came in to pay their respects, and presents of fowls, game, and provisions of all kinds poured in. The table in the banqueting-hall was bountifully spread, casks of wine broached, and all who came received entertainment. As French was still spoken a good deal at the English court and among the nobles and barons, and was considered part of the necessary education of all persons of gentle blood, Guy, who had always used it in his conversation with his father, had no difficulty in performing his duty of seeing that the wants of all who came were well attended to. In a few days guests of higher degree came in, the knights and barons of that part of the province; a few of these expressed surprise at the height of the sturdy men-at-arms and archers loitering about the court-yard. Sir Eustace always answered any remarks made on the subject by saying, "Yes, Dame Margaret and I thought that instead of keeping all our retainers doing nothing in our castle in England, where there is at present no use whatever for their services, we might as well bring a couple of score of them over here. I have no wish to take part in any of the troubles that seem likely to disturb France, but there is never any saying what may happen, and at any rate it costs no more to feed these men here than in England."

The English archers and men-at-arms were well satisfied with their quarters and food, and were soon on good terms with their French associates. The garrison, before their arrival, had consisted of fifty men-at-arms, and although these had no means of communicating verbally with the new arrivals, they were not long in striking up such acquaintance as could be gained by friendly gestures and the clinking of wine-cups. Their quarters were beside those of the English, and the whole of the men-at-arms daily performed their exercises in the court-yard together, under the command of the castellan, while the archers marched out across the drawbridge and practised shooting at some butts pitched there. To the French men-at-arms their performances appeared astounding. The French had never taken to archery, but the cross-bow was in use among them, and half of the French men-at-arms had been trained in the use of this weapon, which was considered more valuable in the case of sieges than of warfare in the field. While they were able to send their bolts as far as the bowmen could shoot their arrows, there was no comparison whatever in point of accuracy, and the archers could discharge a score of arrows while the cross-bowmen were winding up their weapons.

"*Pardieu*, master page," Jean Bouvard said one day as he stood with Guy watching the shooting of the archers, "I no longer wonder at the way in which you English defeated us at Cressy and Poitiers. I have heard from my father, who fought at Poitiers, how terrible was the rain of arrows that was poured upon our knights when they charged up the hill against the English, but I had never thought that men could shoot with such skill and strength. It was but yesterday that I set my men-at-arms to try and bend one of these English bows, and not one of them could draw an arrow anywhere near the head with all their efforts; while these men seem to do so with the greatest ease, and the speed with which they can shoot off arrow after arrow well-nigh passes belief. That tall fellow, who is their chief, but now sent twenty arrows into a space no greater than a hand's-breadth, at a hundred and twenty yards, and that so quickly that he scarce seemed to take time to aim at all, and the others are well-nigh as skilful. Yesterday I put up a breastplate such as is worn by our men-at-arms and asked them to shoot at it at eighty yards. They fired a volley together at it. It was riddled like a colander; not one of the five-and-twenty arrows had failed to pierce it."

"Ay, at that distance, Captain, an English archer of fair skill could not miss it, and it needs Milan armour, and that of the best, to keep out their arrows."

"By our Lady," the captain remarked, "I should be sorry to attack a castle defended by them, and our lord has done well indeed to bring them over with him. Your men-at-arms are stalwart fellows. My own men feel well-nigh abashed when they see how these men take up a stone that they themselves can with difficulty lift from the ground, and hurl it twenty yards away; and they whirl their heavy axes round their heads as if they were reeds."

"They are all picked men," Guy said with a laugh. "You must not take it that all Englishmen are of equal strength, though no doubt Sir Eustace could have gathered five hundred as strong had he wished it."

"If that be so," the captain said, "I can well believe that if France and England meet again on a field of battle France shall be beaten as she was before. However, there is one comfort, we shall not be among the defeated; for our lord, and his father and his grandfather before, him, have ever been with England, and Sir Eustace, having an English wife and mother, and being a vassal of the English crown for his estates in England, will assuredly take their part in case of a quarrel. Of course, at present we hold ourselves to be neutrals, and though our lord's leanings towards England give some umbrage to his neighbours, their enmity finds no expression, since for years now there has been no righting to speak of between the two nations. How it will be if Orleans and Burgundy come to blows I know not; but if they do so, methinks our lord will have to declare for one or the other, or he may have both upon him. A man with broad estates, on which many cast covetous eyes, can scarce stand altogether aloof. However, if Villeroy is attacked, methinks that with the following Sir Eustace has brought with him across the sea even Burgundy himself will find that it would cost him so dearly to capture the castle that it were best left alone."

"How about the vassals?"

"They will fight for their lord," Jean Bouvard answered confidently. "You see their fathers and grandfathers fought under the Black Prince, and it is natural that their leanings should be on that side. Then they know that there is no better lord in all Artois than Sir Eustace, and his dame has made herself much beloved among them all. There is no fear that they will disobey our lord's orders whatever they be, and will fight as he bids them, for Orleans or Burgundy, England or France. He has never exercised to the full his rights of seigneur; he has never called upon them for their full quota of work; no man has even been hung on his estate for two generations save for crime committed; no vassal's daughter has ever been carried into the castle. I tell you there is not a man for over fifty miles round who does not envy the vassals of Villeroy, and this would be a happy land indeed were all lords like ours. Were we to hoist the flag on the keep and fire a gun, every man on the estate would muster here before sunset, and would march against the King of France himself did Sir Eustace order them to do so."

"In that case what force could we put on the walls, Captain?"

"Two hundred men besides the garrison, and we have provisions stored away in the keep sufficient for them and their women and children for a three months' siege. Sir Eustace gave me orders yesterday to procure wood of the kind used for arrows, and to lay in a great store of it; also to set the smiths to work to make arrow-heads. I asked him how many, and he said, 'Let them go on at it until further orders. I should like a store sufficient at least for a hundred rounds for each of these English archers, and if we had double that it would be all the better. They can make their own arrows if they have suitable wood.' It seemed to me that two hundred rounds was beyond all necessity, but now when I see that these men can shoot nigh twenty rounds a minute, I can well understand that a great supply for them is needful."

The time passed very pleasantly at Villeroy. Sometimes Guy rode with his lord and lady when they went out hawking or paid visits to neighbouring castles. Regularly every day they practised for two hours in arms, and although well instructed before, Guy gained much additional skill from the teaching of Jean Bouvard, who was a famous swordsman. The latter was surprised at finding that the page was able to draw the English bows as well as the archers, and that, although inferior to Long Tom and three or four of the best shots, he was quite as good a marksman as the majority. Moreover, though of gentle blood he would join with the men in their bouts of quarter-staff, and took no more heed of a broken head than they did.

GUY HAS HIS HEAD BOUND UP AFTER A BOUT AT QUARTERSTAFF.

"*Pardieu*, master page," he said one day when Guy came in from the court-yard to have his head, which was streaming with blood, bound up, "our French pages would marvel indeed if they saw you. They all practise in arms as you do, save with the shooting; but they would consider it would demean them sorely to join in such rough sports with their inferiors, or to run the risk of getting their beauty spoiled by a rough blow. No wonder your knights strike so mightily in battle when they are accustomed to strike so heavily in sport. I saw one of your men-at-arms yesterday bury his axe to the very head in a block of oak; he wagered a stoup of wine that no two of my men-at-arms would get the axe out, and he won fairly, for indeed it took four of the knaves at the handle to tug it out, and then indeed it needed all their strength. No armour ever forged could have withstood such a blow; it-would have cracked both the casque and the skull inside like egg-shells. It seemed to me that a thousand such men, with as many archers, could march through France from end to end, if they kept well together, and were well supplied with meat and drink by the way—they would need that, for they are as good trenchermen as they are fighters, and indeed each man amongst them eats as much as three of my fellows."

"Yes, they want to be well fed," Guy laughed, "and they are rarely pleased with the provision that you make for them; surely not one of them ever fed so well before."

"Food does not cost much," the captain said; "we have herds of our own which run half wild on the low ground near the river, which our lords always keep in hand for their own uses, and they multiply so fast that they are all the better for thinning; we sell a few occasionally, but they are so wild that it scarce pays the trouble of driving them to the nearest market, and we are always ready to grant permission to any of the vassals, whose cattle have not done as well as usual, to go out and kill one or two for meat."

"I hear from the Governor of Calais," Sir Eustace said, when he returned from a visit to that town, "that a truce has been agreed upon between England and France for a year; it is France who asked for it, I suppose. Both parties here wanted to be able to fight it out without interference. Here, in Artois, where the Burgundians are most numerous, they will profit, as they will have no fear of England trying to regain some of her lost territory, while in the south it will leave Armagnac and his friends equally free from English incursions from Guienne."

"And how will it affect us, Eustace?" his wife asked.

"That I have not been able fully to determine. At any rate they will have no excuse for attacking us upon the ground that we are partly English, and wholly so in feeling; but upon the other hand, if we are attacked either by Burgundians or Orleanists, we cannot hope, as we should have done before, for aid from Calais, lying as we do some fifteen miles beyond the frontier. Amiens has already declared for Burgundy, in spite of the fact that a royal proclamation has been issued, and sent to every town and bailiwick through

France, strictly commanding all persons whatsoever not to interfere, or in any manner to assist the Dukes of Orleans or Burgundy in their quarrels with each other. I hear that the Duke of Burgundy has seized Roye, Nesle, and Ham, and a number of other places, and that both parties are fortifying all their towns. They say, too, that there is news that the king has again been seized with one of his fits of madness. However, that matters little. He has of late been a tool in the hands of Burgundy, and the royal signature has no weight one way or the other. However, now that hostilities have begun, we must lose no time, for at any moment one party or the other may make a sudden attack upon us. Burgundy and Orleans may quarrel, but it is not for love of one or the other that most of the nobles will join in the fray, but merely because it offers them an opportunity for pillaging and plundering, and for paying off old scores against neighbours. Guy, bid John Harpen come hither."

When the esquire entered, Sir Eustace went on:

"Take two men-at-arms, John, and ride round to all the tenants. Warn them that there are plundering bands about, and that either the Burgundians or the Orleanists may swoop down upon us any day. Tell them that they had better send in here all their valuables, and at any rate the best of their cattle and horses, and to have everything prepared for bringing in their wives and families and the rest of their herds at a moment's notice. You can say that if they like they can at once send their wives and families in, with such store of grain and forage as they can transport; the more the better. If the plunderers come, so much the more is saved from destruction; if we are besieged, so much the more food have we here. Those who do not send in their families would do well to keep a cart with two strong horses ready day and night, so that no time would be lost when they get the signal. We shall fire a gun, hoist the flag, and light a bonfire on the keep, so that they may see the smoke by day or the fire by night. Tell Jean Bouvard to come to me."

"There is trouble afoot, Jean, and at any moment we may be attacked. Place two men-at-arms on each of the roads to St. Omer, St. Pol, and Bethune. Post them yourself at the highest points you can find near our boundary. By each have a pile of faggots, well smeared with pitch, and have another pile ready on the keep, and a watch always stationed there. He is to light it at once when he sees smoke or fire from either of the three points. Let the men at the outposts be relieved every four hours. They must, of course, be mounted. Let one of the two remain by the faggots, and let the other ride three or four miles in advance, and so post himself as to see a long distance down the road.

"If he sees a force advancing he must gallop back at full speed to his comrade, and light the fire. Have a gun always loaded on the keep, and have a brazier burning hard by, with an iron in it, so that the piece may be fired the instant smoke is seen. It might be two or three minutes before the beacon would give out smoke enough to be noticed, and every minute may be of the greatest importance to the vassals. As soon as you return from setting the posts see that everything is in readiness here. I myself will make sure that the drawbridge works easily and the portcullis runs freely in its groove. I have already sent off John Harpen to warn the tenants, and doubtless many of them will be in this afternoon. Send Pierre with four men, and tell them to drive up a number of the cattle from the marshes. They need not trouble to hunt them all up today. Let them bring the principal herd, the others we will fetch in to-morrow, or let them range where they are until we have further news."

In a few minutes the castle resounded with the din of preparations under the superintendence of Sir Eustace. The men-at-arms and archers carried up stones from the great pile that had been collected in the court-yard in readiness, to the various points on the walls that would be most exposed to assault. Others were employed in fixing barricades in the court-yard at the rear for the reception of the herd of half-wild cattle. The water was turned from the little rivulet running down to the Somme into the moat. Two or three bullocks were killed to furnish food for the fugitives who might come in, and straw was laid down thickly in the sheds that would be occupied by them. Machines for casting heavy stones were taken from the storehouse and carried up to the walls, and set up there. Large stone troughs placed in the court-yard were filled with water, and before nightfall everything was in readiness.

As Sir Eustace had anticipated, most of the vassals whose farms lay at a distance from the castle came in with their wives and families in the course of the afternoon, bringing carts laden with their household goods, and a considerable number of horses and cattle. Lady Margaret herself saw that they were established as comfortably as possible in the sheds, which were large enough to contain all the women and children on the estate. As for the men, no such provision was necessary, as at this time of the year they could sleep in the open air. Guy was busy all day seeing that the orders of his lord were carried out, and especially watching the operations of putting the ballistas and catapults together on the walls. Cannon, though now in use, had by no means superseded these machines, for they were cumbrous and clumsy, and could only be fired at considerable intervals, and their aim was by no means accurate or their range extensive, as the charge of powder that could be used in them was comparatively small, and the powder itself ill-made and defective in strength.

Guy was struck with the difference of demeanour between the men-at-arms and archers, especially among the English contingent, and that of the fugitives who poured in. What was a terrible blow to the latter was the cause of a scarce concealed gratification among the former. The two months that had been spent at the castle had, to the English, been a somewhat monotonous time, and the prospect of active service and of the giving and taking of blows made their blood course more rapidly through their veins. It was the prospect of fighting rather than of pay that had attracted them to the service of Sir Eustace. Then, as for a century previous and until quite modern days, Frenchmen were regarded as the natural foes of England, and however large a force an English king wished to collect for service in France, he had never any difficulty whatever in obtaining the number he asked for, and they were ready cheerfully to give battle whatever the odds against them. The English archer's confidence in himself and his skill was indeed supreme. Before the shafts of his forefathers the flower of the French chivalry had gone down like rushes before a scythe, and from being a mere accessory to a battle the English archers had become the backbone of the force. Their skill, in fact, had revolutionized warfare, had broken the power of cavalry, and had added to the dignity and value of infantry, who had become, as they have ever since continued to be, the prime factor in warfare. Consequently the English archers and men-at-arms went about their work of preparation with a zest and cheerfulness that showed their satisfaction in it.

"Why, Tom," Guy said to the tall leader of the archers, "you look as pleased as if it were a feast rather than a fray for which you were preparing."

"And so I feel, Master Guy. For what have I been practising with the bow since I was eight years old but that I might, when the time came, send an arrow straight through the bars of a French vizor? In faith, I began to think that I should never have an opportunity of exercising my skill on anything more worthy than a target or peeled wand. Since our kings have given up leading armies across the sea, there was no way but to take service with our lord when I heard that he wanted a small company of archers for the defence of his castle over here, and since we have come it has seemed to us all that we were taking pay and food under false pretences, and that we might as well have stopped at home where, at least, we can compete in all honour and good temper against men as good as ourselves, and with the certainty of winning a few silver pennies, to say nothing of plaudits from the onlookers. 'Tis with our people as with the knights of old; if they win in a tournament they take the armour of the vanquished, the prize from the Queen of Beauty, and many a glance of admiration from bright eyes. It is the same with us; for there is not an English maid but would choose an archer who stands straight and firm, and can carry off a prize when in good company, to a hind who thinks of naught but delving the soil and tending the herd."

# At Agincourt

Guy laughed. "I suppose it is the same, when you put it so, Long Tom; but there will be none of your English maids to watch your prowess here."

"No, Master Guy; but here we shall fight for our own satisfaction, and prove to ourselves that we are as good men as our fathers were. I know naught of this quarrel. Had Sir Eustace taken us into the field to fight for one or other of these factions concerning which we know nothing, we should doubtless have done our duty and fought manfully. But we are all glad that here we are doing what we came for; we are going to defend the castle against Frenchmen of some sort or other who would do ill to our lord and lady, and we shall fight right heartily and joyfully, and should still do so were it the mad king of France himself who marched against us. Besides, master, we should be less than men if we did not feel for the frightened women and children who, having done no wrong, and caring naught for these factions, are forced to flee from their homes for their lives; so we shall strike in just as we should strike in were we to come upon a band of robbers ill-treating a woman at home.... Think you that they will come, master?" he added eagerly.

"That I cannot say surely, Tom; but Sir Eustace has news that the Burgundians have already seized several towns and placed garrisons there, and that armed bands are traversing the country, burning and pillaging. Whether they will feel strong enough to make an attack on this castle I know not, but belike they will do so, for Sir Eustace, belonging as he does, and as his fathers have done before him, to the English party, neither of the others will feel any good-will towards him, and some of his neighbours may well be glad to take advantage of this troubled time to endeavour to despoil him of his castle and possessions."

"They will want to have good teeth to crack this nut, Master Guy— good teeth and strong; and methinks that those who come to pluck the feathers may well go back without their own. We have a rare store of shafts ready, and they will find that their cross-bowmen are of little use against picked English archers, even though there be but twenty-five of us in all."

"You know very well, Long Tom, that you would have come over here whether there was any chance of your drawing your bow on a Frenchman or not."

"That is true enough, Master Guy. Our lady wanted some bowmen, and I, who have been born and bred on the estate, was of course bound to go with her. Then you see, Master Guy, haven't I taught you to use the bow and the quarter-staff, and carried you on my shoulder many a score of times when you were a little lad and I was a big boy? It would not have been natural for you to have gone out with a chance of getting into a fight without my being there to draw a shaft when you needed it. Why, Ruth

Gregory, whose sworn bachelor you know I am, would have cried shame on me if I had lingered behind. I told her that if I stayed it would be for her sake, and you should have seen how she flouted me, saying that she would have no tall lout hiding behind her petticoats, and that if I stayed, it should not be as her man. And now I must be off to my supper, or I shall find that there is not a morsel left for me."

The gates of the castle were closed that night, but it was not considered necessary to lower the drawbridge. Two sentries were posted at the work beyond the moat, and one above the gate, besides the watcher at the top of the keep. The next day things were got into better order. More barricades were erected for the separation of the cattle; a portion was set aside for horses. The provisions brought in from the farms were stored away in the magazines. The women and children began to settle down more comfortably in their sheds. The best of the horses and cattle were removed into the inner court-yard. The boys were set drawing water and filling the troughs, while some of the farm men were told off to carry the fodder to the animals, most of which, however, were for the time turned out to graze near the castle. Many of the men who had come in had returned to their work on the farms. During the day waggons continued to arrive with stores of grain and forage; boys and girls drove in flocks of geese and turkeys and large numbers of ducks and hens, until the yard in which the sheds were was crowded with them. By nightfall every preparation was complete, and even Jean Bouvard himself could find nothing further to suggest.

"If they are coming," he said to Sir Eustace, "the sooner they come the better, my lord; we have done all that we can do, and had best get it over without more ado."

"I still hope that no one will come, Bouvard, but I agree with you, that if it is to come the sooner the better. But there is no saying, it may be to-morrow, it may be months before we are disturbed. Still, in a war like this, it is likely that all will try and get as much as they can as quickly as possible, for at any moment it may suit Burgundy and Orleans to patch up their quarrel again. Burgundy is astute and cunning, and if he sees that the Orleans princes with Armagnac and the Duke of Bourbon are likely to get the best of it, he will use the king and queen to intervene and stop the fighting. Seeing that this may be so, the rogues who have their eye on their neighbours' goods and possessions will, you may be sure, lose no time in stretching out their hands for them."

A week later came the news that Sir Clugnet de Brabant, who styled himself Admiral of France, had gathered two thousand men from the Orleanist garrisons and, with scaling-ladders and other warlike machines, had attacked the town of Rethel. The inhabitants had, however, notice of their coming, and resisted so stoutly that the Orleanists had been forced to retreat, and had then divided into two parties, each of whom had scoured the country, making prisoners all whom they met, firing the villages and driving off the cattle, and then returned to the town of Ham and to the various garrisons from which they had been drawn. Some of the tenants had returned to their farms, but when the news spread they again took refuge in the castle. It was probable that Artois, where almost all the towns were held by the Burgundian party, would be the next object of attack. The Orleanists remained quiet for eight days only, then the news came that they had moved out again from Ham eight thousand strong, and were marching west.

Two days later several fugitives from the country round arrived at the castle with news that the Orleanists were advancing against Bapaume, and the next morning they heard that they had, after a fierce fight, won their way to the gate of the town. The Burgundian garrison had then sallied out and at first met with success, but had been obliged to retreat within the walls again. The Orleanists, however, considering the place too strong to be captured without a long siege, which might be interrupted by a Burgundian force from Flanders, had drawn off from the place, but were still marching north burning and plundering.

"It is likely enough that they will come this way," Sir Eustace said as he and Jean Bouvard talked the matter over. "Assuredly Arras will be too strong for them to attempt. The straight line would take them to St. Pol, but the castle there is a very strong one also. They may sack and burn Avesne and Auvigni, and then, avoiding both St. Pol and Arras, march between them to Pernes, which is large enough to give them much plunder, but has no force that could resist them. As Pernes is but four miles away, their next call may be here."

"But why should they attack us, Sir Eustace? for here, too, they might reckon upon more hard blows than plunder."

"It will depend upon whom they have with them," Sir Eustace replied. "They say that our neighbour Hugh de Fruges went south ten days ago to join the Duke of Bourbon; his castle is but a small place, and as most of Artois is Burgundian he might be afraid he might be captured. He has never borne me good-will, and might well persuade the duke that were my castle and estates in his possession he might do good service to the cause; and that, moreover, standing as we do within twelve miles of the English frontier, its possession might be very valuable to him should the Orleanists ever have occasion to call in the aid of England, or to oppose their advance should the Burgundians take that step."

"Surely neither of these factions will do that, Sir Eustace."

"Why not, Bouvard? Every time that English armies have passed into France they have done it at the invitation of French nobles who have embroiled themselves with their kings. Burgundy and Orleans, Bourbon and Brittany, each fights for his own hand, and cares little for France as a whole. They may be vassals of the Valois, but they regard themselves as being nearly, if not altogether, their equals, and are always ready to league themselves with each other, or if it needs be with the English, against the throne."

At nine o'clock on the following evening Sir Eustace and his family were startled by the report of the gun on the keep, and, running out, saw the signal-fire beginning to blaze up.

"Above there!" Sir Eustace shouted, "where is the alarm?"

"A fire has just blazed up on the road to St. Pol," the warder replied.

"Blow your horn, then, loudly and urgently."

The news that the Orleanists were marching north from Bapaume had caused the greater portion of the farmers to come in on the previous day, and in a short time those who were nearest to the castle, and who had consequently delayed as long as possible, began to arrive. The garrison were already under arms, and had taken the places assigned to them on the walls. All the tenants had brought their arms in with them, and were now drawn up in the court-yard, where a large bonfire, that had been for some days in readiness, was now blazing. The new-comers, after turning their horses into the inclosure with those already there, joined them. All had been acquainted with the share they were to bear should the place be besieged. They were to be divided into two parties, one of which was to be on duty on the walls with the garrison, the other to be held in reserve, and was—every six hours when matters were quiet—to relieve the party on the walls, or, when an attack took place, to be under arms and ready to hasten to any spot where its aid was required. The men were now inspected by Sir Eustace, additional arms were served out from the armoury to those whose equipment was insufficient, and they were then dismissed to join their wives and families until called to the walls.

"THE TWO MEN WHO LIT THE ALARM FIRES RODE INTO THE CASTLE"

# CHAPTER III — A SIEGE

The two men who had lit the alarm fires had already ridden in. They reported that they had, just as it became dark, seen flames rising from a village three miles from them, and that the man in advance had ridden forward until near enough to see that a great body of men were issuing from the village in the direction of the castle.

Ten of the English men-at-arms, and as many French, were now posted in the outwork at the head of the drawbridge under the command of Jean Bouvard. Sir Eustace placed himself with his squire on the wall above the gate, and four men were stationed at the chains of the drawbridge in readiness to hoist it should the order be given. The English archers were on the wall beside Sir Eustace, as their arrows commanded the ground beyond the outwork. Half an hour after the first alarm was given the tale of the tenants was found to be complete, and the guards on the other two roads had also ridden in. Guy, to his great satisfaction, had been ordered by Sir Eustace to don his armour and to take his place beside him.

It was upwards of an hour before a body of horsemen could be heard approaching. They came at a leisurely pace, for the bonfire on the road and that on the keep had apprised them that their hope of taking the castle by surprise had been frustrated by the disobedience of some of their men, who, in defiance of the strictest orders to the contrary, had set fire to several houses in the village after having plundered them. Sir Eustace, accompanied by his esquire and Guy, descended from the wall and crossed the drawbridge to the outwork. As soon as the horsemen came within bow-shot of the castle they lighted some torches, and three knights, preceded by a trooper carrying a white flag, and two others with torches, came towards the work. When within fifty yards of the postern they halted.

"Is Sieur Eustace de Villeroy present?"

"I am here," Sir Eustace replied, and at his order two men with torches took their place one on each side of him. "Who are you that approach my castle in armed force?"

"I am Sir Clugnet de Brabant, Admiral of France. These are Sir Manessier Guieret and Sir Hugh de Fruges, and we come in the name of the

Duke of Orleans to summon you to admit a garrison of his highness's troops."

"I am neither for Orleans nor for Burgundy," Sir Eustace replied. "I am a simple knight, holding my castle and estate as a vassal of the crown, and am ready to obey the orders of the king,—and of him only when he is in a condition of mind to give such orders. Until then I shall hold my castle, and will admit no garrison whether of Orleans or of Burgundy."

"We hold you to be but a false vassal of the crown, and we are told that at heart you are an enemy to France and devoted to England."

"I am a vassal of England for the estates of my wife in that country," Sir Eustace said; "and as at present there is a truce between the two nations, I can serve here the King of France as faithfully as if, in England, I should serve the King of England."

"Nevertheless, Sir Eustace, you will have to receive a garrison of Orleans. I have at my back eight thousand men, and if you compel me to storm this hold of yours I warn you that all within its walls will be put to the sword."

"Thanks for your warning, Sir Knight; and I on my part warn you that, eight thousand though you be, I shall resist you to the death, and that you will not carry eight thousand away. As for Sir Hugh de Fruges, I give him my open defiance. I know it is to him that I owe this raid; and if he be man enough, I challenge him to meet me in the morning on fair ground outside this postern, with lance and battle-axe, to fight to the death. If he conquers, my castle shall be surrendered to him, upon promise of good treatment and a safe-conduct to depart where they will for all within it; but if I slay him, you must give me your knightly oath that you and your following will depart forthwith."

"The conditions would be hardly fair, Sir Eustace," Sir Clugnet said; "and though I doubt not that Sir Hugh would gladly accept them, I cannot permit him to do so. I have brought some eight thousand men here to capture this castle, and hold it for the Duke of Orleans, and I see not why I should march away with them because you may perchance prove a better fighter than Sir Hugh. I am ready, however, to give a safe-conduct to all within the walls if you will surrender."

"That will I not do, Sir Clugnet. I hold this castle neither for Burgundy nor Orleans, and am ready to give pledge that I will not draw sword for either of these princes; but if that will not content you, you must even take my castle if you can, and I give you fair warning that it will cost you dear."

"Then adieu, Sir Knight, until to-morrow morning, when we will talk in other fashion."

"So be it," Sir Eustace replied, "you will not find me backward in returning any courtesies you may pay me."

The knights turned away with their torch-bearers.

"Keep a close watch to-night, Bouvard," Sir Eustace said. "Mark you what the knight said,—adieu till the morning. Had I to deal with a loyal gentleman I could have slept soundly, but with these adventurers it is different. It may be that he truly does not intend to attack till morning, but it is more likely that he used the words in order to throw us off our guard."

"We will keep close ward, Sir Eustace. All the men-at-arms have their cross-bows, and though I say not that they can shoot like these English archers, they can shoot straight enough to do good work should those fellows attempt in force to cross the small moat and attack the gate. But if they come, methinks it will be but to try if we are wakeful; 'tis no light thing to attack even an outwork like this, with this loop from the moat surrounding it, without previous examination of the ground and reconnoitring of the castle."

"They would not attempt to attack the fortress itself," Sir Eustace said; "but if they could seize this outwork by surprise it would mightily aid them in their attack on the fortress; at any rate I will send down five archers, and if any of the enemy crawl up to see how wide the water is here, and how the attempt had best be made, I warrant that they will not return if the archers can but get a sight of them. Post half your men on the wall, and let the others sleep; change them every two hours—we want no sleepy heads in the morning."

By this time the confused sound of a large number of men marching could be made out, and a quarter of an hour later three or four cottages, some five hundred yards away, were fired, and an angry murmur broke from the men as the flames shot up. After sending down the five archers, Sir Eustace returned to his post over the main gate.

"Get cressets and torches in readiness to light if they attack the postern," Sir Eustace said; "we must have light to see how things go, so that we may hoist the drawbridge as soon as our men are upon it, should the enemy get the better of them. Be sure that one is not left behind; it were better that half a dozen of the enemy set foot on the drawbridge than that one of our brave fellows should be sacrificed."

"I should think that there is no fear of their attacking until those flames have burnt down; we should see them against the light," John Harpen said.

"No, there is no fear of their attacking; but the fire would be of advantage if any men were crawling up to spy. Of course they would not cross the slope in a line with the fire, but would work along on either side, reckoning, and with reason, that as our men would have the light in their eyes they would be all the less likely to make out objects crawling along in the shade by the side of the moat. Plant half a dozen bowmen at intervals on the wall, Tom, and tell them to keep a shrewd eye on the ground near the moat, and if they see aught moving there to try it with an arrow."

*There was shouting and noise up by the burning cottages, where the enemy*
*were feasting on the spoils they had taken, and drinking from the*
*wine-barrels that had been brought with them in carts from the last village*
*that they had plundered.*

*"I wish we were somewhat stronger, or they somewhat weaker," Sir Eustace*
*said; "were it so, we would make a sally, and give the knaves a sharp*
*lesson, but with only two hundred men against their eight thousand it*
*would be madness to try it; we might slay a good many, but might lose a*
*score before we were back in the castle, and it would be a heavy loss to*
*us."*

"I was thinking that myself, Sir Eustace," his esquire said. "That is the worst of being on the defence; one sees such chances but cannot avail one's self of them."

In the castle everything was quiet, and all those not on duty were already asleep. Along the wall watchers stood at short intervals peering into the darkness, but the main body there were also stretched on the wall with their arms by their side until required to be up and doing. Now that Sir Eustace was himself at the gate his esquire went round the walls at short intervals to be sure that the men on watch were vigilant. Presently a loud cry was heard from the corner of the moat away to the right.

"Go and see what is doing, Guy," Sir Eustace said, "and bring me news."

Guy ran along to the angle of the wall. Here one of the archers was posted.

"What is it, Dickon?"

"A man crept up to that corner opposite, Master Guy. I could not have sworn to him, it is so pesky dark, but I thought there was something moving there and shot almost at a venture, for I could scarce see the end of my arrow; but it hit there or thereabouts, for I heard him shout. A moment later he was on his feet and running. I could see him more plainly then, so I shot again, and over he went. I fancy that in the morning you will see my arrow sticking up somewhere between his shoulder-blades, though there is no saying precisely, for a nicety of shooting is not to be looked for in the dark."

"You have done very well, Dickon. Keep your eyes open; we may be sure there are more than one of these fellows about."

Guy hurried back with the news.

"That is good," said Sir Eustace, "and it was just as well that the archer did not kill him outright with his first arrow, the cry will show any of his comrades who may be about that they had best keep their distance from the walls."

A minute's silence followed, and then Long Tom said, "There is another has had his lesson, Sir Eustace. I heard a bow twang across there, and as there was no cry you may be sure that the shaft sped straight, and that the man had no time to utter one."

"He may have been missed altogether, Tom."

"Missed altogether! no indeed, Sir Eustace, there is no fear of that. There is not one of the men on the wall who would miss a man whose figure he could make out at fifty yards' distance, and they would scarce see them until they were as close as that. No, my lord, I would wager a month's pay that when morning dawns there is a dead man lying somewhere in front of the outwork."

"Now, Guy, you had best go up to your room and lie down until daylight," Sir Eustace said. "There will be naught doing to-night, and unless I am mistaken, we shall be busy from sunrise till sunset. I shall myself lie down for a couple of hours presently, and then send John Harpen to rest till daylight. Long Tom, see that you yourself and all your men take a short sleep by turns; we shall need your eyes to be open above all others to-morrow."

Guy promptly obeyed the order. Dame Margaret was still up.

# At Agincourt

"Is everything quiet, Guy?" she asked as she entered,

"So quiet, my lady, that Sir Eustace has ordered me to bed, and he said that he himself should come down for a short sleep presently. Two spies who crawled up have been slain by the archers. Sir Eustace is sure that no attack will be made before morning."

Then he went into his little room and threw himself onto his pallet. During the first few minutes he lifted his head several times fancying that he heard noises; then he fell into a sound sleep and did not awake until the day dawned.

In a few minutes Guy was on the wall. The night had passed quietly; so far as was known no fresh attempt at reconnoitring the works had been made, and as the moon had risen soon after he had gone to bed there was reason to believe that the fact that the two spies had not returned was so strong a proof of the vigilance of the garrison, that the enemy had been content to wait until morning. Just as the sun rose the three knights who had summoned the castle on the preceding evening appeared on the brow of the opposite slope, accompanied by a body of men-at-arms, and rode slowly round the castle. From time to time they halted, and were evidently engaged in a discussion as to the point at which it could be best attacked.

"Shall I shoot, my lord?" Long Tom asked. "They are some two hundred and fifty yards away, but from this height methinks that I could reach them."

"It would be useless," Sir Eustace said; "you could hit them, I doubt not, but you would not pierce their armour at this distance, and it is as well that they should not know how far our bows will carry until we are sure of doing execution when we shoot; besides I would rather that they began the fight. The quarrel is not one of my seeking, and I will leave it to them to open the ball. It is true that they did so last night by sending their spies here, but we have balanced that account. Moreover, if they are to attack, the sooner the better. They may have gained news from Sir Hugh of the coming here of the English archers and the men-at-arms, but if they have not done so we shall have a rare surprise in store for them."

After the knights had made a circuit of the castle they retired, and presently a dense mass of men appeared from behind the brow on which the cottages they had burned had stood.

"They have bundles of faggots, Sir Eustace!" Guy exclaimed.

"So they have, Guy! Your eye is a good one. It seemed to me that the outline was a strange one, but doubtless it is as you say—that each man has a faggot on his shoulder. It is evident that they intend, in the first place, to assault the postern, and have brought the faggots to fill up the ditch."

Then he turned to the gunners at the cannon.

"Lay your pieces so as to bear on them when they come half-way down the hill," he said, "and shoot when they are fairly in the line of fire. Take the same orders, Guy, to the men working the ballistas and mangonels on the wall. Tell them not to loose their machines until after the guns are fired. If the fellows take to flight, tell them not to waste their missiles; if they advance, let them be sure that they are well within range before they shoot."

With loud shouts the enemy came down the slope. When they were half-way down the two guns roared out, and their shot ploughed two lanes in the crowded body. There was a movement of retreat, but the three knights and several others threw themselves in front, waving their swords and shouting, and the Orleanists rallied and moved forward, but at a much slower pace than before. They had gone but a short distance when the arrows of the archers in the outwork and the bolts of the cross-bows worked by the men-at-arms there, began to fall among them. So true was the aim of the archers that scarce a shaft was wasted. At the distance at which they were shooting they did not aim at the knights, whose vizors and coats of mail could not have been pierced, but shot at the commonalty, whose faces and throats were for the most part unprotected. Man after man fell, and the cross-bow bolts also told heavily upon the crowd. They had come down but a short distance farther when Long Tom, and the archers with him on the wall, began to send their arrows thick and fast, and the machines hurled heavy stones with tremendous force among them. A moment later the French broke and fled up the slope again, leaving some fifty of their number stretched on the ground. The knights followed more slowly. When they reached the crest a group of them gathered around Sir Clugnet de Brabant.

"By my faith," the latter said bitterly, "we have reckoned without our host, Sir Knights. We came to shear, but in good sooth we seem more likely to go back shorn. Truly those knaves shoot marvellously; scarce an arrow went astray."

"As I mentioned to you, Sir Clugnet," Sir Hugh de Fruges said, "Sir Eustace brought with him from England five-and-twenty bowmen, and I heard tell from men who had seen them trying their skill at targets that they were in no wise inferior to those with whom we have before had to deal to our cost."

"Truly ye did so, Sir Hugh; but the matter made no impression upon my mind, except as a proof that the knight's inclinations were still with England, and that it were well that his castle were placed in better keeping;

but in truth these fellows shoot marvellously, both for strength and trueness of aim. I marked as we came back that of the men we passed lying there, nigh all those who had been struck with arrows were hit in the face or throat, and yet the distance must have been over a hundred and fifty yards."

"I can answer for the force," one of the others said, "for a shaft struck me fairly on the chest, and hurled me to the ground as if it had been the shock of a lance, and it is well my mail was of the best work of Milan; but nevertheless the arrow broke two of the links; if the distance had been shorter, I doubt not that it would have slain me. Well, what shall we do next, gentlemen? For very shame we cannot with eight thousand men march away having accomplished nothing. The question is, where shall our next attack be delivered?"

"Methinks," another knight said, "we delivered our attack too rashly. Had I known that there were English archers there I should have advised waiting until nightfall, and I think that it would be best to do so now. If we take our fellows up while there is light they will suffer so much from the stings of these wasps that they will soon lose heart. The knaves shoot not only straight and strong, but they shoot so fast that though, as you say, there may be but twenty-five of them, the air seemed full of arrows, and had you told us that there were two hundred archers shooting, I should have thought the estimate a reasonable one."

They stood for some time discussing the best method of attack, and as soon as they had settled upon it the men were told to scatter. Some were to go to the farmhouses, and bring up any hides that might be stored there, and to fetch all the hurdles they could lay hands upon; a portion were to go to the woods and cut timber for making mantlets and cover, while two thousand were to remain under arms in case the garrison should make a sortie.

Within the castle all were in high spirits at the easy repulse of the first attack.

"Sir Clugnet must have learned from Sir Hugh of my having English archers and men-at-arms here," Sir Eustace said to his lieutenant, "and yet he advanced as carelessly and confidently as if he had been attacking a place defended only by fat Flemish burghers; however, he has had his lesson, and as it is said he is a good knight, he will doubtless profit by it, and we shall hear no more of him till after the sun has set. Run up to the top of the keep, Guy, and bring me back news what they are doing."

In a few minutes the lad returned. "There are two or three thousand of them, my lord, drawn up in a body beyond the crest; the rest of them are scattering in various directions."

"That is as I expected," Sir Eustace remarked; "they have gone to prepare materials for a regular attack. It may be delivered to-night, or may be delayed for a day or two; however, we shall be ready for them. Jean Bouvard, do you go round the walls and tell all, save a few as sentries, to retire until the watchman blows his horn to warn us if they seem to be gathering for an attack; and do you, Long Tom, give the same orders to your archers. There is no use wasting the men's strength till the work begins in earnest. If Sir Clugnet is wise he will march away at once. He would need heavy machines and cannon to make a breach in our walls, and even had he an abundance of them it would take him some time to do so. If he tries again, you may be sure that it will be the work of Sir Hugh de Fruges, who has no doubt a lively interest in the matter. He is a clever fellow, and will no doubt do his best to work on the feelings of the other knights by representing that it would be disgraceful for so large a force to abandon the enterprise merely because a first hasty attack, delivered without preparation, had been repulsed. The fact that they have made so careful an examination of the castle would seem in itself to show that they intended to renew the attempt in another form if the first onset failed, and, moreover, the scattering of the force afterwards while the knights still remained with a large body here points in the same direction."

Guy on descending from the keep joined Sir Eustace and his wife in their apartments.

"The lad has borne himself bravely," Sir Eustace said approvingly to his wife; "he was standing beside me when their shot was bringing down the dust round our ears, and he neither started nor flinched, though in truth it was far from pleasant, especially as we had nothing to do but to look on. It may be next time we shall have sterner fighting, and I doubt not that he will bear himself well."

"Could I not come up and carry your messages, father?" Henry asked; "I am not strong like Guy, but I could do that."

"He is too young for it yet, Eustace," Dame Margaret broke in.

"Nay, wife," the knight said gently, "the lad is not too young for such service. There will be little danger in it, for his head will not show over the battlements, and it is well that he should learn to hear without fear the whizz of an arrow or the shock of a great stone from a ballista, the clash of arms, and the shouting of men. As he says, he is not yet strong enough to bear arms, but he will learn to brace his nerves and show a bold front in danger; that is a lesson that cannot be learned too young. Yes, Henry, you shall be my messenger. If they try an assault to-night, you shall put on for the first time the steel cap and breastpiece I had made for you in England; there will be no danger of your being hit by crossbow bolt or arrow, but there may be splinters of stone flying when a missile hits the battlement. Take no arms with you, only your dagger; they would be useless to you, and would hamper your movements in getting past the men on the wall, or in running up and down the steps leading to it. Now you had better lie down; both Guy and myself are going to do so. At sunset, if no alarm comes before, you will be called."

"We must not coddle the boy, Margaret," he said as Guy and Henry went off. "I know that he is not physically strong as yet, and sorry I am that it should be so, but he might exert himself more than he does, and he is apt to think too much of his ailments. I was glad when he volunteered to do something, for it is at least as well that he should be able to stand fire even if he cannot learn the use of arms; moreover, it may be that after once bearing a part in a fray he may incline more warmly to warlike exercises than he has hitherto done; it may rouse in him a spirit which has so far been wanting. I have often thought that it would have been better if Agnes had been the boy and he the girl; she has far more courage and fire than he has. You remember when that savage bull chased them, how she saw him first over the stile and got tossed over after him for her pains?"

Dame Margaret nodded. "I am not likely to forget it, Eustace, seeing that her arm was broken and I had to nurse her for six weeks. Do you know that she was up on the top of the keep while the fighting was going on? Of course I was there myself, and she begged so hard to be allowed to remain with me that I had not the heart to say her nay."

"Was Henry there too?"

"Oh, yes; and shouted with the best of them when the enemy fled over the hill. Even Charlie was there, and as excited as either of them. Of course, I had to hold him up sometimes for him to be able to see what was going on; and he looked rather pale at first, when they opened fire, but he soon plucked up when he saw that their shot did no damage near us. You see he is a strong healthy boy; while Henry has always been weak, although I do not think that he lacks courage."

"He ought not, wife; he comes from a fighting stock on either side. But I fear that unless he changes greatly he is cut out rather for a monk than a man-at-arms. And now I will lie down, for you may be sure that I shall not close an eye to-night. Did you note the banner of Hugh de Fruges with the others?"

"Yes, and I felt more uncomfortable after seeing it. He is a crafty man, Eustace."

"He is not a brave one," the knight said scornfully. "I challenged him to meet me outside in a fair field, and the craven did not answer me, and Sir Clugnet had to make speech for him and decline the offer."

"You will need all your vigilance, Eustace. I trust that every man within the walls is faithful to us; but if there be a traitor, be sure that Sir Hugh will endeavour to plot with him, nay, he may already have done so."

"They would have no chance of making communication with him were there a dozen of them, wife. Long Tom and his comrades will take good care that none come near enough for speech."

The day passed away in perfect quiet. From time to time word came down from the look-out that the scattered soldiers were returning laden with a great quantity of young trees, wattles, and doors. Dame Margaret kept watch in her room, and allowed no messengers to enter her husband's apartments.

"If there be need, I will wake him," she said; "but he knows well enough what the French have gone for, and there is naught to do until they advance to the attack."

Guy slept but a short time, and as he frequently started up under the impression that the horn was sounding an alarm, in the afternoon he got up and went down into the courtyard. For some time he wandered about in the quarters occupied by the tenants. These had now settled down; the children were playing about as unconcernedly as if they had been on their fathers' farms; women were washing clothes or preparing the evening meal over little charcoal fires. A certain quantity of meat had been served out to each family, and they were therefore doing better than in their own houses, for meat was a luxury seldom touched by the French peasantry.

Almost all who had entered the castle had brought with them a supply of herbs and vegetables; these, with a handful or two of coarsely-ground meal boiled into broth, constituted their usual fare, and the addition of a portion of meat afforded them great satisfaction. Some of the men were still asleep, in preparation for a long night's work; others were standing about talking in little groups; some were on the walls watching with gloomy faces the smoke wreaths that still rose from what had been their homes. Ducks, geese, and hens walked about unconcernedly looking for any stray grains that had passed unnoticed when they had last been fed, and a chorus of dissatisfied grunting arose from the pigs that had a large pen in the yard next to the huts. These were still smarting under a sense of injury excited not only by their removal from their familiar haunts, but by the fact that most of them had been hastily marked by a clipping of some kind in the ear in order to enable their owners to distinguish them from the others. Boys were carrying buckets of water from a well in the court-yard to the troughs for the cattle and horses, and the men-at-arms were cleaning their armour and polishing their steel caps.

"Well, Tom, I hope we shall get on as well to-night as we did this morning," Guy said to the leader of the archers.

"I hope so, Master Guy, but I would rather fight by day than by night; it is random work when you can neither see your mark nor look straight along your arrow. If we had a moon we should do well enough, but on these dark nights skill does not go for much; still, I doubt not that we shall give a good account of ourselves, for at any rate we shall be able to make them out before they come to close work. The women have been making a great store of torches to-day, and that will help us a bit, though I would that they could be planted fifty yards beyond the moat instead of on the walls, for although they will be of some use to us they will be of even more to the enemy. What think you that their plan will be?"

"I should say that they are intending to march forward covered by mantlets of wattles and hides. They will plant them near the edge of the moat, and throw up some earthworks to shelter them and their machines; no doubt they will use the doors they have fetched from all the farmhouses for the same purpose."

"The doors will be more to the point, certainly," the bowman said. "As to their hides and wattles, at fifty yards I will warrant our arrows go through them as if they were paper; but I cannot say as much about stout oaken doors—that is a target that I have never shot against; I fear that the shock would shiver the shafts. The mantlets too would serve them to some purpose, for we should not know exactly where they were standing behind them. As for their machines, they cannot have many of them."

"They had something like a score of waggons with them, Tom; these would carry the beams for half a dozen big ballistas; besides, they have their cannon."

"I don't make much account of the cannon," the archer said; "they take pretty nearly an hour to load and fire them, and at that rate, however hard a shot may hit, it would be some time before they wrought much damage on the walls. It is the sound more than the danger that makes men afraid of the things, and, for my part, I would not take the trouble of dragging them about. They are all very well on the walls of a castle, though I see not that even there they are of great advantage over the old machines. It is true that they shoot further, but that is of no great use. It is when the enemy come to attack that you want to kill them, and at fifty yards I would kill more men with my shafts in ten minutes than a cannon would do with a week's firing. I wonder they trouble to carry them about with them, save that folks are not accustomed to their noise yet, and might open their gates when they see them, while they would make a stout defence if they had only ballistas and mangonels to deal with. I suppose when they have got the shelters close to the moat they will bring up planks to throw across."

"Yes, no doubt they will try that, Tom; but the moat is over wide for planks, and I think it more likely that they will have provided themselves with sacks, and filled them with earth, so as to make a passage across with them."

"As to the planks not being long enough, Master Guy, they could get over that easy enough. They would only have to send three or four swimmers across the moat, then thrust long beams over for those who had crossed to fix firmly, and then lay short planks across them."

"So they would, Tom; I did not think of that. Well, at any rate, I expect they will manage to get across the moat somehow and plant ladders against the wall."

"And we shall chuck them down again," Tom said.

"They won't care much for that. But as long as they cannot knock a breach in the walls I warrant that we can hold them."

# CHAPTER IV — A FATAL ACCIDENT

As soon as the sun had set, the defenders gathered on the walls. Fires had already been lighted there and cauldrons of water and pitch suspended over them, and sacks of quicklime placed in readiness to be emptied; great piles of stone were placed at short intervals.

"As long as they attack at only one or two places," Sir Eustace said to his wife, "I am quite confident that we shall repulse them. If they attack at a dozen they may succeed, as we should only have a couple of archers and six or seven men-at-arms at each point, besides a score or so of the vassals. I have no doubt that these will fight stoutly, for the sight of their burning homes has roused them, and each man is longing to get a blow at those who have wrought them so much damage. Still, thirty men are but a small party to beat back an assault by hundreds. However, if they carry the outside wall they will have the second to deal with, and there we shall stand much thicker together, and they cannot attack from many points, while if we are driven into the keep, we shall be stronger still. Have you seen that the women and children are ready to retire into the keep as soon as the assault begins?"

"I have been round myself and given orders," Dame Margaret said. "I have told them that the inner gate will be closed as soon as fighting begins, and that those who do not come in before that must remain outside, or else mount to the walls and cross the bridges, for that on no account will the gates be opened again."

"That is well, Margaret. I am now about to station two men-at-arms on the inner wall at the end of each of the three bridges, so that they may be ready on the instant to turn the catches and let the bridges fall behind our men as they rush across. The tenants have already driven as many more of their best horses and cattle into the inner court as can find standing room, so that their loss may be as small as possible. If the outer wall is carried, I have no great fear that the second wall will be taken; the plunderers who form the mass of Sir Clugnet's force will have had enough and more than enough of fighting by the time that they capture the outer one. Whatever happens, do not show yourself on the walls to-night, and see that the children do not leave their beds; you can do naught, and will see but little in the dark. To-morrow morning, wife, I will leave you free to go among the soldiers and give them encouragement as may be needed, but for to-night, I pray you stir not out. I will send Henry from time to time to let you know how matters go."

Rapidly the men gathered on the walls; each had had his post assigned to him, and when Sir Eustace made a tour of inspection he was glad to see how confidently each man bore himself, and how well prepared to give the enemy a warm reception. As soon as it became dark, the outwork on the other side of the moat was abandoned, the defenders called into the castle, and the drawbridge raised, for it was evident to Sir Eustace that although it might be maintained in daylight, by the aid of the archers on the wall, it could not resist an attack by overwhelming numbers when deprived of that assistance. Sir Eustace, after inspecting the men's arms, ordered all those on the walls, with the exception of a few who were to remain on watch, to sit down with their backs against the battlement, and to maintain an absolute silence.

"It is by sound rather than sight that we shall be able to judge of their movements," he said. "All sitting down may sleep, if it so pleases them, till they are roused."

The sentries were ten in number, and were all taken from among the archers. Most of these men had been accustomed to the chase, were skilled in woodcraft, and accustomed to listen to the slightest noises that might tell of the movement of a stag and enable them to judge his position. Sir Eustace, for the present, posted himself in his old position over the gate. Jean Bouvard and Guy were with him, while Long Tom moved round and round the walls to gather news from his sentries. Sometimes Guy accompanied him.

"They are moving," Tom the archer said as he stood listening intently on the wall at the rear of the castle. "It is an hour past sundown, and about the time the knaves will be mustering if they intend to make a regular attack on us. If it had been only an escalade there would have been no sound until nearly morning. I thought I heard them on the other side, but I am sure of it now."

"I can hear singing up at their camp," Guy said, "but I don't hear anything else."

"They are keeping that up to deceive us, I expect. But besides the singing there is a sort of rustle. I don't think that they are coming this way at present, or we should hear it plainer. It seems to me that it is spreading all round."

# At Agincourt

"I will go back and tell Sir Eustace what you think, Tom."

Guy hurried back to the other side of the castle.

"Long Tom thinks, Sir Eustace, that he can hear a stir all round."

"We have noticed it too—at least, all round this side. Tell him not to call the men to their feet until the enemy approaches more closely. I believe that it is the march of a large number of men, and that they are probably moving to the positions assigned to them, but it may be another hour or two before they close in."

In a short time the sound became more distinct; from a rustle it rose to a deep confused murmur, then an occasional clink as of arms striking armour became audible. Most of the men on the walls were now on their feet gazing into the darkness. Presently the sound ceased, first on one side and then on another.

"I fancy they are all at their stations now, Jean Bouvard; we shall soon hear more of them. Do not let your archers shoot, Tom, until they can make them out very distinctly. We may be sure that they will come up with their mantlets, and it would be a waste of arrows to loose at them until they are close to the moat; but of course if separate figures can be distinguished your men will draw on them."

In a quarter of an hour messengers came from various points on the wall saying that there was something moving within sight, and to those at the post over the gate a dark confused mass like a shadow seemed to be slowly coming down towards their outwork.

"Touch off the guns, Jean," Sir Eustace said; "we shall get no further chance of catching them in a body."

The captain stooped, lit two touchfires at the lantern standing in readiness, gave one to a man-at-arms, and went with the other to a cannon. Both the guns had been filled to the muzzle with bits of iron and nails, and had been laid to bear on the slope beyond the outwork. They were fired almost simultaneously, and the sound was followed by yells of pain and dismay. The besiegers, seeing that there was nothing further to gain by concealment, burst into a shout that ran all round the castle, and were answered by one of defiance from the walls. The sound was succeeded by loud orders from the leaders of the various assaulting parties, and the objects before but dimly seen, now approached the walls rapidly. Jean Bouvard hurried away to superintend the defence at other parts.

"You may as well go the other way, Guy, and let me know from time to time how things are getting on. Henry, run down to your mother and tell her that the enemy are moving up to the moat, and that it will be some time before there is any hard fighting; then come back here again."

It was easier to see from the side walls than it had been in front, for in front there was a glow in the sky from the number of fires burning beyond the crest of the slope, and Guy was able to make out what seemed to him a wall extending some fifteen yards, near the edge of the moat. The archers and crossbow-men gathered opposite to it had just begun to shoot. Behind this wall there were other dark masses irregularly placed, and extending back as far as he could see. An occasional cry told that the arrows were doing execution upon the unseen assailants behind the mantlets, and soon the blows of cross-bow bolts against the wall and the sharp tap of arrows told that the enemy had also betaken themselves to their arms. A number of giant torches had been prepared, consisting of sheafs of straw soaked with pitch, and one of these was now lighted and elevated on a pole some fifteen feet above the battlement. Its light was sufficient to enable the scene beyond to be clearly made out. A row of mantlets some eight feet high had been placed by the moat, and others of the same height, and seven or eight feet long, elevated at short intervals behind these, were so placed as to afford shelter to the men coming down to the mantlets in front. They stood in two lines; they were some twenty feet apart, but those in one line alternated with those in the other. Guy soon saw the object of this arrangement. Men were darting to and fro across the interval some six feet wide between the two lines. Thus they had but ten feet to run from the shelter on one side to that on the other, and exposed themselves but for an instant to the aim of the archers. Some of the men carried great bundles of faggots, others had sacks on their shoulders.

"Do not heed the mantlets in front," said Dickon, who was in command of the six archers near Guy, "but pick off those fellows as they come down. Shoot in turn; it is no use wasting two arrows on one man. Don't loose your shaft until a man is within three mantlets from the end; then if one misses, the next can take him when he runs across next time. That is right, Hal," he broke off, as an arrow sped and a man with a sack on his shoulder rolled over. "Now, lads, we ought not to miss them by this light."

Eleven men fell, out of the next twelve who attempted to carry their burdens down. Guy went back to Sir Eustace with the news of the manner in which the attack was being carried on, and of the effect of the archers' defence.

"I have just heard the same from the other side; there is one attack on each side and two behind; Jean Bouvard has posted himself there. I am going round myself now; I do not think there will be any attack made in front. I have sent the archers here to the rear, where they will be more useful; the fellows in the outwork across there have enough to do to shelter themselves."

This Guy could well understand, for although the guns could not be depressed sufficiently to fire down into the *tête du pont*, the mangonels were hurling stones into it, and the men-at-arms shooting cross-bow quarrels whenever a man showed himself. The rear of the outwork was open and afforded no shelter to those who had taken possession of it, and already the greater portion had retired to the other side of the small moat surrounding it, where they lay sheltered by the outwork itself. It was not long before the assailants at the other points, finding that the plan they had formed was defeated by the skill of the archers, poured down in a mass between the two lines of mantlets, each man carrying his burden before him, thus sheltering him to a great extent. Against this method of attack the archers could do little, and now confined themselves to shooting at the men who, having thrown down the fascines or sacks by the edge of the moat, stood for a moment and hesitated before running back to the shelter of the mantlets, and not one in three got off scot-free. Guy on going round the wall found the same state of things at each of the other three points of assault. Numbers of the enemy were falling, but great piles of materials were accumulating at the edge of the moat. After a time a number of knights and men-at-arms, fully protected by armour, came down and began to hurl the sacks and bags into the moat, their operations being covered as much as possible by a storm of missiles shot through holes in the mantlets. In a short time Sir Eustace ordered the archers to desist shooting, for they were obliged, in order to aim at those so much below them, to expose a considerable portion of their bodies, and three were killed by the enemy's missiles.

"We can't prevent them from filling up the moat," he said, "and it is but throwing away life to try to do so."

The archers were accordingly placed in the projecting turrets, where, without being themselves exposed, they could shoot through the loopholes at any point on the face of the walls. It was not long before the moat was bridged at all four points of attack. Ladders were then brought down. This the assailants were able to accomplish without loss, as, instead of carrying them, they were pushed backwards and forwards by men stationed behind the mantlets, and were so zigzagged down to the moat without the defenders being able to offer any opposition. Then rushes were made by parties of knights, the ladders were placed, and the fight began in earnest.

In the great court-yard the leader of the English men-at-arms was placed with twelve of his men as a reserve. They were to be summoned by one, two, three, or four blasts of a horn to the point at which their services were most required. The assaults were obstinate, but the walls were as stoutly defended. Sometimes the ladders were hurled back by poles with an iron fork at the end; buckets of boiling water and tar were poured over on to the assailants as they clambered up, and lime cast over on those waiting to take their turns to ascend; while with spear, axe, and mace the men-at-arms and tenants met the assailants as they endeavoured to get a footing on the wall.

Guy had placed himself with the party to which he had first gone, and, taking a pike from a fallen man, was fighting stoutly. The archers from their turrets kept up a constant flight of arrows on the crowd below. Only once was the horn sounded for the aid of the reserve. Sir Eustace had taken the command at the rear, while Jean Bouvard headed the defence on the side opposite to that at which Guy was fighting. The defenders under Sir Eustace had the hardest work to hold their own, being assaulted at two points. This was evidently the main place of attack, for here Sir Clugnet himself and several of his knights led the assault, and at one time succeeded in gaining a footing on the wall at one point, while Sir Eustace was at the other. Then the knight blew his horn, and at the same time called the archers from the turret nearest to him, while some of the other party on the wall rushed to aid him of their own accord and, pressing through the tenants, opposed themselves to the knights and men-at-arms who had obtained a footing on the wall.

Their strength, and the power with which they wielded their heavy axes, so held the assailants in check that they could not gain space sufficient for others to join them, and when the reserve ran up, so fierce an attack was made upon the knights that several were beaten down and the rest forced to spring over the wall at the risk of life and limb. Sir Clugnet himself was the last to do this, and was carried away insensible. Two or three of his companions were killed by the fall, but the rest, leaping far enough out to alight beyond the solid ground at the foot of the walls, had their fall broken by the yielding mass of materials by which they had crossed the moat. A loud shout of triumph rose from the defenders, and was re-echoed by shouts from the other walls. As soon as the news of the repulse at the rear reached the other parties, and that Sir Clugnet was badly hurt, while several of the knights were killed, the assault ceased at once, and the Orleanists withdrew, followed by derisive cries from the defenders.

"Thanks be to the saints that it is all over," Sir Eustace said, as he opened his vizor; "it was a close thing here, and for a time I feared that the outer wall was lost. However, I think that there is an end of it now, and by the morning we shall find that they have moved off. They must have suffered very heavily; certainly three or four hundred must have fallen, for we must admit that they fought stoutly. You have all done well, my friends, and I thank you heartily. Now, the first thing is to fetch the wounded down to the hall prepared for them. Father Gregory has all in readiness for them there. Guy, go round and find who have fallen, and see them carried reverently down to the court-yard, send me a list of their names, and place two men-at-arms at each point where the assault took place. Tom, do you similarly dispose eight of your archers so that should they send a spy up to see if we sleep, a message can be sent back in the shape of a cloth-yard shaft. Bid all the tenants and retainers leave the wall; a horn will recall them should there be need. I will myself visit them shortly, and thank them for their stout defence. I will send round a cup of spiced wine to each man on the wall as soon as it can be prepared, to that all may slake their thirst after their efforts."

Sir Eustace then made his way down from the wall to his Apartments, where Dame Margaret was awaiting him. She hurried to meet him.

"Wait, wife, till I have removed my helmet, and even then you must be careful how you embrace me, for methinks there is more than one blood-stain on my armour, though happily not of mine own. All has gone well, love, and methinks that we shall hear no more of them; but they fought more stoutly than I had given them credit for, seeing that they were but a mixed rabble, with a small proportion of real men-at-arms among them. I suppose Henry brought you my message to close the inner gates, as they had gained a footing on the walls."

"No, I received no message since the one he brought me half an hour ago, saying that all was going well, and I thought that he was with you. Where can he be, Eustace?" she asked anxiously.

"I know not indeed, Margaret, but will search at once. While I do so will you go to the hall that you have prepared for the wounded, and give what aid you can there? Do not fear for the boy; he turned and ran off when I spoke to him, and as his head reaches not to the top of the battlements no harm can have befallen him, though in truth I cannot think what can have delayed him."

He called to two or three of the men below to take torches, and to accompany him at once, and sent others to the sheds to ask if he had been seen there, then went up to the top of the inner wall and crossed the bridge at the back.

"SIR EUSTACE GAVE A LOUD CRY, FOR LYING AT THE BOTTOM OF
THE STAIR WAS THE FORM OF HIS SON."

"Have any of you seen aught of my son Henry?" he asked the men
there.

"No, my lord," one said in reply. "I marked him by our side just before the French got a footing at the other end of the wall, but I saw him not afterwards."

"He ran towards the steps at the corner there," Sir Eustace said, "with a message from me that the inner doors were to be closed. Come along, men," he said to those with torches, and going to the corner of the wall descended the steps, which were steep and narrow. He took a torch from one of the men and held it over his head. As he neared the bottom he gave a low cry and ran down the last few steps, where, lying at the bottom, was the form of his son. He was stretched at full length, and there was a terrible gash on his forehead. The knight knelt beside him and raised his head, from which the steel cap had fallen; there was a deep stain of blood on the pavement beneath. He placed his hand on the boy's heart and his ear to his lips, and the men with the torches stood silently round. It was but too evident what had happened. In his haste to carry the message Henry's foot had slipped, and he had fallen headforemost down the steep steps, his head coming in contact with the edge of one of them. Without a word Sir Eustace raised the boy gently in his arms. His face was sufficient to tell the men the news; their young lord was dead.

Sir Eustace carried him through the inner gate and up to the boy's own room, and laid him down on his bed, then silently he went out again and crossed the court to the keep. Dame Margaret was seeing to the wounded being laid on the straw in the lower room, and did not notice him until he touched her. She turned sharply round, his face was sufficient to tell her the truth. She gave a low cry and stepped back a pace, and he moved forwards and drew her to him.

"Love," he said tenderly, "God has taken him. He was fitter for heaven than any of us; he was too gentle for this rough world of ours. We shall mourn for him, but with him it is well."

Dame Margaret laid her head on his shoulder, and burst into a passion of tears. Sir Eustace let her weep for a time, then he whispered:

"You must be brave, my love. There will be other mourners here for their dear ones who have died fighting for us; they will need your comfort. A Villeroy could not die better than doing his duty. It was not by man's hand that he fell, but God took him. His foot slipped in running down the stair from the wall, and he must assuredly have died without a pang. Take the priest with you; I will see to the wounded here. Father Gregory," he went on, raising his voice, "Dame Margaret has more need of you at the present moment than have these brave fellows. A grievous misfortune has befallen us. My son is dead; he fell while doing his duty. Do you take her to his room; I give her to your charge for the present. I have my work to do, and will see that your patients are well cared for."

There was a murmur of surprise and regret from the wounded and those who had brought them in. The poor lad had been a general favourite in the castle for his gentle and pleasant ways with all, though many a time the rough soldiers had said among themselves, "'Tis a pity that he was not a girl, and the Lady Agnes a boy. He is more fit for a priest than for a baron in times like these, for assuredly he will never grow into a stout man-at-arms like his father." That a soldier should have been killed in such a fight was to be expected, but that a gentle boy like this should have fallen seemed strange and unnatural, and all sorrowed for him as well as for their lord and lady, and the men forgot for a time the smart of their wounds in their regret at his untimely death.

Sir Eustace went about his work quietly and earnestly, bound up the soldiers' wounds, and saw as far as might be to their comfort. Their number was not large, as it was only in the fight on the wall that aught save their heads had been exposed, and those struck by cross-bow bolts had for the most part fallen as they stood. The eight men brought in had without exception received wounds from the swords of the French knights, and though some of the gashes were broad and deep, none of them were likely to prove fatal. Just as the knight had finished, Guy entered. He had heard the news, which had spread like wildfire through the castle. The lad's eyes were red, for he had been greatly attached to Henry, whose constant companion he had been whenever the family had been at their English home.

"It is a strange fate, lad," Sir Eustace said, laying his hand upon Guy's shoulder. "You who have exposed yourself freely—for I marked you in the fight—have come through scatheless, while Henry, whom I thought to keep out of danger, has fallen. And what is your news?"

"There have been seventeen killed, my lord, besides Jean Bouvard, who was struck in the face by one of the last crossbow bolts shot before they drew off."

"This is bad news indeed. I wondered why he came not to me as soon as we had beaten them off, but I thought not of this. He was a good and trustworthy fellow, and I shall miss him sorely. Seventeen, say you? It is too many; and yet there might have been more. Who are they?"

"Four of our archers, Sir Eustace, one of our English men-at-arms, and six of your French men-at-arms. These were all killed by cross-bow bolts and arrows, Two of your tenants, Pierre Leroix and Jules Beaune, and four of their men fell on the wall when the French gained a footing there; three were, I hear, unmarried men, the other has left a wife and three children."

"They shall be my care," the knight said. "The wives of Leroix and Beaune shall hold their farms free of dues until their eldest sons come of age. Does all seem quiet without?"

"All is quiet, my lord; but as I left the wall but now a knight with a white flag and four torch-bearers was coming down the slope towards the outwork."

"I will go there myself," Sir Eustace said; "'tis likely they do but come to ask for leave to carry off the dead and wounded, which we will gladly let them do, for it will save us much trouble to-morrow."

It was as the knight had supposed, and he at once gave the permission asked for, and in a short time a great number of men with torches came down the slope and for the next two hours were occupied in carrying off their dead and wounded comrades. A close watch was maintained all night, though there was small fear of a renewal of the attack. At daybreak the rear-guard of the enemy could be seen retiring, and a party of men-at-arms, under Sir Eustace himself, on going out to reconnoitre, found that none had remained behind. A mound marked the place where their dead had been buried in one great grave. Many of the mantlets had been removed, and they doubted not that these had been used as litters for the conveyance of the wounded. They afterwards heard that some four hundred and fifty men had been killed, and that over a hundred, too sorely wounded to be able to walk, had been carried away.

In the afternoon Henry was buried beneath the chapel in the castle, while the men-at-arms and others were laid in the inner court-yard. Having learned that the Orleanists, greatly disheartened at their heavy repulse, had marched away to the south, the gates of the castle were opened. A small number of the garrison were retained in the castle, and the rest were sent out to aid the tenants in felling trees and getting up temporary shelters near their former homes until these could be rebuilt as before. For the time their wives and families were to remain in the castle.

All fear of another attack by the Orleanists speedily passed away. Artois was, upon the whole, strongly Burgundian, and an army marching from Flanders speedily brought the whole province over to that side. Nothing was done towards commencing the work of rebuilding the farmhouses, for it was evident that the castle might at any moment be again beleaguered.

Two months passed quietly. Sir Eustace busied himself in seeing that the tenants were comfortably re-established in their temporary homes. The

Burgundians had again obtained several advantages, and as Sir Clugnet was known to have marched away with his following to the assistance of the Orleanists, who had of late fared badly, there was no fear of any fresh attack being made upon the castle. One day a messenger rode in from the Governor of Calais, who was personally known to Sir Eustace. The letter that he carried was an important one. After the usual greeting it read:—

*For the love I bear you, Sir Eustace, I write to let you know that there is a change in affairs. It seems that the Duke of Burgundy has but been playing with our King Henry, and that the offer of a marriage was made only in order to obtain assistance and the countenance of the king. Being now, as it would seem, powerful enough to hold his own against his enemies without such aid, the matter has fallen through. I have received a royal order, which has also been sent to the governors of other English towns, and it has been proclaimed everywhere by sound of trumpets, that none of Henry's subjects of whatever rank should in any way interfere between the two factions in France, nor go into France to serve either of them by arms or otherwise under pain of death and confiscation of fortune. But I would tell you for your private ear, that I have news that our king is in correspondence with the Dukes of Berri, Orleans, and Bourbon, and that it is like that he will shortly declare for that party, being grievously offended at the treatment that he has received at the hands of the Duke of Burgundy after having given him loyal help and assistance which had, in no slight degree, assisted him in making good his cause against his enemies.*

In a short time, indeed, the English from Calais, and from other places held by them in France, began to make sorties and to carry off much plunder from the country round, and especially took by storm the Castle of Banelinghen near Ardres, notwithstanding the truce that prevailed. The intentions of the King of England were made still more manifest by his writing a letter to the Flemish towns, saying that, having heard that the Duke of Burgundy was gathering an army of Flemings to march into Aquitaine to wage war upon and destroy his subjects, and particularly his very dear and well-beloved cousins the Dukes of Berri, Orleans, and Bourbon, and the Counts of Alençon and Armagnac, and the Lord d'Albreth, he therefore begged them to inform him whether they were willing to conform to the truce concluded between them and England without in any way assisting their lord in his wicked purpose.

The Flemish towns replied that they desired in no way to infringe the truce between the two countries, but that they would serve and assist the King of France, their sovereign lord, and their Count the Duke of Burgundy, as heretofore, to the utmost of their power.

In a short time, indeed, it became known that a solemn treaty had been concluded between the King of England and the Orleanist nobles, they engaging to aid him to recover Guienne and the parts of Aquitaine he had lost, while he promised to put an army in the field to assist them.

The position of Sir Eustace was now very difficult. It was uncertain when the English would move, and it was likely enough that if an army set sail it would land in Guienne, and that Calais would be able to render no assistance, so that he would be exposed to the attacks of the Burgundians. Nor was his position improved when he learned that on the 15th of July the two French factions, urged by the Count of Savoy, the Grand Master of Rhodes, and many others, had agreed to terms of peace between them, and that the Orleanists had formally renounced the English alliance.

At the meeting of the leaders of the party, the Duke of Aquitaine, the king's son, presided. For a time all the differences were patched up. The news, however, came too late to arrest the embarkation of the English. Eight thousand men landed at La Hogue, under the Duke of Clarence, overran a wide extent of country, being reinforced by 800 Gascons, who had, according to the agreement with the Orleanists, been raised to join them. They advanced towards Paris, declaring, however, that they would retire if the Duke of Berri and his party kept their engagement with them, and paid them the two hundred thousand crowns he had agreed to do. The Duke had not, however, the means to pay this amount, and the English therefore continued to ravage the country, while a large force from Calais, under the Earl of Warwick, captured the town of Saumer-au-Bois and the Castle of Ruissault. This, however, was scarcely an invasion, and Sir Eustace, being doubtful whether Henry meditated operations upon a large scale now that he had no longer allies in France, took no part in the matter, but remained quietly in his castle.

Towards the end of March, 1413, a royal herald appeared before the gate. He was at once admitted, and was received with all honour in the great hall by Sir Eustace.

"Sir Eustace de Villeroy." he said, "I come to you in the name of the King of France, your lord and suzerain. He bids me to say that he has heard with satisfaction that you refused entry to your castle to those who demanded it altogether without authority from him; but that, seeing the importance of the castle in case of trouble with England, and that you are a vassal of England for estates in that country, he deems it necessary that its safety should be assured, and therefore calls upon you to send, in proof of your loyalty to and affection for him, your wife and children to Paris, where they shall be cared for in all honour and as becomes their condition; or to receive a garrison of royal troops of such strength as to defend it from any fresh assault that may be made upon it, either on the part of those who before attacked it, or of England. He charges you on your fealty to accept one or other of these conditions, or to be deemed a false vassal, which he cannot believe you are, knowing you to be a brave and worthy knight. Here is a document with the king's signature and seal to the effect which I have delivered to you."

"His Majesty's demands come upon me as a surprise," the knight said gravely, "and I pray you to abide with me till to-morrow, by which time I shall have had leisure to consider the alternative and be ready to give you answer."

"Your request is a reasonable one, Sir Eustace," the herald replied, "and I will await the answer for twenty-four hours."

The herald was then conducted to the guest-chamber, and Sir Eustace went out into the court-yard and for some time busied himself with the usual affairs of his estate and talked to the tenants as to their plans; then he went up on to the wall and there paced moodily backwards and forwards thinking over the summons that he had received. He knew that Margaret had been in the gallery in the hall and had heard the message the herald had delivered, and he wished to think it well over before seeing her. His position was, he felt, a perilous one. The last treaty of peace between France and England had drawn the frontier line more straitly in. After Cressy was fought, but a few miles away, Villeroy had stood within the English line as far as it now stood without it. That Henry, who although now old and averse to war, must yet ere long again renew the war that had so long languished he had little doubt; but he had no hope of succour at present, and felt that though able to withstand any sudden attack like that he had recently repulsed, he could not hope to make a successful defence against a great force provided with battering machines.

The message from the king was indeed but a message from Burgundy, but if Burgundy was all-powerful just at present it had the same effect as if it were the king and not he who had sent the summons. He could see no way of temporizing save that Margaret and the children should go as hostages, and the idea of this was wholly repugnant to him. Were he to admit a French garrison the castle would be virtually lost to him; for once powerless, he could easily be set aside in favour of one of Burgundy's followers. The only alternative then seemed to be that he should altogether forsake the castle and estate so long held by his ancestors, and retire to England, until maybe some day Henry might again place him in possession of it. He regretted now that he had not told Margaret that she had best keep her chamber, for she then would have known nothing of the alternative that she should go as a hostage—an alternative, he foresaw, that she was likely to favour, as by so doing the necessity for making an absolute decision and choosing between France and England would be postponed. At length, still undecided in his mind, he descended from the wall and went up to his wife's apartments.

# CHAPTER V — HOSTAGES

Margaret rose to meet her husband when he entered. She had looked pale in her dress of deep mourning before, but he thought that she looked paler now. She, too, had evidently been thinking over the summons that he had received, and there was an expression of firmness and resolution in her face that seemed to say that she had arrived at a more definite conclusion than he had done.

"'Tis a knotty question, wife," Sir Eustace said. "In the first place, it is clear we cannot hope to defend the castle successfully against an attack by Burgundy. The last was but of the character of a raid, the next would be a serious siege by experienced soldiers provided with all proper means and appliances. Before, it was certain that Sir Clugnet would, if he tarried here, be shortly attacked by the Burgundians, whereas now there would be no prospect of assistance. There is no hope of help from England, for there is no force in Calais that could contend with that which would probably be sent against me; therefore I take it that if attacked the castle must in the end fall, in which case probably its defenders would all be put to the sword. I myself should most likely be killed, the estates forfeited, and you and the children taken prisoners to Paris. Now it seems to me that that is not to be thought of. It remains to decide, therefore, whether we shall abandon the castle and journey to England, or whether we will admit a Burgundian garrison, which will in fact, we may be sure, be the first step towards losing the castle and estate altogether. It seems to me that the first will be the best plan. I see no chance of it at present, but in time Henry may invade France; and as we lie only some seven or eight miles from the frontier he would doubtless recapture Villeroy, and we should again become its masters."

"You have not mentioned the other alternative, Eustace, namely, that I and the children should go to Paris as hostages; and this, it seems to me, is the best of the three to follow. If there were indeed a chance of an English invasion I should not say so, but I think not that there is any such prospect. It is many years since England has done aught in earnest, and during all that time her power in France has been waning. I would not that our children should lose this fair estate when it can well be preserved by some slight sacrifice on my part. Were I and the children to go to Paris it would put an end to all doubts as to your loyalty, and you would hold the castle and estates. The peace now patched up between the parties will not last, and as soon as they are engaged with each other, and have no time to spare to think of attacking you here, I will endeavour to escape with the children and rejoin you. I shall assuredly have no cause for complaint. I shall, of course, have honourable treatment, and apartments fitting to our rank assigned to me. It would be no great hardship, and even were it so it would be worth enduring in order that our son Charles should inherit his father's estate."

"I could not part from you, love."

"Nay, Eustace, as I have said, it cannot be for long; and you must remember that twice when the children were infants I remained in England with them while you were some months here. It would be no worse now. I would take Guy with me; the lad has sense and courage, the children are both fond of him, and I myself could, if occasion arose, take counsel with him. Then I could have two or three stout men-at-arms who might ride in my train in peaceful garb as retainers. As to a maid I can, if I need one, hire her in Paris. Surely, husband, it would be far better so than that we should lose castle and land. There could be little danger to one in Paris at any time, still less to the wife of a vassal of the crown, least of all to a hostage. I shall be but staying at the court. If you peril life and limb, Eustace, in defence of your castle, surely it is not much that I should put myself to the slight inconvenience of a stay in Paris for a while."

"I like it not," the knight said moodily. "I see well enough that what you say is true, and that you should be safe at Charles's court, indeed safer than here. The citizens of Paris are indeed turbulent, whether they shout for Orleans or Burgundy, but what if Henry of England should again lead an army here?"

"But why imagine what is not likely to happen? Long ere Henry comes I may have joined you again; should it be otherwise I might perhaps escape, or at the very worst of all they could but keep me in duress in my chamber. Who ever heard of a woman being ill-treated for the disobedience of her lord? All that they could do would be to make you pay ransom for my return."

"I would rather go as a hostage myself."

"Nay, husband, that could hardly be. Who would then take care of your castle? It is not a hard thing that the king asks, merely that I and the children shall for a time live at his court as a proof that you, his vassal, hold your castle for him. Even if the worst comes to the worst we can but lose castle and land, as we must lose it now if I do not go. Nay, my dear lord, do not wrinkle your brow, we cannot strive against the might of France; and at present we must bow our heads and wait until the storm has passed, and hope for better times. There may be an English war; ere long Henry may again extend his frontiers, and you might again become a vassal of England for these possessions of yours even as your fathers were."

"I see that reason is on your side, Margaret, and yet I cannot bring myself to like the plan."

"Nor do I like it, husband; yet I feel that it were a thousand times better that I should be separated from you for a time than that we should risk another siege. The last has cost us dear enough, another might take you from me."

"Well, well, dear, I suppose you must have your way; indeed I do not see that harm can possibly come to you, and it will at any rate ensure peace for a time and enable us to repair our tenants' losses. I shall send over a message at once to Sir Aylmer, and beg him to choose and send me another fifty archers—with that reinforcement I could make head against any attack save in the greatest force—for there is no saying how things may go. The five-and-twenty did wonders, and with thrice that force I should feel confident that Villeroy could withstand any attack save by an army with an abundance of great machines.

"Well, Margaret, since you have decided for me that you are to go—and indeed I myself plainly see that that alternative is really the best—let us talk over who you had best take with you. I quite approve of your choice of Guy; he is a good lad, and will make a brave knight some day. I shall now make him one of my esquires, and as such he will always be in attendance on you; and assuredly Agnes and Charlie will, as well as yourself, benefit by his presence. He will be able to take them out and look after them, and as he talks French as well as English the lad will be useful to you in many ways. Have you any preference as to the four men-at-arms?"

"Could you spare Tom, the leader of the archers? I should like to have another Englishman with me, and he is very good-tempered and obliging. He is shrewd too, and with his strength and courage I should feel that I could wholly rely upon him in any strait, though indeed I see not that there is any probability of such occurring."

"Certainly you can have him, Margaret, and I shall be glad to know that he is with you. Dickon, who is next under him, can act as captain of the archers while he is away. I have noticed that Tom is picking up the language fast. He is always ready to do little kindnesses to the women and children, and I have often heard him talking with them. He will soon get to speak the language fairly. As to the others have you any choice?"

"No, I think you had better choose them for me, Eustace."

"They had better be French," he said; "it would not do for you to surround yourself entirely by English, although of course it is natural enough that you should have an English squire and servant. I think that you could not do better than take Jules Varey and Albert Bongarde. They are both stout men-at-arms, prudent fellows, and not given to the wine-cup. As a fourth I would say Jean Picard's son; he is a stout fellow too, and I know that, but for his father's hopes that he will one day succeed him as butler, he would have taken service regularly as a man-at-arms. He fought stoutly when the French gained the wall, and I marked him exchanging blows with Sir Clugnet himself, and bearing himself as well as any man there. You could choose no better."

"So be it," she said. "I think, Eustace, that with four such defenders, to say nothing of young Guy, you need not feel uneasy about us."

"I don't think that I shall feel uneasy, Margaret; but I know that I can ill spare you. You have ever been at my side since we were married, save when, after the birth of Agnes and Charles, you were forced to stay in England when I came over here. I felt it a dreary time then, and shall feel it so now; but I doubt not that all will go well with you, though it will be a very different life to that to which you have been accustomed."

"I shall do well enough," Margaret said cheerfully, "and maybe I shall get so fond of court that you will have to take me to that of Henry when we return to England."

"Now you had best begin to make your preparations. I will speak to Guy and the others myself."

Sir Eustace went into the court-yard, where Guy was superintending the issue of provisions for the women.

"This can go on without you," he said; "Gervaise will see to it. I would speak to you. You were at the meeting this morning, Guy, and you heard what the herald of France said. The position is a hard one. I cannot hold the castle against the strength of France, while if we take a Burgundian garrison I should cease to be its master, and it would doubtless soon pass into other hands. Again, if I go to England, it would equally be lost to us. Therefore my wife has resolved, in order to gain time until these disorders are over, to go to Paris with the children as a hostage for me. In no case, as it seems to me, are Dame Margaret and the children likely to be in danger; nevertheless, I am greatly loth for them to go. However, seeing no other way out of the business, I have consented, and we have arranged that you shall accompany her. You will go as my esquire, and I shall install you as such this afternoon. You will take Long Tom, two of the men-at-arms, and Robert Picard, all good men and true; but at the same time the burden and responsibility must rest upon your shoulders. You are young yet for so grave a charge, and yet I feel that I can confide it to you. You will have to be the stay and support of your mistress, you will have to be the companion and friend of my children, and I shall charge the four men-at-arms to take orders from you as from me. Tom will be a valuable fellow. In the first place, he is, I know, much attached to you, besides being shrewd, and a very giant in strength. The other three are all honest varlets, and you can rely upon them in any pinch."

"I will do my best, my lord," Guy said quietly; "and I am grateful to you indeed for the confidence that you show in me, and I shall, I hope, prove worthy of it, and of my father."

The news soon spread through the castle that Dame Margaret was going to Paris. The maids wept at the thought, as did many of the tenants' wives, for since the siege began, her kindness and the pains that she had taken to make them comfortable had endeared her greatly to them. On her previous visits they had seen comparatively little of her; she had been to them simply their lord's English wife, now they knew her as a friend. Nevertheless, their regret at her leaving was softened by the thought that her going to be near the king insured peace for them, and that they would now be able to venture out to the houses that were fast rising on the ruins of their former homes, and to take up their life again as they had left it.

Early next morning the little cortege mustered in the court-yard in readiness for a start. Sir Eustace and his wife had said good-bye to each other in their chamber, and she looked calm and tranquil as she mounted her horse; for, having been accustomed from a child to ride with her father hunting and hawking, she could sit a horse well, and scorned to ride, as did so many ladies, on a pillion. Guy rode by her side, with Agnes on a pillion behind him. Long Tom, with Charlie perched in front of him, followed them, and the three men-at-arms brought up the rear. Charlie was in high spirits; he regarded the trip as a sort of holiday, and had been talking, ever since he got up, of the wonders that he should see in Paris. Agnes better understood the situation, and nothing but the feeling that she ought to emulate the calmness of her mother restrained her from bursting into tears when her father lifted her on to her seat. The herald led the way, followed by his two pursuivants. Dame Margaret checked her horse in the middle of the court-yard, and said in a loud clear voice to the tenants and men-at-arms round: "Adieu, good friends; I trust that I shall not be long away from you. I go to stay for a time at the court in Paris, and I leave you with the surety that you will have peace and rest until I return, and be able to repair the damages you suffered from the attack made upon us by men who regard not the law." She turned and waved her hand to Sir Eustace, who was standing immovable on the steps, and then, touching the horse with her heel, they moved on after the herald.

"Do not fear to speak, Tom," Dame Margaret said, after they had left the castle behind them; "the journey is a long one, and it will go all the quicker for honest talk. What think you of this expedition to Paris?"

"I would as lief go there as anywhere else, my lady. Indeed, men say that it is a fine city, and as I have never seen a bigger town than Southampton, I doubt not that I shall find plenty to interest me at times when you may not require our services."

"I see that you have brought your bow with you."

"Ay, my lady, I could not bring myself to part with it. Sir Eustace told me that I could not carry it, as its length would be a matter of remark, and point me out at once as being an Englishman, seeing that the French archers carry no bows of such length; so I have, even as you see, wrapped it round with straw, and fastened it to the saddle beneath my leg. I have also put fourscore arrows among the valises on the pack-horses."

"There is no chance of your needing them, Tom."

"I trust that it is so," the archer replied; "but, indeed, there is never any saying, and an archer without his bow is but a poor creature,—though, indeed, I trust that I can swing an axe as well as another."

"And much better than most, Tom; still, I hope that neither axe nor bow will be required."

"To that I say amen also; for, although a fray may sometimes be to my taste, I have no desire to be mixed up in a mêlée without some of my own stout comrades with me."

"Shall we get to Paris to-night, Lady Mother?" Charlie asked.

"No, indeed; it will be five days, if not six, for I see by the way that we are travelling we are bearing east, and shall sleep at Lille or may be at Tournay; then, doubtless, we shall bear south, and may stop the next night at Cambrai, and make to Noyon on the following day, and thence to Compiègne or to Senlis, and the next day will take us to Paris. It all depends how far and how fast we ride each day. But these matters will be arranged by the herald. Were we to go by the shortest route we should get there more quickly; but Amiens is held by the party to whom the men who attacked our castle belong, and by the way we are travelling we shall keep for some time in Artois, and so escape all risk of trouble on the road."

"I don't care for trouble," Charlie said stoutly; "we have got Long Tom and Robert Picard and the other two, and Guy can fight also."

# At Agincourt

"That would be all very well, my son," his mother said smiling, "if we were only attacked by half a dozen vagrants, but brave as they all are they could do naught if a large body surprised us; but be assured that there is no fear of that—by the way we are travelling we shall meet with none but friends."

"I should like to be attacked by the vagrants, mother. The last time you made us stay with you when there was fighting going on, except just at the first, but here we should see it all."

"Well, I don't want to see it, Charlie, and I am glad that we are not likely to do so; and you must remember that you and I and Agnes would sorely hamper our friends."

Nevertheless whenever a party of peasants was met upon the road Charlie looked out hopefully and heaved a sigh of disappointment when, after doffing their caps in respect, they passed on quietly. Several times they encountered bodies of knights and men-at-arms, but the presence of the royal herald saved them from all question. At each halting-place Dame Margaret, her children and maid, were lodged in the house of one of the principal citizens, while Guy and the men-at-arms lay at an inn. The troubled state of the times was only manifest by the number of men-at-arms in the streets, and the strict watch kept at the gates of the towns. Many of these were kept shut, and were only opened once an hour to let people pass in and out. This, however, did not affect the travellers, for the gates were opened the moment the emblazonings on the surcoat of the herald could be made out.

"We have assuredly nothing to complain of so far, Guy," Dame Margaret said, as they set out on their last day's journey; "had we been the king's special guests we could not have been more honourably treated, and I have no doubt that although we shall be much less important personages at Paris than as travellers under the royal protection, we shall yet be made comfortable enough, and shall have naught to grieve over save the separation from our lord."

"I cannot doubt that it will be so, lady," Guy replied; "and that at any rate there will be no trouble, unless the Armagnacs lay siege to Paris or there are riots in the city. I heard last night at the inn from some travellers who had just left it, that although the majority of the people there are in favour of Burgundy, yet that much discontent exists on account of the harsh measures of the officers he has appointed, and especially of the conduct of the guild of butchers, who, as it seems, are high in favour with the duke, and rule the city as if it belonged to them."

"It matters little to us, Guy, though it seems strange that the nobles of France and the respectable citizens of Paris should allow themselves to be ruled over by such a scum as that; but it was the same in Flanders, where Von Artevelde, our ally, a great man and the chief among them, was murdered by the butchers who at the time held sway in Ghent, and who were conspicuous for many years in all the tumults in the great towns there."

"I hear, madam, that the king is ill, and can see no one."

"Yes, I have heard the same from the herald. It will be John of Burgundy who will, for the time, be our master."

"I could desire a better," Guy said bluntly; "but we shall at any rate know that his fair words are not to be trusted. For my part, however, I wonder that after the (agreement with) the Duke of Orleans, with whom he had sworn a solemn peace, any man should hold converse with him."

"Unfortunately, Guy, men's interests count for more than their feelings, and a great noble, who has it in his power to grant favours and dispense honours, will find adherents though he has waded through blood. Burgundy, too, as I hear, has winning manners and a soft tongue, and can, when it pleases him, play the part of a frank and honest man. At least it must be owned that the title of 'Fearless' does not misbecome him, for, had it been otherwise, he would have denied all part in the murder of Orleans, instead of openly avowing that it was done by his orders."

They had started at an earlier hour than usual that morning, as the herald had pointed out to Dame Margaret, that it were best to arrive in Paris as early as possible, in order that the question of their lodging might be settled at once. Accordingly, they had been up at daybreak, and arrived in Paris at noon.

"How long will it be, I wonder," Dame Margaret said, as they rode through the gates, "before we shall pass through here again?"

"Not very long I hope, my lady," Guy said; "but be sure that if at any time you wish to leave we shall be able to procure disguises for you all, and to make our way out without difficulty."

"Nay, Guy, you forget that it is only so long as we are here that Villeroy is safe from attack. Whatever happens, nothing, save the news that an English army has landed at Calais, and is about to invade France, would leave me free to attempt an escape. If not released before that, I must then, at all hazards, try to escape, for Sir Eustace, knowing that I am here, would be placed in a sore strait indeed; both by his own inclinations and as a vassal of England, for he would want to join the English as soon as they advanced, and yet would be hindered by the knowledge that I was a hostage here. It would be for me to relieve him of that fear; and the same feeling that induced me to come hither would then take me back to Villeroy."

"Then, madam, I fear that our stay here will be a long one, for Henry has never pushed on the war with France vigorously, and though plenty of cause has been given by the capture of his castles in Guienne, he has never drawn sword either to regain them or to avenge the insults put upon the English flag."

"King Henry is old, Guy; and they say that his son is as full of spirit and as fiery as his father is peaceful and indisposed for war. When the king dies, my lord thinks that it will be but a short time before the English banner will be unfurled in France; and this is one of the reasons why he consented to my becoming an hostage, thinking that no long time is likely to elapse before he will have English backing, and will be able to disregard the threats of France."

"How narrow and sombre are these streets!" Guy said, after a pause, "one seems to draw one's very breath with difficulty."

"They are well-nigh as narrow in London," his mistress replied; "but they are gay enough below. See how crowded they are, and how brilliant are some of the costumes!"

"Some of them indeed, madam, but more are poor and miserable; and as to the faces, they are so scowling and sombre, truly were we not on horseback I should keep my hand tight upon my pouch, though in truth there is nothing in it worth stealing."

"Ay, ay, Master Guy," Long Tom broke in, "methinks that there are a good many heads among these scowling knaves that I would gladly have a chance of cracking had I my quarter-staff in my hand and half a dozen stout fellows here with me. See how insolently they stare!"

"Hush, Tom!" Dame Margaret said, turning round, "if you talk of cracking skulls I shall regret that I brought you with me."

"I am not thinking of doing it, my lady," the archer said apologetically. "I did but say that I should like to do it, and between liking and doing there is often a long distance."

"Sometimes, Tom, but one often leads to the other. You must remember that above all things it behoves us to act prudently here, and to avoid drawing the attention of our foes. We English are not loved in Paris, and the less you open your mouth here the better; for when Burgundians and

Armagnacs are ready to cut each other's throats over a name, fellow-countrymen though they be, neither would feel any compunction about killing an Englishman."

After riding for half an hour they entered the court-yard of a large building, where men-at-arms and varlets wearing the cognizance of Burgundy were moving about, a group of nobles were standing on the steps, while some grooms were walking their horses round the court-yard. The herald made his way to the door, and here all alighted.

"Whom have we here, I wonder?" one of the young nobles said to another as they came up. "A royal herald and his pursuivants; a young dame and a very fair one; her daughter, I suppose, also fair; the lady's esquire; and a small boy."

"Hostages, I should say," the other replied, "for the good conduct of the lady's lord, whoever he may be. I know her not, and think that she cannot have been at court for the last ten years, for I could hardly have forgotten her face."

Dame Margaret took the hands of her two children and followed the herald up the steps. She had made a motion of her head to Guy to attend her, and he accordingly followed behind.

"A haughty lady as well as a fair one," the young knight laughed. "She did not so much as glance at us, but held her head as high as if she were going in to rate Burgundy himself. I think that she must be English by her looks, though what an English woman can be doing here in Paris is beyond my understanding, unless it be that she is the wife of a knight of Guienne; in that case she would more likely be with Orleans than here."

"Yes, but you see the herald has brought her. It may be her lord's castle has been captured, and she has come under the safe-conduct of a herald to lay a complaint; but I think with you that she is English. The girl was fair too, though not so fair as her mother, and that curly-headed young esquire is of English stock too."

"He is a stout-looking fellow, De Maupas, and will make a powerful man; he looks as if he could strike a shrewd blow even now. Let us question their knaves, one of whom, by the way, is a veritable giant in point of height."

He beckoned to the four men, and Robert Picard came forward.

"Who is your lady, young man?"

"Dame Margaret de Villeroy, may it please you, sir. She is the wife of Sir Eustace de Villeroy."

"Then we were right, De Maupas, for De Villeroy is, I know, a vassal of England for his wife's estates, and his people have always counted themselves English, because for over a hundred years their castle stood inside the English line."

"He is a stout knight. We heard a month ago how bravely he held his castle against Sir Clugnet de Brabant with 8000 Orleanists, and beat him off with a loss of five knights and 400 men. Sir Clugnet himself was sorely wounded. We all ought to feel mightily obliged to him for the check, which sent them back post-haste out of Artois, where they had already done damage enough, and might have done more had they not been so roughly handled. I wonder what the lady is here for?"

"It may be that he would have fought the Burgundians as stoutly as he fought the Armagnacs," the other said, "and that the duke does not care about having so strong a castle held by so stout a knight within a few miles of the English line."

The other shrugged his shoulders. "The English are sleeping dogs," he said; "there is no Edward and no Black Prince to lead them now."

"No, but you must remember that sleeping dogs wake up sometimes, and even try to bite when they do so; moreover we know of old that these particular dogs can bite hard."

"The sooner they wake up the better, I say, De Maupas. We have a long grudge to wipe off against them, and our men are not likely to repeat the mistakes that cost us so dearly before. Besides, the English have had no real fighting for years, and it seems to me that they have altogether given up any hope of extending their possessions in France."

"One can never tell, De Revelle. For my part I own that I care not that they should again spread their banner on this side of the sea. There can be no doubt that they are stout fighting-men, and seeing how France is divided they might do sore damage did they throw their weight into one side of the scale."

"Methinks that there is no fear of that. The dukes both know well enough that their own followers would not fight side by side with the English; and though they might propose an alliance with the Islanders, it would only be for the purpose of bringing the war to a close by uniting both parties against our old enemy."

In the meantime Dame Margaret had followed her conductor to the great chamber, where John of Burgundy held audience in almost royal state. Several nobles were gathered round him, but at the entrance of the herald these fell back, leaving him standing by himself. An eminently politic man, the duke saw at once by the upright figure and the fearless air with which Dame Margaret entered the hall, that this was a case where courtesy and deference were far more likely to bring about the desired end of winning her husband over to his interests, than any menaces or rough speaking; he therefore advanced two or three steps to meet her.

"My lord duke," the herald said, "this lady, Dame Margaret of Villeroy, has journeyed hither with me in accordance with the wish expressed by His Majesty the king."

"As the king's representative in Paris, lady," the duke said to Margaret, "I thank you for your promptness in thus conceding to his wish."

"His Majesty's wish was naturally a command to me, Sir Duke," Margaret said with quiet dignity. "We, my husband and I, understood that some enemy had been influencing His Majesty's mind against my lord, and in order to assure him of my lord's loyalty as a faithful vassal for the land he holds, I have willingly journeyed here with my children, although in much grief for the loss of my eldest son, who died in the attack lately made upon our castle by a large body of men, of whom we knew naught, save that they did not come in the name of our lord the king."

"I have heard of the attack, lady, and of the gallant and successful defence made by Sir Eustace, and the king was greatly pleased to hear of the heavy check thus inflicted upon the men who had raised the banner of revolt, and were harassing His Majesty's faithful subjects."

"That being so, my lord duke," Margaret said, "'tis strange, after my lord had shown how ready and well prepared he was to protect his castle against ill-doers, that he should have been asked to admit a garrison of strangers to aid him to hold it. Sir Eustace has no desire to meddle with the troubles of the times; he holds his castle as a fief directly from the crown, as his ancestors have held it for two hundred years; he wishes only to dwell in peace and in loyal service to the king."

THE LADY MARGARET MAKES HER OBEISANCE TO THE DUKE OF
BURGUNDY.

"Such we have always understood, madam, and gladly would the king
have seen Sir Eustace himself at his court. The king will, I trust, shortly be
recovered from his malady; until he is so I have—for I was made
acquainted with your coming by messenger sent forward by Monjoie—

arranged for you to be lodged in all honour at the house of Master Leroux, one of the most worshipful of the citizens of Paris, and provost of the guild of silversmiths. My chamberlain will at once conduct you thither."

"I thank you, my lord duke," Margaret said with a stately reverence, "and trust that when I am received by my lord the king I shall be able to prove to him that Sir Eustace is his faithful vassal, and can be trusted to hold his castle for him against all comers."

"I doubt it not, lady," the duke said courteously. "Sir Victor Pierrepoint, I pray you to see this lady to the entrance. Sir Hugo will already be waiting her there."

# CHAPTER VI — IN PARIS

"A bold dame and a fair one," John of Burgundy said to the gentlemen round him when Margaret left the chamber. "Methinks that she would be able to hold Villeroy even should Sir Eustace be away."

"That would she," one of the knights said with a laugh. "I doubt not that she would buckle on armour if need were. But we must make some allowance for her heat; it is no pleasant thing to be taken away from her castle and brought hither as a hostage, to be held for how long a time she knows not."

"It was the safest way of securing the castle," the duke said. "Can one doubt that, with her by his side, her husband would open his gates to the English, should they appear before it? He himself is a vassal both of England and France, and should the balance be placed before him, there can be little doubt that her weight would incline him to England. How well these English women keep their youth! One might believe her to be but a few years past twenty, and yet she is the mother of that girl, who is well-nigh as tall as herself."

"And who bids to be as fair, my lord duke."

"And as English, De Porcelet. She would be a difficult eaglet to tame, if I mistake not; and had she been the spokeswoman, methinks she would have answered as haughtily as did her mother. But it might be no bad plan to mate her to a Frenchman. It is true that there is the boy, but the fief might well be bestowed upon her if so mated, on the ground that the boy would likely take after his father and mother and hold Villeroy for England rather than for France. However, she is young yet; in a couple of years, De Porcelet, it will be time for you to urge your suit, if so inclined."

There was a general smile from the circle standing round, but the young knight said gravely, "When the time comes, my lord duke, I may remind you of what you have said. 'Tis a fair young face, honest and good, though at present she must naturally feel with her mother at being thus haled away from her home."

Sir Victor escorted Margaret to the court-yard. As they appeared at the entrance a knight came up and saluted her.

"I am intrusted by the duke with the honour of escorting you to your lodgings," he said; "I am Hugo de Chamfort, the duke's chamberlain."

After assisting her into the saddle he mounted a horse which an attendant brought up and placed himself by her side. Two men-at-arms with their surtouts embroidered with the cognizance of Burgundy led the way, and the rest of the party followed in the same order in which they had come. The distance was short, and beyond a few questions by the knight as to the journey and how she had been cared for on the way, and Margaret's replies, little was said until they reached the house of the provost of the silversmiths. As they rode up to the door Maître Leroux himself came out from the house.

"Welcome, lady," he said, "to my abode. My wife will do all that she can to make you comfortable."

"I am sorry indeed, good sir," Margaret said, "to be thus forced upon your hospitality, and regret the trouble that my stay will impose upon you."

"Say not so, lady," he said, "we deem it an honour that his grace the Duke of Burgundy should have selected us for the honour of entertaining you. The house is large, and we have no family. Chambers are already prepared for yourself, your daughter, and son, while there are others at your disposal for your following."

"I would not trespass too much upon you," she said. "My daughter can sleep with me, and I am sure that my esquire here, Master Guy Aylmer, will gladly share a room with my boy. I can obtain lodgings for my four followers without."

"You will grieve me much if you propose it, lady. There is a large room upstairs unoccupied, and I will place pallets for them there; and as for their meals they can have them apart."

By this time they had mounted a fine flight of stairs, at the top of which Dame Leroux was standing to receive her guests. She was a kindly-looking woman between thirty and forty years of age.

"Welcome, Lady Margaret," she said with a cordiality that made Margaret feel at once that her visit was not regarded as an infliction. "We are quiet people, but will do our best to render your stay here a pleasant one."

"Thanks indeed, mistress!" Margaret replied. "I feared much that my presence would be felt as a burden, and had hardly hoped for so kind a welcome. This is my daughter Agnes, and my son Charles." Then she turned to Sir Hugo: "I pray you to give my thanks to his grace the Duke of

Burgundy, and to thank him for having so well bestowed me. I thank you also for your courtesy for having conducted me here."

"I will convey your message to the duke," he said, "who will, I am sure, be pleased to hear of your contentment."

Maître Leroux accompanied the knight downstairs again, and when he had mounted and ridden off he called two servitors, and bade one carry the luggage upstairs, and the other conduct the men to the stables he had taken for the horses.

"After you have seen to their comfort," he said to Robert Picard, "you will return hither; you will find a meal prepared for you, and will be bestowed together in a chamber upstairs."

In the meantime his wife had ushered Dame Margaret into a very handsomely furnished apartment. "This is at your entire service, Lady Margaret," she said. "The bedroom behind it is for yourself, the one next to it for your daughter, unless you would prefer that she should sleep with you."

"I thank you. I was telling your husband that I should prefer that; and my son and esquire can therefore occupy the second room. But I fear greatly that I am disturbing yourself and your husband."

"No, indeed; our sitting-room and bedroom are on the other side of the landing. These are our regular guest-chambers, and your being here will make no change whatever in our arrangements. I only regret that the apartments are not larger."

"Do not apologize, I beg of you, madam. I can assure you that the room is far handsomer than that to which I have been accustomed. You citizens of Paris are far in advance of us in your ideas of comfort and luxury, and the apartments both at Villeroy and in my English home cannot compare with these, except in point of size. I never dreamt that my prison would be so comfortable."

"Say not prison, I pray you, lady. I heard, indeed, that your visit to the court was not altogether one of your own choice; but, believe me, here at least you will be but a guest, and an honoured and welcome one. I will leave you now. If there is aught that you desire, I pray you to ring that bell on the table; refreshments will be quickly served. Had I known the precise hour at which you would come we should have been in readiness for you, but I thought not that you would arrive till evening."

"I hope that you will give me much of your company, mistress," Margaret said warmly. "We know no one in this great city, and shall be glad indeed if, when you can spare time, you will sit with us."

"Well, children, what do you think of this?" she asked when their hostess had left the room.

"It is lovely, mother," Agnes said. "Look at the inlaid cabinets, and the couches and tables, and this great warm rug that covers all the floor, how snug and comfortable it all is. Why, mother, I never saw anything like this."

"You might have seen something like it had you ever been in the house of one of our rich London traders, Agnes; at least so I have heard, though in truth I have never myself been in so luxuriously furnished a room. I only hope that we may stay here for some time. The best of it is that these good people evidently do not regard us as a burden. No doubt they are pleased to oblige the Duke of Burgundy, but, beyond that, their welcome seemed really sincere. Now let us see our bedroom. I suppose that is yours, Charlie, through the door in the corner."

The valises had already been brought to the rooms by another entrance, and Margaret and her daughter were charmed with their bedroom. A large ewer and basin of silver stood on a table which was covered with a white cloth, snowy towels hung beside it; the hangings of the bed were of damask silk, and the floor was almost covered by an Eastern carpet. An exquisitely carved wardrobe stood in one corner.

"It is all lovely!" Agnes said, clapping her hands. "You ought to have your room at home fitted up like this, mother."

"It would take a large slice out of a year's revenue, Agnes," her mother said with a smile, "to furnish a room in this fashion. That wardrobe alone is worth a knight's ransom, and the ewer and basin are fit for a king. I would that your father could see us here; it would ease his anxiety about us. I must ask how I can best despatch a messenger to him."

When they returned to the other apartment they found the table already laid, and in a short time a dainty repast was served. To this Guy sat down with them, for except when there were guests, when his place was behind his lord's chair, he had always been treated as one of the family, and as the son of Sir Aylmer rather than as a page.

"Well, Master Guy, what think you of affairs?"

"They seem well to the eye, mistress, but I would not trust that Duke of Burgundy for an hour. With that long face of his and the hooked nose and his crafty look he resembles little a noble of France. He has an evil face, and one which accords well with the foul murder of the king's brother. However, as I see not that he has aught to gain by holding you here,—save that he thinks it will ensure our lord's keeping his castle for him,—there is no reason why he should not continue to treat you honourably and courteously. We have yet to learn whether Master Leroux is one of his party, or whether he is in favour of Armagnac."

"I should think that he cannot be for Armagnac," she said, "or Duke John would hardly have quartered us upon him. No doubt it was done under the semblance of goodwill, but most men would have considered it a heavy tax, even though, as I expect, we shall not remain here long. Doubtless, however, the trader considers that his complaisance in the matter would be taken by the duke as a sign of his desire to show that at least he is not hostile to him."

When they rose from the table Guy, at his mistress's suggestion, went below and found the four men sitting in the great kitchen, where they had just finished an ample meal.

"You have seen to the horses, Robert?"

"Yes, Master Guy, they are comfortably bestowed, with an abundance of provender."

"I am going out to see how matters stand in the town. Our lady says that at all times two of you must remain here, as it may be necessary to send messages, or should she wish to go out, to escort her, but the other two can be out and about as they please, after first inquiring of me whether there is aught for them to do. You can arrange among yourselves which shall stay in, taking turns off duty. Tom, you had better not go out till after dark. There is something in the cut of your garments which tells that you are not French. Robert will go out with me now, and find a clothier, and bid him send garments here for you to choose from, or if he has none to fit, which may likely enough be, send him to measure you. It might lead to broils and troubles were any of the rabble to notice that you were a stranger."

"That is right enough, Master Guy; and in sooth I have no desire to go out at present, for after riding for the last six days I am well content to sit quiet and take my ease here."

Guy then started with Robert Picard. Except in the streets where the principal merchants dwelt, the town struck him as gloomy and sombre. The palaces of the nobles were veritable fortresses, the streets were ill-paved and evil-smelling, and the people in the poorer quarters had a sinister aspect.

"I should not care to wander about in this district after nightfall, Robert," Guy said to the man-at-arms, who kept close to his elbow.

"Nor I," the man growled. "It is as much as I can do to keep my hands off my dagger now, for methinks that nine out of ten of the fellows loitering about would cut our throats willingly, if they thought that we had but a crown in our pockets."

Presently they found themselves on the quays, and, hailing a boat, rowed up the river a little beyond the walls. Hearing the sound of music they landed, and on seeing a number of people gather round some booths they discharged the boat and went on. They found that it was a sort of fair. Here were sword-players and mountebanks, pedlars who vended their wares at a lower price than those at which they were sold within the limits of the city, booths at which wine and refreshments could be obtained. Here many soldiers were sitting drinking, watching the passers-by, and exchanging ribald jests with each other, and sometimes addressing observations to the wives and daughters of the citizens, amid fits of laughter at the looks of indignation on the part of their husbands or fathers.

"It is evidently a holiday of some sort," Guy remarked, as they found that the fair extended for a considerable distance, and that the crowd was everywhere large. They stopped for a minute or two in front of a booth of more pretensions than the generality. In front of it a man was beating a drum, and a negro walking up and down attired in showy garments. The drum ceased and the latter shouted:

"Those of you who wish to see my master, the famous Elminestres, the most learned doctor in Europe, who can read the stars, cast your horoscope, foretell your future, and cure your ailments, should not lose this opportunity."

The curtains opened behind, and a man dressed in dark garments with a long black cloak spotted with silver stars came forward.

"You have heard, good people, what my slave has said. He speaks with knowledge. I saved his life in the deserts of Africa when he was all but dead with fever, by administering to him one of my wonderful potions; he at once recovered and devoted himself to my service. I have infallible remedies for every disease, therefore do you who are sick come to me and be cured; while for you who do not suffer I can do as much or more, by telling you of your future, what evils to avoid and what chances to grasp."

He stood for a minute silent, his eyes wandering keenly over the spectators. "I see," he said, "one among you who loves a fair maiden standing beside him. At present her parents are unfavourable to his suit, but if he will take my advice he will be able to overcome their objections and to win the damsel. Another I see who has come to Paris with the intention of enlisting in the service of our good duke, and who, I foresee, will attain rank and honour and become a distinguished soldier if he does but act prudently at the critical moment, while if he takes a wrong turn misfortune and death will befall him. I see a youth of gentle blood who will become a brave knight, and will better his condition by marriage. He has many dangers to go through before that, and has at present a serious charge for one so young; but as he has circumspection as well as courage he may pass through them unharmed. To him too I could give advice that may be valuable, more especially as he is a stranger to the land, as are those of whom he is in charge."

"It is wonderful, Master Guy!" Robert Picard whispered in Guy's ear in a tone of astonished awe.

"The knave doubtless saw us ride in this morning, and recognized me again. There is naught of magic in it, but the fellow must be shrewd, or he would not have so quickly drawn his conclusions. I will go in and speak to him presently, for though I believe not his prophecies one jot, a fellow of this sort may be useful. Let us be moving on at present."

They passed two monks, who were scowling angrily at the man, who was just exciting the laughter of the crowd by asserting that there was a holy man present who usually preferred a flask of good wine to saying his vespers.

"Rogues like this should be whipped and branded, Brother Anselmo."

"Ay, ay," the other agreed: "and yet," he added slyly, "it may be that he has not altogether missed his mark this time. We are not the only two monks here," he went on as the other turned upon him angrily, "and it may well be that among them is one who answers to the fellow's lewd description."

On the outskirts of the fair were many people of higher degree. Knights and ladies strolled on the turf exchanging greetings, looking for a minute or two at the gambols of a troupe of performing dogs, or at a bout of cudgel play—where two stout fellows belaboured each other heartily, and showed sufficient skill to earn from the crowd a shower of small pieces of money, when at last they ceased from pure exhaustion. Half an hour later Guy returned to the booth of the doctor, and went in by a side entrance, to which those who wished to consult the learned man had been directed by the negro. The latter was at the entrance, and, observing that Guy's condition was above that of the majority of his master's clients, at once took him into an inner apartment divided from the rest of the tent by a hanging. Over the top of this was stretched a black cloth spotted with silver stars, and similar hangings surrounded it; thus all light was cut off, and the room was dimly illuminated by two lamps. A table with a black cloth stood at the back. On this stood a number of phials and small boxes, together with several retorts and alembics. The doctor was seated on a tripod stool. He rose and was about to address Guy in his usual style, when the latter said:

"So you saw us ride in this morning, Master Doctor, and guessed shrewdly as to our condition and nationality. As to the latter, indeed, it needed no sorcery, for it must have been plain to the dullest that my mistress and her daughter were not of French blood, and though I am much less fair, it was a pretty safe guess to suppose that I also was of their country. I need not tell you that I have not come here either for charms or nostrums, but it seemed to me that being, as you said, strangers here, we might benefit by the advice of one who like yourself notes things quickly, and can form his own conclusions."

The doctor removed his tall conical cap, and placed it on the table.

"You guess rightly," he said with a smile. "I was in the crowd and marked you enter, and a soldier standing next to me observed to a comrade that he had heard that Burgundy had sent the herald to demand the surrender of a castle held by one Sir Eustace, a knight who was known to have friendly leanings towards the English, being a vassal of their king for estates that had come to him with an English wife, and that doubtless this was the lady. When my eye fell on you in the crowd I said: Here is a youth of shrewdness and parts, he is alone and is a foreigner, and maybe I can be of service to him; therefore I shot my shaft, and, as you see, with success. I said to myself: This youth, being a stranger, will know of no one to whom he can turn for information, and I can furnish him with almost any that he may require. I come in contact with the highest and the lowest, for the Parisians are credulous, and after dark there are some of rank and station who come to my doors for filtres and nostrums, or to have their horoscope cast and their futures predicted. You will ask why one who has such clients should condescend to stand at a booth and talk to this rabble; but it has its purpose. Were I known only as one whom men and women visit in secret, I should soon become suspected of black arts, the priests would raise an outcry against me, and one of these days I might be burned. Here, however, I ostensibly earn my living as a mountebank vendor of drugs and nostrums, and therefore no one troubles his head about me."

"There is one thing that you have not told me," Guy said when he ceased speaking. "Having, as you say, good clients besides your gains here, why should you trouble to interest yourself in our affairs?"

"Shrewdly put, young sir. I will be frank with you. I too am a stranger, and sooner or later I may fall into discredit, and the power of the church be too much for me. When I saw your mistress to-day I said to myself: Here is an English lady of rank, with a castle and estate in England; should I have to fly—and I have one very dear to me, for whose sake I value my life—it might be well for me that I should have one friend in England who would act as protectress to her should aught befall me. Your mistress is a stranger here, and in the hands of enemies. I may be of use to her. I know this population of Paris, and can perhaps give her better information of what is going on both at the court and in the gutter than any other man, and may be able to render her assistance when she most needs it; and would ask but in payment that, should I come to England, she will extend her protection to my daughter until I can find a home and place her there. You see I am playing an open game with you."

"I will reply as frankly," Guy said. "When I came in here it was, as I told the man-at-arms my companion, with the thought that one who had noticed us so shrewdly, and had recognized me so quickly in the crowd, was no ordinary mountebank, but a keen, shrewd man who had some motive for thus addressing me, and I see that my view was a right one. As to your proposal I can say naught before I have laid it before my mistress, but for myself I may say at once that it recommends itself to me as excellent. We are, as you say, strangers here, and know of no one from whom we might obtain information as to what is going on. My mistress, if not an actual prisoner, is practically so, being held with her children as hostages for my lord's loyalty to France. She is the kindest of ladies, and should she authorize me to enter into further communication with you, you may be sure that she would execute to the full the undertaking you ask for on behalf of your daughter. Where can I see you again? This is scarce a place I could often resort to without my visits being noticed, if, as is likely enough, the Duke of Burgundy may occasionally set spies to inform him as to what we are doing, and whether my mistress is in communication with any who are regarded as either doubtful or hostile to his faction."

"If you will be in front of Notre Dame this evening at nine o'clock, I will meet you there and conduct you to my abode, where you can visit me free of any fear of observation."

"What name shall I call you?" Guy asked.

"My name is Montepone. I belong to a noble family of Mantua, but mixing myself up with the factions there, I was on the losing side, and unfortunately it happened that in a fray I killed a noble connected with all the ruling families; sentence of death was passed upon me in my absence, my property was confiscated. Nowhere in Italy should I have been safe from the dagger of the assassin, therefore I fled to France, and for ten years have maintained myself by the two arts which so often go together, astrology and buffoonery. I had always been fond of knowledge, and had learned all that could be taught in the grand science of astrology, so that however much I may gull fools here, I have obtained the confidence of many powerful personages by the accuracy of my forecasts. Had Orleans but believed my solemn assurance he would not have ridden through the streets of Paris to his death that night, and in other cases where I have been more trusted I have rendered valuable assistance."

The belief in astrology had never gained much hold upon the mass of the English people, many as were the superstitions that prevailed among them. Guy had never even given the matter a thought. Montepone, however, evidently believed in his powers of foreseeing the future, and such powers did not in themselves seem altogether impossible to the lad; he therefore made no direct reply, but saying that he would not fail to be at the appointed place at nine that evening, took his leave.

"Truly, Master Guy, I began to be uneasy about you," Robert Picard said when he rejoined him, "and was meditating whether I had best enter the tent, and demand what had become of you. It was only the thought that there might have been others before you, and that you had to wait your turn before seeing him, that restrained me. You have not been taking his nostrums, I trust; for they say that some of those men sell powders by which a man can be changed into a wolf."

Guy laughed. "I have taken nothing, Robert, and if I had I should have no fear of such a change happening to me. I have but talked to the man as to how he came to know me, and it is as I thought,—he saw us as we entered. He is a shrewd fellow, and may well be of some use to us."

"I like not chaffering with men who have intercourse with the devil," Picard said, shaking his head gravely; "nothing good comes of it. My mother knew a man who bought a powder that was to cure his wife of jealousy; and indeed it did, for it straightway killed her, and he was hung. I think that I can stand up against mortal man as well as another, but my blood ran cold when I saw you enter yon tent, and I fell into a sweat at your long absence."

"The man is not of that kind, Robert, so you can reassure yourself. I doubt not that the nostrums he sells are perfectly harmless, and that though they may not cure they will certainly not kill."

They made their way back to the house of the provost of the silversmiths.

"Well, what do you think of Paris, Guy?" Dame Margaret asked when he entered.

"It is a fine city, no doubt, lady, but in truth I would rather be in the country than in this wilderness of narrow streets. But indeed I have had somewhat of an adventure, and one which I think may prove of advantage;"

and he then related to his mistress his visit to the booth of the supposed doctor.

"Do you think that he is honest, Guy?" she asked when he concluded.

"I think so, madam. He spoke honestly enough, and there was a ring of truth in what he said; nor do I see that he could have had any motive for making my acquaintance save what he stated. His story seemed to me to be a natural one; but I shall be able to judge better when I see him in his own house and with this daughter he speaks of; that is, if your ladyship is willing that I should meet him."

"I am willing enough," she said, "for even if he is a spy of Burgundy's there is nothing that we wish to conceal. I have come here willingly, and have no thought of making my escape, or of mixing myself up in any of the intrigues of the court. Therefore there is no harm that he can do us, while on the other hand you may learn much from him, and will gather in a short time whether he can be trusted. Then by all means go and meet him this evening. But it would be as well to take Tom with you. It does not seem to me at all likely that any plot can be intended, but at any rate it will be well that you should have one with you whom you can thoroughly trust, in case there is any snare set, and to guard you against any lurking cut-throats."

"I will tell him to be in readiness to go with me. It will be his turn to go out with one of the others this evening, and he might not be back in time if I did not warn him."

"What arms shall I take with me?" Long Tom said, when Guy told him of their expedition.

"Nothing but your sword and quarter-staff. I see that many of the beggars and others that one meets in the streets carry long staffs, and yours is not much longer than the generality. You brought it tied up with your bow, so you would do well to carry it, for in a street broil, where there is room to swing it, you could desire no better weapon, in such strong hands as yours, Tom. Besides, you can knock down and disable with it and no great harm is done, whereas if you used your sword there would be dead men; and although by all I hear these are not uncommon objects in the streets of Paris, there might be trouble if the town watch came up, as we are strangers. I shall carry a stout cudgel myself, as well as my sword."

Accordingly at half-past eight they set out. Guy put on a long cloak and a cap such as was worn by the citizens, but strengthened inside by a few bands of steel forming sufficient protection to the head against any ordinary blow. This he had purchased at a stall on his way home. Tom had put on the garments that had been bought for him that afternoon, consisting of a doublet of tanned leather that could be worn under armour or for ordinary use, and was thick enough to afford considerable protection. The streets were already almost deserted; those who were abroad hurried along looking with suspicion at all whom they met, and walking in the middle of the road so as to avoid being taken by surprise by anyone lurking in the doorways or at the corners of alleys. Once or twice men came out and stared at Guy and his companion by the light of the lanterns suspended across the streets, but there was nothing about their appearance to encourage an attack, and the stalwart figure of the archer promised hard blows rather than plunder. Arriving at the square in front of Notre Dame they waited awhile. Here there were still people about, for it was a rendezvous both for roistering young gallants, thieves, and others starting on midnight adventures. After walking backwards and forwards two or three times Guy said, "You had best stand here in the shadow of this buttress while I go and place myself beneath that hanging lamp; seeing that we are together, and he, looking perhaps only for one, may not recognize me."

On reaching the lamp, Guy took off his hat, so that the light should fall on his face, waited for a minute, and then replaced it. As soon as he did so a slightly-built lad came up to him.

"Were you not at the fair by the river to-day, sir, and are you not expecting some one to meet you here?"

"That is so, lad. If you will tell me whom I am expecting I shall know that he has sent you, though, indeed, I looked to meet himself and not a messenger."

"Montepone," the lad said.

"That is right. Why is he not here himself?"

"He received a message before starting that one whose orders he could not neglect would call upon him this evening, and he therefore sent me to the rendezvous. I have been looking anxiously for you, but until now had not seen you."

"I have a companion with me; being a stranger here in Paris, I did not care to be wandering through the streets alone. He is a countryman of mine, and can be trusted."

"It is indeed dangerous to be out alone. It is seldom that I am in the streets after dark, but the doctor came with me and placed me in a corner of the porch, and then returned by himself, telling me to stir not until I saw you; and that should you not come, or should I not be able to make you out, I was to remain until he came for me even if I waited until morning."

"I will fetch my follower," Guy said, "and am ready to accompany you."

The lad was evidently unwilling to be left there for a moment alone, and he walked back with Guy to the buttress where the archer was standing.

"This is our guide, Tom," Guy said, as the archer stepped out to join him; "the person I expected was unable to come himself. Now, lad, I am ready; you see we are well guarded."

The boy nodded, evidently reassured by the bulk of the archer, and was about to step on ahead of them, when Guy said, "You had best walk with us. If you keep in front, it will seem as if you were guiding us, and that would point us out at once as strangers. Is it far to the place you are taking us to?"

"A short quarter of an hour's walk, sir."

# CHAPTER VII — IN THE STREETS OF PARIS

They crossed the bridge to the right bank of the river, and followed the stream down for some distance. Passing through some narrow lanes, they presently emerged into a street of higher pretensions, and stopped at the door of a small house wedged in between two of much larger size. The boy took a key from his girdle, opened the door, and entered.

"Stand here a moment, I pray you," he said; "I will fetch a light."

In a few seconds he appeared with a lantern. He shut and barred the door, and then led the way upstairs and showed them into a small but well-furnished room, which was lighted by a hanging lamp. He then went to a buffet, brought out a flask of wine and two goblets, and said: "Will it please you to be seated and to help yourselves to the wine; my master may possibly be detained for some little time before he is able to see you." Then he went out and closed the door behind him.

"It is evident, Tom," Guy said, as he took off his hat and cloak, and seated himself, "that the doctor has a good idea of making himself comfortable. Sit down, we may have to wait some time."

"Do you think that it will be safe to touch the wine, Master Guy? Perchance it may be drugged."

"Why should it be?" Guy asked. "We are not such important personages that anyone can desire to make away with us. I am convinced that the doctor was in earnest when he told me that story that I repeated to you this evening. It is possible that he may not be able to give us as much information as he said, but that he means well by us I am certain; and I think we may be sure that his wine is as good as his apartments are comfortable."

This turned out to be the case; the wine was excellent, and the archer soon laid aside any doubt he might have entertained. From time to time steps could be heard in the apartment above, and it was evident that it was here that the interview between the doctor and his visitor was taking place. Presently a ring was heard below.

# At Agincourt

"Another visitor," Guy said. Getting up, he slightly drew aside a thick curtain that hung before a casement, a moment later he let it fall again. "There are two men-at-arms standing on the other side of the street and one at the door." He heard the door opened, then the boy's step was heard on the stairs, two or three minutes later there was a movement above and the sound of the footsteps of two men coming down. Presently the outside door closed, two or three minutes elapsed; then the door opened and the Italian entered.

"I regret that I have kept you so long," he said courteously, "but my visitor was not to be got rid of hastily. It was a lady, and there is no hurrying ladies. When a man comes in, I have already ascertained what he desires to know; he listens to my answer and takes his departure. A woman, on the contrary, has a thousand things to ask, and for the most part they are questions quite beyond my power to answer."

"I have, as you see, Signor Montepone, brought my tall countryman with me; as you noticed me, I doubt not for a moment that you also marked him when we entered the city. Knowing nothing of the ways of Paris, but having heard that the streets were very unsafe after dark, I thought it best to bring him with me; and I am indeed glad that I did so, for we met with several very rough-looking characters on our way to Notre Dame, and had I been alone I might have had trouble."

"You did quite right," the Italian said; "I regretted afterwards that I did not myself advise you to bring some one with you, for indeed it is not safe for one man to go abroad alone after dark. And now, will you accompany me upstairs; this tall fellow will doubtless be able to pass the time with that flask of wine until you return."

"He should be able to do so," Guy said with a smile, "for indeed it is the best wine I have tasted, so far as my judgment goes, since I crossed the Channel, and indeed the best I have ever tasted."

"'Tis good wine. I received a cask of it from the grower, a Burgundian noble, who had, as he believed, gained some advantage from following my advice."

The man led the way upstairs. The room he entered there was much larger than that which they had left, extending over the whole floor. It was draped similarly to that in the booth, but was far more handsomely and elaborately got up. The hangings were of heavy cloth sprinkled with stars, the ceiling was blue with gold stars, a planisphere and astrolabe stood in the centre of the room, and a charcoal fire burned in a brazier beside them. A pair of huge bats with outstretched wings hung by wires from the ceiling, their white teeth glistening in the light of four lamps on stands, some six feet high, one in each corner of the room. The floor was covered with a dark Eastern carpet, a large chair with a footstool in front stood at a short distance from the planisphere; at one end was a massive table on which were retorts, glass globes, and a variety of apparatus new to Guy. At the other end of the room there was a frame some eight feet square on which a white sheet was stretched tightly.

"Now, Master Guy," the Italian said, "firstly, I beg you to give me the date of your birth and if possible the hour, for I would for my own information if not for yours, cast your horoscope. I like to know for my own satisfaction, as far as may be, the future of those with whom I have to deal. If I perceive that misfortunes and perhaps death threaten them, it is clearly of no use my entering into relations with them. In your case, of course, it is with your mistress that I am chiefly concerned; still as your fortunes are at present so closely mixed up with hers, I may learn something of much utility to me from your horoscope."

"I was born on the 8th of December, 1394, and shall be therefore seventeen in a fortnight's time. I was born a few minutes after midnight, for I have heard my mother say that the castle bell had sounded but a few minutes before I was born. She said that she had been anxious about it, because an old woman had predicted that if she ever had a child born on the 7th day of the month, it would be in every way unfortunate; so my mother was greatly pleased that I had escaped the consequences predicted."

"And now," the Italian went on, having made a note in his tablets, "what said your lady?"

"She bid me say, sir, that she was very sensible of the advantage that it would be to her to receive news or warning from one so well informed as yourself; and that she on her part promises that she will befriend and protect your daughter should you at any time bring her to her castle in England, or should she come alone with such tokens from you as that she might be known; and this promise my lady vows on the sacraments to keep."

"Then we are in agreement," the Italian said; "and right glad am I to know that should aught befall me, my daughter will be in such good hands. As far as worldly means are concerned her future is assured, for I have laid out much of the money I have received in jewels of value, which will produce a sum that will be an ample dowry for her. Now I can give you some news. The Duke of Berri with the queen came two days since from Melun to Corbeil, and Louis of Bavaria came on here yesterday to the Duke of Aquitaine with a message to Burgundy and to the butchers, asking that they would allow him to attend the queen to Paris, and that she might reside in his house of Nasle. Burgundy was minded to grant her leave, but at a meeting of the chiefs of the guild of butchers this afternoon they resolved to refuse the request; and this evening they have broken every door and window of the Duke of Berri's house, and committed great damages there, so that it should not be habitable; they resolved that Berri should not enter Paris, but that the queen might come. I hear that it has been determined that the king shall be placed in the Louvre, where the citizens of Paris can keep guard over him and prevent any attempt by the Orleanists to carry him away.

"All this will make no difference to your mistress directly; the point of it is that the power of these butchers, with whom go the guild of skinners and others, is so increasing that even the Duke of Burgundy is forced to give in to them. Some of the other guilds and the greater part of the respectable traders are wholly opposed to these men. They themselves may care little whether Orleans or Burgundy sways the court and the king, but this usurpation of the butchers, who have behind them the scum of Paris, is regarded as a danger to the whole city, and the feeling may grow into so hot a rage that there may be serious rioting in the streets. I tell you this that you may be prepared. Assuredly the butchers are not likely to interfere with any save such of the townspeople as they may deem hostile to them, and no harm would intentionally be done to her or to any other hostage of Burgundy. But the provost of the silversmiths is one of those who withstands them to the best of his power, and should matters come to serious rioting his house might be attacked. The leaders of the butchers' guild would be glad to see him killed, and their followers would still more like to have the sacking of his rich magazine of silver goods and the spoiling of his furniture.

"I say not that things are likely to come to that yet, but there is no telling how far they may be carried. It is but a dark cloud in the distance at present, but it may in time burst into a storm that will deluge the streets of Paris with blood. I may tell you that, against you as English there is no strong feeling at present among the Burgundians, for I am informed that the duke has taken several bodies of English archers into his pay, and that at Soissons and other towns he has enlisted a score or two of these men. However, I am sure to gain information long before matters come to any serious point, except a sudden outbreak arise from a street broil. I may tell you that one result of the violence of the butchers to-day may be to cause some breach between them and the Burgundian nobles, who are, I am told, greatly incensed at their refusing to give permission to the Duke of Berri to come here after Burgundy had acceded to his request, and that these fellows should venture to damage the hotel of one of the royal dukes seemed to them to be still more intolerable. The Duke of Burgundy may truckle to these fellows, but his nobles will strongly resent their interference and their arrogant insolence, and the duke may find that if he is to retain their support he will have to throw over that of these turbulent citizens. Moreover, their conduct adds daily to the strength of the Orleanists among the citizens, and if a strong Armagnac force approaches Paris they will be hailed by no small portion of the citizens as deliverers."

"In truth I can well understand, Signor Montepone, that the nobles should revolt against this association with butchers and skinners; 'tis past all bearing that fellows like these should thus meddle in public affairs."

"The populace of Paris has ever been turbulent," the Italian replied. "In this it resembles the cities of Flanders, and the butchers are ever at the bottom of all tumults. Now I will introduce my daughter to you; it is well that you should know her, for in case of need she may serve as a messenger, and it may be that I may some day ask you to present her to your lady."

He opened the door. "Katarina!" he said without raising his voice, and at once a girl came running up from the floor below.

"This is my daughter, Master Aylmer; you have seen her before."

Katarina was a girl of some fourteen years of age. She was dressed in black, and was tall and slight. Her complexion was fairer than that of her father, and she already gave promise of considerable beauty. Guy bowed to her as she made her reverence, while her face lit up with an amused smile.

"Your father says I have seen you before, signora, but in sooth I know not where or how, since it was but this morning that I arrived in Paris."

"We parted but half an hour since, monsieur."

"Parted?" Guy repeated with a puzzled expression on his face. "Surely you are jesting with me."

"Do you not recognize my messenger?" the Italian said with a smile. "My daughter is my assistant. In a business like mine one cannot trust a stranger to do one service, and as a boy she could come and go unmarked when she carries a message to persons of quality. She looks a saucy page in the daytime when she goes on the business, but after nightfall she is dressed as you saw her this evening. As a girl she could not traverse the streets unattended, and I am far too busy to bear her company; but as a boy she can go where she likes, and indeed it is only when we are alone, and there is little chance of my having visitors, that she appears in her proper character."

"You must be very courageous, signora," Guy said; "but, indeed, I can well imagine that you can pass where you will without anyone suspecting you to be a girl, for the thought that this was so never entered my head."

"I am so accustomed to the disguise," she said, "that I feel more comfortable in it than dressed as I now am, and it is much more amusing to be able to go about as I like than to remain all day cooped up here when my father is abroad."

"And now, Master Aylmer, that you have made my daughter's acquaintance, and I have told you what news I have gathered, it needs not that I should detain you longer; the hour is getting late already, and your lady may well be getting anxious at your absence. Can you read?"

"Yes, signor; the priest at my lady's castle in England, of which my father is castellan during my lord's absences, instructed me."

"It is well; for sometimes a note can be slipped into a hand when it would not be safe to deliver a message by word of mouth. From time to time if there be anything new you shall hear from me, but there will be no occasion for you to come hither again unless there is something of importance on which I may desire to have speech with you, or you with me. Remain here, Katarina, until my return; I will see monsieur out, and bar the door after him."

GUY AND LONG TOM COME TO THE RESCUE OF COUNT CHARLES.

Passing downstairs Guy looked in at the room where he had left the archer. The latter sprung to his feet as he entered with a somewhat dazed expression on his face, for indeed, he had fallen off into a sound sleep.

# At Agincourt

"We are going now, Tom," Guy said. "I have concluded my business with this gentleman. We will not go back the way we came," he went on, as they issued into the street, "for I am sure we should never find our way through those alleys. Let us keep along here until we come to a broader street leading the way we wish to go; fortunately, with the river to our left, we cannot go very far wrong."

They presently came to a street leading in the desired direction. They had scarcely entered it when they heard ahead of them the sound of a fray. A loud cry arose, and there was a clashing of sword-blades.

"Come on, Tom!" Guy said; "it may be that some gentleman is attacked by these ruffians of the streets."

Starting off at a run, they soon arrived at the scene of combat, the features of which they were able to see by the light of the lamp that hung in the centre of the street. A man was standing in a narrow doorway, which prevented his being attacked except in front, and the step on which he stood gave him a slight advantage over his adversaries. These were nearly a dozen in number, and were evidently, as Guy had supposed, street ruffians of the lowest class. Without hesitation Guy and the archer fell upon them, with a shout of encouragement to the defender of the doorway, who was evidently sorely pressed. Tom's quarter-staff sent two of the men rolling on the ground almost before they realized that they were attacked, while Guy ran another through the body. For a moment the assailants scattered, but then, seeing that they were attacked by only two men, they fell upon them with fury.

Guy defended himself stoutly, but he would have fared badly had it not been for the efforts of Long Tom, whose staff descended with such tremendous force upon the heads of his assailants that it broke down their guard, and sent man after man on to the pavement. Guy himself received a sharp wound in the shoulder, but cut down another of his assailants; and the defender of the door, leaving his post of vantage, now joined them, and in a couple of minutes but four of the assailants remained on their feet, and these, with a shout of dismay, turned and took to their heels. Guy had now opportunely arrived. As the latter took off his hat he saw time to look at the gentleman to whose assistance he had so that the stranger was but a year or two older than himself.

"By our Lady, sir," the young man said, "you arrived at a lucky moment, for I could not much longer have kept these ruffians at bay. I have to thank you for my life, which, assuredly, they would have taken, especially as I had disposed of two of their comrades before you came up. May I ask to whom I am so indebted? I am Count Charles d'Estournel."

"My name is Guy Aylmer, sir; I am the son of Sir James Aylmer, an English knight, and am here as the esquire of Dame Margaret de Villeroy, who arrived but this morning in Paris."

"And who is this stalwart fellow whose staff has done more execution than both our sword-blades?" the young count asked; "verily it rose and fell like a flail on a thrashing-floor."

"He is one of Dame Margaret's retainers, and the captain of a band of archers in her service, but is at present here as one of her men-at-arms."

"In truth I envy her so stout a retainer. Good fellow, I have to thank you much, as well as Monsieur Guy Aylmer, for your assistance."

"One is always glad of an opportunity to stretch one's arms a bit when there is but a good excuse for doing so," the archer said; "and one needs no better chance than when one sees a gentleman attacked by such scum as these ruffians," and he motioned to the men lying stretched on the ground.

"Ah, you are English!" D'Estournel said with a slight smile at Tom's very broken French. "I know all about you now," he went on, turning to Guy. "I was not present today when your lady had audience with Burgundy, but I heard that an English dame had arrived, and that the duke came but badly out of the encounter in words with her. But we had best be moving on or we may have the watch on us, and we should be called upon to account for these ten fellows lying here. I doubt not but half of them are only stunned and will soon make off, the other six will have to be carried away. We have a good account to give of ourselves, but the watch would probably not trouble themselves to ask any questions, and I have no fancy for spending a night locked up in the cage with perhaps a dozen unsavoury malefactors. Which way does your course lie, sir?"

"We are lodged at the house of Maître Leroux, provost of the silversmiths."

"Then you are going in the wrong direction. You return up this street, then turn to your right; his house is in the third street to the left. I shall do myself the honour of calling in the morning to thank you more fully for the service you have rendered me, which, should it ever fall into my power, you can count on my returning. My way now lies in the opposite direction."

After mutual salutes they parted, and Guy followed the directions given to them.

"That was a sharp skirmish, Master Guy," Long Tom said contentedly; "the odds were just enough to make it interesting. Did you escape scatheless?"

# At Agincourt

"Not altogether, Tom, I had a sword-thrust in my shoulder; but I can do with it until I get back, when I will get you to bandage it for me."

"That will I; I did not get so much as a scratch. A quarter-staff is a rare weapon in a fight like that, for you can keep well out of the reach of their swords. In faith I have not had so pleasant an exercise since that fight Dickon and I had in the market-place at Winchester last Lammas fair."

"I am afraid Dame Margaret will scold us for getting into a fray."

"Had it not been for your wound we need have said nothing about it; but you may be sure that you will have to carry your arm in a sling for a day or two, and she will want to know the ins and outs of the matter."

"I think the affair has been a fortunate one, for it has obtained for me the friendship of a young Burgundian noble. Friendless as we are here, this is no slight matter, and I by no means grudge the amount of blood I have lost for such a gain. There is a light in Dame Margaret's casement; she said that she should sit up till my return, and would herself let me in, for the household would be asleep two hours ago; and as Maître Leroux and his wife have shown themselves so kindly disposed towards us, she should not like the household disturbed at such an hour. I was to whistle a note or two of *Richard Mon Roi*, and she would know that we were without."

He whistled a bar or two of the air, they saw a shadow cross the casement, then the light disappeared, and in a minute they heard the bolts undrawn and the door opened.

"You are late, Guy," she said; "I have been expecting you this hour past. Why, what has happened to you?" she broke off as she saw his face.

"It is but a trifle, lady," he said; "a sword-thrust in the shoulder, and a little blood. Long Tom will bind it up. Our delay was caused partly by the fact that the Italian was engaged, and it was half-an-hour before I could see him. Moreover, we had been kept at the trysting-place, as the guide did not recognize me owing to Tom being with me; and lastly, we were somewhat delayed by the matter that cost me this sword-thrust, which I in no way grudge, since it has gained for us a friend who may be useful."

Tom had by this time barred the door and had gone upstairs. "I am disappointed in you, Guy," Dame Margaret said severely when they entered the room. "I told you to keep yourself free from frays of all kinds, and here you have been engaged in one before we have been twelve hours in Paris."

"I crave your pardon, madam, but it is not in human nature to stand by without drawing a sword on behalf of a young gentleman defending himself against a dozen cut-throats. I am sure that in such a case your ladyship would be the first to bid me draw and strike in. The matter did not last three minutes. Tom disposed of six of them with his quarter-staff, the gentleman had killed two before we arrived, and I managed to dispose of two others, the rest took to their heels. The young gentleman was Count Charles d'Estournel; he is, as it seems, in the Duke of Burgundy's train; and as we undoubtedly saved his life, he may turn out a good and useful friend."

"You are right, Guy; I spoke perhaps too hastily. And now about the other matter."

Guy told her all that had taken place.

"And what is this man like?" she asked when he had concluded.

"Now that I saw him without the astrologer's robe and in his ordinary costume he seemed to me a very proper gentleman," Guy replied. "He is my height or thereabouts, grave in face and of good presence. I have no doubt that he is to be trusted, and he has evidently resolved to do all in his power to aid you, should it be necessary to do so. He would scarce have introduced his daughter to me had it not been so."

"He must be a strange man," Dame Margaret said thoughtfully.

"He is certainly no common man, lady. As I have told you, he believes thoroughly in his science, and but adopts the costume in which I first saw him and the role of a quack vendor of nostrums in order that his real profession may not be known to the public, and so bring him in collision with the church."

"It seems to me, Guy," Dame Margaret said the next morning, "that as you have already made the acquaintance of a young French noble, and may probably meet with others, 'twill be best that, when we have finished our breakfast, you should lose no time in sallying out and providing yourself with suitable attire. Spare not money, for my purse is very full. Get yourself a suit in which you can accompany me fitly if I again see the duke, or, as is possible, have an interview with the queen. Get two others, the one a quiet one, and not likely to attract notice, for your ordinary wear; the other a more handsome one, to wear when you go into the company of the young men of station like this Burgundian noble whom you succoured last night. Your father being a knight, you may well, as the esquire of my lord, hold your head as high as other young esquires of good family in the train of French nobles."

On Agnes and Charlie coming into the room, the latter exclaimed, "Why have you got your arm in a scarf, Guy?"

"He was in a fray last night, Charlie. He and Tom came upon a number of ruffians fighting a young gentleman, so they joined in and helped him, and Guy was wounded in the shoulder."

"Did they beat the bad men, mother?"

"Yes, dear; Guy had taken a sword with him, as it was after dark, and Tom had his quarter-staff."

"Then the others can have had no chance," Charlie said decidedly. "I have often seen Long Tom playing with the quarter-staff, and he could beat anyone in the castle. I warrant he laid about him well. I should have liked to have been there to have seen it, mother."

"It will be a good many years yet, Charlie, before you will be old enough to go out after dark in such a place as Paris."

"But I saw real fighting at the castle, mother, and I am sure I was not afraid even when the cannon made a great noise."

"No, you behaved very well, Charlie; but it is one thing to be standing on the top of a keep and another to be in the streets when a fray is going on all round."

"Did you kill anyone, Guy?" the boy asked eagerly.

"Some of them were wounded," Guy replied, "but I cannot say for certain that anyone was killed."

"They ought to be killed, these bad men who attack people in the street. If I were King of France I would have all their heads chopped off."

"It is not so easy to catch them, Charlie. When the watch come upon them when they are doing such things there is not much mercy shown to them."

As soon as breakfast was over Guy went out, after learning from Maître Leroux the address of a tradesman who generally kept a stock of garments in store, in readiness for those passing through Paris, who might not have time to stop while clothes were specially made for them. He returned in the course of an hour, followed by a boy carrying a wooden case with the clothes that he had bought. He had been fortunate in getting two suits which fitted him perfectly. They had been made for a young knight who had been despatched by the duke to Flanders just after he had been measured for them, and the tailor said that he was glad to sell them, as for aught he knew it might be weeks or even months before the knight returned, and he could make other suits for him at his leisure. Thus he was provided at once with his two best suits; for the other he had been measured, and it was to be sent in a couple of days. On his return he went straight to his room, and attired himself in readiness to receive the visit of Count Charles d'Estournel.

The suit consisted of an orange-coloured doublet coming down to the hips, with puce sleeves; the trousers were blue, and fitting closely to the legs; the shoes were of the great length then in fashion, being some eighteen inches from the heel to the pointed toe. The court suit was similar in make, but more handsome—the doublet, which was of crimson, being embroidered with gold; the closely-fitting trousers were striped with light blue and black; the cap with the suit in which he was now dressed was yellow, that with the court suit crimson, and both were high and conical, resembling a sugar-loaf in shape. From his sword-belt he carried a light straight sword, instead of the heavier one that would be carried in actual warfare, and on the right side was a long dagger.

Charlie clapped his hands as he entered the sitting-room.

"That will do very well, Master Esquire," Dame Margaret said with a smile; "truly you look as well fitted as if they had been made for you, and the colours are well chosen."

Guy told her how he had obtained them.

"You are very fortunate," she said, "and this afternoon, when I mean to take a walk to see the city, I shall feel that I am well escorted with you by my side."

"Shall you take us, mother?" Charlie asked anxiously.

"I intend to do so. You are so accustomed to be in the open air that you would soon pine if confined here, though indeed the air outside is but close and heavy compared with that at home. I have been speaking to Master Leroux while you have been away, and he tells me that a post goes once a week to Lille, and that he will send a letter for me to Sir Eustace under cover to a worthy trader of that town, who will forward it thence to Villeroy by a messenger. Therefore I shall write this morning; my lord will be pleased indeed to learn that we are so comfortably bestowed here, and that there is no cause for any uneasiness on his part."

# CHAPTER VIII — A RIOT

While Dame Margaret was speaking to Guy, one of the servitors came up with word that Count Charles d'Estournel was below desiring to speak with Master Guy Aylmer.

"Show the count up. Or no, you had best go down yourself to receive him, Guy. Pray him to come up with you; it will be more fitting."

Guy at once went down.

"So this is my saviour of last night," the count said gaily as Guy joined him. "I could scarce get a view of your face then, as the lamps give such a poor light, and I should hardly have known you again. Besides, you were wrapped up in your cloak. But you told me that you were an esquire, and I see that you carry a sword. I want to take you out to introduce you to some of my friends. Can you accompany me now?"

"I shall do so willingly, Count; but first will you allow me to present you to my lady mistress? She prayed me to bring you up to her apartments."

"That shall I right willingly; those who were present yesterday speak of her as a noble lady."

They went upstairs together.

"My lady, this is Count Charles d'Estournel, who desires me to present him to you."

"I am glad to meet you, Sir Count," Dame Margaret said, holding out her hand, which he raised to his lips, "seeing that my esquire, Master Guy Aylmer, was able to render you some slight service last night. This is my daughter Agnes, and my son Charles."

"The service was by no means a slight one," the young count said, returning a deep salute that Agnes and Charlie made to him, "unless indeed you consider that my life is a valueless one, for assuredly without his aid and that of your tall retainer, my father would have been childless this morning. I was indeed in sore plight when they arrived; my arm was tiring, and I could not have defended myself very much longer against such odds, and as I had exasperated them by killing two of their comrades, I should have received no mercy at their hands. In my surprise at being so suddenly attacked I even forgot to raise a shout for the watch, though it is hardly likely that they would have heard me had I done so; the lazy knaves are never on the spot when they are wanted. However, we gave the ruffians a lesson that those of them who escaped are not likely to forget readily, for out of the fourteen who attacked me we accounted for ten, of whom your retainer levelled no less than six with that staff of his, and I doubt whether any of the other four came off scatheless. I imagine that those levelled by your retainer got up and made off,—that is, if they recovered their senses before the watch came,—but I am sure that the other four will never steal pouch or cut throat in future. 'Tis a shame that these rascals are suffered to interfere with honest men, and it would be far better if the city authorities would turn their attention to ridding the streets of these pests instead of meddling with things that in no way concern them."

"It would no doubt be much wiser," Dame Margaret replied; "but since their betters are ever quarrelling among themselves, we can hardly wonder that the citizens do not attend to their own business."

"No doubt you are right," the young count said with a smile; "but it is the highest who set the bad example, and we their vassals cannot but follow them, though I myself would far rather draw my sword against the enemies of France than against my countrymen. But methinks," and here he laughed, "the example of the wars that England has so often waged with Scotland might well cause you to take a lenient view of our misdoings."

"I cannot gainsay you there, Sir Count, and truly those quarrels have caused more damage to England than your disputes between Burgundy and Orleans have, so far, inflicted on France; but you see I am a sufferer in the one case and not in the other. Even now I am ignorant why I have been brought here. There is a truce at present between England and France, and assuredly there are more English in the service of nobles of Burgundy than in those of Orleans, and at any rate I have seen no reason why there can at present be any doubt at all of the conduct of my lord, who has but lately defended his castle against the followers of Orleans.'"

"So I have heard, madame, and I know that there are some of my friends who think that Duke John has behaved hardly in the matter; but he seldom acts without reason, though it may not be always that one which he assigns for any action." Then, changing the subject, he went on. "I have come to take Master Guy for a walk with me, and to introduce him to some of my friends. My father is absent at present, but on his return he will, I know, hasten to express his gratitude. I trust that you can spare your esquire to go out with me."

"Certainly, so that he does but return in time to escort me for a walk through the streets this afternoon."

"I will be sure to come back, madam," Guy said. "You have but to say the hour at which you will start; but indeed I think that I shall probably be in to dinner at one."

"I cannot see," Guy said, when he had sallied out with the young count, "why they should have called upon Sir Eustace to furnish hostages. As the Duke of Burgundy has English archers in his pay, and France is at truce with England, there seems less reason than at other times to demand sureties of his loyalty, especially as he has shown that he is in no way well disposed to the Armagnacs."

"Between ourselves, Guy, I think that the duke in no way expected that hostages would be given, and that he was by no means well pleased when a messenger arrived from the herald to say that he was returning with your lady and her children. What was his intention I know not, but in times like these it is necessary sometimes to reward faithful followers or to secure doubtful ones, and it may be that he would have been glad to have had the opportunity of finding so fair a castle and estate at his disposal. You know the fable of the wolf and the lamb; a poor excuse is deemed sufficient at all times in France when there is a great noble on one side and a simple knight on the other, and I reckon that the duke did not calculate upon the willingness of your Sir Eustace to permit his wife and children to come here, or upon the dame's willingness to do so, and in no way expected matters to turn out as they have done, for there is now no shadow of excuse for him to meddle with Villeroy. Indeed, I question whether the condition about hostages was of his devising; but it may well be that the king or the queen wished it inserted, and he, thinking that there was no chance of that alternative being accepted, yielded to the wish. Mind, all this is not spoken from my own knowledge, but I did hear that Duke John was much put out when he found that the hostages were coming, and there was some laughter among us at the duke being for once outwitted."

"Then you do not love him overmuch, Count?"

"He is our lord, Guy, and we are bound to fight in his cause, but our vows of fealty do not include the word love. The duke his father was a noble prince, just and honourable, and he was loved as well as honoured. Duke John is a different man altogether. He is brave, as he proved in Hungary, and it may be said that he is wise, but his wisdom is not of the kind that Burgundian nobles love. It might have been wise to remove Orleans from his path, although I doubt it, but it was a dastardly murder all the same; and although we are bound to support him, it alienated not a few. Then he condescends to consort with these sorry knaves the butchers, and others of low estate, to take them into his counsels, and to thrust them upon us, at which, I may tell you, there is grievous discontent. All this is rank treason to the duke, I have no doubt, but it is true nevertheless. Here we are at our first stopping-place. This is as it is kept by a Burgundian master, who has with him two or three of the best swordsmen in France, and here a number of us meet every morning to learn tricks of fence, and to keep ourselves in good exercise, which indeed one sorely needs in this city of Paris, where there is neither hawking nor hunting nor jousting nor any other kind of knightly sport, everyone being too busily in earnest to think of amusement. Several of my best friends are sure to be here, and I want to introduce you to them."

When they entered the salon they found some thirty young knights and nobles gathered. Two or three pairs in helmet and body-armour were fighting with blunted swords, others were vaulting on to a saddle placed on a framework roughly representing a high war-horse; one or two were swinging heavy maces, whirling them round their heads and bringing them down occasionally upon great sand-bags six feet high, while others were seated on benches resting themselves after their exercises. D'Estournel's arrival was greeted with a shout, and several of those disengaged at once came over to him.

"Laggard!" one exclaimed, "what excuse have you to make for coming so late? I noted not that De Jouvaux's wine had mounted into your head last night, and surely the duke cannot have had need of your valuable services this morning?"

"Neither one nor the other befell, D'Estelle. But first let me introduce to you all my friend Guy Aylmer, an English gentleman, the son of a knight of that country, and himself an esquire of Sir Eustace de Villeroy. I am sure you will welcome him when I tell you that he saved my life last night when attacked by a band of cut-throats. Guy, these are my friends Count Pierre d'Estelle, Count Walter de Vesoul, the Sieur John de Perron, and the Knights Louis de Lactre, Sir Reginald Poupart, Sir James Regnier, Sir Thomas d'Autre, and Sir Philip de Noisies."

"I can assure you of our friendship," the first-named of these gentlemen said cordially to Guy, "for indeed you have rendered us all a service in thus saving to us our friend D'Estournel. Tell us how the matter occurred, Charles; in sooth, we shall have to take these ruffians of Paris in hand. So long as they cut each other's throats no great harm is done, but if they take to cutting ours it is time to give them a lesson."

"The matter was simple enough," D'Estournel said. "As you know, it was late before we broke up at De Jouvaux's last night, for I heard it strike half-past ten by the bell of St. Germain as I sallied out. I was making my way home like a peaceful citizen, when two men came out from a narrow lane and stumbled roughly across me. Deeming that they were drunk, I struck one a buffet on the side of his head and stretched him in the gutter."

"That was not like a peaceful citizen, Charles," one of the others broke in.

"Well, hardly, perhaps; but I forgot my character at the moment. However, an instant later there was a shout, and a dozen or so armed men poured out from the lane and fell upon me. I saw at once that I had been taken in a trap. Luckily there was a deep doorway close by, so I sprang into it, and, drawing my sword, put myself in a posture of defence before they were upon me. I ran the first through the body, and that seemed to teach the others some caution. Fortunately the doorway was so deep that only two could assail me at once, and I held my ground for some time pretty fairly, only receiving a few scratches. Presently I saw another opening, and, parrying a thrust, I ran my sword through the fellow's throat. He fell with a loud outcry, which was fortunate, for it came to the ears of my friend here, and brought him and a stout retainer—a prodigiously tall fellow, with a staff longer than himself—to my aid. They were but just in time, for the ruffians, furious at the fall of another of their companions, were pressing me hotly, and slashing so furiously with their swords that it was as much as I could do to parry them, and had no time to thrust back in reply. My friend here ran two of them through, his tall companion levelled six to the ground with his staff, while I did what I could to aid them, and at last the four that remained still on their legs ran off. I believe they thought that the man with the staff was the Evil One himself, who had got tired of aiding them in their villainous enterprises."

"It was a narrow escape indeed, Charles," Count Walter de Vesoul said gravely, "and it was well for you that there was that doorway hard by, or your brave friend would have found but your body when he came along. It is evident, gentlemen, that when we indulge in drinking parties we must go home in couples. Of course, Charles, you must lay a complaint before the duke, and he must let the Parisians know that if they do not keep their cut-throats within bounds we will take to sallying out at night in parties and will cut down every man we find about the streets."

"I will lay my complaint, but I doubt if much good will come of it. The duke will speak to the provost of the butchers, and nothing will be done."

"Then we will take them in hand," the other said angrily. "If the Parisians won't keep order in their streets we will keep it for them. Such doings are intolerable, and we will make up parties to scour the streets at night. Men passing peaceably along we shall not of course molest, but any parties of armed men we find about we will cut down without hesitation."

"I shall be heartily glad to join one of the parties whenever you are disposed, De Vesoul," D'Estournel said. "Perchance I may light on one or more of the four fellows who got away last night. Now I am ready to have a bout with swords."

"We have all had our turn, Charles," the other said.

"Then I must work with the mace," the count said. "My friend here, you see, did not come off as scatheless last night as I did, or else I would have asked him to have a bout with me. He held his own so well against two of them who fell on him together that I doubt not I should find him a sturdy adversary."

"I fear not, Count," Guy said smiling. "I can use my sword, it is true, in English fashion, but I know little of feints and tricks with the sword such as I am told are taught in your schools."

"A little practice here will amend that," D'Estournel said. "These things are well enough in a *salle d'armes*, and are useful when one man is opposed to another in a duel, but in a battle or *mêlée* I fancy that they are of but little use, though indeed I have never yet had the chance of trying. We will introduce you to the master, and I hope that you will come here regularly; it will give real pleasure to all. This salon is kept up by the duke for our benefit, and as you are one of his most pressingly invited guests you are certainly free of it."

They went up in a body to the master. "Maître Baudin," Count Charles said, "I have to introduce to you a gentleman who is our mutual friend, and who last night saved my life in a street brawl. He is at present an esquire of Sir Eustace de Villeroy, and has travelled hither with the knight's dame, who has come at the invitation of the duke. His father is an English knight, and as the friend of us all we trust that you will put him upon the list of your pupils."

"I shall be pleased to do so, Count Charles, the more so since he has done you such service."

"I am afraid that you will, find me a very backward pupil," Guy said. "I have been well taught in English fashion, but as you know, maître, we were more famed for downright hard hitting than for subtlety and skill in arms."

"Downright hard hitting is not to be despised," the master said, "and in a battle it is the chief thing of all; yet science is not to be regarded as useless, since it not only makes sword-play a noble pastime, but in a single combat it enables one who is physically weak to hold his own against a far stronger antagonist."

"That I feel greatly, maître. I shall be glad indeed of lessons in the art, and as soon as my shoulder is healed I shall take great pleasure in attending your school regularly, whenever my lady has no need of my presence. I am now in the position of the weak antagonist you speak of, and am therefore the more anxious to acquire the skill that will enable me to take my part in a conflict with full-grown men."

"You showed last night that you could do that," Count Charles said with a smile.

"Nay, men of that sort do not count," Guy said. "They are but rough swordsmen, and it was only their number that rendered them dangerous. There is little credit in holding one's own against ruffians of that kind."

"Well, I will be lazy this morning," the young count said, "and do without my practice. Will you all come round to my rooms, gentlemen, and drink a glass or two of wine and make the better acquaintance of my friend? He is bound to be back at his lodgings by one, and therefore you need not be afraid that I am leading you into a carouse."

Guy passed an hour in the count's lodgings and then returned to the provost's. The count accompanied him, saying that he had not yet seen his tall friend of the night before, and must personally thank him. Long Tom was called down, he being one of the two who had remained in for the morning.

"I must thank you again for the service that you rendered me last night," the count said frankly, holding out his hand to the archer. "I hope that you will accept this ring in token of my gratitude; I have had it enlarged this morning so that it may fit one of your strong fingers. It may be useful some day to turn into money should you find yourself in a pinch."

"I thank you, sir," Tom said. "I will wear it round my neck, for in truth rings are not for the use of men in my condition. As to gratitude, I feel that it is rather the other way, for my arms were beginning to get stiff for want of use. I only wish that the fray had lasted a bit longer, for I had scarce time to warm to it, and I hope that the next time your lordship gets into trouble I may have the good luck to be near at hand again."

"I hope you may, my friend; assuredly I could want no better helper."

After the count had taken his leave Guy went upstairs and told Lady Margaret how he had spent the morning.

"I am very glad to hear what you say about the fencing school, Guy; it will be good for you to have such training. And indeed 'tis well that you should have some employment, for time would hang but wearily on your hands were you to remain long caged up here. I shall be very glad for you to go. It will make no difference to us whether we take our walk in the morning or in the afternoon."

After dinner they went out. Guy escorted Dame Margaret, Agnes and Charlie followed, Long Tom and Jules Varoy bringing up the rear, both armed with swords and carrying in addition heavy cudgels. First of all they visited the cathedral, where Dame Margaret and her daughter knelt for some time in prayer before one of the shrines; then crossing the bridge again they followed along the broad pavement between the foot of the walls and the river, which served as a market, where hucksters of all sorts plied their trade; then entering the next gate on the wall they walked down the street to the Place de la Bastille, which had been finished but a few years.

"'Tis a gloomy place and a strong one," Dame Margaret said with a shiver as she looked at its frowning towers; "the poor wretches who are once entombed there can have but little hope of escape. Surely there cannot be so many state prisoners as to need for their keeping, a building so large as that. Still, with so turbulent a population as this of Paris, it doubtless needs a strong castle to hold them."

"It seems to me, madame, that, though useful doubtless as a prison, the castle was never really built for that purpose, but as a stronghold to overawe Paris."

"That may be so, Guy; at any rate I am glad that they did not use it as our place of detention instead of the house of Maître Leroux."

"They see well enough, madame, that you are more securely held than bolts and bars could detain you. I imagine that they would like nothing better than for you to get away back to Villeroy, since it would give them an excuse for an attack on the castle."

"Doubtless that is so, Guy; I came freely, and I must stay freely until some change takes place that will leave it open to us to fly. But in sooth it seems to me that nothing short of the arrival of an English army could do that. Were the Armagnacs to get the better of the Burgundians our position would be even worse than it is now."

"That is true enough, madame, for the Burgundians have no cause of hostility whatever to Sir Eustace and you, while we have given the Armagnacs good reasons for ill-will against us. Still, were they to come here it would be open to you to fly, for all Artois is Burgundian; and though the duke might not be able to hold his position here, Artois and Flanders would long be able to sustain themselves, and you would therefore be safe at Villeroy, for they would have other matters to attend to without meddling with those who only ask to be let alone."

On their way back from the Bastille they saw a crowd in the street and heard loud shouts.

"We had best turn off by this side street, madame," Guy said; "doubtless it is a body of the scoundrel butchers at their work of slaying some enemy under the pretext of his being an Orleanist. Do you hear their shouts of 'Paris and Burgundy!'?"

Turning down a side street they made a circuit round the scene of the tumult, and then coming up into the main street again resumed their way. After walking a considerable distance they came to a large building.

"What place is this, Guy?"

"It is the Louvre, madame. It should be the abode of the King of France, but he is only sometimes lodged there; but often stays at one of the hotels of the great lords. These palaces are all fortified buildings. Our country castles are strong, but there is no air of gloom about them; these narrow streets and high houses seem to crush one down."

"We will go back again, Guy; I do not think that I shall often go out in future."

"You can take a boat on the river, madame, and row up or down into the country. They say it is pretty; once fairly away from Paris, there are hills and woods and villages."

"That may be pleasant. If they would but let me go and live in one of those quiet spots I should be as contented as it is possible for me to be away from my husband.

"Nothing can be kinder than are Maître Leroux and his wife, but one cannot but feel that one is a burden upon them. My hope is that when the king comes to his senses I may be able to obtain an interview with him, and even if I cannot have leave to return to Villeroy I may be allowed to take up my abode outside the walls, or at any rate to obtain a quiet lodging for ourselves."

For the next three weeks the time passed quietly. Guy went every morning to the *salle d'armes*, for his wound being on his left shoulder he was able to use his sword arm as soon as it began to heal.

"You underrated your skill," the fencing-master said when he had given him his first lesson. "It is true that you do not know the niceties of sword-playing, but indeed you are so quick of eye and wrist that you can afford to do without them. Still, doubtless after a couple of months' practice here you will be so far improved that he will need to be a good swordsman who holds his own with you."

Guy paid only one visit during this time to the lodgings of the Italian.

"You have not heard from me, Master Aylmer," the latter said, "because indeed there has been nothing of importance to tell you. The Armagnacs are, I hear, collecting a great army, and are likely ere long to march in this direction. The butchers are becoming more and more unpopular and more and more violent; not a day passes but many citizens are killed by them under the pretence that they are Armagnacs, but really because they had expressed themselves as hostile to the doings of these tyrants. I have cast your horoscope, and I find that the conjunction of the planets at your birth was eminently favourable. It seems to me that about this time you will pass through many perilous adventures, but you are destined to escape any dangers that threaten you. You will gain honour and renown, and come to fortune through a marriage. There are other things in your career that are uncertain, since I cannot tell at what date they are likely to occur and whether the planets that were favourable at your birth may again be in the ascendant; but, for as much as I have told you, I have no doubt whatever."

"I thank you for the trouble that you have taken, Count Montepone," for Guy had now learned the rank that the Italian held in his own country, "and can only trust that your predictions will be verified. I would rather win fortune by my own hand than by marriage, though it will not come amiss."

"Whatever way it may happen, you will be knighted," the astrologist said gravely, "after a great battle, and by the hand of a sovereign; though by whom the battle will be fought and who the sovereign may be I cannot say, but methinks that it will be the English king."

"That I can wish more than anything," Guy said warmly. "Fortune is good, but to be knighted by a royal hand would be an honour greater than any other that could befall me."

"Bear your destiny in mind," the Italian said earnestly, "remember that in many cases predictions bring about their own fulfilment; and truly I am rejoiced that I have found that the stars point out so prosperous a future for you."

Guy was not free from the superstition of the time, and although in his English home he had seldom heard astrology mentioned, he had found since he had been in France that many even of the highest rank had an implicit belief in it, and he was convinced that at any rate the count himself believed in the power of the stars. He was gratified, therefore, to be told that his future would be prosperous; and, indeed, the predictions were not so improbable as to excite doubt in themselves. He was already an esquire, and unless he fell in combat or otherwise, it was probable that he would attain the honour of knighthood before many years had passed. The fact, however, that it was to be bestowed by royal hand added greatly to the value of the honour. Knighthood was common in those days; it was bestowed almost as a matter of course upon young men of good birth, especially if they took up the profession of arms. Every noble had some, while not a few had many knights in their service, discharging what would now be the duties of officers when their levies were called out, and they could themselves bestow the rank upon any man possessing a certain amount of land; but to be knighted by a distinguished leader, or by a sovereign, was a distinction greatly prized, and placed its recipient in quite another category to the knights by service. It was a testimony alike of valour and of birth, and was a proof that its bearer was a warrior of distinction. The prophecy that he would better his fortune by marriage weighed little with him; marriage was a matter that appeared to him at present to be a very remote contingency; at the same time it was pleasant to him to be told that his wife would be an heiress, because this would place him above the need of earning his living by his sword, and would enable him to follow his sovereign, not as one of the train of a powerful noble, but as a free knight.

# CHAPTER IX — A STOUT DEFENCE

The Duke of Burgundy had left Paris upon the day after he had received Dame Margaret, and as the king had a lucid interval, the Duke of Aquitaine, his son, was also absent with the army. In Paris there existed a general sense of uneasiness and alarm. The butchers, feeling that their doings had excited a strong reaction against them, and that several of the other guilds, notably that of the carpenters, were combining against them, determined to strike terror into their opponents by attacking some of their leaders. Several of these were openly murdered in the streets, and the houses of others were burnt and sacked. One evening when Guy had returned at nine o'clock from a supper at Count Charles's lodgings, it being the first time he had been out after dark since his first adventure, he had but just gone up to his room, when he heard a loud knocking at the door below. Going to the front window he looked out of the casement.

"Who is it that knocks?" he asked.

"It is I—the lad of Notre Dame."

He recognized the voice and ran down and opened the door.

"What is it, signora?"

"My father bids me tell you, sir, that he but learned the instant before he despatched me that the butchers are going to attack this house this evening, under the pretext that there are English spies here, but really to slay the provost of the silversmiths, and to gratify their followers by the sack of his house. I fear that I am too late, for they were to march from the *abattoirs* at nine, and it is already nearly half-past. Look! I see torches coming up the street."

"It is too late, indeed, to fly, even if we wished to," Guy said. "Dame Margaret and the children retired to bed an hour ago. Will you take this ring," and he took off from his finger one that D'Estournel had given him, "and carry it at once to the lodgings of Count Charles d'Estournel? They are in the house on this side of the Hotel of St. Pol. He is still up, and has some of his friends with him. Tell him from me that this house is being attacked, and beg him to gather a party, if he can, and come to our assistance. Say that we shall defend it until the last."

The girl took the ring and ran off at the top of her speed. The roar of the distant crowd could now be distinctly heard. Guy put up the strong bars of the door and then rushed upstairs. First he knocked at the door of Maître Leroux.

"The butchers are coming to attack your house!" he shouted. "Call up your servants; bid them take to their arms." Then he ran up to the room where his men slept. Long Tom, who had met him at D'Estournel's door and accompanied him home, sprang to his feet from his pallet as Guy entered. "The butchers are about to attack the house, Tom; up all of you and arm yourselves; bring down your bow and arrows. Where do the men-servants sleep?"

"There are five of them in the next room, and the two who serve in the shop are in the chamber beyond," the archer replied, as he hastily buckled on his armour. Guy rushed to the door and awoke the inmates of the rooms, telling them to arm and hasten down to defend the house, which was about to be attacked. A moment later Maître Leroux himself appeared and repeated the order.

"Art sure of what you say, Master Guy?" he asked.

"Look from the window and you will see them approaching," Guy replied, and going to the casement window which was at the front of the house he threw it open. Some four hundred yards away a dense throng was coming along; a score of torches lighted up the scene.

"Resistance is vain," the silversmith said. "It is my life they seek; I will go down to them."

"Resistance will not be in vain," Guy said firmly. "I have already sent for aid, and we shall have a body of Burgundian men-at-arms here to our assistance before long. Your life will not satisfy them; it is the plunder of your shop and house that they long for, and you may be sure that they will put all to the sword if they once break in. Now let us run down and see what we can do to strengthen our defences."

"The shutters and doors are all strong," the provost said as they hurried downstairs, followed by the four men-at-arms and the servants—for in those days men removed but few of their garments as they lay down on their rough pallets.

"In the first place," Guy said, "we must pile everything that we can find below against these doors, so that when they yield we can still make a defence here, before we retire. Are there other stairs than these?"

"No."

"So much the better. As soon as we have blocked the door we will barricade the first landing and defend ourselves there. Jean Bart, do you take the command below for the present. Seize everything that you can lay hands on, logs from the wood-store, sacks of charcoal, cases, everything heavy that you can find, and pile them up against the door. Tom, do you come with us; an arrow or two will check their ardour, and it is not likely they have brought bows or cross-bows with them. Try to parley with them as long as you can, Maître Leroux, every minute is of value."

"What is all this, Guy?" Dame Margaret asked as she entered the apartment. Having been aroused by the noise she had hastily attired herself, and had just come into the front room.

"The butchers are about to attack the house, lady; we are going to defend it. I have sent to D'Estournel, and we may hope for aid before long."

At this moment there was a loud knocking at the door and a hoarse roar of voices from the street. The silversmith went to the casement and opened it, and he and Guy looked out. A shout of fury arose from the street, with cries of "Death to the English spies!" "Death to the Armagnac provost!"

Leroux in vain endeavoured to make his voice heard, and so tell the crowd that his guests were not spies, but had been lodged at his house by the Duke of Burgundy himself. A tall man on horseback, one of several who were evidently leaders of the mob, pressed his way through the crowd to the door and evidently gave some orders, and a din of heavy sledge-hammers and axes beating against it at once mingled with the shouts of the crowd. The horseman crossed again to the other side of the street and shook his fist threateningly at Leroux.

"That is Jacques Legoix," the silversmith said, as he retired from the window; "one of the great leaders of the butchers; his family, and the St. Yons and Taiberts rule the market."

"Tom," Guy said to the archer, who was standing behind him. "Begin by picking off that fellow on horseback opposite."

Tom had already bent his bow and had an arrow in readiness, a moment later the shaft flew and struck the butcher between the eyes, and he fell dead from his horse. A yell of consternation and rage rose from the crowd.

"Now you can distribute a few arrows among those fellows at the door," Guy said.

# At Agincourt

The archer leant far out of the low casement. "It is awkward shooting, Master Guy," he said quietly, "but I daresay I can make a shift to manage it." Disregarding the furious yells of the crowd, he sent arrow after arrow among the men using the sledges and axes. Many of them had steel caps with projecting rims which sheltered the neck, but as they raised their weapons with both hands over their heads they exposed their chests to the marksman above, and not an arrow that was shot failed to bring down a man. When six had fallen no fresh volunteers came forward to take their places, although another horseman made his way up to them and endeavoured by persuasions and threats to induce them to continue the work. This man was clad in armour, and wore a steel cap in the place of the knightly helmet.

"Who is that fellow?" Guy asked the merchant.

"He is the son of Caboche, the head of the flayers, one of the most pestilent villains in the city."

"Keep your eye on him, Tom, and when you see a chance send an arrow home."

"That armour of his is but common stuff, Master Guy; as soon as I get a chance I will send a shaft through it."

The man with a gesture of anger turned and gave instructions to a number of men, who pushed their way through the crowd, first picking up some of the fallen hammers and axes. The fate of his associate had evidently taught the horseman prudence, for as he moved away he kept his head bent down so as not to expose his face to the aim of the terrible marksman at the window. He halted a short distance away and was evidently haranguing the crowd round him, and in his vehemence raised his arm. The moment he did so Tom's bow twanged. The arrow struck him at the unprotected part under the arm-pit, and he fell headlong from his horse. Maddened with rage the crowd no longer hesitated, and again attacked the door. Just as they did so there was a roar of exultation down the street as twelve men brought up a solid gate that they had beaten in and wrenched from its hinges from a house beyond.

"TOM'S BOW TWANGED, AND THE ARROW STRUCK THE HORSE-
MAN UNDER THE ARM-PIT."

"You can shoot as you like now, Tom. I will go down and see how the men are getting on below; the mob will have the door in sooner or later."

Guy found that the men below had not wasted their time. A great pile of logs, sacks, and other materials was piled against the door, and a short distance behind stood a number of barrels of wine and heavy cases ready to be placed in position.

"Get them upstairs, Jean," Guy said; "they will make a better barricade than the furniture, which we may as well save if possible."

The nine men set to work, and in a very short time a strong barricade was formed across the top of the wide staircase.

"Have you all the cases out of the shop?"

"Yes, we have not left one there, Master Guy. If they are all full of silver there must be enough for a royal banqueting-table."

Some, indeed, of the massive chests were so heavy that it required the efforts of six men to carry them upstairs.

"How do matters go, Guy?" Dame Margaret asked quietly as he re-entered the apartment.

"Very well," he replied. "I don't think the door will hold out much longer; but there is a strong barricade behind it which it will take them some time to force, and another on the landing here that we ought to be able to hold for an hour at least, and before that yields we will have another ready on the landing above."

"I will see to that," she said. "I will take Agnes and Charlie up with me, and then, with the women, I will move out the clothes' and linen chests and build them up there."

"Thank you, madame; I trust long before the barricade here is carried we shall have D'Estournel and his friends to our assistance. Indeed, I doubt whether they will be able to carry it at all; it is as solid and almost as strong as a stone wall, and as there are thirteen or fourteen of us to defend it, it seems to me that nothing short of battering the cases to pieces will enable them to force a way."

"I wish I could do something," Agnes broke in; "it is hard not to be able to help while you are all fighting for us. I wish I had brought my bow with me, you know I can shoot fairly."

"I think that it is just as well that you have not," Guy said with a smile. "I do not doubt your courage for a moment, but if you were placing yourself in danger we should all be anxious about you, and I would much rather know that you were safe with your mother upstairs."

# At Agincourt

Guy now went to the window. Maître Leroux had been directing his servants in the formation of the barricades.

"I can do nothing to protect the door," the archer said; "they have propped up that gate so as to cover the men who are hammering at it. I have been distributing my arrows among the crowd, and in faith there will be a good many vacancies among the butchers and flayers in the market tomorrow morning. I am just going up to fill my quiver again and bring down a spare armful of arrows."

"Leave those on the landing here, Tom, and bring your full quiver down below. The door will not hold many minutes longer: I could see that it was yielding when I was down there just now. I don't think that we shall be able to make a long defence below, for with their hooked halberts they will be able to pull out the logs, do what we will."

One of the servants now ran in.

"They have broken the door down, sir. It is only kept in place by the things behind it."

Guy ran out, climbed the barricade—which on the landing was four feet high, but as it was built on the edge of the top stair it was nine inches higher on that face—let himself drop on to the stairs, and ran down into the passage.

"I think, Maître Leroux," he said, "that you and your men had better go up at once and station yourselves at the barricade. There is no room here for more than five of us to use our arms, and when we retire we shall have to do so quickly. Will you please fasten a chair on the top step in such a way that we can use it to climb over the barricade without delay? We are like to be hard pressed, and it is no easy matter to get over a five-foot wall speedily with a crowd of armed men pressing hotly on your heels."

The provost told two of his men to pick out a square block of firewood, as nearly as possible the thickness of the height of one of the steps. After trying several they found one that would do, and on placing it on the stair next to the top it formed with the step above it a level platform. On this the chair was placed, a strong rope being attached to it so that it could be pulled up over the barricade when the last of the defenders had entered. By the time this was finished the battle below began in earnest. The infuriated assailants had pulled the doors outwards and were making desperate efforts to climb the pile of logs. This they soon found to be impossible, and began with their halberts to pull them down, and it was not long before they had dislodged sufficient to make a slope up which they could climb. Their work had not been carried on with impunity, for the archer had stationed himself on the top and sent his arrows thick and fast among them.

"In faith, master," he said to Guy, who stood close behind, "methinks that I am doing almost as much harm as good, for I am aiding them mightily in making their slope, which will presently contain as many dead men as logs."

As soon as they deemed the slope climbable the furious assailants charged up. They were met by Guy and the four men-at-arms. Tom had now slung his bow behind him and had betaken himself to his heavy axe, which crashed through the iron caps of the assailants as though they had been eggshells. But in such numbers did they press on that Guy saw that this barricade could not be much longer held.

"Get ready to retire when I give the word!" he shouted to his companions. "Tom, you and Jules Varoy and Robert Picard run first upstairs. When you have climbed the barricade, do you, Tom, take your place on the top. Jean Bart and I will come up last, and you can cover us with your arrows. Tell Maître Leroux to remove the light into the room, so that they will not be able to see what there is to encounter, while these torches here and those held by the crowd will enable you to see well enough to take aim. Now!" he shouted, "fall back!"

Tom and the two men-at-arms sprang up the stairs, Guy and Jean Bart followed more slowly, and halted a few steps from the top.

"All up, master!" Tom shouted, and Jean and Guy were able to cross the barricade before the foremost of their pursuers reached them. There had indeed been confusion below, for several of those who had first climbed the barricade had, instead of pressing hotly in pursuit, run along the hall and through the door into the shop, in their eagerness to be the first to seize upon the plunder. They expected the others to follow their example, but one of their leaders placed himself in their way and threatened to cut them down if they did not first assault the stairs.

"Fools!" he shouted, "do you think that the old fox has wasted the time we have given him? You may be sure that the richest prizes have been carried above."

There was an angry altercation, which was continued until those who had first run into the shop returned with the news that it had been completely stripped of its contents. There was now no longer any hesitation in obeying their leader, and the men poured up the stairs in a mass. Suddenly some torches appeared above, and those in front saw with consternation the obstacle that stood between them and their prey. They had little time for consideration, however, for the arrows from the archer now smote them, and that with a force and rapidity that bewildered them. Five or six of those in front fell shot through the brain.

"Heads down!" a voice shouted. There was no retreat for those in front, for the mass behind pressed them forward, and, instinctively obeying the order, they ran up. But neither helm nor breast-plate availed to keep out the terrible English arrows, which clove their way through the iron as if it had been pasteboard. Stumbling over the bodies of those who had fallen, the front rank of the assailants at last reached the barricade, but here their progress was arrested. A line of men stood behind the smooth wall of massive cases, and those who strove to climb it were smitten with axe or sword, while they themselves could not reach the defenders above them. They could but thrust blindly with pike or halbert, for if a face was raised to direct the aim one of the deadly arrows struck it instantly. In vain they strove by the aid of the halberts to haul down a case from its position, the weight was too great for one man's strength to move, and before several could grasp the handle of the halbert to aid them, the shaft was cut in two by the blow of an axe.

Hopeless as the attempt seemed, it was persevered in, for the crowd below, ignorant of the nature of the obstacle, maddened with fury and with the wine which had been freely served out before starting, still pressed forward, each fearing that the silversmith's treasures would be appropriated before he could obtain his share. For half an hour the fight continued, then there was a roar in the street, and Dame Margaret, who, after seeing the barricade above completed, had come down to her room and was gazing along the street, ran out on to the landing.

"Help is at hand!" she cried, "the knights are coming!"

Then came the loud tramp of horses, mingled with shouts of "Burgundy!" The crowd at the entrance at once turned and ran out, and as the alarm reached those within, they too rushed down, until the stairs were untenanted save by the dead. Bidding the others hold their places lest the assailants should return, Guy ran in and joined Lady Margaret at the window. A fierce conflict was going on in the street, with shouts of "Burgundy!" "A rescue!" "A rescue!"

The knights, who were followed by some fifty men-at-arms, rode into the mob, hewing them down with their swords. The humiliations that they had received from the arrogance and insolence of the butchers had long rankled in their minds, and they now took a heavy vengeance. The windows of all the houses opposite, from which men and women had been peering timidly out, were now crowded; women waving their handkerchiefs to the knights, and men loudly shouting greetings and encouragements. The whole of the traders of Paris were bitterly opposed to the domination of the market guilds, and while they cared but little for the quarrel between the rival dukes, the alliance between Burgundy and the butchers naturally drove them to sympathize with the opposite party. The proof afforded by the charge of the knights upon the mob delighted them, as showing that, allied with them though they might be, the Burgundians were determined no longer to allow the rioting and excesses of the men of the market guilds to continue.

In two or three minutes all was over. The resistance, though fierce, was short, and the mob was driven down the side streets and chased until the trading quarter was cleared of them. As the knights returned Guy went down to the door, to which Maître Leroux had already descended to thank his rescuers for their timely aid.

"I thank you, my lords and knights," the silversmith said, "for the timely succour you have rendered me. I would pray you to enter and to allow me to thank you in more worthy fashion, but indeed the stairs and passage are encumbered with dead."

"Dame Margaret of Villeroy prays me to say that she also desires greatly to thank you," Guy said.

"I feared that we should have been too late," Count Charles replied. "We lost no time when your messenger came, Guy, but it took some time to rouse the men-at-arms and to saddle our horses. You must have made a stout defence indeed, judging by the pile of dead that encumber your passage."

"There are many more inside," Guy said, "and methinks that we could have held out for another hour yet if it had been needed. Indeed, the only thing that I feared was that they might set fire to the lower part of the house."

"I should like to see your defences, Maître Leroux," Count Walter de Vesoul said, "What say you, my friends, shall we mount and see the scene of this battle? Methinks we might well gain something by it, for 'tis no slight thing that an unfortified house should for over an hour defend itself against a mob full a couple of thousand strong. I doubt not, too, that Master Leroux will serve us with a flagon of wine; and, moreover, we should surely pay our respects to this English lady,—who while a hostage of the duke has been thus sorely ill-treated by the scum of Paris,—if she will please receive us at this hour of the evening."

The other knights, of whom there were ten in number, at once dismounted. The silversmith's servants brought torches, and after ordering two of them to broach a cask of wine and to regale the men-at-arms, the provost led the way upstairs.

"Wait a moment, good provost," the Count de Vesoul said, "let us understand the thing from the beginning. I see that the knaves lying here and many of those in the road are pierced by arrows, which, as I note, have in some cases gone through iron cap or breast-piece; how comes that?"

"That is the work of one of my lady's retainers. He is an English archer, and one of the most skilful. He comes from her English estate, and when she chose him as one of the four men-at-arms to accompany her, he begged leave to bring his bow and arrows, and has in truth, as you see, made good use of them."

"That is the same tall fellow who, as I told you, Walter, did me such good service in that fray," said D'Estournel.

"By Saint Anne, Guy, I would that I had a dozen such men among my varlets. Why, there are a round dozen lying outside the door."

"There would have been more," Guy said, "had they not brought up that great gate and used it as a screen while they battered in the door here."

"Then you built the barricade behind it?" Count Walter said as he climbed over the heap of logs.

"Yes, Count, it was built against the door, but when that gave way they pulled it down with halberts until they could climb over it. But, as you see, no small portion of slope on the outside is composed of their bodies. The archer's arrows did good execution as they worked at it, and when they made the assault we—that is to say, Dame Margaret's four retainers and I— held it for some time, then we retired up the stairs and defended that barricade we had built across the top."

The knights picked their way among the bodies that encumbered the stairs.

"By Saint Denis, Charles, this is a strong work indeed!" the count said to D'Estournel, as they reached the top; "no wonder the knaves found it too much for them. What are all these massive cases?"

"They contain the goods from my shop," Maître Leroux said. "Master Aylmer had them carried here while the archer was defending the door, and by so doing not only made, as you see, a stout breast-work, but saved them from being plundered."

"They were well fitted for it," Guy said, "for they are very weighty; and though the fellows tried hard they could not move them with their hooks, and as fast as they strove to do so the provost's men and ours struck off the heads of the halberts with axes; and the work was all the more difficult as our archer had always a shaft fitted to let fly whenever they lifted their heads."

"But how did you manage to get over safely when they won the barricade below?" D'Estournel asked; "it was not an easy feat to climb this wall with a crowd of foemen behind."

Guy explained how they had arranged a chair to form a step. "There was, however," he went on, "no great need for haste. The archer and two others went first, and he took his stand on the top of the chests in readiness to cover the retreat of the fourth man-at-arms and myself. But happily many of the knaves wanted to sack the shop more than to follow us, and there was such confusion below, that we had time to climb over and pull up the chair before they had mustered to the attack."

While they were talking Long Tom and the others had removed one of the chests and made a passage by which they could pass through, and Maître Leroux led them into his private apartments, which were similar to, although larger than, Dame Margaret's. A number of candles had already been lighted, and in a minute Mistress Leroux entered, followed by two of her maids carrying trays with great beakers of wine and a number of silver goblets, and she and the provost then poured out the wine and offered it with further expressions of thanks to the knights.

"Say naught about it, madame," Count Walter said; "it was high time that a check was put on these rough fellows who lord it over Paris and deem themselves its masters. I doubt not that they will raise some outcry and lay their complaint before the duke; but you, I trust, and other worthy citizens, will be beforehand with them, and send off a messenger to him laying complaints against these fellows for attacking, plundering, and burning at their will the houses of those of better repute than themselves. We have come to your help not as officers of the duke, but as knights and gentlemen who feel it a foul wrong that such things should be done. Moreover, as Dame Margaret of Villeroy, a hostage of the duke, was lodged here at his request, it was a matter that nearly touched his honour that her life should be placed in danger by these scurvy knaves, and we shall so represent the matter to the duke."

Just as the knights had drunk their wine, Guy, who had left them on the landing, entered, escorting Dame Margaret and her two children. Count Charles d'Estournel, after saluting her, presented his companions to her, and she thanked each very heartily for the succour they had brought so opportunely.

"In truth, lady," the Count de Vesoul said, "methinks from what we saw that you might even have managed without us, so stoutly were you defended by your esquire and your retainers, aided as they were by those of the provost, though in the end it may be that these must have succumbed to numbers; for I can well imagine that your assailants, after the loss that they have suffered, would have spared no effort to avenge themselves, and might indeed, as a last resource, have fired the house. This they would no doubt have done long before had it not been that by so doing they would have lost all the plunder that they counted on. This stout defence will no doubt teach these fellows some moderation, for they will see that citizens' houses are not to be plundered without hard fighting and much loss. As for ourselves, we shall see the Duke of Burgundy's lieutenant to-morrow morning and lay the matter before him, praying him to issue a proclamation saying that in order to suppress the shameful disorders that have taken place, he gives notice that all who attack the houses of peaceful citizens will henceforth be treated as evildoers and punished accordingly."

After some further conversation the knights prepared to leave.

"I shall do myself the honour, sirs," Maître Leroux said, "of sending to your lodgings to-morrow the cups that you have used, as a small testimony of my gratitude to you, and as a memorial of the events of this evening."

While they were upstairs the men-at-arms and servants had been employed in clearing the stairs, throwing the bodies that had encumbered it out into the street. The men-at-arms of the knights had, after drinking the wine that had been sent out to them, aided in clearing the passage; buckets of water had been thrown down on the stairs, and the servitors by a vigorous use of brooms had removed most of the traces of the fray. The work had just been finished, and Dame Margaret's men had, by Guy's orders, stationed themselves on the landing to do honour to the knights as they set out.

"Ah, my tall friend," D'Estournel said to the archer, "so you have been at work again, and I can see that you are even more doughty with the bow than with that long staff of yours. Well, this time there must have been enough fighting to please even you."

"It has been an indifferent good fight, my lord," Tom said; "but in truth, save for the stand on that pile of logs below, when things were for a time brisk, it has been altogether too one-sided to please me."

"Most people would think that the one-sidedness was all the other way," D'Estournel laughed. "Well, men, you have all done your duty to your lady right well this night, and there is not one of us here who would not gladly have such brave fellows in his service. I see that you are all four wounded."

"They are scarce to be called wounds, Sir Count, seeing that they are but flesh cuts from their halberts which we got in the fray below. These slaughterers can doubtless strike a good blow with a pole-axe, but they are but clumsy varlets with other weapons. But to give them their due, they fought stoutly if with but little skill or discretion."

Several of the others also said a few words of commendation to the men. The provost and Guy escorted the knights to the door below. The latter had ordered twenty of their men-at-arms to remain in the house until morning, after which ten were to stay there until the doors had been repaired and refixed. As soon as the knights had ridden off the silversmith ordered several bundles of rushes to be strewn in the shop for the guard, and a meal of cold meat to be set for their supper. Two of them were posted as sentinels at the door.

"I shall not open the shop to-morrow," he said as he ascended the stairs with Guy, "nor indeed shall I do so until things have settled down. There will be for some time a mighty animosity on the part of these butchers and skinners against me, and it is only reasonable that after such an attack I should close my shop. Those who have dealings with me will know that they can do their business with me in private. And now methinks we will retire to bed; 'tis past midnight, and there is no fear of our being disturbed again. If they send anyone to spy out whether we are on the watch, the sight of the Burgundian soldiers below will suffice to tell them that there is nothing to be done. The first thing tomorrow I will set the carpenters to work to make me an even stronger pair of doors than those that have been spoilt."

# CHAPTER X — AFTER THE FRAY

On going into Dame Margaret's apartments Guy found that she had again retired to rest, and at once threw himself on his bed without disrobing himself further than taking off his armour, for he felt that it was possible the assailants might return after finding that the Burgundian knights and men-at-arms had ridden away. He had told the men-at-arms to keep watch by turns at the top of the stairs, where the barricade still remained, and to run in to wake him should they hear any disturbance whatever at the door below. He slept but lightly, and several times went out to see that the watch was being well kept, and to look up and down the street to assure himself that all was quiet.

"You did nobly last night, Guy," Dame Margaret said as she met him in the morning; "Sir Eustace himself could have done no better had he been here. When I next write to my lord I shall tell him how well you have protected us, and pray him to send word of it to your father."

"I did my best, lady; but it is to Long Tom that it is chiefly due that our defence was made good. It was his shooting that caused the long delay in breaking open the door, and that enabled us to hold the barricade below, and he also stoutly aided in the defence of the landing."

"Nevertheless, Guy, it was under your direction that all things were done. It is to the leader who directs that the first praise is due rather than to the strongest and bravest of his men-at-arms. It was, too, owing to your interference on behalf of Count Charles d'Estournel that we owe it that succour came to us; it was his friendship for you that prompted him to gather his friends to come to our aid; and it was the warning, short though it was, sent us by that strange Italian that enabled you to send to the count for aid. I must see his daughter and thank her personally for the part she played in the matter. No, Guy, had it not been for you this house would now have been an empty shell, and all of us would have been lying under its ruins. I have been thinking during the night that you must be most careful when you go abroad; you know that the son of that monster Caboche, the leader of the skinners, and doubtless many leaders of the butchers, among them Legoix, were killed, and their friends are certain to endeavour to take vengeance on you. They saw you at the window, they will know that you are my esquire, and will doubtless put down their defeat entirely to you. You cannot be too careful, and, above all, you must not venture out at night save on grave occasion. Agnes," she broke off as the girl entered the room, "you too must thank our brave esquire for having so stoutly defended us."

"I do thank you most heartily, Guy," the girl said, "though I felt it very hard that I could do nothing to help you. It was terrible sitting here and hearing the fight so close to us, and the dreadful shouts and screams of those people, and to have nothing to do but to wait. Not that I was frightened, I felt quite confident that you would beat them, but it was so hard to sit quiet. I should not have minded so much if I could have been standing there to see the brave deeds that were being done."

"Like the queen of a tournament, Agnes," her mother said with a smile. "Yes, indeed, it is one of the hardships of us women. It is only when a castle is besieged and her lord is away that a woman may buckle on armour and set an example to her retainers by showing herself on the wall and risking the enemies' bolts, or even, if necessary, taking her place with her retainers on the breach; at other times she must be passive and wait while men fight."

"If I had only had my bow," Agnes said regretfully, "I could really have done something. You would have let me go out then, mother, would you not?"

"I don't know, dear; no, I don't think I should. It was anxious work enough for me as it was. If you had gone out I must have done so, and then Charlie would have wanted to go too. No; it was much better that we all sat together as we did, waiting quietly for what might come, and praying for those who were fighting for us."

"I was glad that Madame Leroux stayed upstairs with her maid instead of coming down here as you asked her, mother; she looked so scared and white that I do think it would have been worse than listening to the fighting to have had to sit and look at her."

Dame Margaret smiled. "Yes, Agnes, but I think that she was more frightened for her husband than for herself, and I don't suppose that she had ever been in danger before. Indeed, I must say that to look out at that crowd of horrible creatures below, brandishing their weapons, shouting and yelling, was enough to terrify any quiet and peaceable woman. As a knight's wife and daughter it was our duty to be calm and composed and to set an example, but a citizen's wife would not feel the same obligation, and might show her alarm without feeling that she disgraced herself or her husband."

On going out Guy found their host already engaged in a conference with a master carpenter as to the construction of the new doors. They were to be very strong and heavy, made of the best oak, and protected by thick sheets of iron; the hinges were to be of great strength to bear the weight. A smith had also arrived to receive instructions for making and setting very strong iron bars before the shop, the front of which would require to be altered to allow of massive shutters being erected on the inside. Iron gates were also to be fixed before the door.

"That will make something like a fortress of it, Master Aylmer," the silversmith said, "and it will then need heavy battering-rams to break into it. Several others of my craft similarly protect their shops; and certainly no one can blame me, after the attack of last night, for taking every means to defend myself. I intend to enlist a party of ten fighting men to act as a garrison until these troubles are all over."

"I think that you will act wisely in doing so," Guy said. "Your servants all bore themselves bravely last night, but they had no defensive armour and were unaccustomed to the use of weapons. Only I would advise you to be very careful as to the men that you engage, or you may find your guard within as dangerous as the mob without."

"I will take every pains as to that, you may be sure, and will engage none save after a careful inquiry into their characters."

The streets had already been cleared of the slain. All through the night little parties had searched for and carried off their dead, and when at early morning the authorities sent a party down to clear the street there remained but some twenty-five bodies, evidently by their attire belonging to the lowest class, and presumably without friends. That day petitions and complaints were sent to the king by the provosts of the merchants, the gold and silver smiths, the cloth merchants, the carpenters and others, complaining of the tumults caused by the butchers and their allies, and especially of the attack without cause or reason upon the house of Maître Leroux, the worshipful provost of the silversmiths. Several skirmishes occurred in the evening between the two parties, but an order was issued in the name of the king to the Maire and syndics of Paris rebuking them for allowing such disturbances and tumults, and ordering them to keep a portion of the burgher guard always under arms, and to repress such disturbances, and severely punish those taking part in them.

Maître Leroux and his wife paid a formal visit to Dame Margaret early in the day to thank her for the assistance that her retainers had given in defending the house.

"You were good enough to say, madame," the silversmith said, "that you regretted the trouble that your stay here gave us. We assured you then, and truly, that the trouble was as nothing, and that we felt your presence as an honour; now you see it has turned out more. Little did we think when you came here but a few days since that your coming would be the means of preserving our lives and property, yet so it has been, for assuredly if it had not been for your esquire and brave retainers we should have been murdered last night. As it is we have not only saved our lives but our property, and save for the renewal of the doors we shall not have been the losers even in the value of a crown piece. Thus, from being our guests you have become our benefactors; and one good result of what has passed is, that henceforth you will feel that, however long your stay here, and however much we may try to do for you, it will be but a trifle towards the discharge of the heavy obligation under which we feel to you."

After a meeting of the city council that afternoon, a guard of ten men was sent to the silversmith's to relieve the Burgundian men-at-arms. Five of these were to be on duty night and day until the house was made secure by the new doors and iron grill erected in front of the shop. Guy proposed to Dame Margaret that he should give up his visit to the *salle d'armes*, but this she would not hear of.

"I myself and the children will go no more abroad until matters become more settled, but it is on all accounts well that you should go to the school of arms. Already the friends that you have made have been the means of saving our lives, and it is well to keep them. We know not what is before us, but assuredly we need friends. Maître Leroux was telling me this morning that the Armagnacs are fast approaching, and that in a few days they will be within a short distance of Paris. Their approach will assuredly embitter the hostility between the factions here, and should they threaten the town there may be fierce fighting within the walls as well as without. At present, at any rate, there are likely to be no more disturbances such as that of last night, and therefore no occasion for you to remain indoors. Even these butchers, arrogant as they are, will not venture to excite the indignation that would be caused by another attack on this house. That, however, will make it all the more likely that they will seek revenge in other ways, and that the house will be watched at night and any that go out followed and murdered.

"You and Tom the archer are no doubt safe enough from the attack of ordinary street ruffians, but no two men, however strong and valiant, can hope to defend themselves successfully against a score of cut-throats. But I pray you on your way to the school go round and thank, in my name, this Italian and his daughter, and say that I desire much to thank the young lady personally for the immense service she has rendered me and my children. Take the archer with you, for even in the daytime there are street brawls in which a single man who had rendered himself obnoxious could readily be despatched."

"In faith, Master Guy," Long Tom said as they sallied out, "it seems to me that if our stay in Paris is a prolonged one I shall return home rich enough to buy me an estate, for never did money so flow into my pocket. We have been here but a short time, and I have gained as much and more than I should do in a year of hard service. First there was that young French count, the very next morning when he called here he gave me a purse with thirty crowns, telling me pleasantly that it was at the rate of five crowns for each skull I cracked on his behalf. Then this morning Maître Leroux came to me and said, 'Good fellow, it is greatly to your skill and valour that I owe my life, and that of my wife; this will help you to set up housekeeping; when you return home,' and he gave me a purse with a hundred crowns in it; what think you of that, master? The other three also got purses of fifty crowns each. If that is the rate of pay in Paris for a couple of hours' fighting, I do not care how often I take a share in a fray."

"You are doing well indeed, Tom, but you must remember that sooner or later you might go into a fray and lose your life, and with it the chance of buying that estate you speak of."

"We must all take our chances, master, and there is no winning a battle without the risk of the breaking of casques. Are we going to the house we went to the first night we came here, Master Guy? Methinks that this is the street we stopped at."

"Yes, Tom. It was the man who lives here who sent me word that the butchers were going to attack the provost's house, by the same messenger who met us before Notre Dame, and who last night, after warning me, carried my message to Count Charles, praying him to come to our aid."

"Then he did us yeoman service," the archer said warmly, "though I think not that they would have carried the barricade had they fought till morning."

"Perhaps not, though I would not say so for certain, for they might have devised some plan such as they did for covering themselves while they assaulted the door. But even had they not done so they would have been sure before they retired to have fired the house."

"That is what I thought of when they were attacking us," the archer said, "and wondered why they should waste men so freely when a torch would have done their business just as well for them."

"That would have been so, Tom, had they only wished to kill us; but though, no doubt, the leaders desired chiefly the life of the provost, the mob simply fought for plunder. If they had found all the jeweller's store in his shop, they would have fired the house very quickly when they discovered that they could not get at us. But it was the plunder that they wanted, and it was the sight of those chests full of silver-ware that made them venture their lives so freely, in order to have the handling of it. I do not think that I shall be long here, Tom. Do not wait for me at the door, but stroll up and down, keeping a short distance away, so that I can see you when I come out."

A decrepit old woman opened the door, and on Guy giving his name she said that she had orders to admit him if he called. The girl came out dressed in her female attire as he went upstairs.

"Ah, signor," she said, "I am glad indeed to see that you are safe."

"Thanks to you," he said warmly; "we are all your debtors indeed."

"I had but to run a mile or two," she said; "but what was there in that? But indeed I had an anxious time, I so feared that I should be too late. When I had seen the Count d'Estournel and delivered your message to him and had shown him your ring, and he and his friends had declared that they would call up their men and come at once to your aid, I could not go back and wait until this morning to learn if they arrived in time, so I ran to your street again and hid in a doorway and looked out. Just as I got there they broke in the door and I saw some of them rush in. But there was a pause, though they were all pressing to enter. They went in very slowly, and I knew that you must be defending the entrance. At last there was a sudden rush, and I almost cried out. I thought that it was all over. A great many entered and then there was a pause again. The crowd outside became more and more furious; it was dreadful to hear their shouts and to see the waving of torches and weapons.

"They seemed to be almost mad to get in. The crush round the door was terrible, and it was only when two or three horsemen rode in among them shouting, that the press ceased a little. One horseman obtained silence for a moment by holding up his hand. He told them that their friends inside were attacking a barricade, and would soon carry it, and then there would be silver enough for all; but that by pressing forward they did but hamper the efforts of their comrades. It seemed, oh, such a long, long time before I saw the Burgundians coming along, and I could not help throwing my cap up and shouting when they charged into the crowd. I waited until it was all over, and then I ran back home and had a rare scolding for being out so late; but I did not mind that much, after knowing that you were all safe."

At this moment a voice from the landing above said: "Are you going to keep Master Aylmer there all day with your chattering, Katarina?" The girl made a little face and nodded to Guy to go upstairs.

# At Agincourt

"Katarina is becoming a madcap," the astrologer said, as he led Guy into the room. "I cannot blame her altogether; I have made a boy of her, and I ought not to be shocked at her acting like one. But she gave me a rare fright last night when she did not return until close on midnight. Still, it was natural for her to wish to see how her mission had turned out."

"Her quickness saved all our lives," Guy said. "Had it not been for her carrying my message to the Count d'Estournel we should have been burnt alive before morning."

"It was unfortunate that I sent you the message so late, Master Aylmer. I was busy when a medical student who sometimes gathers news for me in the butchers' quarter came here, and left a missive for me. Had he sent up a message to me that it was urgent, I would have begged the personage I had with me to wait a moment while I read the letter. As it was, it lay downstairs till my visitor departed. When I learned the news I sent off Katarina at once. She had but a short time before come in, and was fortunately still in her boy's dress, so there was no time lost. I went out myself at ten o'clock to see what was going on, and must have been close to her without either of us knowing it. I looked on for a short time; but seeing that nothing could be done, and feeling sure that the house must be taken,—knowing nothing of the chance of the Burgundians coming to the rescue,—I returned here and was surprised to find that Katarina had not returned.

"I did not think that she could have reached the shop and warned you before the mob arrived, and therefore I became greatly alarmed as the time went by without her appearing. Indeed, my only hope was that she must have been looking on at the fight and would return when it was all over, as indeed it turned out; and I should have rated her much more soundly than I did had she not told me how she had fetched the Burgundians and that they had arrived in time. I hear that there is a great stir this morning. The number of men they have lost, and specially the deaths of Legoix and of the young Caboche, have infuriated the butchers and skinners. They have already sent off two of their number to lay their complaint before the Duke of Burgundy of the conduct of some of his knights in attacking them when they were assailing the house of a noted Armagnac. But they feel that they themselves for the moment must remain quiet, as the royal order has emboldened the Maire, supported by the traders' guilds, and notably by the carpenters, who are a very strong body, to call out a portion of the city guard, and to issue an order that all making disturbances, whomsoever they may be and under whatsoever pretext they are acting, will be summarily hung if captured when so engaged.

"In spite of this there will no doubt be troubles; but they will not venture again to attack the house of the silversmith, at any rate until an order comes from the Duke of Burgundy to forbid his knights from interfering in any way with their doings."

"Which I trust he will not send," Guy said; "and I doubt if the knights will obey it if it comes. They are already much enraged at the insolence of the butchers, and the royal proclamation this morning will justify them in aiding to put down disturbances whatsoever may be the duke's orders. And now, Sir Count, I have come hither this morning on behalf of my lady mistress to thank you for sending the news, and still more for the service your daughter rendered in summoning the knights to her assistance. She desires much to return thanks herself to your daughter, and will either call here to see her or would gladly receive her at her lodging should you prefer that."

"I should prefer it, Master Aylmer. Your lady can scarce pass through the streets unnoticed, for her English appearance marks her at once; and as all know she lodges at the silversmith's, she will be more particularly noticed after the events of last night, and her coming here will attract more attention to me than I care for. Therefore I will myself bring Katarina round and will do myself the honour of calling upon your lady. I can wrap the girl up in a cloak so that she shall not attract any observation, for no one knows, save the old woman below, that I have a daughter here; and with so many calling at the house, and among them some reckless young court gallants, I care not that it should be known, if for no other reason than, were it so, it would be soon suspected that the lad who goes so often in and out is the girl in disguise, and I could then no longer trust her in the streets alone."

"You will find my lady in at whatever hour you come, signor, for she has resolved not to go abroad again until order is restored in Paris."

"The decision is a wise one," the Italian said; "though indeed I think not that she would be in any danger, save that which every good-looking woman runs in troubled times like these, when crime is unpunished, and those in authority are far too occupied with their own affairs to trouble their heads about a woman being carried off. But it is different with you and your comrade. The butchers know well enough that it was your work that caused their failure last night. Your appearance at the window was noticed, and it was that tall archer of yours who played such havoc among them. Therefore I advise you to be ever on your guard, and to purchase a mail shirt and wear it under your doublet; for, however watchful you may be, an assassin may steal up behind you and stab you in the back. You may be sure that Caboche and the friends of Legoix will spare no pains to take vengeance upon you."

Guy presently rejoined the archer in the street. "Henceforth, Tom," he said, "you must always put on breast-and-back piece when you go out. I have been warned that our lives will almost surely be attempted, and that I had best put on a mail shirt under my doublet."

"Perhaps it would be best, Master Guy. I fear not three men if they stand up face to face with me, but to be stabbed in the back is a thing that neither strength nor skill can save one from. But as I care not to be always going about in armour I will expend some of my crowns in buying a shirt of mail also. 'Tis better by far than armour, for a man coming up behind could stab one over the line of the back-piece or under the arm, while if you have mail under your coat they will strike at you fair between the shoulders, and it is only by striking high up on the neck that they have any chance with you. A good coat of mail is money well laid out, and will last a lifetime; and even if it cost me all the silversmith's crowns I will have a right good one."

Guy nodded. He was wondering in his own mind how he should be able to procure one. His father had given him a purse on starting, but the money might be needed for emergencies. He certainly could not ask his mistress for such a sum, for she too might have need of the money that she had brought with her. He was still turning it over in his mind when they reached the fencing-school. He was greeted with acclamations as he entered by the young count and his friends.

"Here is our defender of houses," the former exclaimed. "Truly, Guy, you have given a lesson to the butchers that they sorely needed. They say that the king himself, who is in one of his good moods to-day, has interested himself mightily in the fray last night, and that he has expressed a wish to hear of it from the esquire who he has been told commanded the defence. So it is not unlikely that there will be a royal message for you to attend at the palace. Fortunately we had the first say in the matter this morning. My father returned last night, and as he is rather a favourite of his majesty, we got him to go to the king and obtain audience as soon as he arose, to complain of the conduct of the butchers in attacking the house of the provost of the silversmiths, and where, moreover, Dame Villeroy, who had arrived here in obedience to his majesty's own commands, was lodged. The king when he heard it was mightily offended. He said he had not been told of her coming, and that this insult to her touched his honour. He sent at once for the Maire and syndics, and upbraided them bitterly for allowing such tumults to take place, and commanded them to put a stop to them under pain of his severe displeasure.

"That accounts, you see, for the Maire's proclamation this morning. The king desired my father to thank me and the other knights and gentlemen for having put down the riot, and said that he would at once send off a message to the Duke of Burgundy commanding him to pay no attention to any reports the butchers might send to him, but to give them a stern answer that the king was greatly displeased with their conduct, and that if any fresh complaint about them was made he would straightway have all their leaders hung.

"It is one thing to threaten, and another to do, Guy; but at any rate, so long as the duke is away they will see that they had best keep quiet; for when the king is in his right senses and is not swayed by others, he is not to be trifled with.

"You can imagine what an excitement there was last night when that boy you sent arrived. The ring was sent up first, and when I gave orders that he should be admitted he came in well-nigh breathless. There were six or eight of us, and all were on the point of leaving. Thinking that it might be something private, they had taken up their hats and cloaks. The boy, as he came in, said, 'Which of you is Count Charles d'Estournel?' 'I am,' I said. 'You are the bearer of a message from Guy Aylmer?' 'I am, my lord. He prays you hasten to his assistance, for the butchers and skinners are attacking Maître Leroux's house, and had begun to hammer on the door when I was still in the street. If they make their way in, they will surely kill all they find in there. They are shouting, 'Death to the Armagnacs! Death to the English spies!'

"I called upon my comrades to join me, and all were eager to do so. We had long been smarting under the conduct of these ruffians, and moreover I was glad to discharge a part of my debt to you. So each ran to his lodgings and despatched servitors to summon their men-at-arms, and to order the horses to be saddled, and to gather in front of my lodging with all speed. Two or three of my friends who had left earlier were also summoned; but though we used all the speed we could it was more than an hour before all were assembled. The men-at-arms were scattered, and had to be roused; then there was the work of getting the stables open, and we had to force the doors in some places to do it. I was on thorns, as you may well imagine, and had little hope when we started that we should find any of you alive. Delighted indeed we were when, on getting near enough, we could see the crowd were stationary, and guessed at once that you were still holding out— though how you could have kept so large a number at bay was beyond us. We struck heartily and heavily, you may be sure, and chased the wolves back to their dens with a will. I hear that, what with those you slew in the house and street and those we cut down, it is reckoned that a couple of hundred were killed; though as to this none can speak with certainty, seeing that so many bodies were carried away before morning."

"I trust that none of you received wounds, Count Charles?"

"None of us; though several of the men-at-arms had gashes from the rascals' weapons, but naught, I think, that will matter."

At this moment one of the attendants of the salon came in.

"An usher from the palace is here, my lords and gentlemen. He has been to the lodging of Master Guy Aylmer, and has learned that he will most likely be here. If so, he has the king's command to conduct him to the palace, as His Majesty desires to have speech with him."

"I told you so, Guy; my father's story has excited the king's curiosity, and he would fain hear all about it. Make the most of it, for His Majesty loves to be entertained and amused."

"Had I better ask the usher to allow me to go back to my lodging to put on a gayer suit than this?" Guy asked.

"Certainly not; the king loves not to be kept waiting. Fortunately no time has been wasted so far, as this is on the road from the silversmith's to the palace."

The Louvre at that time bore no resemblance to the present building. It was a fortress surrounded by a strong embattled wall, having a lofty tower at each corner and others flanking its gates. On the water-face the towers rose from the edge of the river, so that there was no passage along the quays. The building itself was in the castellated form, though with larger windows than were common in such edifices. Eight turret-shaped buildings rose far above it, each surmounted with very high steeple-like roofs, while in the centre rose another large and almost perpendicular roof, terminating in a square open gallery. The building was further protected by four embattled towers on each side, so that if the outer wall were carried it could still defend itself. In the court-yard between the outer wall and the palace were rows of low barracks, where troops were lodged. Two regiments of the best soldiers of Burgundy were quartered here, as the duke feared that some sudden rising of the Armagnac party might put them in possession of the king's person, in which case the Orleanists would easily persuade him to issue proclamations as hostile to Burgundy as those which were now published in his name against the Orleanists. The Louvre, indeed, differed but slightly from palaces of several of the great nobles within the walls of Paris, as all of these were to some extent fortified, and stood as separate fortresses capable of offering a stout resistance to any attack by the populace.

"I would rather face those villains of last night for another hour than go before the king," Guy said, as he prepared to follow the attendant; "but I trust that good may come of my interview, and that I can interest the king in the case of my mistress."

# At Agincourt

Joining the usher, who was waiting at the entrance, and who saluted him courteously—for the manner in which the message had been communicated to the usher showed him that the young squire was in no disgrace with the king—Guy walked with him to the Louvre, which was a short half-mile distant. Accompanied as he was by a royal officer, the guard at the gate offered no interruption to his passage, and proceeding across the court-yard he entered the great doorway to the palace, and, preceded by the usher, ascended the grand staircase and followed him along a corridor to the apartments occupied by the king.

# CHAPTER XI — DANGER THREATENED

On being ushered into the royal apartment Guy was led up to the king, who was seated in a large arm-chair. He was stroking the head of a greyhound, and two or three other dogs lay at his feet. Except two attendants, who stood a short distance behind his chair, no one else was present. The king was pale and fragile-looking; there was an expression of weariness on his face, for in the intervals between his mad fits he had but little rest. He was naturally a kind-hearted man, and the troubles that reigned in France, the constant contention among the great lords, and even among the members of his own family, were a constant source of distress to him. Between the Duke of Burgundy, the queen, his nephew of Orleans, and the other royal dukes he had no peace, and the sense of his inability to remedy matters, and of his position of tutelage in the hands of whoever chanced for the moment to be in the ascendant, in no slight degree contributed to the terrible attacks to which he was subject. At the present moment the Duke of Burgundy was away, and therefore, feeling now comparatively free, he looked up with interest when the usher announced Guy Aylmer.

"You are young, indeed, sir," he said, as Guy made a deep bow, "to be the hero of the story that I heard this morning. I hear that you have been slaying many of the good citizens of Paris!"

"Some have certainly been slain, sire; but I think not that any of them could be considered as good citizens, being engaged, as they were, in attacking the house of the worshipful provost of the silversmiths, Maître Leroux."

"I know him," the king said, "and have bought many rare articles of his handiwork, and more than once when I have needed it have had monies from him on usance. 'Tis a grave scandal that so good a citizen should thus be attacked in my city, but I will see that such doings shall not take place again. And now I would hear from your own lips how you and a few men defended the house so long, and, as I hear, with very heavy loss to those attacking it. I am told that you are English."

"Yes, sire, I have the honour to be an esquire to Sir Eustace de Villeroy, and am here in attendance upon his dame, who, with her two children, have been brought as hostages to Paris under your royal order."

A look of pain passed across the king's face. "Your lord is our vassal for his castle at Villeroy?"

"He is, sire, and is also a vassal of England for the estates of his wife."

"Since England and France are not at present on ill terms," the king said, "he may well discharge both duties without treason to either Henry or myself; but they told me that his vassalage to me has sat but lightly upon him."

"His father and grandfather, sire, were vassals of England, as Villeroy was then within the English bounds, but he is, I am assured, ready faithfully to render any service that your majesty might demand of him, and is willing to submit himself, in all respects, to your will. But since he wishes not to take any part in the troubles between the princes, it seems that both regard him with hostility. Two months since his castle was attacked by some eight thousand men from Ham, led by Sir Clugnet de Brabant. These he repulsed with heavy loss, and deemed that in so doing he was acting in accordance with your majesty's proclamation, and was rendering faithful service to you in holding the castle against your enemies, and he had hoped for your majesty's approbation. He was then deeply grieved when your royal herald summoned him, in your name, either to receive a garrison or to send his wife and children hither as hostages."

"I will see into the matter," the king said earnestly. "And so your mistress was bestowed at the house of Maître Leroux?"

"She was, sire, and is most hospitably entertained by him."

"Now let us hear of this defence. Tell me all that took place; withhold nothing."

Guy related the details of the defence.

"THE KING EXTENDED HIS HAND TO GUY, WHO WENT ON ONE
KNEE TO KISS IT."

"Truly it was well done, young sir, and I owe you thanks for having given so shrewd a lesson to these brawlers, Maître Leroux has good reasons for being thankful to the duke for lodging your lady in his house, for he would doubtless have lost his life had you and your four men not been

142

there. When the Duke of Burgundy returns I will take council with him touching this matter of your mistress. I know that he gave me good reasons at the time for the bringing of her hither, but in the press of matters I do not recall what they were. At any rate, as she is here as my hostage her safety must be ensured, and for the present I will give orders that a guard be placed at the house."

He extended his hand to Guy, who went on one knee to kiss it and then retired.

He took the news back to Dame Margaret.

"I knew well enough that the poor king had nothing to do with the matter," she said. "Were it otherwise I would myself have asked for an audience with him; but I knew that it would be useless, he would but have replied to me as he has to you, that he must consult the duke."

In the afternoon the Italian called with his daughter upon Dame Margaret. The former was now dressed in accordance with his rank as an Italian noble, and the girl, on laying aside her cloak, was also in the costume of a young lady of position. Guy presented the count to his mistress.

"I am greatly indebted to you, Count Montepone," she said, "for the timely warning that you sent us, and still more for the service rendered to us by your daughter in summoning the Burgundian knights to our aid. Truly," she added with a smile, "it is difficult to believe that it was this young lady who was so busy on our behalf. I thank you, maiden, most heartily. And, believe me, should the time ever come when you require a friend; which I hope may never be the case, you will find one in me on whom you can confidently rely.

"This is my daughter Agnes. She is, methinks, but a year or so younger than yourself, though she is as tall or taller, and she will gladly be your friend also."

Katarina replied quietly and composedly, and Guy, as he watched her and Agnes talking together, was surprised at the way in which she adapted herself to circumstances. As a boy she assumed the character so perfectly that no one would suspect her of being aught else. She was a French gamin, with all the shrewdness, impudence, and self-confidence of the class. As he saw her at her father's in female attire something of the boy's nature seemed still to influence her. There was still a touch of sauciness in her manner, and something of defiance, as if she resented his knowledge of her in her other character. Now she had the quiet composure of a young lady of rank. As Dame Margaret had said, she was but little older than Agnes; but though less tall than the English girl, she looked a woman beside her. Guy stood talking with them while Dame Margaret and the count conversed apart. Gradually as they chatted Katarina's manner, which had at first been somewhat stiff, thawed, and Guy left her and Agnes together and went to look through the window.

He could vaguely understand that Katarina at first, knowing that Dame Margaret and Agnes must be aware of her going about as a boy, was standing a little on her dignity. The simple straightforwardness of Agnes and her admiration of the other's boldness and cleverness had disarmed Katarina, and it was not long before they were chatting and laughing in girlish fashion. There was a difference in their laughter, the result of the dissimilar lives they had led. One had ever been a happy, careless child, allowed to roam about in the castle or beyond it almost unattended, and had only to hold herself as became the position of a maiden of rank on special occasions, as when guests were staying in the castle; the other had been for years her father's assistant, engaged in work requiring shrewdness and quickness and not unattended at times with danger. She had been brought into contact with persons of all ranks and conditions, and at times almost forgot her own identity, and was in thought as well as manner the quick-witted messenger of her father. After the latter had chatted for some time with Dame Margaret he beckoned her to him.

"Dame Margaret has promised me to be your protector should aught befall me, child," he said, "and I charge you now in her hearing should anything happen to me to go at once to her castle at Villeroy, and should she not be there to her castle at Summerley, which lies but twelve miles from the English port of Southampton, and there to place yourself under her guardianship, and to submit yourself to her will and guidance wholly and entirely. It would be well indeed for you to have a quiet English home after our troubled life. To Italy you cannot go, our estates are long since confiscated; and did you return there you would find powerful enemies and but lukewarm friends. Besides, there would be but one mode of life open to you, namely, to enter a convent, which would, methinks, be of all others the least suited to your inclinations."

"I can promise you a hearty welcome," Dame Margaret said kindly. "I trust that you may never apply for it; but should, as your father says, aught happen to him, come to me fearlessly, and be assured that you will be treated as one of my own family. We shall ever be mindful of the fact that you saved our lives last night, and that nothing that we can do for you will cancel that obligation."

"I trust that I may never be called upon to ask your hospitality, Lady Margaret," the girl said quietly, "but I thank you with all my heart for proffering it, and I feel assured that I should find a happy home in England."

"'Tis strange how it has all come about," her father said. "'Tis scarce a month since I saw Dame Margaret enter Paris with her children, and the thought occurred to me that it would be well indeed for you were you in the charge of such a lady. Then, as if in answer to my thoughts, I saw her young esquire in the crowd listening to me, and was moved at once to say words that would induce him to call upon me afterwards, when I saw that I might possibly in these troublous times be of use to his mistress. And thus in but a short time what was at first but a passing thought has been realized. It is true that there are among my clients those whose protection I could obtain for you; but France is at present as much torn by factions as is our native Italy, and none can say but, however highly placed and powerful a man may be to-day, he might be in disgrace to-morrow."

Carefully wrapping his daughter up in her cloak again, the Italian took his leave, refusing the offer of Dame Margaret for two of her men-at-arms to accompany them.

"There is no fear of trouble of any sort to-day," he said. "The loss that was suffered last night was so severe that the people will be quiet for a few days, especially as the king, as well as the city authorities, are evidently determined to put a stop to rioting. Moreover, the fact that the Burgundian nobles have, now that the duke is away, taken a strong part against the butchers' faction has for the moment completely cowed them. But, apart from this, it is my special desire to return to my house unnoticed. It is seldom that I am seen going in and out, for I leave home as a rule before my neighbours are about, and do not return till after nightfall. I make no secret of my being a vendor of drugs at the fairs, and there are few can suspect that I have visitors after dark."

"I like your astrologer, Guy," Dame Margaret said when they had left. "Before I saw him I own that I had no great faith in his countship. Any man away from his native country can assume a title without anyone questioning his right to use it, so long as he is content to live in obscurity, and to abstain from attracting the attention of those who would be likely to make inquiries. But I have no doubt that our friend is, as he represents himself, the Count of Montepone, and I believe him to be sincere in the matter of his dealings with us. He tells me that he has received more than one hint that the reports that he deals with the stars and exercises divinations have come to the ears of the church, and it is likely ere long he may be forced to leave Paris, and indeed that he would have done so before now had it not been that some of those who have had dealings with him have exercised their influence to prevent things being pushed further.

"No doubt it is true that, as he asserts, he in no way dabbles in what is called 'black art,' but confines himself to reading the stars; and he owned to me that the success he has obtained in this way is to some extent based upon the information that he obtains from persons of all classes. He is evidently a man whose nature it is to conspire, not so much for the sake of any prospect of gain or advantage, but for the pleasure of conspiring. He has dealings with men of both factions. Among the butchers he is believed to be an agent of the duke, who has assumed the character of a vendor of nostrums simply as a disguise, while among the Armagnacs he is regarded as an agent of Orleans. It is doubtless a dangerous game to play, but it both helps him in his profession of astrologer and gives him influence and power. I asked him why he thus mingled in public affairs. He smiled and said: 'We are always conspiring in Italy; we all belong to factions. I have been brought up in an atmosphere of conspiracy, and it is so natural to me that I could scarce live without it. I am rich: men who trade upon the credulity of fools have plenty of clients. My business of a quack doctor brings me in an income that many a poor nobleman would envy. I travel when I like; I visit alternately all the great towns of France, though Paris has always been my head-quarters.

"'As an astrologer I have a wide reputation. The name of the Count Smarondi—for it is under that title that I practise—is known throughout France, though few know me personally or where I am to be found. Those who desire to consult me can only obtain access to me through some of those whose fortunes I have rightly foretold, and who have absolute faith in me, and even these must first obtain my consent before introducing anyone to me. All this mystery adds both to my reputation and to my fees. Could anyone knock at my door and ask me to calculate his horoscope he would prize it but little; when it is so difficult to obtain an introduction to me, and it is regarded as a matter of favour to be allowed to consult me, people are ready to pay extravagant sums for my advice. And,' he said with a smile, 'the fact that ten days or a fortnight always elapses between the time I am asked to receive a new client and his or her first interview with me, enables me to make such minute inquiries that I can not only gain their complete confidence by my knowledge of certain events in their past, but it will aid me in my divination of their future.

"'I believe in the stars, madame, wholly and implicitly, but the knowledge to be gained from them is general and not particular; but with that general knowledge, and with what I know of men's personal character and habits, of their connections, of their political schemes and personal ambitions, I am able in the majority of cases so to supplement the knowledge I gain from the stars, as to trace their future with an accuracy that seems to them astonishing indeed. For example, madame, had I read in the stars that a dire misfortune impended over you last night, and had I learned that there was a talk among the butchers that the provost of the silversmiths was a strong opponent of theirs, and that steps would shortly be taken to show the Parisians the danger of opposing them, it would have needed no great foresight on my part to tell you that you were threatened with a great danger, and that the danger would probably take the form of an attack by the rabble on the house you occupied. I should naturally put it less plainly. I should tell you to beware of this date, should warn you that I saw threatening faces and raised weapons, and that the sounds of angry shouts demanding blood were in my ears.

"'Any astrologer, madame, who works by proper methods can, from the conjunction of the stars at anyone's birth, calculate whether their aspect will be favourable or unfavourable at any given time, and may foretell danger or death; but it needs a knowledge of human nature, a knowledge of character and habits, and a knowledge of the questioner's surroundings to be able to go much farther than this. That I have had marvellous successes and that my counsels are eagerly sought depends, then, upon the fact that I leave nothing to chance, but that while enveloping myself in a certain amount of mystery I have a police of my own consisting of men of all stations, many, indeed most of whom, do not know me even by sight. They have no idea of the object of my inquiries, and indeed believe that their paymaster is the head of the secret police, or the agent of some powerful minister.'

"You see, Guy, the count spoke with perfect frankness to me. His object naturally was to gain my confidence by showing himself as he is, and to explain why he wished to secure a home for his daughter. He took up his strange profession in the first place as a means of obtaining his living, and perhaps to secure himself from the search of private enemies who would have had him assassinated could he have been found; but he follows it now from his love for an atmosphere of intrigue, and for the power it gives him, because, as he told me, he has already amassed a considerable fortune, and could well retire and live in luxury did he choose. He said frankly that if he did not so interest himself his existence would be simply intolerable to him.

"'I may take my daughter to England,' he said; 'I may stay there until I see her established in life, but when I had done so I should have to return here. Paris is always the centre of intrigues; I would rather live on a crust here than be a prince elsewhere.'

"He certainly succeeded in convincing me wholly of his sincerity, as far as we are concerned. Devoted to intrigue himself, he would fain that his daughter should live her life in peace and tranquillity, and that the money for which he has no use himself should be enjoyed by her. 'I have lost my rank,' he said, 'forfeited it, if you will; but she is the Countess Katarina of Montepone, and I should like to know that she and my descendants after her should live the life that my ancestors lived. It is a weakness, a folly, I know; but we have all our weak points and our follies. At any rate I see that that fancy could not well be carried out in France or in Italy, but it may be in England.' At any rate, after all he has told me I feel that he has it in his power to be a very useful friend and ally to us here; I am convinced that he is truly desirous of being so."

"And how did you like the girl, Agnes?" she said, raising her voice. Agnes had fetched Charlie in, and they were looking together down into the street while their mother was talking to Guy.

"I hardly know, mother; she seemed to be so much older than I am. Sometimes when she talked and laughed, I thought I liked her very much, and then a minute later it seemed to me that I did not understand her one bit. But I do think that she would be very nice when one came to know her thoroughly."

"She has lived so different a life to yourself, Agnes, that it is no wonder that you should feel at first that you have nothing in common with her. That she is very clever I have no doubt, and that she is brave and fearless we know. Can you tell us anything more, Guy?"

"Not very much more, Lady Margaret. I should say that she was very true and loyal. I think that at present she enters into what she has to do in something of the same spirit as her father, and that she thoroughly likes it. I think that she is naturally full of fun and has high spirits, and that she enjoys performing these missions with which she is entrusted as a child enjoys a game, and that the fact that there is a certain amount of danger connected with them is in itself attractive to her. I am glad that you have told me what he said to you about himself, for I could not understand him before. I think I can now, and understanding him one can understand his daughter."

At eight o'clock all retired to bed. They had had little sleep the night before, and the day had been full of events. Guy's last thought was that he was sorry for the king, who seemed to wish to do what was right, but who was a mere puppet in the hands of Burgundy or Queen Isobel, to be used as a lay figure when required by whichever had a temporary ascendency.

For the next fortnight Guy worked hard in the *salle d'armes*, being one of the first to arrive and the last to depart, and after taking a lesson from one or other of the masters he spent the rest of the morning in practising with anyone who desired an adversary. Well trained as he was in English methods of fighting, he mastered with a quickness that surprised his teachers the various thrusts and parries that were new to him. At the end of that time he was able to hold his own with the young Count d'Estournel, who was regarded as an excellent swordsman.

The attendance of the Burgundian nobles had now fallen off a good deal. The Armagnac army had approached Paris, St. Denis had opened its gates to them, and there were frequent skirmishes near the walls of Paris between parties of their knights and the Burgundians. Paris was just at present more quiet. Burgundy was still absent, and the future seemed so uncertain, that both factions in the city held their hands for a time.

The news that a reconciliation between Orleans and Burgundy had been fully effected, and that the great lords would soon enter Paris together, was received with a joy that was modified by recollections of the past. Burgundy and Orleans had once before sworn a solemn friendship, and yet a week or two later Orleans lay dead in the streets of Paris, murdered by the order of Burgundy. Was it likely that the present patching up of the quarrel would have a much longer duration? On the former occasion the quarrel was a personal one between the two great houses, now all France was divided. A vast amount of blood had been shed, there had been cruel massacres, executions, and wrongs, and the men of one faction had come to hate those of the other; and although neither party had dared to put itself in the wrong by refusing to listen to the mediators, it was certain that the reconciliation was a farce, and that it was but a short truce rather than a peace that had been concluded. Nevertheless Paris rejoiced outwardly, and hailed with enthusiasm the entry of the queen, the Dukes of Aquitaine, Burgundy, Berri, and Bourbon.

The Duke of Aquitaine was now acting as regent, though without the title, for the king was again insane. He had married Burgundy's daughter, but it was rumoured that he was by no means disposed to submit himself blindly to the advice of her father. The only effect of the truce between the parties was to add to the power of the Burgundian faction in Paris. But few of the Armagnac party cared to trust themselves in the city that had shown itself so hostile, but most of them retired to their estates, and the great procession that entered the town had been for the most part composed of adherents of Burgundy. Three days after their arrival in the town Guy, on leaving the *salle d'armes*, found Katarina in her boy's attire waiting for him at the corner of the street.

"My father would speak with you, Master Guy," she said shyly, for in the past two months she had always been in her girl's dress when he had met her. "Pray go at once," she said; "I will not accompany you, for I have other matters to attend to."

"Things are not going well," the count said when Guy entered the room; "the Orleanists are discouraged and the butchers triumphant. At a meeting last night they determined that a body of them should wait upon the Dukes of Aquitaine and Burgundy to complain of the conduct of the knights who fell upon them when attacking the silversmith's, and demand in the name of Paris their execution."

"They would never dare do that!" Guy exclaimed indignantly.

"They will assuredly do it, and I see not how they can be refused. The duke has no force that could oppose the Parisians. They might defend the Louvre and one or two of the strongly fortified houses, but the butchers would surround them with twenty thousand men. Burgundy's vassals might come to his assistance, but the gates of Paris would be closed, and it would need nothing short of an army and a long siege before they could enter Paris. When they had done so they might punish the leaders, but Burgundy would thereby lose for ever the support of the city, which is all-important to him. Therefore if you would save your friends you must warn them that it will be necessary for them to make their way out of Paris as quickly and as quietly as may be. In the next place, and principally, you yourself will assuredly be murdered. There was a talk of the meeting demanding your execution and that of your four men; but it was decided that there was no need to do this, as you could all be killed without trouble, and that possibly the Duke of Aquitaine might refuse on the ground that, as your lady had come here under safe-conduct as a royal hostage, you were entitled to protection, and it would be contrary to his honour to give you up.

"There are others who have displeased the Parisians whose lives they will also demand, and there are several women among them; therefore, it is clear that even the sex of your lady will not save her and her children from the fury and longing for revenge, felt by the family of Legoix and by Caboche the skinner. The only question is, where can they be bestowed in safety? I know what you would say, that all this is monstrous, and that it is incredible that the Parisians will dare to take such steps. I can assure you that it is as I say; the peril is most imminent. Probably to-night, but if not, to-morrow the gates of Paris will be closed, and there will be no escape for any whom these people have doomed to death. In the first place, you have to warn your Burgundian friends; that done, you must see to the safety of your four men. The three Frenchmen may, if they disguise themselves, perchance be able to hide in Paris, but your tall archer must leave the city without delay, his height and appearance would betray him in whatever disguise he were clad.

"Now as to your lady and the children, remain where they are they cannot. Doubtless were she to appeal to the Duke of Burgundy for protection he would place her in the Louvre, or in one of the other castles— that is, if she could persuade him of the intentions of the Parisians, which indeed it would be difficult for her to do; but even could she do so she would not be safe, for if he is forced to surrender some of his own knights and ladies of the court to these miscreants, he could not refuse to hand over Lady Margaret. They might, it is true, possibly escape from Paris in disguise, but I know that there is already a watch set at the gates. The only resource that I can see is that she should with her children come hither for a time. This is but a poor place for her, but I think that if anywhere she might be safe with me. No one knows that I have had any dealings whatever with you, and no one connects me in any way with politics. What should a vendor of nostrums have to do with such affairs? Thus, then, they might remain here without their presence being in the slightest degree suspected. At any rate I have as good means as any for learning what is being done at their councils, and should receive the earliest information were it decided that a search should be made here; and should this be done, which I think is most unlikely, I shall have time to remove them to some other place of concealment.

"Lastly, as to yourself, I take it that nothing would induce you to fly with your Burgundian friends while your lady is in hiding in Paris?"

"Assuredly not!" Guy said. "My lord appointed me to take charge of her and watch over her, and as long as I have life I will do so."

"You will not be able to aid her, and your presence may even add to her danger. Still, I will not say that your resolution is not honourable and right. But, at least, you must not stay here, for your detection would almost certainly lead to hers. You, however, can be disguised; I can darken your skin and hair, and, in some soiled garb you may hope to pass without recognition. Where to bestow you I will talk over with my daughter. As soon as it becomes dusk this evening she will present herself at the house-door of Maître Leroux. She will bring with her disguises for your lady, the children, and yourself—I have many of them here—and as soon as it is quite dark she will guide here Dame Margaret with her daughter and son. You had best not sally out with them, but can follow a minute or two later and join them as soon as they turn down a side street. As to the men, you must arrange with them what they had best do. My advice is that they should this afternoon saunter out as if merely going for a walk. They ought to go separately; you can decide what they had best do when outside."

# CHAPTER XII — IN HIDING

The news of this terrible danger was so wholly unexpected that Guy for a moment felt almost paralyzed.

"It seems almost incredible that such wickedness could take place!" he exclaimed.

"My information is certain," the count replied. "I do not say that I think your Burgundian friends are in so much danger as some of those of the king's party, as Burgundy's influence with these Parisians goes for something; still, he might not be able to save them if they waited till the demand was made, although he might warn them if he learned that they were to be among those demanded."

"Does the duke, then, know what is intended?"

The count smiled. "We know what followed the last reconciliation," he said, "and can guess pretty shrewdly at what will happen now. *Then* the duke murdered Orleans, *now* he may take measures against the supporters of the present duke. It was certain that the struggle would begin again as soon as the kiss of peace had been exchanged. Last time he boldly avowed his share in the murder; this time, most conveniently for him, the Parisians are ready and eager to do his work for him. Dismiss from your mind all doubt; you can rely upon everything that I have told you as being true. Whether you can convince these young knights is a matter that concerns me not; but remember that if you fail to convince your mistress, her life and those of her children are forfeited; and that, so far as I can see, her only hope of safety is in taking refuge here."

"I thank you with all my heart," Guy said, "and will now set about carrying out your advice. First, I will return to my lady and consult with her, and see what we had best do with the men. As to Count Charles d'Estournel and his friends, I will see them as soon as I have arranged the other matter. Their case is not so pressing, for, at least, when once beyond the gates they will be safe. I will see that my lady and the children shall be ready to accompany your daughter when she comes for them."

"Look well up and down the street before you sally out," the count said; "see that there are but few people about. It is a matter of life and death that no one who knows you shall see you leave this house."

Guy followed his advice, and waited until there was no one within fifty yards of the door, then he went out, crossed the street, took the first turning he came to, and then made his way back to the silversmith's as fast as he could.

"What ails you, Guy?" Dame Margaret said as he entered the room, "you look sorely disturbed, and as pale as if you had received some injury."

"Would that that were all, my lady. I have had news from the Count of Montepone of so strange and grave a nature that I would not tell you it, were it not that he is so much in earnest, and so well convinced of its truth that I cannot doubt it."

He then related what the count had told him, and repeated the offer of shelter he had made.

"This is, indeed, beyond all bounds," she said. "What, is it credible that the Duke of Burgundy and the king's son, the Duke of Aquitaine, can hand over to this murderous mob of Paris noble gentlemen and ladies?"

"As to Burgundy, madame, it seems to me from what the count said that he himself is at the bottom of the affair, though he may not know that the Parisians demand the lives of some of his own knights as well as those of his opponents. As he did not of old hesitate to murder Orleans, the king's own brother, we need credit him with no scruples as to how he would rid himself of others he considers to stand in his way. As to Aquitaine, he is a young man and powerless. There are no Orleanist nobles in the town to whom he might look for aid; and if a king's brother was slain, why not a king's son? It seems to me that he is powerless."

"That may be; but I cannot consent to what the count proposes. What! disguise myself! and hide from this base mob of Paris! It would be an unworthy action."

"It is one that I knew you would shrink from, madame; but pardon me for saying that it is not your own life only, but those of your children that are at stake. When royal princes and dukes are unable to oppose these scoundrel Parisians, women and children may well bend before the storm."

Dame Margaret sat for some time with knitted brows. At last she said: "If it must be, Guy, it must. It goes sorely against the grain; but for the sake of the children I will demean myself, and will take your advice. Now you had best summon the four men-at-arms and talk over their case with them."

Guy went upstairs and fetched the four men down.

"We have sure news, my friends," Dame Margaret said calmly, "that to-night we and many others shall be seized by the mob and slain."

An exclamation of rage broke from the four men.

"There will be many others slain before that comes about," Long Tom said.

"That I doubt not, Tom, but the end would be the same. An offer of refuge has been made to me and the children, and for their sake, unwilling as I am to hide myself from this base mob, I have brought myself to accept it. My brave esquire will stay in Paris in disguise, and do what may be to protect us. I have now called you to talk about yourselves. The gates will speedily be guarded and none allowed to sally out, therefore what is to be done must be done quickly."

"We will all stay and share your fate, madame. You could not think that we should leave you," Robert Picard said, and the others murmured their agreement.

"You would add to my danger without being able to benefit me," she said, "and my anxiety would be all the greater. No, you must obey my commands, which are that you forthwith quit Paris. Beyond that I must leave you to judge your own course. As French men-at-arms none would question you when you were once beyond the gate. You may find it difficult to travel in this disturbed time, but you are shrewd enough to make up some story that will account for your movements, and so may work your way back to Villeroy. The difficulty is greater in the case of your English comrade—his height and that light hair of his and ruddy face would mark him anywhere, and if he goes with you would add to your danger, especially as his tongue would betray him as being English the first time he spoke. However, beyond ordering you to quit Paris, I must leave this matter in your hands and his, and he will doubtless take counsel with my esquire and see if any disguise can be contrived to suit him. I will see you again presently. You had best go with them, Guy, and talk the matter over."

"This thing cannot be done, Master Guy," the archer said doggedly when they reached their apartments; "it is not in reason. What should I say when I got home and told them at Summerley that I saved my own skin and left our dear lady and the children to be murdered without striking a blow on their behalf? The thing is beyond all reason, and I will maintain it to be so."

"I can understand what you say, Tom, for I feel exactly as you do. The question is, how is the matter to be arranged?" Then he broke into French, which the archer by this time understood well enough, though he could speak it but poorly.

"Tom is saying that he will not go, men," he said, "and I doubt not that you feel as he does. At the same time our lady's orders must be carried out in the first place, and you must leave Paris. But I say not that you need travel to any distance; on the contrary, I should say that, if it can be arranged, you must return here in a few days, having so changed your attire and aspect that there is no fear of your being recognized, and bestow yourself in some lodging where I may find you if there be need of your services."

"That is what will be best, Master Guy," Robert Picard said. "We have but to get steel caps of another fashion to pass well enough, and if need be we can alter the fashion of our hair. There are few here who have noticed us, and I consider that there is no chance whatever of our being recognized. There are plenty of men among the cut-throats here who have served for a while, and we can easily enough get up some tale that will pass muster for us three. That matter is simple enough, the question is, what are we to do with Tom? We cannot shorten his stature, nor give his tongue a French twist."

"No, that is really the difficulty. We might dye that hair of his and darken his face, as I am going to do myself. There are tall men in France, and even his inches would not matter so much; the danger lies in his speech."

"I would never open my mouth, Master Guy; if need were I would sooner cut out my tongue with a dagger."

"You might bleed to death in the doing of it, Tom. No; we must think of something better than that. You might perhaps pass as a Fleming, if we cannot devise any other disguise."

"Leave that to me, Master Guy, I shall think of something. I will at any rate hide somewhere near Paris, and the lads here will let me know where they are to be found, and I shall not be long before I join them in some such guise as will pass muster. But it will be necessary that we should know where you will be, so that you can communicate with us."

"That I don't know myself yet; but I will be every evening in front of Notre Dame when the bell strikes nine, and one of you can meet me there and tell me where you are bestowed, so that I can always send for you in case of need. Now I think that you had better lose no time, for we know not at what hour a guard will be placed on the gate. You had better go out in pairs as if merely going for a walk. If you are stopped, as may well happen, return here; but as you come purchase a length of strong rope, so that you may let yourselves down from the wall. Now that peace has been made, there will be but slight watch save at the gates, and you should have no difficulty in evading the sight of any who may be on guard."

"That will be easy enough," Robert Picard said confidently. "We had best not come back here, for there may be a watch set upon the house and they may follow us."

"The only thing that troubles me," Tom said, "is that I must leave my bow behind me."

"You can get another when you get back to Villeroy; there are spare ones there."

"Yes, yes, but that is not the same thing, Master Guy; a man knows his own bow, and when he takes to a fresh one his shooting is spoilt until he gets to know it well. Every bow has its niceties; for rough shooting it makes but little matter, but when it comes to aiming at the slit in a knight's vizor at eighty yards one makes poor shooting with a strange bow."

"Well, you must practise with your new one, that is all, Tom; and if you hide yours here it may be that you will be able to recover it before we start for Villeroy. You must leave your bundles behind, it would look suspicious if you were to attempt to take them with you. I should advise you to put on one suit over the other, it will not add greatly to your bulk. When you are ready to start, come below and our lady will say good-bye to you. Do not give her a hint that you are thinking of staying near Paris; if she asks any questions say that you intend to disguise Tom, and he will travel with you."

A few minutes later there was a tapping at Dame Margaret's door; Guy opened it and the four men entered.

"I wish you good fortunes, my friends," Dame Margaret said. "Here is a letter, Robert, that I have written to my lord telling him that you have all served me faithfully and well, and that I commend you to him. I have told him that you are leaving me by my special orders, and that you would willingly have stopped and shared my danger, but that, as I feel that force would avail nothing and your presence might lead to the discovery of my hiding-place, I bid you go. Here are four purses to pay the expenses of your journey and of any disguises you may find it necessary to adopt. And now farewell. Tarry not an instant, my heart will be lighter when I know that you are beyond the walls."

She held out her hand to them; each in turn knelt and kissed it, the three Frenchmen in silence but with tears running down their cheeks. Tom was the last, and said as he rose:

"I am obeying your orders, Lady Margaret, but never before have I felt, as I feel now, that I am doing a mean and cowardly action. I would rather stay by your side, though I knew that I should be cut in pieces this very night, than leave you thus."

"I doubt it not, Tom. I know well how your inclinations lie, and yet I feel that it is necessary that you should go. If the great nobles cannot withstand this cruel mob of Paris, the arm of a single man can avail nothing, and your presence would bring danger rather than safety to me."

"I feel that, my lady; did I not do so I would not go even at your command. You are my liege lady, and I have a right to give my life for you, and would do it were it not that I see that, as you say, my staying here would bring danger upon you."

As soon as they had gone Dame Margaret said: "Now, Guy, I will detain you no longer; hasten and warn your friends."

Guy hurried away; he found that Count Charles was on the point of mounting to go for a ride with some of his friends.

"Stay a moment I beg of you, Count," Guy said as he hurried up, "I have a matter of most serious import to tell you."

"Wait, my friends," the young count said to Sir Pierre Estelle, Count Walter de Vesoul, and the Sieur John de Perron, who were already mounted; "I shall not detain you many minutes."

"Well, what is it, friend Guy?" he asked as he entered his room.

"I have come to warn you of a great danger, Count. This evening a mob of Parisians, I know not how numerous, but at least of great strength, will demand from Burgundy and the Duke of Aquitaine the surrender to them of you and the others who took part in defeating them the other night, besides other gentlemen, and, as I hear, ladies."

"*Pardieu*! if it be so the duke will give the impudent knaves their answer."

"Ten thousand armed men are not apt to take an answer, Count. You know that many times already the Duke of Burgundy has been overborne by the leaders of these Parisians and forced to do things that must have displeased him, as they displeased you all, therefore I implore you to ride off while you may. Even now it is possible that the gales may be closed, but if so, they are not likely to be strongly guarded. It is evident that your going would at any rate save the duke from grave embarrassment."

"Are you sure that this news is true?" the count asked.

"Absolutely certain. If you would save yourself and your friends I pray you to call upon them at once to mount and ride in a body to one of the gates. You may bid some of your retainers mount and follow you at a short distance, and if you find the gates closed and the fellows will not let you out, call them up and fight your way out. You can stay for to-night at Sèvres, and if you find in the morning that I have not spoken truly you can return and upbraid me as you will. If, however, you find that strange events have happened here, then you had best ride away to Burgundy and stay there until you find that these villainous knaves here have been reduced to order, which methinks it will need an army to undertake."

The count went to the window, opened it, and called his friends below to come up.

"No, no," D'Estelle said laughing; "if we once come up we shall stay there. If you cannot come now, join us at the Lion d'Or at Sèvres, where you will find us eating the dinner that we have sent on to order."

"The matter is urgent," D'Estournel said. "I am not joking with you, but pray you to come up at once."

Seeing that the matter was serious the three knights dismounted and went up. They were at first absolutely incredulous when they heard from Count Charles what Guy had told them.

"That the knaves owe us no good-will I know well enough," Count Walter said, "for they have over and over again laid their complaint against us before the duke; but it is hard to believe that they would dare to demand what Burgundy would never grant."

Guy repeated the arguments that he had used with D'Estournel.

"There is no limit," he said, "to the arrogance of these knaves, and in truth it cannot be denied that they are masters here, and that even the duke cannot altogether withstand them; and you know, moreover, how essential is their goodwill to him. But even should he ever so obstinately refuse their demands they might well take their way without his leave. What can he, with a handful of knights and a few hundred armed men, do against the mob of Paris? I earnestly pray you, gentlemen, to treat the matter as serious. Warn your eight friends without delay; bid your retainers mount and ride to the gate. If it is open, all the better, it is but a party of pleasure bound for Sèvres, and if you learn to-morrow morning that all is quiet here you can return. If it seems better to you, and this may save you much argument, merely ask your friends to mount and ride with you to dine there; if any refuse, say you have a motive that they will learn when they get there, and almost compel them to go with you. I pledge you my honour that you will have no reason to regret having taken my advice."

"Well, what do you say, gentlemen?" Count Walter asked. "As Master Aylmer says, it will at worst be but a carouse, which I hope he will share with us."

"That I would right gladly do," Guy replied, "but I have the safety of my lady and her children to look after, for she too, as well as our four men-at-arms, have incurred the enmity of these butchers. I have sent the men out of the town, and a place of safety has been prepared for her and the children. I shall see them safely bestowed there at nightfall."

"Since you have thought such preparations necessary we will at any rate act on the information that you have given us, and will promise not to blame you unduly should it turn out that the affair you speak of does not come off. Let us lose no time, gentlemen; let us each go to two of our friends and take no denial from them to our invitation to dine with us at Sevres. Let us say nothing to them about bringing their men-at-arms and grooms with them. We can ourselves muster some thirty fighting men, and that should be enough with our own swords to bring these knaves to reason if they keep their gates shut against us."

"As my arrangements are all made," Guy said, "and I have an hour to spare, I shall walk down towards the gate and see what comes of it."

The four gentlemen at once mounted and rode off,—after giving directions to their grooms to order their men-at-arms to mount at once and to wait for them at a spot a quarter of a mile from the gate,—and Guy strolled off in the same direction. In half an hour he had the satisfaction of seeing the men-at-arms ride up and halt as ordered. Walking a little further on he saw that something unusual had happened. Groups of people were standing about talking, and each man who came up from the gate was questioned. Joining one of the groups he soon learned that the excitement was caused by the unusual closing of the gates, no one being allowed either to enter or pass out. None could account for this proceeding. It was certain that it had not been done by the orders either of the Dukes of Aquitaine or Burgundy,—for there were no royal guards or men-at-arms with the duke's cognizance,—but by men of the city, who, as all agreed, must be acting under the orders of the butchers.

"It is a bold deed," one said, "for which they will have to account. It is a usurpation of authority, and one the Duke of Aquitaine, who is now king in all but name, will surely resent hotly."

"How strong is the party?" one of the bystanders asked, putting the question that Guy had on his lips.

"Some forty or fifty, all stout fellows with steel caps and breast-pieces, and well armed."

Guy turned and walked back to the spot where the Burgundian men-at-arms were drawn up. In ten minutes D'Estournel and his party rode up. Guy was glad to see that he had with him the whole of his companions. He at once went up to them.

"The gates are closed, Count, and held by forty or fifty of the townsmen in arms, so you see that my information was correct. Had you not better tell your friends of the truth now, for otherwise they might hesitate to take so grave a step as to attack them?"

D'Estournel nodded, and, riding to the others, said in a low voice: "Gentlemen, we had not intended to let you into this little mystery until we had left Paris, but I find it necessary to do so now. I have learned surely that the rabble of Paris have resolved upon massacring us to-night for the share we took in that little affair at the provost of the silversmiths. To that end they have shut the gates, and hold it with some fifty armed men. It is as well that some of us have brought our men-at-arms here. I can hardly fancy that these rascals will try to prevent us from passing out, seeing that they have no warrant but their own for closing the gates against us, but if they do there is nothing for it but to open them ourselves. Let us ride forward at once, gentlemen, for these fellows may receive a reinforcement at any time."

So saying, he put spurs to his horse, calling upon the men-at-arms to follow. His three companions, who were already in the secret, joined him at once; and the others, after a pause of astonishment and almost incredulity, followed, in no way loath at the chance of another fight with the followers of the butchers. As they approached the gate the townsmen hastily drew up in front of it.

"What means this?" Count Walter de Vesoul said haughtily, as he reined up his horse a few paces from the line. "By what authority do you dare close the gates and thus stand armed before them?"

"By the authority of the city of Paris," the leader of the party said insolently.

"I recognize no such authority while the king and the Duke of Aquitaine, who holds his full powers, are resident here. Clear the way, my man, and open the gates, or I will ride over you."

The butcher answered him with a derisive laugh. "It will cost you your lives if you attempt it," he said.

"Gentlemen, draw your swords and give these rough fellows the lesson they need;" and, setting the example, he rode at the butcher and cut him down. The idea that the Burgundian knights would venture to force a passage in the teeth of the prohibition of the master of the butchers had apparently not so much as entered the minds of the guard, and as soon as the knights and their followers fell upon them, the greater portion of them flung down their arms and fled, a few only fighting stoutly until overpowered. As soon as the skirmish was over the keys were brought out from the guard-room, and the gate unlocked and the massive bars taken down. In the meantime some of the men-at-arms had run up on to the wall, hoisted the portcullis, and lowered the drawbridge across the fosse. As soon as they returned and mounted the party rode through. As they did so, four men ran out from a lane near the wall and followed them; and Guy at once recognized in them the archer and his three companions. Greatly pleased, he returned to the city and informed Dame Margaret of what had taken place.

"No doubt," he said, "when they found the gates shut they remembered what I had said, that I was going to warn Count Charles and his friends, and went back to observe what these were doing; and the sight of their retainers going towards the gate must have told them which way they intended to leave; and they, no doubt, went down and hid up near the gate to watch the conflict, and to take advantage of it, if a chance offered, to get off themselves."

"That is indeed a satisfaction, Guy; and I am glad, too, that your friends got away. There can be no doubt now that the count's information was accurate; the gates having been closed, as he said they would be, vouches for this. Katarina has been here; she was dressed this time as an apprentice in the service of some trader, and brought a large box containing our disguises and yours. For you there is a bottle of dye for your hair, a mixture for darkening your skin, and clothes—the latter such as would be worn by a workman. Charlie is to wear a girl's dress, at which he is mightily offended; nor is Agnes better pleased, for a boy's suit has been sent for her. My disguise is simply a long cloak with a hood, such as is worn by the wives of small traders. Katarina explained that it had been thought better to change the sex of Agnes and Charlie, so that, when a hue and cry is raised for a missing woman, with a girl of fourteen, and a boy of ten, no one should associate the woman with two lads and a little girl, whom they passed in the street, as being the party for which search is being made. And now, Guy, do you not think that we should warn our good host of the danger that threatens, for, doubtless, he also has been marked out as a victim?"

"I will see him at once, and will tell him as much as it is necessary for him to know. Assuredly it is now too late for him to escape beyond the walls, unless he were to take his wife with him, and bring his serving-men to let them down from the walls; but this, I should think, he will not do, he would rather take refuge in the house of some of his friends."

The silversmith listened gravely when Guy told him that he had received sure information that the butchers would that evening make a slaughter of some of their opponents, that they would be in such force that resistance would be hopeless, and that the few royal troops and the followers of Burgundy would be insufficient to make head against them.

"Your news does not surprise me, and though I know not how you came by it, I fear that it is true. The news that the city gates have been all shut and are being guarded by strong parties of the butchers' rabble, shows but too surely that there is danger in the air. In the first place, there is your lady to be thought of; I must endeavour to obtain for her also shelter among my friends."

"We have already arranged for a hiding-place for her and the children, Maître Leroux. I may not name where it is to anyone, but suffice that it is a quiet house where there is little fear of any suspicions resting upon them, and where they will be able to remain until order is restored."

"I fear that that will be a long time," the silversmith said. "The butchers boast that they can place 20,000 men under arms, and indeed the terror excited by them is so great, that very many who hate their doings as much as I do myself have been forced to make a semblance of joining them. Next about your men-at-arms, they are brave fellows and I owe them much."

"They are all safe outside the walls. Some Burgundian knights, indignant that this rabble should dare stop them, cut their way out through the Port St. Denis, and our men took advantage of the gates being open to follow them."

"And as to yourself, Master Aylmer?"

"I have dyes to blacken my hair and a tincture for darkening my face. I have also a disguise by which I may pass as an apprentice to a trader. I shall at all hazards remain in Paris, but what I shall yet do I know not. And now about yourself and Madame Leroux—you will not, I hope, think of defending the house as you did before."

"Certainly not; it would not avail to save our lives, and would assuredly cost those of my servitors and most likely of the women. I have friends, who will, I hope, gladly take us in. Maître Lepelletiere, the Master

# At Agincourt

Carpenter, who has been doing my doors, is an old friend of mine, and after the last attack, urged me to withdraw for a time from the attention of the mob, and offered me refuge in his place. He lives in the Rue des Fosses; which is close to the old inner wall that is now for the most part in ruins. You pass along by the hospital, and when beyond the old wall turn to the right; 'tis the third doorway. There are no houses facing it, but it looks straight upon the wall, the ground between being some thirty or forty yards wide; and doubtless when the house was built, it was before the present wall was erected, and stood on the outer side of the fosse round the old one. There are many others of the same trade who live in that quarter, and as they are for the most part opposed to the butchers, I doubt not that my friend will have no difficulty in obtaining a lodging for you among them should no other have been settled upon."

"Thank you indeed," Guy replied; "the arrangement has been made by others, and I know not for certain what has yet been decided upon, but should not a suitable place have been chosen I will gladly accept your offer."

"And now I must set to work," the silversmith said.

"In what way?" Guy asked in surprise.

"In hiding my wares. In a city like Paris, with its sieges and its tumults, a prudent man having goods of great value will assuredly prepare a place of safety for them. I will set my men to work at once; the business must be finished before it becomes dark, for as soon as it does so we must leave the house and close it."

"I have nothing to do at present, and shall be glad to help your men," Guy said.

He followed the silversmith downstairs. Maître Leroux called his head man.

"We must move, Jacques, and that quickly; you have heard that the gates are shut."

"Yes, master, people are talking of nothing else."

"I have news that there will be trouble to-night, so we must set to work at once to place the chests in safety. First let them clear out the wood-cellar."

This was done in a few minutes by the seven men, then Jacques told the others to go back into the shop and pack up all the silver goods in the chests. As soon as they were gone Jacques looked inquiringly at his master, who nodded. Then he touched a brick in the wall some seven feet above the floor; it sprung back.

"Will you lift me up?" the man said to Guy. The lad did as he was asked, and the man thrust his arm into the orifice. A moment later he asked Guy to set him down.

"Go to the doorway," he said, and hurried across to where Maître Leroux was standing; then kneeling down he pushed his hand under the sill of the doorway and then stood up.

"Do you hear that?" the silversmith said.

"I hear a dull rumbling somewhere," Guy replied. As he spoke he saw half the floor, which was apparently of solid flags, beginning to rise.

"This was done in my father's time," Maître Leroux said, "and it was made for him by Maître Lepelletiere's father with the aid of two or three good smiths, who put the machinery together at his house and were in ignorance where it was intended to be placed."

The trap-door was now raised, and Guy to his astonishment saw a stream of running water three feet below the opening.

"Whence comes this?" he asked in astonishment.

"No wonder you are surprised," the silversmith said; "it was a piece of rare good-luck that my father hit upon it. A map that he had showed him that in the old days, before there were any houses on this side of the river, a narrow branch left the stream some hundred yards above the position of his house, made a circuit and came into it again as much below. He inquired among some old men, and learned that they had heard their grandfathers say that they knew that at some time or other this stream had been built over when Paris began to grow in this direction. After he had contrived this apparatus that you see, which is worked by a heavy counterpoise in the wall, he began to dig, and a foot below the surface came upon an arch of brickwork, so my father concluded that his house was exactly over the old stream.

"On breaking through the crown he discovered, as you see, that the water still flowed through this tunnel, which is some three and a half yards wide and eight feet deep. My men, all of whom are trusty fellows, know of the existence of this hiding-place, but Jacques is the only one besides myself who knows the secret of the opening. Now, Jacques, fetch the chests along as fast as they are ready."

The chests were soon brought up and one by one lowered. Chains were attached from the handle of each to that of the one that followed; they were almost the weight of the water and sank until within an inch-or two of the surface. Each was floated down as it was lowered, until twenty great chests had been taken down. Then one more heavy and ponderous than the rest was attached to the train, and a sloping board being placed from the cellar floor to the bottom of the stream, the case was allowed to slide down this until it rested on the bottom several feet beyond the trap-door.

"There you see," the silversmith said, "even if they discovered the trap-door and broke up the floor with sledgehammers, which would be no easy matter, and probed the stream with lances, they would find nothing. As you saw, there is a chain to the end of the last box, which is, as it were, an anchor to the rest; this chain Jacques will now attach to a strong wire, and fasten that to a ring below the water's edge, and a foot beyond the trap-door, so that when danger is past we shall haul up the chain and recover the cases one by one in the order in which they have been sent down."

As soon as Jacques had fastened the wire to the ring he touched another heavy spring under the sill, then pulled hard on the trap-door; this gradually began to sink, and in a minute was in its place again. At the same time the brick that had been pushed in above came out into its place again, dust was then swept into the crack at the edge of the trapdoor, and no one who had not seen the latter raised would have dreamt of its existence.

# CHAPTER XIII — THE MASTERS OF PARIS

The trap-door closed, the firewood was carried back again, and Guy went upstairs, where he found that Dame Margaret, Agnes, and Charlie had already put on their disguises. Their faces had been slightly darkened; Agnes had coiled her hair up under a cap, while Dame Margaret's would be completely hidden under the hood. She and Charlie could, have passed very well even in daylight, but Agnes by no means looked her character. Her mother had darkened the skin at the back of her neck as well as on her face, but the girl's evident discomfort and shyness were so unboylike that they would at once be noticed. Guy fetched a short cloak reaching only to his hips from his room and brought it in to her.

"I think that you will be more comfortable in this," he said.

"Yes, indeed," she exclaimed gratefully, as she put it over her shoulders; "I shall not mind now."

It reached nearly down to her knees, and the high collar concealed the back of her head effectually.

"I did not expect that you would be ready so soon," he said, turning to Dame Margaret; "it will not be dark for two hours yet."

"No; but I thought it much better to be prepared to leave at any moment. Mistress Leroux has shown me a door opening from the yard into a very narrow lane behind. She says that it has not been used for years, but she has been down herself with the key and has unlocked it, so that we have only to let a bar down to open it, and if there should be an attack on the front of the house we can escape that way."

"It would be best to leave that way in any case," Guy said, "and thereby you will avoid observation by anyone who may be watching. It is evident that the citizens of this quarter are very anxious and alarmed; looking from the window I have seen them standing in groups, or going in and out of each other's houses. They cannot know what is going to take place, but the closing of the gates by the butchers without any warrant has, of course, shown them that something serious is going to occur."

"You had better disguise yourself at once, Guy."

"I will do so, mistress, but I do not think that there is any fear of disturbance until evening; men who are engaged in work, that may some day bring punishment upon those concerned in it, prefer darkness. Besides, at that time all careful men will be in their houses, and will not dare to come out whatever sounds they may hear."

Maître Leroux presently came up.

"I have been out and trying to gather news. There are all sorts of rumours abroad, but none know aught with certainty. They say that the butchers have stationed guards at the end of all the streets leading to the market quarter, and they allow none to pass in or out. It is reported that Aquitaine has sent an officer to the butchers to demand under what warrant they have closed the gates of the city, and to order them to open them forthwith, and to withdraw the men stationed there. It is said that their answer was that they had acted for the good of the state, and for the safety of the king's person, and that they would presently call upon his highness and explain matters to him. This may be true or merely rumour, but it is generally believed. Everyone is talking of the fight at the gate of St. Denis. Some say that it was forced open by order of the Duke of Burgundy, while others affirm that Caboche, and that mischievous varlet John de Troyes, went in great haste to the duke when they received the news, that he declared to them that he knew nothing whatever of the affair, and that whatever was done was certainly done without his orders. Most of my men have already left; it were better that they should go off one by one than that they should move off together. 'Tis well that my wife bethought her of that back entrance. It has never been used in my time, for the lane is but three feet wide, and the houses beyond are of no very good repute. I talked at one time of having it bricked up, and only refrained from doing so from the thought that it might be useful on some such occasion as this. Your esquire has not gone out, I suppose, Lady Margaret?"

"No, he is putting on his disguise—at least, he is colouring his hair and face, and so altering himself that he would not be known; but he will not put on his full disguise until later."

Guy soon came out. He was in his ordinary garments, but having put on his best suit beneath them he looked broader and bulkier than usual, while his blackened hair and darkened face had made so great a change in his appearance that both Agnes and her mother agreed that they would not have known him.

"You could certainly go anywhere, Guy, and mix with any crowd, and no one would have a suspicion that you were the young Englishman for whom the whole town was searching."

Half an hour before it became dark, Guy went down to the front door. Standing there listening attentively, he presently heard three little knocks given, as by a hand on the door. He opened it a little, Katarina slipped in, and he again fastened it and put up the bar.

"I brought the disguises early," she said, "as I thought they might be required in haste, but my father has learned that it will be eight o'clock before the butchers sally out with their forces from the markets."

"All here are ready and prepared to start at a moment's notice, and have arranged to go out by a door behind, that leads into a narrow lane."

"That is good!" the girl said. "I have been near for the last half-hour and have noticed two or three men hanging about, and by their furtive glances in the direction of the house I have no doubt that they are watching it. I had to wait until there happened to be a group of people before the door, and then slipped in behind them, and got in without, I am sure, their having seen me. I have been uneasy as to how we should leave, for if they saw a party of three or four issuing out together, one of them would be sure to follow."

They were now upstairs. The fact that Agnes was in the same disguise as herself freed Katarina from the shame-facedness that she would otherwise have felt at being seen by Dame Margaret in her present attire.

"You are well disguised," the latter said as she entered. "I no longer wonder that you are able to go about as a boy without suspicion; you look one to the life, while Agnes is so awkward that she would be detected in a moment."

"She has not had the practice that I have had," Katarina said with a laugh; "the awkwardness will soon wear off if she has to dress like this for a short time. As for me, I have learnt all a boy's tricks and ways. I can whistle and shout with any of them, can quarrel, and bluster, be saucy on occasion, and have only once been in trouble."

"How was that, Katarina?"

"A boy who was a bit taller than I ran against me and declared that it was my fault, and gave me a cuff on the head. I might have run away, and of course I ought to have done so, but I was angry, for he really hurt me; so I had to do what any boy would have done, and I flew at him so fiercely, and cuffed and scratched and kicked so savagely that at last he turned and ran. He had hit me too, but I did not feel it at the time, and next morning I was all sorts of colours round the eyes. Father was very angry, but when I asked what else he would have done if he had been cuffed, he could not tell me. I had a very important message to carry that morning for him. At first he said I could not go out in that state; but, as I told him, I had never looked so much like a boy before."

All were glad when it became dark enough for them to make a start. The men and maids had all been sent away, and none remained save Maître Leroux and his wife. They were not in any disguise, but were wrapped up in cloaks, and in the badly-lighted streets could pass unrecognized.

"Do you go out first, Master Aylmer," the silversmith said. "I have no fear of anyone watching behind, for it is not likely that any of them know of this entrance to my house; still, it is as well to make certain. When you get out of the lane you had best stay there until the others have passed on, then you can follow them. We will wait for a few minutes after they have gone, and lock the door behind us. You have not forgotten where you are to find us."

"No, I have the name and house right. Shall I ask for you as Maître Leroux?"

"I have not thought of that. No, it will be better, perhaps, to ask for Philip Sampson; it were just as well that none should know my name there except Lepelletiere and his wife."

As arranged Guy went out first; there was still light enough for him to make his way along the narrow lane without falling over piles of dirt and rubbish that at some points almost blocked it. The street into which it opened was also a very narrow one, and no one was about. In a minute Dame Margaret, walking with Katarina, and with Agnes close behind, holding Charlie's hand, passed him.

"It is all quite clear," he said. Keeping some fifteen yards behind he followed them until they entered a broader street. There were a good many people about here. The nearest way would have been to have crossed the road and passed by another small street facing that from which they had come, but somewhat to his surprise they turned and went along the broader street. He soon acknowledged to himself that this was the wiser course, for there were so many people about that their passage would be unnoticed, while in the narrow lanes some rough fellow might have accosted them. Keeping always in frequented streets they made a long detour before they reached that in which the count resided, and it was with a feeling of great relief that Guy saw them enter the house. He himself, as arranged, did not approach it for another quarter of an hour, then he went and knocked on the door with his hand, which was at once opened by Katarina.

"All is well," she said; "your lady is in the room where you first waited
—my father is with her."

As Guy entered the count was just saying: "Yes, it would certainly be
best, madame, that your daughter should continue at present in that disguise.
In the first place, she will get accustomed to it, and should she have
occasion to move again she would be able to do so without attracting notice;
in the second place, it would be desirable that, even accidentally, no one
should know that there is a young lady of her age here. I have no visitors
save on business, but possibly either she or your boy might come out on to
the stairs when one is going up or down. It would be unfortunate that he
should see them at all, but if it were but a boy he caught sight of he would
not at any rate associate them with your party. These precautions may seem
to you absurd, but it is often by little accidents that things are discovered
when as it seemed everything had been provided against."

"I shall not mind," Agnes said. "When I first went out it seemed
dreadful, but when I found that nobody noticed me I began to be
accustomed to it, and as your daughter is dressed as a boy too I shall not
mind it."

"I shall not like being dressed as a girl," Charlie said sturdily.

The count smiled. "Well, we will see what we can do in your case;
anyhow, you must keep on that dress—for a day or two. And now, Guy,
about yourself. I have arranged for you to lodge with a man who gets news
for me; it is in the butchers' quarter, which is the last place where anyone
would think of looking for you. Besides, there you will see all that is going
on. I have two other disguises in addition to that I sent you; one is that of a
young butcher, another is that of one of the lads who live in misery, who
sleep at the market where they can earn a few sous by doing odd jobs, and
beg or steal when they can do nothing else. I hear that you have also
arranged for a shelter in the quarter between the walls; that too may be very
useful, and it will be well for you to go thither to-morrow and arrange so
that you can have a place to go to when you choose; it will doubtless be
much more pleasant for you there than in the market quarter. Lastly, I have
got you a white hood, which may be most useful of all." Guy looked
surprised. "Henceforth," the count went on, "white is to be the butchers'
colour. All who march this evening are to be so clad, and as soon as it is
known to-morrow, you will find three-fourths of the people wearing it, for
not to do so will be taken as a sign of hostility to their faction. They will
have started by this time, and if it pleases you to put on the butcher's dress
and the white hood over it you can mingle in safety with them and see all
that is done; then when they return to their quarter, you can go with them.
The house to which you are to go is the third on the left-hand side of the
Rue des Couteaux. My man lodges at the top of the house, the room to the

left when you mount the stair—his name is Simon Bouclier. The lane is at the back of the butchers' market. The man has no idea who you are. I have simply told him that I will send a young man to help gather news for me of what is going on, that you would work separately, but that he was to do all in his power to aid you, and that at any time if he wanted to send a message to me and could not himself come, he was to intrust it to you, and similarly he was to bring any message that you might want to send to the spot where he meets my messenger. The man works for one of the Thiberts. He does not know who I am, but I think he believes me to be an agent of Burgundy's, and that I collect the information so that he may be privately informed of what is doing. I have encouraged that idea, because it is more likely to keep him truthful to me, since he would think that were he to play me false the duke would see that some harm or other befell him. Therefore, it is as well that you should drop a word as if by accident that will confirm that notion, and will lead him to believe that you too are working under the orders of the duke. This will lull any suspicion that he might feel on seeing, as he must do, that you live in a position far higher than would appear from your garb. And now, if you would see to-night's doings, you had best put on that disguise and the white hood, and be off without delay; you will find the things in the room above."

In a few minutes Guy was ready to start. He could not help looking with disfavour at the greasy and stained garments, and he put them on with an expression of strong disgust. The two suits that he had taken off he made up into a bundle, placed the disguise he had brought with him with them, putting up separately that of which the count had spoken, and which was so ragged and dirty that he inwardly hoped he might never be obliged to assume it; then he went downstairs again. He had strapped round his waist a heavy sword placed beside the clothes, and carried in his hand a short pike. Dame Margaret smiled when he entered, and Katarina laughed aloud at the expression of his face.

"Truly, Guy," the former said, "you might go anywhere in that garb without a soul suspecting you. This journey with me is leading you into strange disguises and adventures, which will give you much matter for talk when we are safely back at Summerley."

"I have left my other disguises above," he said to the count. "The decent one of an apprentice I have placed with my own clothes, and will take them with me to any lodging that I may get among the carpenters, but that beggar suit I will take to Simon Bouclier's the next time I come. I suppose you would not wish me to come here during the day."

"No, unless it is very important; and to that end I think you had better carry the apprentice's disguise also to your lodging in the market. You would not gain favour among the carpenters were you to go among them in the dress you now wear, and your calling upon me here in your apprentice's dress would excite no attention; therefore, if you have need to come here during the day, you had best come as an apprentice."

Guy now went down into the street through which the butchers' force would pass. In a short time he heard a deep dull sound, and soon they came along, a host of armed men.

He fell in unnoticed near the head of the column. Soon after he had joined them they halted, and three or four knights came up and entered into conversation with their leaders. Guy recognized among them Sir Robert de Mailly, Sir Charles de Lens, and several others of the household of the Duke of Burgundy. These talked for some time with the Sieur de Jacqueville, Governor of Paris, who had joined the butchers' faction and was now riding at the head of the column, whereupon the force went no farther, but turned and retraced its steps. Guy wondered greatly where the butchers could be going, but soon found that they were making for the Bastille. After much parley between De Jacqueville and the governor, the latter consented, on the order of the Duke of Burgundy's friends, to hand over to them Sir Peter des Essars and his brother Sir Anthony, who were both supporters of the Orleanists and had come to Paris secretly, and had by the orders of the Duke of Aquitaine been admitted as guests to the Bastille.

These were marched back to the Louvre, the gates of which were opened by the orders of Burgundy's friends, and the two knights were thrown into the prison of the palace. On the way back the houses of a very rich upholsterer and of a cannon-founder of great repute, both of whom had withstood the butchers, were broken into and their owners both murdered. After this the mob marched to the house of Maître Leroux. No reply being given to their summons to open, an attack was made upon the door. While they were engaged in doing this, screens of wattles covered with two or three thicknesses of hides were placed so as to shelter the assailants from the arrows that had proved so deadly on the occasion of their last attack. It was thus evident that the outrage was a planned one. Guy looked on with some amusement until the door gave way under the action of some very heavy sledge-hammers wielded by a party of brawny smiths; the moment it did so the crowd made a tremendous rush.

So great was the pressure that many were thrown down and trampled to death in the doorway. It was not long before several of the windows were thrown open and voices shouted down that the house was deserted. A yell of fury burst from the crowd below, but the pressure at the door was even greater than before. The loss incurred during the first attack had caused all but the bravest and most determined to hang back somewhat; now, however, that it seemed that the silversmith's stores could be ransacked without danger, all were anxious to have a hand in it. Presently one of the leaders appeared at a casement on the first floor and waved his arms for silence. The roar of voices ceased and the man cried:

"Citizens, 'tis of no use to press forward into the house, not only has the traitor and those with him fled from the just vengeance of the people, but he has taken away with him the whole of his silverware."

A yell of disappointment and rage rose, then as it ceased for a moment a voice shouted out:

"They are trying to cheat us, my friends; those who got in first have divided up the spoil and wish us to have no share in it."

This caused a fresh outburst of commotion. At a signal from the leader above a number of well-armed men, who were evidently a sort of body-guard, pressed forward to the door and drove back the crowd with blows from the staves of their pikes. Presently those who had entered began to pour out, and in a quarter of an hour the house was cleared. As soon as it was so the windows were lit up by a lurid light which showed that it had been fired on each floor, and the flames very soon burst out through the casements. Satisfied with having done this the butchers returned to their quarter, and Guy mounted to the chamber of Simon Bouclier. The man had evidently just returned, as he too wore a white hood. He had been carrying a torch in the procession, and this was stuck into a ring on the wall.

"WELL, COMRADE," SAID SIMON, "I SUPPOSE YOU ARE THE MAN I WAS TOLD WOULD COME TO-NIGHT?"

"Well, comrade," he said as Guy entered, "I suppose you are the man I was told would come here to-night."

"I am so," Guy said. "I should have been here before, but I joined the procession, as I guessed that you would be there also."

"Yes," the man said; "though I should not have gone had I not thought that more would come of it. What have we done? Captured two knights and killed two bourgeois! Pooh, it did not need five thousand men for that."

"No, but it was just as important as if we had killed a hundred."

"How so?" the other asked.

"Because it has shown the Armagnacs that Paris and Burgundy are as united as ever, and that they will stand no intrigues by the court party."

"That is true. We are all sound here; there were but five thousand out to-night, because that was enough for the work, but there will be four times as many next time we go to the Louvre. To-morrow morning, you know, we are going to pay a visit to the Duke of Aquitaine at his hotel, to teach that young man that he has to do as we and Burgundy order him, or that it will be worse for him."

"So I understand," Guy said carelessly. "As long as all hold together in this quarter everything will go right. My duty principally is to find out if there are any signs of wavering; there are no signs, of course, among the butchers, but some of the others are thought to be but half-hearted."

"The butchers and skinners are all right, never fear," the man said; "and if there are others in the quarter who may not be quite so hot in the matter as we are, they know better than to open their mouths. Of course, in the other quarters there may be a strong party who would thwart us; the smiths and the carpenters and masons are ever jealous of us of the markets, but they have no leaders, and hold not together as we do. Besides, they know that we have Burgundy with us, so whatever they think they are not likely to say much, for if it came to a battle we could sweep them out of the city."

"Yes, yes, I know that there is no fear of that, the great thing is to make sure that some of those who seem to be hottest in the matter, are not taking money from the other party; there are one or two I am specially to observe."

"I understand you, comrade. I myself have never had much confidence in John de Troyes nor his medical students. He is good at talking, no one will deny that; but for myself I would rather that we kept among ourselves and had nothing to do with such cattle, who have no interest in the privileges of the guilds, and who take part with us no one knows why. But I am sleepy; that bundle of fresh rushes in the corner is yours, I got them in the hay-market to-day when I heard that you were coming. You can keep beside me to-morrow morning and I will get you a good place in the ranks.

From whence shall I say that you come, as many will ask the question, seeing that your face is strange?"

"You can say I am from Nancy."

"Yes, that will be good enough; that is the right quarter of France for a man to have come from just at present."

Guy was thoroughly fatigued with the long excitement of the day. At eleven in the morning everything had been going on as usual, now Dame Margaret and the two children were in hiding, her four men-at-arms fugitives, and Paris was virtually in a state of insurrection against the royal authority, stirred up thereto by the Duke of Burgundy, who had thus openly leagued himself with the scum of Paris. That what he had seen that evening was but the beginning of a series of crimes, Guy could not doubt; and although this man had expressed his confidence in the power of the market-men to sweep the craftsmen out of Paris, he felt sure from what he had heard, that this could not be done until a fierce and doubtful battle had been fought in the streets. At eight next morning he went out with his companion.

"It is well not to go into a place where we shall meet many till your face is better known," the latter said; and he led the way to a small *trattoir* a quarter of a mile away. Here they sat down and breakfasted, then they returned to the market where the White Hoods were mustering. Simon, who was evidently well known to most of the butchers, took his place near the head of the column, and at nine o'clock it got into motion. When it issued from its own quarters it was evident that its approach excited general apprehension. The streets were deserted as it passed along. None of the casements were opened, and although the traders dared not put up their shutters, none of them appeared at the doors, where their apprentices and workmen gathered to look at the procession. Passing along steadily and in good order, and headed as before by the knights of the Duke of Burgundy's household, they drew up before the palace of the Duke of Aquitaine. Caboche, John de Troyes, and one of the butchers entered the house. The guards having no orders, and seeing how strong was the force that was at their back, did not venture to oppose their entrance, and they pushed on into the private apartments of the duke and informed him that they, on behalf of the good town of Paris and for the welfare of his father and himself, required the delivery to them of certain traitors now in the hotel.

The duke, furious at their insolence, told them that such affairs were not their business, and that there were no traitors in the hotel. In the meantime many of the White Hoods had followed their leaders, Simon and Guy entering with them. They scattered through the apartments and seized the duke's chancellor, the Duke of Bar, a cousin of the king, and twelve other knights and gentlemen, some of whom were in the apartment of the Duke of

Aquitaine himself. While this was going on the Dukes of Burgundy and Lorraine arrived, and Aquitaine, turning to the former angrily, said:

"Father-in-law, this insurrection has been caused by your advice; those of your household are the leaders of it; you shall some day repent of this. The state shall not be always governed according to your will and pleasure."

However, in spite of his indignation and remonstrance, the twelve gentlemen were carried away and confined in different prisons; and presently discovering the king's secretary, they killed him and threw the body into the river. They compelled the Duke of Aquitaine himself to leave his palace, and with the king, his father, to take up his abode in the Hôtel de St. Pol. Placing a strong guard round it, so as to prevent them from leaving Paris, the mob then compelled all the nobles and even the prelates, they met, to put on white hoods, and their leaders sent off letters to the chief towns in France to inform them that what they had done was for the welfare of the king and kingdom, and requiring them to give aid should there be any necessity for it; they then published an edict in the name of the king ordering that it should be proclaimed in every bailiwick that no person, under penalty of death and confiscation of goods, should obey any summons from their superior lord to take up arms or to trouble the kingdom. The mad king was made to sign this after the Dukes of Aquitaine, Berri, and Lorraine, and other nobles of the council had put their names to it.

At nine o'clock that evening Guy went to the square before Notre Dame. Here many groups of people were talking over the events of the day. Guy had, as soon as he left the market quarter, taken off his white hood, and before starting he put on his dress as an apprentice. There was no doubt that the opinion of the great majority of those in the square was hostile to the authors of the events of the day, and that the consternation among the citizens was very great. After thus forcing the great nobles to obey their will and outraging the palace of the Duke of Aquitaine, there was no saying to what length they would go, and fears were expressed that ere long they might sack the whole of the better quarters of Paris.

It was so evident, however, that they had the support of the Duke of Burgundy that no one saw any way out of their trouble, and that nothing but the arrival of a powerful army of Orleanists could relieve them from their peril. As Guy had no real expectation of seeing any of his followers,— although the gates had been opened that afternoon after the seizure of the knights,—he attended more to the conversations going on about him than to the matter on which he had come. Presently, however, he saw a rough-looking fellow watching him attentively. He walked close to him, but not recognizing him would have passed on, had not the man taken a step forward and said in a low voice:

"Villeroy!"

"Is it you, Robert? In faith I did not recognize you in that attire."

"And I was not sure that it was you, Master Guy; I should certainly not have known you by your face. Your figure and walk, when a short distance away, attracted my attention, and knowing your disguise was that of an apprentice I made sure it was you. Then as you came closer I doubted, and though I ventured upon saying the name of our lord, I scarce thought that you would reply."

"Where are the others, Robert?"

"They are walking about separately seeking for you. We are to meet on the steps of the cathedral at half-past nine."

"What has become of Tom?"

The man laughed. "If you will come along this way, master, you will see." They went to a quiet corner of the square. As they approached it they heard angry voices, and standing under a lamp Guy saw a tall man of wild and unkempt appearance, with black hair and a begrimed face, and a basket of vegetables strapped to his shoulders, threatening angrily with a staff three or four gamins who were making fun of him. He spoke in a wild, incoherent way, and seemed to be half-witted.

"What are you worrying this poor fellow for?" Robert said angrily to the boys. "If you do not be off, and that quickly, I will lay my cudgel about your shoulders."

This threat was much more efficacious than those of the half-witted man had been, and the boys at once took to their heels. The tall man shuffled towards the new-comers.

"Is it really you, Tom?" Guy said in a low tone.

"It is me, sure enough, Master Guy. I should not know myself, and am not surprised that you do not know me; in faith, my back aches with walking with a stoop, and my legs with shuffling along as if I had scarce the use of them, instead of stepping out manfully. Is all well? We have heard of strange doings—that the butchers have, with the countenance of Burgundy, bearded the Duke of Aquitaine, and even carried off some of his friends from before his face; also that the houses of three of those who had withstood them had been burned, among them that of Maître Leroux; also that two traders had been killed, though which two they were we have not been able to learn."

"All is well, Tom; our lady and her children were safely bestowed, as was also the silversmith and his wife."

"I am right glad of that; they were a worthy couple. And so his house is burned and sacked?"

"Burned, but not sacked, Tom; for he had, before they came, stowed away in a hiding-place where they could not be found all those chests of his, and not a single piece of silver fell into the hands of the butchers."

"That was well done," the archer said, rubbing his hands. "I should like to have seen the dogs' faces when they burst in and found nothing. And my bow, Master Guy?"

"I fear that the flames will not have spared it. I went past the house to-day, and naught but the bare walls are standing."

At this moment the bell of the cathedral struck the half-hour, and Robert Picard said: "Will you stay here, Master Guy? I must go and meet the others, and forthwith bring them to you here."

# CHAPTER XIV — PLANNING MASSACRE

In a short time Robert Picard returned with his two companions, and leaving the square, they all went along the quays to a quiet spot. "We cannot be overheard here," Guy said, "and now, in the first place, let me know how you have fared. I knew that you had got safely away, for I was near the gate of St. Denis when the Burgundians fought their way out, and I saw you follow."

"We had no difficulty," Robert Picard said. "We went into the wood, and thence I went across to St. Cloud and bought these garments that you see us in, and we hid away our steel caps and harness in some bushes in the heart of the wood, where they are not likely to be found. Then after a long talk with Tom we agreed that he had best go as a half-witted man with a basket of vegetables for sale, and I went into St. Cloud again, dressed as I now am, and found a little shop where they sold rags and old garments, and got his outfit for a couple of francs, and dear at that. We thought in that way he would not have to say much, and that any confusion of speech would be set down to the fact that his brain was weak. Hearing that the gates were open this afternoon, we came in just before they were closed for the night. We have got a room in a lane which honest folk would not care to pass through even in daylight; 'tis a vile hole, but consorts well with our appearance."

"I will try and find you a better place to-morrow, Robert. I am going to see the people with whom Maître Leroux is in hiding. I hear that they have no sympathy with these butchers, and when I tell them that you are stout fellows and good fighters methinks they will find quarters for you; and you may be able to put on safer disguises than those you wear at present, except that of Tom's, which I think we cannot better. Besides, he can lie there quietly, and need not, except when he chooses, sally out. I myself am lodging at present among the butchers. I hear that Caboche and the Legoix are furious at our having slipped through their fingers, and they declare that, as we cannot have escaped from Paris, they will lay hands on us very soon."

"I should like to lay hands on a few of them myself, Master Guy," Tom said earnestly, "say out in that wood there with a quarter-staff, and to deal with four of them at a time. They have burnt my bow, and I shall not get even with them till I have cracked fully a dozen of their skulls."

"I shall be likely to be near you in the quarter where I hope to get you lodging, Tom, for I too am going to have a room there, though I shall generally live where I now am, as I can there obtain news of all that is going on, and might be able to warn our lady in time if they should get any news that may set them on her track. Heard you aught at St. Cloud of any Orleanist gathering?"

"I heard a good deal of talk about it, but naught for certain; but methinks that ere long they will be stirring again. The news that I have heard of the insolence of the mob here to the Duke of Aquitaine, and of the seizure of their friends who were with him, is like to set them on fire, for they will see that all the promises made by Burgundy meant nothing, and that, with the aid of the Parisians, he is determined to exercise all authority in the state, and to hold Aquitaine as well as the king in his hands."

The next morning Guy went to the house of Maître de Lepelletiere, and inquired for Philip Sampson. Maître Leroux was in.

"I have spoken to my friend about you," he said, after they had talked over the events of the last two days, "and he has arranged for a room for you in a house three doors away; and I have no doubt that your four men can be lodged there also, for 'tis a large house, and is let out, for the most part, as he told me, to journeymen carpenters. But since the troubles began there has been little building, and men who can find no work here have moved away to seek for it in places less afflicted by these troubles. That is one of the reasons why the carpenters have not made a firmer stand against the butchers. I will ask him to come up here. You already know him, as you have spoken with him several times when he was looking after his men putting up the new doors."

The master carpenter soon came in. "I will gladly get a lodging for your men," he said, when Guy had explained the matter to him. "We may come to blows with these market people, and four stout fellows are not to be despised. There will be a meeting of the council of our guild this afternoon, and on my recommendation they will give me the necessary documents, saying that the men—you can give me their names—have received permission to work as carpenters in Paris. They can then put on dresses suitable for craftsmen, and the papers will suffice to satisfy anyone who may inquire as to their business. I think that your tall archer may safely lay aside the disguise you say he has assumed, it might be likely to get him into trouble; the change in the colour of the hair and the darkening of his eyebrows should be quite sufficient disguise, and if he is always when abroad with one of his comrades, he has but to keep his mouth shut, and if questioned the man with him can say that he is dumb."

"That would be excellent," Guy said, "and I am greatly obliged to you. Doubtless, too, they will soon make acquaintance with some of the other workmen, and by mixing with these there will be less suspicion excited than if they always went about together."

"I will tell my foreman to present them to the men who work for me, and they will soon get known in the quarter. Five or six of my men lodge in the house where I took the room for you. It might be useful, too, were I to give you a paper of apprenticeship, and if you were similarly introduced. In that case it might be convenient to exchange the small room that I have taken for you for a larger one; as an apprentice you would ordinarily lodge with your master, and if you did not you would scarce have a room to yourself, but were you to lodge with your four men it would seem natural enough."

"That would be a capital plan, Maître Lepelletiere."

"You see, in that way, too," the carpenter went on, "you would only have to place a plank on your shoulder and then go where you will without exciting the least attention. I will furnish you with a list of the houses where I have men at work, and this again would be an assistance to you. It is my foreman who took the lodging for you; I am expecting him here shortly for orders, and he shall go round with you. As you say that your fellows are dressed at present in rough fashion it will be as well that they should provide themselves with their new disguises before they come here, as, if they were seen in their present guise, it would prejudice them with the others in the house, for craftsmen look down greatly upon the rough element of the street."

"They shall do so," Guy said, "and I will come with them myself this evening."

Guy presently went in with the foreman and arranged for a large attic with a dormer window, at the top of the house. At midday he met Robert Picard and told him the arrangements that had been made, supplying him with money for the purchase of the four dresses. "As soon as it becomes dark," he said, "you had best go to some quiet spot and change them. Bring the clothes you now have on in a bundle, for they may yet prove useful, and meet me at eight o'clock at the corner of the Rue des Fosses."

Guy then went to the Italian's and told Dame Margaret of the arrangements he had made.

"Since you have managed it all so well, Guy, I am glad to hear that the men are all back in Paris. I before wished that they should make straight for Villeroy, but since they are so safely bestowed it were best perhaps that they should be within reach. Long Tom is the only one I shall feel anxious about, for of course he is less easy to disguise than the others."

"He has plenty of shrewdness, my lady, and will, I have no doubt, play his part well. I know that I myself feel very glad that there are four true men upon whom we can rely if any difficulty should arise."

"Some evening, mother," Agnes said, "when I have grown more accustomed to this boy's dress I will go with Katarina to this house so that I can carry a message there, should she happen to be away when there is need for sending one."

Lady Margaret hesitated, but Guy said: "By your leave, my lady, I think that the idea is a very good one, saving that I myself will escort the two ladies there as soon as Mistress Agnes feels confident enough to go."

"In that case I should have no objection, Guy. Under your charge I have no doubt Agnes would be perfectly safe, but I could hardly bring myself to let her go out without escort in so wild a city as this is at present."

The Italian and his daughter presently joined them, and heard with satisfaction where Guy and the four men had obtained a safe lodging.

"Still," he said, "I should advise you sometimes to sleep at your lodging by the market-place. Simon is not the sort of companion you would choose. I have only seen him once, and I was then so disguised that he would not recognize me again—for none of those with whom I have dealings know who I am or where I live—but that once was sufficient to show me that the fellow might be trusted to serve me well as long as he was paid well, especially as he believed that I was an agent of the duke's; still, he is a rough and very unsavoury rascal, and had I been able to think at the moment of anywhere else where you could for the time safely shelter I should not have placed you with him."

"I do not mind," Guy said; "and at any rate with him I have opportunities of seeing what is going on, as, for example, when they insulted the Duke of Aquitaine, and it is certainly well to be able to learn what the intentions of the fellows are. As an Englishman I care naught for one party or the other, but as one of gentle blood it fills me with anger and disgust to see this rabble of butchers and skinners lording it over nobles and dragging knights and gentlemen away to prison; and if it were in my power I would gladly upset their design, were it not that I know that, for my lady's sake, it were well to hold myself altogether aloof from meddling in it."

"You are right," the Italian said gravely. "I myself am careful not to meddle in any way with these affairs. I try to learn what is doing, because such knowledge is useful to me and gains me credit as well as money with those who consult me, and may possibly be the means of saving their lives if they do but take my warning. Thus, having learned what was proposed to be done yesterday morning, I was able to warn a certain knight who visited me the evening before that it might cost him his life were he to remain in Paris twelve hours. He was incredulous at first, for I would give him no clue as to the nature of the danger; however, by a little trick I succeeded in impressing him sufficiently for him to resolve to leave at daybreak. This he did; at least they searched for him in vain at the Duke of Aquitaine's, and therefore I have no doubt that he took my advice, engaged a boat, and made his escape by the river. It was his first A to me, and I doubt not that henceforth he will be a valuable client, and that he will bring many of his friends to me. If I mistake not, I shall have more opportunities of doing such services and of so increasing my reputation ere long."

For a time things went on quietly. Tom and his companions were on friendly terms with the other men in the house, who all believed them to be carpenters who had come to Paris in search of employment. Long Tom was supposed by them to be dumb, and never opened his lips save when alone with his companions, and seldom left the house. The room was altogether unfurnished, but furniture was regarded as by no means a necessity in those days. Five bundles of rushes formed their beds, and Guy, as there was little to learn in the markets, generally slept there. An earthenware pan, in which burned a charcoal fire over which they did what cooking was necessary, a rough gridiron, and a cooking pot were the only purchases that it was necessary to make. Slices of bread formed their platters, and saved them all trouble in the matter of washing up. Washing was roughly performed at a well in the court-yard of the house.

Things had now quieted down so much that a considerable number of great nobles resorted to Paris, for the king had now a lucid interval. Among them were the Dukes of Berri, Burgundy, and Lorraine, with Duke Louis of Bavaria, the queen's brother, with the Counts de Nevers, De Charolais, De St. Pol, the Constable of France, and many other great lords and prelates. The queen was also with her husband.

"There will shortly be trouble again," the Italian said one day to Guy. "Simon told my daughter yesterday evening that the butchers were only biding their time to get as many fish into their net as possible, and that when they would draw it they would obtain a great haul. You have not been down there for some time; it were best that you put on your butcher's garb again and endeavour to find out what is intended."

"I was expecting you," Simon said, when that evening Guy entered his room. "There will be a meeting at midnight in the butchers' hall, and I cannot take you in with me, but I will tell you what happens."

"That will do as well as if I went myself," Guy said, "though in truth I should like well to see one of these councils."

"No one is admitted save those known to be, like myself, thoroughly devoted to the cause."

"That I can well understand, Simon; a traitor might mar all their plans."

"Some time I may take you," Simon said, "for doubtless I could smuggle you in; but to-night—" and he hesitated, "to-night it will be specially important, and they have to be more particular than usual as to who are admitted."

Guy noticed the hesitation, and replied carelessly that one occasion would be as good as another for him, and presently lay down in his corner. He wondered to himself what the business could be that his companion was evidently anxious that he should hear nothing of. He might wish that he should alone have the merit of reporting it, or it might be something that it was deemed the Duke of Burgundy himself, the butchers' friend and ally, would not approve of. At any rate he was determined, if possible, to find it all out; he therefore feigned sleep. At eleven o'clock Simon got up and went down; Guy waited for two or three minutes and then rose and followed. As soon as he was out of the door he made direct for the hall of the butchers' guild. He knew that Simon was not going straight there, as the meeting was not, he said, for an hour, and that he would be stopping to drink at some cabaret with his associates. The hall was but a short distance away.

When Guy approached it he saw that as yet it was not lighted up. On three sides it was surrounded by a garden with high trees; near the front entrance some twenty men were gathered talking together. He, therefore, went round to the back; several trees grew near the wall, and the branches of one of these extended over it. With considerable difficulty Guy succeeded in climbing it, and made his way along the branch and got upon the top of the wall. This was about fourteen feet high, and, lowering himself by his arms, he dropped into the garden and crossed to the building. He took off his white hood and thrust it into his doublet. The windows were six feet from the ground, and were, as usual at this time, closed by wooden shutters on the inside. Putting his fingers on the sill he raised himself up. There was plenty of room for him to stand, and, holding on by the iron bars, he took out his dagger and began to cut a hole in the shutter.

The wood was old, and after half an hour's hard work he succeeded in making a hole three inches long and an inch wide. By the time this was finished the hall had been lighted up with torches, and men were pouring in through the doors at the other end. Across the end next to him was a platform on which was a table. For a time no one came up there, for the members as they entered gathered in groups on the floor and talked earnestly together. After a few minutes ten men came up on to the platform; by this time the body of the hall was full, and the doors at the other end were closed. A man, whom Guy recognized as John de Troyes, stepped forward from the others on the platform and, standing in front of the table, addressed his comrades.

"My friends," he said, "it is time that we were at work again. Paris is becoming infested by enemies of the people, and we must rid ourselves of them. The nobles are assembled for the purpose, as they say, of being present at the marriage of Louis of Bavaria with the widow of Peter de Navarre, but we know well enough that this is but a pretext; they have come to consult how best they can overthrow the power of our Duke of Burgundy and suppress the liberty of this great city. The question is, are we tamely to submit to this?"

A deep shout of "No!" ran through the multitude.

"You are right, we will not submit. Were we to do so we know that it would cost the lives of all those who have made themselves prominent in the defence of the liberties of Paris; they might even go so far as to suppress all our privileges and to dissolve our guilds. In this matter the Duke of Burgundy hesitates and is not inclined to go with us to the full, but we Parisians must judge for ourselves what is necessary to be done. The duke has furnished us with a list of twelve names; these men are all dangerous and obnoxious to the safety of Paris. But there must be a longer list, we must strike at our own enemies as well as at those of the duke, and the council has therefore prepared a list of sixty names, which I will read to you."

Then, taking out a roll of paper, he read a list of lords and gentlemen, and also, to Guy's indignation, the names of several ladies of rank.

"These people," he said when he had finished, "are all obnoxious, and must be cast into prison. They must be tried and condemned."

Even among the greater portion of those present the boldness of a proposal that would array so many powerful families against them created a feeling of doubt and hesitation. The bolder spirits, however, burst into loud applause, and in this the others speedily joined, none liking to appear more lukewarm than the rest. Then up rose Caboche, a big, burly man with a coarse and brutal expression of face.

"I say we want no trials," he cried, striking one hand on the palm of the other. "As to the number, it is well enough as a beginning, but I would it were six hundred instead of sixty. I would that at one blow we could destroy all the nobles, who live upon the people of France. It needs but a good example to be set in Paris for all the great towns in France to follow it. Still, paltry as the number is, it will, as I said, do as a beginning. But there must be no mistake; if trials they must have, it must be by good men and true, who will know what is necessary and do it; and who will not stand upon legal tricks, but will take as evidence the fact that is known to all, that those people are dangerous to Paris and are the enemies of the king and the Duke of Burgundy. Last time we went, we marched with five thousand men; this time we must go with twenty thousand. They must see what force we have at our command, and that Paris is more powerful than any lord or noble even of the highest rank, and that our alliance must be courted and our orders obeyed. The Duke of Burgundy may pretend to frown, but at heart he will know that we are acting in his interest as well as our own; and even if we risk his displeasure, well, let us risk it. He needs us more than we need him. Do what he will, he cannot do without us. He knows well enough that the Orleanists will never either trust or forgive him, and he committed himself so far with us last time that, say what he will, none will believe that he is not with us now. For myself, I am glad that De Jacqueville and his knights will not this time, as last, ride at our head; 'tis best to show them that Paris is independent even of Burgundy, and that what we will we can do."

The hall rang with the loud acclamations, then John de Troyes got up again.

"I agree, we all agree, with every word that our good friend has spoken, and can warrant me that the judges shall be men in whom we can absolutely trust, and that those who enter the prisons will not leave them alive. The day after to-morrow, Thursday, the 11th of May, we shall hold a great assembly, of which we shall give notice to the king and the royal dukes, and shall make our proposals to the Duke of Aquitaine. Now, my friends, let each come forward with a list of the number of his friends who he will engage shall be present on Thursday."

At this point, Guy, seeing that the main business of the meeting had been declared, and that there now remained but to settle the details, got down from his post. With the aid of some ivy he climbed the wall and dropped down beyond it, and made his way back to his lodging. When Simon returned an hour later, Guy was apparently as fast asleep as before. When sleeping at the butchers' quarter he always rose at a very early hour, so that none who might have noticed him in his butcher's attire should see him go out in that of an apprentice, and he was obliged to walk about for some time before he could call at the count's. As soon as he thought that they would be likely to be stirring he knocked at the door. The old woman opened it.

"Is your master up yet?" he asked.

She nodded, and without further question he made his way upstairs to the Italian's chamber.

"You are early, Master Aylmer," the latter said in surprise as he entered. "Have you news of importance?"

"I have indeed, Count," and he at once related all that he had heard through the hole in the shutter.

"The insolence of these people surpasses all bounds," the count said angrily as he walked up and down the room. "Were there any force in the town that could resist them I would warn the Duke of Aquitaine what was intended, but as it is, nothing would be gained by it. You can only remember the eight or ten names that you have given me?"

"That is all; they were names that I was familiar with, while the others were strange to me."

"Two or three of them I can at least save from the grasp of these rascals," he said, "but I will take them all down on my tablets. What need was there for you," he went on after he had done this, "to run such risk as you did—for you would assuredly have been killed without mercy had they caught you spying upon them—when Simon, who you say was present, could have sent me full particulars of all that passed?"

Guy stated his reasons for fancying that upon this occasion Simon did not intend to send a full account.

"I thought so before I started," he said, "but I was well assured of it when I heard that, although Burgundy had given the names of twelve persons whom he desired to be arrested, he would go no further in the matter, and that he had no knowledge of their further pretensions. It seems to me, Count, that, believing as he does that you are an agent of the duke's, he was unwilling to say anything about this matter, as Burgundy might thwart the intentions of the butchers. The man is heart and soul with them, and though he is willing to sell you information that can do no harm to their plans, he will say nothing that might enable Burgundy to thwart them."

"If I thought that Burgundy could, or would do so, I would inform him as well as Aquitaine what is doing; but in the first place he has not the power, and in the second he would not have the will. What are a few score of lives to him, and those mostly of men of the Orleanist faction, in comparison with the support of Paris? I am vexed, too, at this failure of Simon, that is to say, if it be a failure. That we shall know by mid-day. My daughter will meet him in the Place de Grève at eleven, and we shall hear when she comes back how much he has told her. I am going after breakfast to my booth outside the walls, where you first saw me. I must send notes to the three gentlemen whom I know, begging them to see me there."

"Can I take them for you? I have nothing to do, and shall be glad of anything to occupy me."

"I shall be obliged if you will; you are sure to find them in at this hour."

He sat down and wrote three short communications. The wording was identical, but the times fixed for the interview were an hour apart. They ran as follows:

"*My Lord,—Consulting the stars last night I find that danger menaces you. It may be averted if you quit Paris when you receive this, for it seems to me that it is here only that your safety is menaced. Should you wish to consult me before doing so, come, I pray you, to my booth in the fair at two, but come mounted.* "

Instead of a signature a cabalistic figure was drawn below it, and then the words were added:

*The bearer can be trusted.*

The slips of parchment were then rolled up and sealed; no addresses were put on.

"If they question you," he said, "say nothing, save that I told you that the matter contained in the letter was sure and certain, and that a great risk of life would assuredly be run unless my advice was taken. Deliver them into the hands of those they concern, and trust them to no others, Master Aylmer. If you cannot obtain access to them, say to the varlets that they are to inform their lords that one from the man in the Rue des Essarts desires urgently to see them, and that should be sufficient if the message is given. If they refuse to take it, then I pray you wait outside for a while on the chance of the gentlemen issuing out. This, on which you see I have made one dot, is for the Count de Rennes, who is at present at the Hotel of St. Pol, being in the company of the Duke of Berri; this is for Sir John Rembault, who is at the Louvre, where he is lodging with the governor, who is a relation of his; the third is for the Lord of Roubaix, who is also lodged at the Louvre."

"They shall have them," Guy said as he placed them in his doublet, "if I have to stop till midnight to get speech with them; the matter of waiting a few hours is but a trifle in comparison with the life of a man. I would that I could warn others."

The Italian shook his head. "It could not be done without great danger," he said. "Were you to carry an anonymous letter to others you might be seized and questioned. The three to whom you now carry notes have all reason for knowing that my predictions are not to be despised, but the others would not accept any warning from an unknown person. They might take it for a plot, and you might be interrogated and even put to torture to discover who you are and whence you obtained this information. Things must go on as they are; assuredly this is no time for meddling in other people's affairs. We are only at the beginning of troubles yet, and know not how great they may grow. Moreover, you have no right to run a risk for strangers when your life may be of vital service to your mistress. Should you succeed in handing these three letters to the gentlemen to whom they are written by noon, I shall be glad if you will bring the news to me at my booth, and I shall then be able to tell, you how much information the butcher has sent of the proceedings last night."

Guy went first to the Louvre. As many people were going in and out, no question was asked him, and on reaching the entrance he inquired of some varlets standing there for the lodgings of the Lord de Roubaix and Sir John Rembault.

"I am in the service of the Lord de Roubaix; what would you with him?"

"I am charged with a message for him; I was told to deliver it only to himself."

"From whom do you come? I cannot disturb him with such a message from I know not who."

"That is reasonable," Guy replied, "but if you tell him that I come from the man in the Rue des Essarts I warrant that he will see me. You don't suppose that I am joking with you," he went on as the varlet looked at him suspiciously, "when I should likely be whipped for my pains. If you will give the message to your lord I doubt not that he will give me audience."

"Follow me," the varlet said, and led the way upstairs and through several corridors, then he motioned to him to wait, and entered a room. He returned in a minute.

"My lord will see you," he said, and led the way into the room. "This is the person, my lord," he said, and then retired.

The Lord of Roubaix was a tall man of some forty years of age. Guy bowed deeply and handed to him the roll of parchment. The count broke the seal and read it, and when he had finished looked fixedly at Guy.

"The writer tells me that you are to be trusted?"

"I hope so, my lord."

"Do you know the contents of this letter?"

"I know so much, my lord, that the writer told me to assure you that the matter was urgent, and that he could not be mistaken as to what was written in the letter."

The count stood irresolute for a minute or two; then he said:

"Tell him that I will act upon his advice. He has before now proved to me that his warnings are not to be neglected. You seem by your attire to be an apprentice, young sir, and yet your manner is one of higher degree."

"Disguises are convenient in times like these, my lord," Guy said.

"You are right, lad." He put his hand to his pouch, but Guy drew back with a smile.

"No, my lord, had you offered me gold before you remarked that I was but playing a part, I should have taken it in order to keep up that part; as it is I can refuse it without your considering it strange that I should do so."

The count smiled. "Whoever you are, you are shrewd and bold, young sir. I shall doubtless see you when I return to Paris."

Guy then left, and delivered the other two missives. In each case those who received them simply returned an answer that they would be at the place at the hour named, and he then went beyond the walls, observing as he passed out through the gates that a party of White Hoods had stationed themselves there. However, they interfered with no one passing in or out. On reaching the booth he informed the count of the success of his visits.

"I doubt, however," he said, "whether either of the three gentlemen will be here at the time appointed, for the White Hoods are watching at the gate."

# At Agincourt

"I think that they will not stop anyone to-day, Master Aylmer. They intend to make a great haul to-morrow, and would not wish to excite suspicion by seizing anyone to-day. Were it known that they had done so, many others who have reason to believe they are obnoxious to Burgundy or to the Parisians, might conceal themselves or make their escape in various disguises. I hear that a request has been made that a deputation of the citizens of Paris shall be received by the Duke of Aquitaine to-morrow morning, and that the great lords may be present to hear the request and complaints of the city."

# CHAPTER XV — A RESCUE

Guy had found his mornings hang heavy on his hands, as of course he had been obliged to give up attending the fencing-school. Going down to the river now, he sat there watching the passing boats until nearly one o'clock, and then returned to the fair. Before reaching the booth Katarina joined him.

"I have been watching for you, Monsieur Guy. Father said it was as well that you should not, twice in a day, be seen entering his place. He bade me tell you that the three gentlemen have been to him and will not re-enter Paris."

"Did you see Simon this morning?"

"Yes, he only told me that the market men would have an interview with the Duke of Aquitaine to-morrow, and would demand the arrest of those whom the Duke of Burgundy had pointed out as his enemies. He said that they would go in such force that the duke would be unable to refuse their request. Although it was so early, I think that the man had been drinking. My father, when I told him, said I should go no more to meet him."

"I am very glad to hear it," Guy said. "He is a low scoundrel, and though I say not but that the information obtained from him may have been of some advantage, for indeed it was the means of my being enabled to save our lives and those of my Burgundian friends, I like not the thought of your going to meet him; and I am sure that if he were to take the idea into his thick head that it was not for the advantage of the Duke of Burgundy that the information he had given was being used, he is capable of denouncing you."

"I did not mind meeting him,", the girl said. "I never went into the rough quarters, but always met him in one of the better squares or streets. Still, I am glad that I have not to go again. I think that he had been drinking all night, and with his unwashed face and his bloodshot eyes and his foul attire I was ashamed even in my present dress to speak with him."

"I hope that I have done with him too," Guy said. "Of course, for my mistress's sake, I shall go again if there be aught to be learnt by it, but as it seems he is now no longer to be trusted it is not likely that any advantage is to be gained by visiting him. However, I shall hear what your father thinks this evening."

Upon talking over the matter with the astrologer the latter at once said that he thought that it would be better for him not to go to Simon's again.

"When he finds that my daughter meets him no more he will feel aggrieved. I myself shall go in disguise to-morrow to meet him in the Place de Grève, and tell him that for the present there will be no occasion for him to come to the rendezvous, as the events of the meeting which will have taken place before I see him show that there can be no doubt that the butchers are ready to go all lengths against the Orleanist party; but that if any change should occur, and private information be required, you would go to his lodging again, I shall make no allusion to his having given me none of the names save those furnished by the duke, or remark on the strangeness that, having been at the meeting, he should have heard nothing of the measures proposed against the others; his own conscience will no doubt tell him that his failure is one of the causes of my no longer desiring any messages from him. I have other means of gaining information, as I have one of the medical students who follow that cracked-brained fellow, John de Troyes, in my pay. Hitherto I have not employed him largely, but shall now, if need be, avail myself of his services. But I do not think that I shall have any occasion to do so. After the demand by the Parisians for so many nobles and gentlemen to be arrested, it will be clear to all adhering to Orleans that Paris is no longer a place for them, and even the followers of Burgundy will see that those the duke regarded as his servants have become his masters, and there will be but few persons of quality remaining in Paris, and therefore, save when some citizen wishes to consult me, I shall have little to do here save to carry on my work as a quack outside the gates. Even this I can drop for a time, for the people of Paris will not be inclined for pleasure when at any moment there may be fierce fighting in the streets. I shall be well content to look on for a time. I have been almost too busy of late. And it was but yesterday that I received news from a Carthusian monk,—whom I thought it as well to engage to let me know what is passing,—that there have been debates among some of the higher clergy upon reports received that persons, evidently disguised, call upon me at late hours, and that I practise diabolic arts. A determination has been arrived at that an inquisition shall be made into my doings, my house is to be searched, and myself arrested and tried by the judge for having dealings with the devil. This news much disturbed me; however, when you told me that the Archbishop of Bourges was among those on the list of accused, and also Boisratier, confessor to the queen, it is evident that these good ecclesiastics will have ample matter of another sort to attend to, and are not likely to trouble themselves about sorcery at present."

# At Agincourt

On the following morning some twelve thousand White Hoods marched to the Hôtel de St. Pol, and the leaders, on being admitted, found all the great lords assembled. After making various propositions they presented a roll to the Duke of Aquitaine containing the names of those they charged with being traitors. He at first refused to take it; but so many of their followers at once poured into the great hall that he was obliged to do so, and to read out the names. Twenty of those mentioned in the list were at once, in spite of the protest of the duke, arrested and carried off; a proclamation was made by sound of trumpet in all the squares of Paris summoning the other forty named to appear within a few days, under penalty of having their property confiscated. A week later the king, having recovered his health, went to the church of Notre Dame, he and all the nobles with him wearing white hoods. Four days later the Parisians rose again, seized the gates, drew up the bridges, placed strong guards at each point, and a cordon of armed men outside the walls all round the city, to prevent any from escaping by letting themselves down from the walls.

Groups of ten armed men were placed in every street, and the sheriffs and other leaders marched a large body of men to the Hôtel de St. Pol and surrounded it by a line three deep. They then entered and found the king, dukes, and nobles all assembled in the great hall.

They then ordered a Carmelite friar, named Eustace, to preach to the king. He took for his text, *"Except the Lord keep the city, the watchman waketh but in vain,"* and upon this discoursed on the bad state of the government of the kingdom, and of the crimes committed. The Chancellor of France demanded of the friar when he had concluded who were those who had incited him thus to speak, and the leaders at once said they had done so, and called up a number of other leaders, who on bended knees declared to the king that Father Eustace had spoken their sentiments; that they had the sincerest love for the king and his family, and that what they had done had been for the welfare of himself and the kingdom. While this was going on, the Duke of Burgundy, at once indignant and alarmed at this insolence of the Parisians, had gone out, and, finding the lines of armed men surrounding the hotel, had earnestly entreated them to retire, saying that it was neither decent nor expedient that the king, who had but just recovered from his illness, should thus see them drawn up in battle array round his abode. Those he addressed replied like the leaders within, that they were there for the good of the kingdom, and then gave him a roll, saying that they should not depart until those written on it were delivered up to them.

With the names of Louis of Bavaria, five knights, an archbishop and priest, were those of nine ladies of high rank, including the eldest daughter of the constable. The duke found that neither his authority nor powers were of the slightest avail, and returning to the queen, showed her the list. She was greatly troubled, and begged him to go with the Duke of Aquitaine and beg the Parisians in her name to wait for eight days, and that she would at the end of that time allow them to arrest her brother. The two dukes went out to the Parisians, but they positively refused to grant the request, and declared that they would go up to the queen's apartments and take those named by force, even in her or the king's presence, unless they were given up. On their return to the queen they found Louis of Bavaria and the king with her. On their report of the Parisians' demands the Duke of Bavaria went out and begged them to take him into custody, and that if he were found guilty they could punish him, but that if found innocent he should be allowed to go back to Bavaria, under a promise not to return to France again. He begged them to be content with taking him a prisoner, and to arrest no others.

They would not, however, abate one jot of their pretensions, and the whole of those demanded were at once brought out, including the ladies. They were put two and two on horseback, each horse escorted by four men-at-arms, and were carried to various prisons. The Duke of Burgundy now, with his usual craft, professed to be well satisfied with what the Parisians had done, and handed over to them the Duke of Bar and the other prisoners confined in the Louvre, for whose security he had solemnly pledged himself. The Parisians then obliged the king to appoint twelve knights, nominated by themselves, and six examiners, to try the prisoners and punish all found guilty, while the dukes were obliged to draw up a statement and send it to the University for their seal of approval of what had been done.

The University, however, to their honour, stood firm; and while king and nobles had quailed before the violence of the crowd, they declared in full council before the king that they would in nowise intermeddle or advise in the business; and that so far from having advised the arrests of the dukes and other prisoners, they were much displeased at what had taken place. The University was a power; its buildings were strong, and the students were numerous, and at all times ready to take part in brawls against the Parisians; and even the butchers, violent as they were, were afraid to take steps against it.

They foresaw, however, that the position taken up by the University might lead some day to an inquiry into their conduct, and therefore obtained from the king an edict declaring that all that had been done was done by his approval and for the security of his person and the state, and that the arrests and imprisonments were therefore to be considered and regarded as having been done for the true honour and profit of the crown, and that he accordingly commanded all his councillors, judges, and officers to proclaim that this was so in all public places. This was signed by the king in council, the Dukes of Berri and Burgundy, and several other nobles and ecclesiastics, by the Chancellor of Burgundy, and other knights attached to the duke.

# At Agincourt

Many nobles quitted Paris at once, either openly or in disguise, including many of the Burgundian party, who were to the last degree indignant at what was going on; for the mock trials were at once commenced, and many of the prisoners, without regard to sex, were daily either put to death in prison or drowned in the Seine. Some of the bodies were exhibited on gibbets, the heads of others were fixed on lances, and some of them were beheaded in the market-place. During this time Paris remained in a state of terror, bands of armed butchers parading the streets were loud in their threats as to what would be done to all who did not join heartily with them. None of the better class ventured from their houses, and the mob were absolute masters of the city. The leaders, however, maintained for the time a certain degree of order. For the time they were anxious to appear in the light of earnest friends of the king, and as carrying out in his name the punishment of his enemies. But many tumults, murders, and conflagrations occurred in the city, and the country in general soon perceived the real nature of their doings. It was known that the Orleanist forces were marching against the city. The Count d'Eu had left Paris and returned to his estates, where he raised two thousand men-at-arms and marched to Verneuil, where the Dukes of Orleans, Brittany, and Bourbon were assembled, with a number of great lords, among whom were the Counts of Vettus and D'Alençon, the king's sons. The former had made his escape from Paris, and brought letters from the Duke of Aquitaine declaring that he himself, with the king and queen, were prisoners in the hands of the Parisians.

All these nobles met in a great assembly, and letters were written to the king, his great council, and to the Parisians, ordering them to allow the Duke of Aquitaine to go wherever he pleased, and to set at liberty the Dukes of Bar and Bavaria and all other prisoners. Should they refuse to comply, they declared war against the town of Paris, which they declared they would destroy, with all within it except the king and the princes of royal blood. The Parisians compelled the king to send a friendly answer, putting them off with excuses, and in the meantime to despatch commissaries to all the towns and baronies of France assuring them that the trials and executions of the traitors had been fairly conducted and their guilt proved, and calling upon the country to take up arms to aid Paris against various nobles who were traitorously advancing against it.

During this time Guy remained quietly in his lodging with the four retainers, seldom stirring abroad. The men were now regarded by all their neighbours as honest carpenters, and they shared the indignation of the great body of the craft at this usurpation by the market men of the government of France, and at the murders of knights and ladies that were daily taking place. At present, however, the opponents of the butchers dared not resort to arms. So great had been the fear that they excited that most men, however much at heart opposed to them, had been constrained to appear to side with and agree with them, and as there was no means of knowing who could be counted upon to join the carpenters were these to take up arms, the latter could not venture alone to enter the lists against the armed host of the other party.

One evening Guy, who had not been near the Italian's for over a fortnight, received a message from Dame Margaret to say that she wished to speak to him, for that she had determined, if any way of escape could be decided on, to quit Paris, and to endeavour to make her way to Villeroy. He was greatly pleased at the news. He had himself ventured to urge this step on the day after the Duke of Bar and his companions were seized, pointing out that it was evident that the Duke of Burgundy had neither the power nor the inclination to thwart the Parisians, and that although both parties were now nominally hostile to the English, neither were likely, at so critical a time, to give so much as a thought to Villeroy. Dame Margaret had agreed to this, but considered the difficulties of getting out of Paris and traversing the intervening country were so great that she preferred to wait until some change took place in the situation of Paris. But it was now too evident that the changes were entirely for the worse, and that if discovered the butchers would undoubtedly add her and her children to their long list of victims.

His companions were equally glad when Guy told them the news.

"The sooner the better, Master Guy," Long Tom said. "I own that I should like to have a tussle with these rascals before I go; their doings are so wicked that every honest man must want to get one fair blow at them. Still, I don't see any chance of that, for although the good fellows round here grumble under their breath, there does not seem any chance of their doing anything. There is not an hour passes that my heart is not in my mouth if I hear a step on the stairs, thinking that they may have found out where my lady is hidden."

Guy had just turned into the street where the astrologer dwelt when he heard loud voices from a little group in front of him. Four armed men, whose white hoods showed that they were one of the butchers' patrols, were standing round a slight figure.

"It is well you stopped him, comrade," a voice said, that Guy recognized at once as being that of Simon Bouclier. "I know the young fellow; he has been to me many a time on the part of a knave who professed to be an agent of Burgundy's, making inquiries of me as to the doings in our quarter. I have found out since that the duke employed no such agent, and this matter must be inquired into. We will take him with us to the market; they will soon find means of learning all about him and his employer."

Guy felt at once that if Katarina were carried to the butchers, not only would the consequences to herself be terrible, but that she would be forced to make such disclosures as would lead to the arrest of the count, and to the discovery of Dame Margaret. He determined at all hazards to get her out of these men's hands. The girl made a sudden attempt to free herself, slipped from the grasp that one of the men had of her shoulder, dived between two others, and would have been off had not Simon seized her by the arm. Guy sprung forward and threw himself on the butcher, and with such force that Simon rolled over in the gutter.

"Run, run!" he shouted at the same moment to Katarina, who darted down a lane to the left, while he himself ran forward and turned down the first lane to the right with the three men in hot pursuit of him. Young, active, and unencumbered by armour, he gained on them rapidly; but when he neared the end of the lane he saw some five or six White Hoods, whose attention had been called by the shouts of his pursuers, running to meet him. He turned and ran back till close to those who had been following him, and then suddenly sprung into a doorway when they were but three or four paces from him. They were unable to check their speed, and as they passed he brought his sword down on the neck of the one nearest, and as he fell to the ground Guy leapt out and ran up the street again. He had gone but ten paces when he met Simon, who rushed at him furiously with an uplifted axe. Springing aside as the blow descended he delivered a slashing cut on the butcher's cheek, dashed past him, and kept on his way. He took the first turning, and then another, leading, like that in which he had been intercepted, towards the river. His pursuers were fifty yards behind him, but he feared that at any moment their shouts would attract the attention of another patrol. More than once, indeed, he had to alter his direction as he heard sounds of shouts in front of him, but at last, after ten minutes' running, he came down on to the main thoroughfare at the point where the street leading to the bridge across to the island issued from it.

"GUY DELIVERED A SLASHING BLOW ON THE BUTCHER'S CHEEK,
AND DASHED PAST HIM."

His pursuers were still but a short distance away, for fresh parties who had joined them had taken up the chase, and Guy was no longer running at the speed at which he had started. His great fear was that he should be stopped at the gate at the end of the bridge; but as there was no fear of attack this had been left open, so as not to interfere with the traffic between that quarter of the city on the island and those on the opposite banks. Guy was now again running his hardest, in order to get across far enough ahead of his pursuers to enable him to hide himself, when a strong patrol of some twenty White Hoods issued from the gate at the other side of the bridge. Without a moment's hesitation he climbed the parapet and threw himself over. It would, he knew, be as bad for his mistress were he captured as if Katarina had fallen into their hands, for if caught he felt sure that tortures would be applied to discover who he was and where his mistress was hidden, and he had made up his mind that if he was overtaken he would fight until killed rather than be captured.

When he came to the surface of the water Guy turned on his back and suffered himself to float down until he recovered his breath. When he did so he raised his head and, treading the water, listened attentively. He was now nearly a quarter of a mile below the bridge. There was no sound of shouting behind him, but he felt sure that the pursuit was in no way abandoned. Already torches were flashing on the quay between the wall and the river, and in a short time others appeared on his left. On both sides there were dark spaces where the walls of the great chateaux of the nobles extended down to the water's side, and obliged those pursuing him along the quays to make a detour round them to come down again to the bank. He could hardly succeed in reaching one of these buildings without being seen, for the light of the torches on the opposite shore would be almost certain to betray his movements as soon as he began to swim, and even if he did reach the shore unseen he might at once be handed over to the White Hoods by those in the hotel. He therefore remained floating on his back, and in twenty minutes was beyond the line of the city wall. He could now swim without fear of being discovered, and made for the southern shore.

It was now the middle of June, and the water was fairly warm, but he was glad to be out of it. So far as Guy had heard he had not been caught sight of from the moment that he had sprung from the bridge. It might well be supposed that he had been drowned. Climbing up the bank he gained, after walking a quarter of a mile, the forest that surrounded Paris on all sides. Going some distance into it he threw himself down, after first taking off his doublet and hanging it on a bush to dry. He had escaped the first pressing danger, that of being taken and tortured into confession, and the rest was now comparatively easy. He had but to obtain another disguise of some sort and to re-enter Paris; he would then be in no greater danger than before, for in the sudden attack on Simon, and in the subsequent flight through the ill-lighted streets, he was certain that beyond the fact that he was young and active, and that he was evidently not a noble, no one could have noted any details of his dress, and certainly no one could have had as much as a glance at his face.

He started at daybreak, walked through the woods up to Meudon, and thence to Versailles, which was then little more than a village. By the time that he reached it his clothes had thoroughly dried on him, and being of a dark colour they looked little the worse, save that his tight pantaloons had shrunk considerably. The stalls were just opening when he arrived there, and he presently came upon one where garments of all sorts were hanging. The proprietor's wife, a cheery-looking woman, was standing at the door.

"I have need of some garments, madame," he said.

"You look as if you did," she said with a smile, glancing at his ankles. "I see that you are an apprentice, and for that sort of gear you will have to go to Paris; we deal in country garments."

"That will suit me well enough, madame. The fact is that, as you see, I am an apprentice; but having been badly treated, and having in truth no stomach for the frays and alarms in Paris (where the first man one meets will strike one down, and if he slays you it matters not if he but shout loud enough that he has killed an Orleanist), I have left my master, and have no intention of returning as an apprentice. But I might be stopped and questioned at every place I pass through on my way home did I travel in this 'prentice dress, and I would, therefore, fain buy the attire of a young peasant."

The woman glanced up and down the street.

"Come in," she said. "You know that it is against the law to give shelter to a runaway apprentice, but there are such wild doings in Paris that for my part I can see no harm in assisting anyone to escape, whether he be a noble or an apprentice, and methinks from your speech that you are as like to be the former as the latter. But," she went on, seeing that Guy was about to speak, "tell me naught about it. My husband, who ought to be here, is snoring upstairs, and I can sell what I will; therefore, look round and take your choice of garments, and go into the parlour behind the shop and don them quickly before anyone comes in. As to your own I will pay you what they are worth, for although those pantaloons are all too tight for those strong limbs of yours they may do for a slighter figure."

Guy was soon suited, and in a few minutes left the shop in a peasant's dress, and made his way along the village until beyond the houses. Then he left the road, made a long detour, and returned to Sèvres. Here he first purchased a basket, which he took outside the place and hid in a bush. Then he went down into the market and bargained for vegetables, making three journeys backwards and forwards, and buying each time of different women, until his basket was piled up. Then he got a piece of old rope for two or three sous, slung the basket on his shoulders, crossed the ferry, and made for Paris. He felt strange without his sword, which he had dropped into the water on landing; for although in Paris every one now went armed, a sword would have been out of character with his dress, in the country, and still more so in the disguise in which he had determined to re-enter the town. He passed without question through the gate, and made his way to his lodgings. As he entered Long Tom leapt up with a cry of joy.

"Thank God that you are safe, Master Guy! We have been grievously disturbed for your safety, for the count came here early this morning in disguise to ask if we had heard aught of you. He said that his daughter had returned last night saying that you had rescued her from the hands of the White Hoods, and that beyond the fact that they had followed you in hot pursuit she had no news of you, and that the countess was greatly alarmed as to your safety. The other three men-at-arms started at once to find out if aught could be learned of you. I would fain have gone also, but the count said that I must bide here in case you should come, and that there was trouble enough at present without my running the risk of being discovered. An hour since Robert Picard returned; he had been listening to the talk of the White Hoods, and had learned that one of their number had been killed and another sorely wounded by a man who had rescued a prisoner from the hands of a patrol. He had been chased by a number of them, and finally threw himself off the bridge into the Seine to avoid falling into their hands. The general idea was that he was one of the nobles in disguise, of whom they were in search, and that the capture would have been a very important one.

"All agreed that he could never have come up alive, for there were bands of men with torches along both banks, and no sign of him had been perceived. However, they are searching the river down, and hope to come upon his body either floating or cast ashore. Robert went out again to try and gather more news, leaving me well-nigh distraught here."

"The story is true as far as it goes, Tom. I did catch one of them a back-handed blow just under his helmet as he ran past me, and I doubt not that it finished him; as to the other, I laid his cheek open. It was a hot pursuit, but I should have got away had it not been that a strong patrol came out through the gate at the other end of the bridge just as I was in the middle, and there was no course but to jump for it. I thrust my sword into the sheath, and went over. It added somewhat to my weight in the water, and it sunk my body below the surface, but with the aid of my hands paddling I floated so that only my nose and mouth were above the water; so that it is little wonder that they could not make me out. I landed on the other bank a quarter of a mile beyond the walls, slept in the forest, started this morning from Versailles, where I got rid of my other clothes and bought these. I purchased this basket and the vegetables at Sèvres, then walked boldly in. No one could have seen my face in the darkness, and therefore I am safe from detection, perhaps safer than I was before."

"Well done, Master Guy; they would have killed you assuredly if they had caught you."

"It was not that that I was afraid of—it was of being taken prisoner. You see, if they had captured me and carried me before the butchers in order to inquire who I was before cutting my throat, they might have put me to the torture and forced me to say who I was, and where my mistress was in hiding. I hope if they had, that I should have stood out; but none can say what he will do when he has red-hot pincers taking bits out of his flesh, and his nails, perhaps, being torn out at the roots. So even if I could not have swam a stroke I should have jumped off the bridge."

"You did well, Master Guy," the archer said admiringly; "for indeed they say that the strongest man cannot hold out against these devilish tortures."

At this moment a step was heard on the stairs, and Jules Varoy entered.

"The saints be praised!" he exclaimed as he recognized Guy. "I thought that you were drowned like a rat, Master Guy; and though Tom here told us that you could swim well, I never thought to see you again."

Guy told him in a few words how he had escaped, and begged him to carry the news to his mistress. He was about to give him the address—for up till now he had refrained from doing so, telling them that it was from no doubt of their fidelity, but that if by any chance one of them fell into the hands of the White Hoods they might endeavour to wring from them the secret, and it was therefore best that they should not be burdened with it—but the man stopped him.

"The count told us that he would be at his booth at the fair at eleven o'clock, and that if any of us obtained any news we were to take it to him there. He said that there were several parties of White Hoods in the streets, and that as he went past he heard them say that the boy of whom they were in search was a messenger of some person of importance at court, and that doubtless the man who had rescued him was also in the plot, and that a strict watch was to be kept on the quarter both for the boy and for the man, who was said to be tall and young. Simon, who had been wounded by him, had declared that he knew him to be connected with the boy; that he was a young man with dark hair, and was in the habit of using disguises, sometimes wearing the dress of an apprentice, and at other times that of a butcher's assistant. He said that he was about twenty-three."

Guy smiled. He understood that the butcher, who was a very powerful man, did not like to own that the man who had killed one of his comrades and had severely wounded himself was but a lad.

"As you go, Jules," he said, "will you see Maître Leroux and ask him if he can come hither, for I would consult him on the matter."

# CHAPTER XVI — THE ESCAPE

Maître Leroux came in shortly after Jules Varoy had left. He had not, until the man told him, heard of the events of the night before, and Guy had to tell him all about it before anything else was said.

"It was a lucky escape, Master Aylmer, if one can call luck what is due to thought and quickness. Is there anything I can do for you?"

"This black hue that I gave my hair has been of good service to me hitherto, but as it is a youth with black hair that they are now looking for, I would fain change its hue again."

"What dye did you use?"

"It was bought for me at a perfumer's in the Rue Cabot. As you see, it is fading now, and the ducking last night has greatly assisted to wash it out. The shopman said that it was used by court ladies and would last for a long time, but I have already had to renew it four or five times. I would now colour my hair a red or a reddish-brown; if I cannot do that I must crop it quite short. It matters nothing in this disguise whether it is altogether out of the fashion or not. What think you?"

"Doubtless you could get dyes of any shade at the perfumer's you speak of, for he supplies most of the court ladies with dyes and perfumes; and I should say that reddish-brown dye would suit you well, since that differs a good deal from your hair's original colour and still more from what it is at present. I will ask one of Lepelletiere's daughters to fetch it for you. It would be better than cutting it short, though that might not go badly with your present disguise, but should you need to adopt any other it would look strange, since in our days there is scarce anyone but wears his hair down to his shoulders. In the meantime I would have you wash your hair several times with a ley of potash, but not too strong, or it will damage it. I warrant me that will take out the dye altogether; but be sure that you wash it well in pure water afterwards, so as to get rid of the potash, for that might greatly affect the new dye. I will send a boy up with some potash to you at once, so that you may be ready to apply the dye as soon as you get it."

Late in the afternoon Guy sallied out in the disguise in which he had arrived. His hair was a tawny brown. He had left his basket behind him, and carried a heavy cudgel in his hand. He sauntered quietly along, stopping often to stare at the goods on the stalls, and at nobles who rode past followed generally by two or three esquires. No one would doubt that he was a young countryman freshly arrived in Paris.

He had sent a message to the count by Jules Varoy that he would pass along the street in the disguise of a young peasant as the clock struck seven, and that if he saw no White Hoods about he would look up at the casement, return a minute or two afterwards, and then try if the door was unfastened. If so he would come in, while if it were fastened he should consider that it was judged unsafe for him to enter. He caught sight of Katarina's face at the window as he glanced up. There was a patrol of the White Hoods in sight, but it was far down the street, and after going a few yards past the house he crossed the road, and as he returned he pushed at the door. It yielded at once, and with a glance round to see that no one was watching he entered quickly and closed it behind him.

"The Madonna be thanked that you are safe!" Katarina, now in her girl's dress, exclaimed as she seized his hand. "Oh, Monsieur Guy, how I have suffered! It was not until two o'clock that my father returned and told us that you were safe; I should never have forgiven myself if harm had come to you from your noble effort to save me. I heard their shouts as they ran in pursuit of you, and scarce thought it possible that you could escape when there was so many of their patrols about in the street. I cried all night at the thought that you should have thrown away your life to try to save mine, for I knew well enough what would have happened had that evil butcher dragged me to his quarter. After my father had been out early and brought back the news that you had leapt into the Seine we had some little hope, for Dame Margaret declared that she knew that you could swim well. We had no one we could send out, for the old woman is too stupid, and my father now strictly forbids me to stir outside the door. So here we all sat worn with anxiety until my father returned from the booth with the news. He could not come back earlier, and he had no one to send, for the black man must keep outside amusing the people as long as my father is there."

All this was poured out so rapidly that it was said by the time they reached the door upstairs. Dame Margaret silently held out her hands to Guy as he entered, and Agnes kissed him with sisterly affection, while Charlie danced round and round him with boisterous delight.

"I hardly knew how much you were to me and how much I depended upon you, Guy," Dame Margaret said presently, "until I feared that I had lost you. When, as I thought must be the case from what Katarina said, I believed you were killed or a prisoner in the hands of those terrible people, it seemed to me that we were quite left alone, although there still remained the four men. Neither Agnes nor I closed our eyes all night Charlie soon cried himself to sleep, Katarina sat up with us till nigh morning, and we had hard work to console her in any way, so deep was her grief at the thought that it was owing to her that you had run this peril. All night we could hear the count walking up and down in the room above. He had pointed out the peril that might arise to us all if you had fallen into the hands of the butchers, but at the time we could not dwell on that, though there were doubtless grounds for his fears."

"Great grounds, madame. That is what I most feared when I was flying from them, and I was resolved that I would not be taken alive, for had I not gained the bridge I was determined to force them to kill me rather than be captured. It was fortunate, indeed, that I came along when I did, Katarina, for had I not heard what Simon said I should have passed on without giving a thought to the matter. There are too many evil deeds done in Paris to risk one's life to rescue a prisoner from the hands of a patrol of the White Hoods."

"As for me, I did not realize it until it was all over," Katarina said. "I felt too frightened even to think clearly. It was not until the shouts of your pursuers had died away that I could realize what you had saved me from, and the thought made me so faint and weak that I was forced to sit down on a door-step for a time before I could make my way home. As to my father, he turned as pale as death when I came in and told him what had happened."

Shortly afterwards the count, who had been engaged with a person of consequence, came down. He thanked Guy in the warmest terms for the service he had rendered his daughter.

"Never was a woman in greater peril," he said, "and assuredly St. Anthony, my patron saint, must have sent you to her rescue. She is all that I have left now, and it is chiefly for her sake that I have continued to amass money, though I say not that my own fancy for meddling in such intrigues may not take some part in the matter. After this I am resolved of one thing, namely, that she shall take no further part in the business. For the last year I had often told myself that the time had come when I must find another to act as my messenger and agent. It was difficult, however, to find one I could absolutely trust, and I have put the matter off. I shall do so no longer; and indeed there is now the less occasion for it, since, as I have just learned, fresh negotiations have been opened for peace. That it will be a lasting one I have no hope, but the Orleanists are advancing in such force that Burgundy may well feel that the issue of a battle at present may go against him. But even though it last but a short time, there will still come so many of the Orleanist nobles here with doubtless strong retinues that Paris will be overawed, and we shall have an end of these riots here. I shall, therefore, have no need to trouble as to what is going on at the markets. As to other matters I can keep myself well informed. I have done services to knights and nobles of one party as well as the other, and shall be able to learn what is being done in both camps. The important point at present is, Lady Margaret, that there is like to be a truce, at any rate for a time. As soon as this is made and the Duke of Aquitaine has gained power to act you may be sure that the leaders of the White Hoods will be punished, and there will be no more closing of gates and examination of those who pass in and out. Therefore, madame, you will then be able to do what is now well-nigh impossible, namely, quit the town. At present the orders are more stringent than ever, none are allowed to leave save with orders signed by John de Troyes, who calls himself keeper of the palace, Caboche, or other leaders and even peasants who come in with market goods must henceforth produce papers signed by the syndics of their villages saying they are the inhabitants of his commune, and therefore quiet and peaceable men going about their business of supplying the city with meat or vegetables, as the case may be. These papers must also be shown on going out again. Until a change takes place, then, there is no hope of your making your way out through the gates with your children; but as soon as the truce is concluded and the Orleanists come in you will be able to pass out without trouble."

It was not, indeed, for another month that the truce was settled, although the terms were virtually agreed upon at Pontois, where the Dukes of Berri and Burgundy met the Dukes of Orleans and Bourbon and the other Orleanist nobles, and the conditions were considered at a council to which the delegates of the University and the municipality of Paris were admitted. The conduct of the insurgents of Paris was now repudiated by the Duke of Burgundy, and the severest, censure passed upon them, in the conditions of the treaty. The greatest alarm was excited in the market quarter, and this was increased when, immediately afterwards, the Dukes of Bar and Bavaria were liberated. On the 12th of August and on the 4th of September the rest of the prisoners still left alive were also set free. The bells of the churches rang a joyful peal. De Jacqueville, John de Troyes, Caboche, and many of the leaders of the butchers at once fled from Paris.

Most of the knights who had been agents for the insurgents in the mock trials also left Paris, and shortly afterwards the duke himself, finding how strongly the tide had set against him, and fearing that he himself might shortly be seized and thrown into prison, went out from Paris under the pretence of hunting, and fled. During this time Guy had remained with the four men-at-arms. As soon as the power of the butchers diminished and the guards were removed from the gates, and all who pleased could enter or leave, Dame Margaret prepared for flight. Along with the Burgundian knights and nobles who returned after the truce was proclaimed came Count Charles d'Estournel, and several of those who had fled with him. Guy met the former riding through the street on the day after his return to Paris. Not caring to accost him there, he followed him and saw him dismount at his former lodging. As soon as he had entered Guy went up to the door.

"What do you want?" one of the count's valets said.

"I want to see your master, fellow," Guy said sharply, "and I will pull your ears for your insolence if you accost me in that style."

The valet stared at him open-mouthed, then thinking that this peasant might be deputed by the terrible butchers to see his lord, he inquired in a changed tone what message he should give to the count.

"Say to him that the man of the street fray wants to see him."

A minute later the young count himself ran downstairs and warmly embraced Guy, to the astonishment of the valet.

"My dear friend," he exclaimed, "I am indeed delighted to see you! Twice have you saved my life, for assuredly had we not got through the Port St. Denis that day not one of us would ever have left Paris alive, and we are all under the deepest obligation to you. But even after our skirmish at the gate we scarcely realized the danger that we had escaped, for we believed that even had the Parisians been insolent enough to demand our arrest for stopping them when engaged in attacking the houses of peaceable citizens, the duke would treat their demand with the scorn that it deserved. However, when next day we heard that some of the officers of his household had headed them when they forced their way into the Duke of Aquitaine's hotel, and carried off the Duke of Bar and others from before his eyes, and that the duke in all things assisted them, we knew that he would not have hesitated to deliver us up to the villains.

"We held a council as to what we should do. We could not affirm that he had failed, as our lord, in giving us protection, for he had not done so, seeing that we had taken the matter in our own hands. Had he actually consented to hand us over to the Parisians, we should have issued a declaration laying the matter before all the great vassals of Burgundy and denouncing him as a false lord. There are many who would have been very glad to have taken up the matter, for his truckling to these knaves has greatly displeased all save the men who are mere creatures of his. However, as we had no proof that he was willing to surrender us to the fury of the mob of Paris, we could do nothing, and the crafty fox called upon my father the next day and expressed his satisfaction that we had all ridden away, though at the same time saying that there was no reason whatever for our having done so, as he should of course have refused to give any satisfaction to the mob of Paris, and he caused several letters to the same effect to be sent to my friends who escaped with me.

# At Agincourt

"My father was very short with him, and told him that as it seemed the Parisians were the masters of the city, and that he had no power to restrain them, however monstrous their doings, he thought that we had all acted very wisely in going. He himself left Paris the next day, and several other nobles, relations or friends to some of us, took the earliest opportunity also of leaving for their estates. Now that the power of the butchers has been broken and that their leaders have fled, I came back again, chiefly to find out what had become of you, and whether you and your charges have passed through these evil times unharmed."

"We have all been in hiding, and save for an adventure or two have passed the time quietly. Now that the gates are open we are going to make our escape, for you see everything points to the probability that the Orleanists will very shortly be supreme here, and after the defeat Sir Eustace gave Sir Clugnet de Brabant they might be glad still to retain our lady as hostage, though methinks they would treat her more honourably than the Duke of Burgundy has done."

"Possibly they might, but I would not count upon it, for indeed wherever they have taken a town they have treated those who fell into their hands most barbarously. 'Tis true that they have some excuse for it in the treatment of so many knights and ladies here. Indeed it seems to me that France has been seized with madness, and that Heaven's vengeance will fall upon her for the evil things that are being done. And now, can we aid you in any way? The duke was extremely civil when I saw him on my arrival here yesterday. He said that I and my friends were wrong in not having trusted in him to protect us from the demands of the butchers. I told him frankly that as he had in other matters been so overborne by them, and had been unable to save noble knights and ladies from being murdered by them under the pretence of a trial that all men knew was a mockery, it was just as well that we had taken the matter into our own hands without adding it to his other burdens; and that I and my friends felt that we had no reason to regret the step we had taken, and we knew that our feelings were shared by many other nobles and knights in Burgundy.

"He looked darkly at me, but at the present pass he did not care to say anything that would give offence, not only to me, but to my friends, who with their connections are too powerful to be alienated at a time when he may need every lance. I could not, however, well ask from him a free conduct for your people without naming them, but I might get such a pass from his chancellor, and if your former host, Maître Leroux, be still alive, he might doubtless get you one from the municipality. As an additional protection I myself shall certainly ride with you. It is for that that I have returned to Paris. I shall simply say to the chancellor that I am riding to Arras on my own business, and that though in most places I should be known to Burgundians, yet that it would be as well that I should have a pass lest I be met by any rude body of citizens or others who might not know me, and I shall request him to make it out for me personally and for all persons travelling in my train. So that, as far as Flanders at any rate, there should be no difficulty. I only propose that you should also get a document from the city in case of anything befalling us on the way.

"I see not indeed what can befall us; but it is always well in such times as these, when such strange things occur, to provide for all emergencies. I may tell you that Louis de Lactre and Reginald Poupart have arrived with me in Paris bent on the same errand, and anxious like myself to testify their gratitude to you; so that we shall be a strong body, and could if necessary ride through France without any pass at all, since one or other of us is sure to find a friend in every town which we may traverse."

"Truly, I am thankful indeed to you and to your friends, Count. I own that it has been a sore trouble to me as to how we should be able, however we might disguise ourselves, to travel through the country in these disturbed times, without papers of any kind, when bodies of armed men are moving to and fro in all directions, and travellers, whoever they may be, are questioned at every place on the road where they stop."

"Do not speak of thanks, Guy; I twice owe you my life, and assuredly 'tis little enough to furnish you in return with an escort to Artois. Now, tell me all that you have been doing since we left."

Guy gave a short account of all that had happened.

"It has been fortunate for us both," the Count Charles said when he had finished, "that this astrologer should have made your acquaintance; it was his warning that enabled you to save us as well as your lady. I have heard several times of him as one who had wondrous powers of reading the stars, but now I see that it is not only the stars that assist him."

"I can assure you that he himself believes thoroughly in the stars, Count; he says that by them he can read the danger that is threatening any person whose horoscope he has cast. I had not heard much of such things in England, but I cannot doubt that he has great skill in them. To my knowledge he has saved several lives thereby."

"He certainly saved ours, Guy, and should he like to join your party and ride with us he will be heartily welcomed."

"I will return at once," Guy said, "and give my lady the good news. I will not ask you to go with me now, for if the count—for he is really a nobleman though an exile—decides to stay here he would not care to attract the attention of his neighbours by the coming of a noble to his house in daylight. Though I cannot without his permission take you there, I will return here this evening at eight o'clock, if you will be at home at that hour."

"I will be here, and De Lactre and Poupart will be here to meet you. I will go now direct to the chancellor and obtain the pass both in their names and mine, then we shall be ready to start whenever your lady is prepared. We have all brought some spare horses, so that you will have no trouble on that score. Your men-at-arms will, of course, ride with ours. We have brought eight horses, knowing the number of your company; if your Italian and his daughter go with us Lady Agnes and Charles can ride behind some of us."

Dame Margaret, Agnes, and Charlie were delighted indeed when they heard from Guy of his meeting with the young Count d'Estournel, and of the latter's offer to escort them to Artois.

"The saints be praised!" his lady said. "I have spoken little about it, Guy, but I have dreaded this journey far more than any of the dangers here. In times so disturbed I have perceived that we should run innumerable risks, and eager as I am to return to my lord I have doubted whether, with Agnes with me, I should be right in adventuring on such a journey. Now there can be no risk in it, saving only that of falling in with any of the bands of robbers who, as they say, infest the country, and even these would scarce venture to attack so strong a party. We shall be ready to start to-morrow, if Count d'Estournel is prepared to go so soon. We will be veiled as we ride out. It is most unlikely that anyone will recognize us, but 'tis as well for his sake that there should be no risk whatever of this being known. The count is out and will not return until six, therefore it will be best that you should go at once and warn the others that we start to-morrow."

The pleasure of Long Tom and his companions at the news was scarcely less than had been that of Dame Margaret, and they started at once to recover their steel caps and armour from the place where they had been hidden, saying that it would take them all night to clean them up and make them fit for service. Then Guy went in to Maître Lepelletiere and saw the silversmith, who was also sincerely glad at the news he gave him.

"I was but yesterday arranging for a house where I could open my shop again until my own was rebuilt," he said, "for there is an end now of all fear of disturbances, at any rate for the present, and I was heartily greeted by many old friends, who thought that I was dead. I will go down with Lepelletiere this afternoon to the offices of the municipality and ask for a pass for madame—what shall I call her?"

"Call her Picard: it matters not what surname she takes."

"Madame Picard, her daughter and son, and her cousin Jean Bouvray of Paris, to journey to St. Omer. It does not seem to me that the pass is likely to be of any use to you; at the same time it is as well to be fortified with it. Now that the tyranny of the market-men is over they will be glad to give us the pass without question."

On the Italian's return that afternoon Dame Margaret herself told him of the offer the Count d'Estournel had made. He sat silent for a minute or two and then said: "I will talk it over with Katarina; but at present it does not seem to me that I can accept it. I am a restless spirit, and there is a fascination in this work; but I will see you presently."

An hour later he came down with Katarina.

"We have agreed to stay, Lady Margaret," he said gravely, "I cannot bring myself to go. It is true that I might continue my work in London, but as a stranger it would be long before I found clients, while here my reputation is established. Two of the knights I enabled to escape have already returned. One called upon me last night and was full of gratitude, declaring, and rightly, that he should have been, like so many of his friends, murdered in prison had I not warned him. I have eight requests already for interviews from friends of these knights, and as, for a time at any rate, their faction is likely to be triumphant here, I shall have my hands full of business. This is a pleasant life. I love the exercise of my art, to watch how the predictions of the stars come true, to fit things together, and to take my share, though an unseen one, in the politics and events of the day. I have even received an intimation that the queen herself is anxious to consult the stars, and it may be that I shall become a great power here. I would fain that my daughter should go under your protection, though I own that I should miss her sorely. However, she refuses to leave me, and against my better judgment my heart has pleaded for her, and I have decided that she shall remain. She will, however, take no further part in my business, but will be solely my companion and solace. I trust that with such protection as I shall now receive there is no chance of even the Church meddling with me, but should I see danger approaching I will send or bring her to you at once."

"I shall be glad to see her whenever she comes, and shall receive her as a daughter. We owe our lives to your shelter and kindness, and we already love her."

"The shelter and the kindness have already been far more than repaid by the inestimable service your esquire rendered us," the Italian said. "I have since blamed myself bitterly that I neglected to consult the stars concerning her. I have since done so, and found that a most terrible danger threatened her on that day; and had I known it, I would have kept her indoors and would on no account have permitted her to go out. However, I shall not be so careless of her safety in future. I see that, at any rate for some time, her future is unclouded. She herself will bitterly regret your absence, and has already been weeping sorely at the thought of your leaving. Save myself she has never had a friend, poor child, and you and your daughter have become very dear to her."

Dame Margaret had no preparations to make, for in their flight from the silversmith's each had carried a bundle of clothes. Guy brought Count d'Estournel round in the evening, and the arrangements were then completed. It was thought better that they should not mount at the house, as this would be certain to attract considerable observation and remark, but that Count Charles should come round at seven in the morning and escort them to his lodging. There the horses would be in readiness, and they would mount and ride off. Guy then went round to the Rue des Fosses and warned the men of the hour at which they were to assemble at the count's. He found them all hard at work burnishing up their armour.

"We shall make but a poor show, Master Guy, do what we will," Tom said; "and I doubt whether this gear will ever recover its brightness, so deeply has the rust eaten into it. Still, we can pass muster on a journey; and the swords have suffered but little, having been safe in their scabbards. I never thought that I should be so pleased to put on a steel cap again, and I only wish I had my bow slung across my shoulder."

"It will be something for you to look forward to, Tom, and I doubt not that you will find among the spare ones at Villeroy one as good as your own, and that with practice you will soon be able to shoot as truly with it."

Tom shook his head doubtfully. "I hope so, but I doubt whether I shall be suited again till I get home, and Master John the bowyer makes one specially suitable for me, and six inches longer than ordinary. Still, I doubt not that, if it be needed, I shall be able to make shift with one of those at Villeroy."

The evening before the departure of Dame Margaret and her children, Maître Leroux and his wife, with a man bearing a large parcel, had called upon Dame Margaret at the house of the astrologer, whose address Guy had given, the provost that day.

"We could not let you leave, Lady Margaret," his wife said, "without coming to wish you God speed. Our troubles, like yours, are over for the present, and I trust that the butchers will never become masters of Paris again, whatever may happen."

"Maître Lepelletiere," said the silversmith, "is going to organize the whole of his craft, the workmen and apprentices, into an armed body, and the master of the smiths will do the same. I shall endeavour to prevail upon all the traders of my own guild and others to raise such a body among their servitors; and while we have no wish whatever to interfere in the political affairs of state, we shall at least see that the market people of Paris shall not become our masters again. Master Aylmer, I have brought hither for you a slight token of my regard and gratitude for the manner in which you saved not only our property but our lives. Within this package are two suits of armour and arms. One is a serviceable one suitable to your present condition of an esquire; the other is a knightly suit, which I hope you will wear in remembrance of us as soon as you obtain that honour, which I cannot but feel assured will not be far distant. Had you been obliged to leave Paris in disguise I should have made an endeavour to send them to you in England by way of Flanders; but as you will issue out in good company, and without examination or question asked, you can wear the one suit and have the other carried for you."

Guy thanked the silversmith most heartily, for, having lost his armour at the burning of the house, he had felt some uneasiness at the thought of the figure that he would cut riding in the train of the three Burgundian knights. But at the same time his own purse had been exhausted in the purchase of the disguises for himself and the men-at-arms, and that of his mistress greatly reduced by the expenses of the keep of the men, and he had determined not to draw upon her resources for the purchase of armour. His thanks were repeated when, on the package being opened, the beauty of the knightly armour was seen. It was indeed a suit of which any knight might be proud. It was less ornate in its inlaying and chasing than some of the suits worn by nobles, but it was of the finest steel and best make, with every part and accessory complete, and of the highest workmanship and finish.

"It is a princely gift, sir," Guy said as he examined it, "and altogether beyond my poor deserts."

"That is not what I think, Master Aylmer. You have shown all through this business a coolness and courage altogether beyond your years, and which would have done honour to an experienced knight. My store of silver-ware that was saved by your exertions, to say nothing of our lives, was worth very many times the value of this armour, and I am sure that your lady will agree with me that this gift of ours has been well and honourably earned."

"I do indeed, Maître Leroux," Dame Margaret said warmly; "and assure you that I am as pleased as Guy himself at the noble gift you have made him. I myself have said but little to him as to the service that he has rendered here, leaving that until we reach our castle in safety, when Sir Eustace, on hearing from me the story of our doings, will better speak in both our names than I can do."

# At Agincourt

In the morning Dame Margaret and her children set out for the lodging of D'Estournel, escorted by the count and Guy, followed by a porter carrying the latter's second suit of armour and the valises of Dame Margaret. Guy himself had charge of a casket which the Count de Montepone had that morning handed to Dame Margaret.

"These are gems of value," he said, "In the course of my business I more often receive gifts of jewels than of money. The latter, as I receive it, I hand to a firm here having dealings with a banker of Bruges, who holds it at my disposal. The gems I have hitherto kept; but as it is possible that we may, when we leave Paris, have to travel in disguise, I would fain that they were safely bestowed. I pray you, therefore, to take them with you to your castle in England, and to hold them for us until we come."

Dame Margaret willingly took charge of the casket, which was of steel, strongly bound, and some nine inches square.

"Its weight is not so great as you would think by its appearance," the Italian said, "for it is of the finest steel, and the gems have been taken from their settings. It will, therefore, I hope, be no great inconvenience to you."

At parting, Katarina, who was greatly affected, had given Guy a small box.

"Do not open it until you reach Villeroy," she said; "it is a little remembrance of the girl you saved from deadly peril, and who will never forget what she owes to you."

On reaching the count's lodgings they found the other two knights in readiness. Dame Margaret's four men-at-arms were holding the horses.

"I am glad to see you all again," she said as she came up. "This is a far better ending than our fortunes seemed likely to have at one time, and I thank you all for your faithful service."

"I am only sorry, my lady, that we have had no opportunity of doing aught since we were cooped up," Tom replied; "nothing would have pleased us better than to have had the chance again of striking a stout blow in your defence."

"We may as well mount at once, if it is your pleasure, Dame Margaret," Count d'Estournel said, "for the other men-at-arms are waiting for us outside the gates."

The packages were at once fastened on the two pack-horses that were to accompany them; all then mounted. The three knights with Dame Margaret rode first, then Guy rode with Agnes by his side, and the four men-at-arms came next, Charlie riding before Jules Varoy, who was the lightest of the men-at-arms, while two of the count's servants brought up the rear, leading the sumpter horses.

# CHAPTER XVII — A LONG PAUSE

A quarter of a mile beyond the gate the party was joined by eighteen men-at-arms, all fully armed and ready for any encounter; eight of them fell in behind Dame Margaret's retainers, the other ten took post in rear of the sumpter horses. With such a train as this there was little fear of any trouble with bands of marauders, and as the road lay through a country devoted to Burgundy there was small chance of their encountering an Orleanist force. They travelled by almost the same route by which Dame Margaret had been escorted to Paris. At all the towns through which they passed the Burgundian knights and their following were well entertained, none doubting that they were riding on the business of their duke. One or other of the knights generally rode beside Guy, and except that the heat in the middle of the day was somewhat excessive, the journey was altogether a very pleasant one. From Arras they rode direct to Villeroy. As soon as their coming was observed from the keep the draw-bridge was raised, and as they approached Sir Eustace himself appeared on the wall above it to hear any message the new-comers might have brought him. As they came near, the knights reined back their horses, and Dame Margaret and Agnes rode forward, followed by Guy having Charlie in front of him. As he recognized them Sir Eustace gave a shout of joy, and a moment later the drawbridge began to descend, and as it touched the opposite side Sir Eustace ran across to the outwork, threw open the gate, and fondly embraced his wife and children, who had already dismounted.

"Ah, my love!" he exclaimed, "you cannot tell how I have suffered, and how I have blamed myself for permitting you and the children to leave me. I received your first letter, saying that you were comfortably lodged at Paris, but since then no word has reached me. I of course heard of the dreadful doings there, of the ascendency of the butchers, of the massacres in the streets, and the murders of the knights and ladies. A score of times I have resolved to go myself in search of you, but I knew not how to set about it when there, and I should assuredly have been seized by Burgundy and thrown into prison with others hostile to his plans. But who are these with you?"

"They are three Burgundian knights, who from love and courtesy, and in requital of a service done them by your brave esquire here, have safely brought us out of Paris and escorted us on our way. They are Count Charles d'Estournel, Sir John Poupart, and Sir Louis de Lactre."

Holding his hand she advanced to meet them and introduced them to him.

"Gentlemen," Sir Eustace said, "no words of mine can express the gratitude that I feel to you for the service that you have rendered to my wife and children. Henceforth you may command me to the extent of my life."

"The service was requited before it was rendered, Sir Eustace," Count Charles said; "it has been service for service. In the first place your esquire, with that tall archer of yours, saved my life when attacked by a band of cutthroats in Paris. This to some small extent I repaid when, with my two good friends here and some others, we charged a mob that was besieging the house in which your dame lodged. Then Master Aylmer laid a fresh obligation on us by warning us that the butchers demanded our lives for interfering in that business, whereby we were enabled to cut our way out by the Port St. Denis and so save our skins. We could not rest thus, matters being so uneven, and therefore as soon as the king's party arrived in a sufficient force to put down the tyranny of the butchers, we returned to Paris, with the intention we have carried out—of finding Dame Margaret in her hiding-place, if happily she should have escaped all these perils, and of conducting her to you. And now, having delivered her into your hands, we will take our leave."

"I pray you not to do so, Count," the knight said; "it would mar the pleasure of this day to me, were you, who are its authors, thus to leave me. I pray you, therefore, to enter and accept my hospitality, if only for a day or two."

The knights had previously agreed among themselves that they would return that night to Arras; but they could not resist the earnestness of the invitation, and the whole party crossed the drawbridge and entered the castle, amid the tumultuous greeting of the retainers.

"You have been away but a few months," Sir Eustace said to his wife, as they were crossing the bridge, "though it seems an age to me. You are but little changed by what you have passed through, but Agnes seems to have grown more womanly. Charlie has grown somewhat also, but is scarcely looking so strong!"

"It has been from want of air and exercise; but he has picked up a great deal while we have been on the road, and I, too, feel a different woman. Agnes has shared my anxiety, and has been a great companion for me."

"You have brought all the men back, as well as Guy?"

"You should rather say that Guy has brought us all back, Eustace, for 'tis assuredly wholly due to him that we have escaped the dangers that threatened us."

The knights and men-at-arms dismounted in the courtyard, and Sir Eustace and Dame Margaret devoted themselves at once to making them welcome with all honour. The maids hurried to prepare the guest-chambers, the servitors to get ready a banquet. Guy and his men-at-arms saw to the comfort of the knights' retainers and their horses, and the castle rang with sounds of merriment and laughter to which it had been a stranger for months. After the cup of welcome had been handed round Sir Eustace showed the knights over the castle.

"We heard the details of the siege, Sir Eustace, from your esquire, and it is of interest to us to inspect the defences that Sir Clugnet de Brabant failed to capture, for, foe though he is to Burgundy, it must be owned that he is a very valiant knight, and has captured many towns and strong places. Yes, it is assuredly a strong castle, and with a sufficient garrison might well have defeated all attempts to storm it by foes who did not possess means of battering the walls, but the force you had was quite insufficient when the enemy were strong enough to attack at many points at the same time, and I am surprised that you should have made good your defence against so large a force as that which assailed you.

"But it was doubtless in no slight degree due to your English archers. We saw in Paris what even one of these men could do."

"I am all anxiety to know what took place there," Sir Eustace said, "and I shall pray you after supper to give me an account of what occurred."

"We will tell you as far as we know of the matter, Sir Eustace; but in truth we took but little share in it, there was just one charge on our part and the mob were in flight. Any I can tell you that we did it with thorough good-will, for in truth we were all heartily sick of the arrogance of these butchers, who lorded over all Paris; even our Lord of Burgundy was constrained to put up with their insolence, since their aid was essential to him. But to us, who take no very great heed of politics and leave these matters to the great lords, the thing was well-nigh intolerable; and I can tell you that it was with hearty good-will we seized the opportunity of giving the knaves a lesson."

As soon as the visitors had arrived, mounted men had ridden off to the tenants, and speedily returned with a store of ducks and geese, poultry, wild-fowl, brawn, and fish; the banquet therefore was both abundant and varied. While the guests supped at the upper table, the men-at-arms were no less amply provided for at the lower end of the hall, where all the retainers at the castle feasted royally in honour of the return of their lady and her children. The bowmen were delighted at the return of Long Tom, whom few had expected ever to see again, while the return of Robert Picard and his companions was no less heartily welcomed by their comrades. After the meal was concluded Dame Margaret went round the tables with her husband, saying a few words here and there to the men, who received her with loud shouts as she passed along.

Then the party from the upper table retired to the private apartment of Sir Eustace, leaving the men to sing and carouse unchecked by their presence. When they were comfortably seated and flagons of wine had been placed on the board, the knight requested Count Charles to give him an account of his adventure with the cut-throats and the part he had subsequently played in the events of which he had spoken. D'Estournel gave a lively recital, telling not only of the fray with the White Hoods, but of what they saw when, after the defeat of the mob, they entered the house. "Had the passage and stairs been the breach of a city attacked by assault it could not have been more thickly strewn with dead bodies," the count said; "and indeed for my part I would rather have struggled up a breach, however strongly defended, than have tried to carry the barricade at the top of the stairs, held as it was. I believe that, even had we not arrived, Master Aylmer could have held his ground until morning, except against fire."

"I wonder they did not fire the house," Sir Eustace remarked.

"Doubtless the leaders would have done so as soon as they saw the task they had before them; but you see plunder was with the majority the main object of the attack, while that of the leaders was assuredly to get rid of the provost of the silversmiths, who had powerfully withstood them. The cry that was raised of 'Down with the English spies!' was but a pretext. However, as all the plate-cases with the silverware were in the barricade, there would have been no plunder to gather had they set fire to the house, and it was for this reason that they continued the attack so long; but doubtless in the end, when they were convinced that they could not carry the barricade, they would have resorted to fire."

Then he went on to recount how Guy had warned himself and his friends of the danger that threatened, and how difficult it had been to persuade them that only by flight could their safety be secured; and how at last he and the two knights with him had returned to Paris to escort Dame Margaret.

"Truly, Count, your narrative is a stirring one," Sir Eustace said; "but I know not as yet how Guy managed to gain the information that the house was going to be attacked and so sent to you for aid, or how he afterwards learned that your names were included with those of the Duke of Bar and others whom the butchers compelled the Duke of Aquitaine to hand over to them."

"Dame Margaret or your esquire himself can best tell you that," the count said. "It is a strange story indeed."

"And a long one," Dame Margaret added. "Were I to tell it fully it would last till midnight, but I will tell you how matters befell, and to-morrow will inform you of the details more at length."

She then related briefly the incidents that had occurred from the day of her interview with the Duke of Burgundy to that of her escape, telling of the various disguises that had been used, the manner in which Guy had overheard the councils of the butchers before they surrounded the hotel of the Duke of Aquitaine and dragged away a large number of knights and ladies to prison, and how the four men-at-arms had re-entered Paris after their escape, and remained there in readiness to aid her if required.

Guy himself was not present at the narration, as he had, after staying for a short time in the room, gone down into the banqueting-hall to see that the men's wants were well attended to, and to talk with the English men-at-arms and archers.

"It seems to me," Sir Eustace said when his wife had finished the story, "that my young esquire has comported himself with singular prudence as well as bravery."

"He has been everything to me," Dame Margaret said warmly; "he has been my adviser and my friend. I have learned to confide in him implicitly. It was he who secured for me in the first place the friendship of Count Charles, and then that of his friends. He was instrumental in securing for us the assistance of the Italian who warned and afterwards sheltered us—one of the adventures that I have not yet told, because I did not think that I could do so without saying more than that person would like known; but Guy rendered him a service that in his opinion far more than repaid him for his kindness to us. The messenger he employed was a near relation of his."

And she then related how Guy had rescued this relation from the hands of the butchers, how he had himself been chased, and had killed one and wounded another of his assailants; and how at last he escaped from falling into their hands by leaping from the bridge into the Seine.

"You will understand," she said, "that not only our host but we all should have been sacrificed had not the messenger been rescued. He would have been compelled by threats, and if these failed by tortures, to reveal who his employer was and where he lived, and in that case a search would have been made, we should have been discovered, and our lives as well as that of our host would have paid the penalty."

"It is impossible to speak too highly of the young esquire," Sir John Poupart said warmly. "For a short time we all saw a good deal of him at the fencing-school, to which D'Estournel introduced him. He made great progress, and wonderfully improved his swordsmanship even during the short time he was there, and the best of us found a match in him. He was quiet and modest, and even apart from the service he had rendered to D'Estournel, we all came to like him greatly. He is a fine character, and I trust that ere long he may have an opportunity of winning his spurs, for the courage he has shown in the defence of his charges would assuredly have gained them for him had it been displayed in battle."

The knights were persuaded to stay a few days at the castle, and then rode away with their retainers with mutual expressions of hope that they would meet again in quieter times. Guy had opened the little packet that Katarina had given him at starting. It contained a ring with a diamond of great beauty and value, with the words "With grateful regards."

He showed it to Sir Eustace, who said:

"It is worth a knight's ransom, lad, and more, I should say. Take it not with you to the wars, but leave it at home under safe guardianship, for should it ever be your bad luck to be made a prisoner, I will warrant it would sell for a sufficient sum to pay your ransom. That is a noble suit of armour that the silversmith gave you. Altogether, Guy, you have no reason to regret that you accompanied your lady to Paris. You have gained a familiarity with danger which will assuredly stand you in good stead some day, you have learned some tricks of fence, you have gained the friendship of half a score of nobles and knights; you have earned the lasting gratitude of my dame and myself, you have come back with a suit of armour such as a noble might wear in a tournament, and a ring worth I know not how much money. It is a fair opening of your life, Guy, and your good father will rejoice when I tell him how well you have borne yourself. It may be that it will not be long before you may have opportunities of showing your mettle in a wider field. The English have already made several descents on the coast, and have carried off much spoil and many prisoners, and it may not be long before we hear that Henry is gathering a powerful army and is crossing the seas to maintain his rights, and recover the lands that have during past years been wrested from the crown.

"I propose shortly to return to England. My dame has borne up bravely under her troubles, but both she and Agnes need rest and quiet. It is time, too, that Charlie applied himself to his studies for a time and learnt to read and write well, for methinks that every knight should at least know this much. I shall take John Harpen back with me. Such of the men-at-arms and archers as may wish to return home must wait here until I send you others to take their places, for I propose to leave you here during my absence, as my castellan. It is a post of honour, Guy, but I feel that the castle will be in good hands; and there is, moreover, an advantage in thus leaving you, as, should any message be sent by Burgundian or Orleanist, you will be able to reply that, having been placed here by me to hold the castle in my absence, you can surrender it to no one, and can admit no one to garrison it, until you have sent to me and received my orders on the subject. Thus considerable delay may be obtained.

"Should I receive such a message from you, I shall pass across at once to Calais with such force as I can gather. I trust that no such summons will arrive, for it is clear that the truce now made between the two French factions will be a very short one, and that ere long the trouble will recommence, and, as I think, this time Burgundy will be worsted. The Orleanists are now masters of Paris and of the king's person, while assuredly they have the support of the Duke of Aquitaine, who must long to revenge the indignities that were put upon him by Burgundy and the mob of Paris. They should therefore be much the stronger party, and can, moreover, issue what proclamations they choose in the king's name, as Burgundy has hitherto been doing in his own interest. The duke will therefore be too busy to think of meddling with us. Upon the other hand, if the Orleanists gain the mastery they are the less likely to interfere with us, as I hear that negotiations have just been set on foot again for the marriage of King Henry with Katherine of France. The English raids will therefore be stopped, and the French will be loath to risk the breaking off of the negotiations which might be caused by an assault without reason upon the castle of one who is an English as well as a French vassal, and who might, therefore, obtain aid from the garrison of Calais, by which both nations might be again embroiled."

"If you think well, my lord, to leave me here in command I will assuredly do the best in my power to prove myself worthy of your confidence; but it is a heavy trust for one so young."

"I have thought that over, Guy, but I have no fear that you will fail in any way. Were the garrison wholly a French one I might hesitate, but half the defenders of the castle are Englishmen; and in Tom, the captain of the archers, you have one of whose support at all times you will be confident, while the French garrison will have learned from the three men who went with you that they would as readily follow you as they would a knight of experience. Moreover, good fighters as the English are, they are far more independent and inclined to insubordination than the French, who have never been brought up in the same freedom of thought. Therefore, although

I have no doubt that they will respect your authority, I doubt whether, were I to put a Frenchman in command, they would prove so docile, while with the French there will be no difficulty. I might, of course, appoint John Harpen, who is ten years your senior, to the command; but John, though a good esquire, is bluff and rough in his ways, and as obstinate as a mule, and were I to leave him in command he would, I am sure, soon set the garrison by the ears. As an esquire he is wholly trustworthy, but he is altogether unfitted for command, therefore I feel that the choice I have made of you is altogether for the best, and I shall go away confident that the castle is in good hands, and that if attacked it will be as staunchly defended as if I myself were here to direct the operations."

Two days later Sir Eustace with his family started, under the guard of ten English and ten French men-at-arms, for Calais. Before starting he formally appointed Guy as castellan in his absence, and charged the garrison to obey his orders in all things, as if they had been given by himself. He also called in the principal tenants and delivered a similar charge to them. The English men-at-arms were well pleased to be commanded by one whom they had known from childhood, and whose father they had been accustomed to regard as their master during the absences of Sir Eustace and Dame Margaret. The archers had not, like the men-at-arms, been drawn from the Summerley estate, but the devotion of their leader to Guy, and the tales he had told them of what had taken place in Paris rendered them equally satisfied at his choice as their leader. As for the French men-at-arms, bred up in absolute obedience to the will of their lord, they accepted his orders in this as they would have done on any other point. Sir Eustace left Guy instructions that he might make any further addition to the defences that he thought fit, pointing out to him several that he had himself intended to carry out.

"I should have set about these at once," he had said, "but it is only now that the vassals have completed the work of rebuilding their houses, and I would not call upon them for any service until that was completed. I have told them now that such works must be taken in hand, and that, as they saw upon the occasion of the last siege, their safety depends upon the power of the castle to defend itself, I shall expect their services to be readily and loyally rendered, especially as they have been remitted for over six months. It would be well also to employ the garrison on the works—in the first place, because they have long been idle, and idleness is bad for them; and in the second place because the vassals will all work more readily seeing that the garrison are also employed. While so engaged an extra measure of wine can be served to each man, and a small addition of pay. Here are the plans that I have roughly prepared. Beyond the moat I would erect at the centre of each of the three sides a strong work, similar to that across the drawbridge, and the latter I would also have strengthened.

"These works, you see, are open on the side of the moat, so that if carried they would offer the assailants no shelter from arrows from the walls, while being triangular in shape they would be flanked by our fire. Each of these three forts should have a light drawbridge running across the moat to the foot of the wall, thence a ladder should lead to an entrance to be pierced through the wall, some fifteen feet above the level of the moat; by this means the garrison could, if assailed by an overwhelming force, withdraw into the castle. These outposts would render it—so long as they were held—impossible for storming-parties to cross the moat and place ladders, as they did on the last occasion. The first task will, of course, be to quarry stones. As soon as sufficient are prepared for one of these outworks you should proceed to erect it, as it would render one side at least unassailable and diminish the circuit to be defended. As soon as one is finished, with its drawbridge, ladder, and entrance, proceed with the next. I would build the one at the rear first. As you see from this plan, the two walls are to be twenty feet high and each ten yards long, so that they could be defended by some twenty men. After they are built I would further strengthen them by leading ditches from the moat, six feet deep and ten feet wide, round them. The earth from these ditches should be thrown inside the walls, so as to strengthen these and form a platform for the defenders to stand on. If the earth is insufficient for that purpose the moat can be widened somewhat."

"I will see that your wishes are carried out, Sir Eustace; assuredly these little outworks will add greatly to the strength of the castle. Are the bridges to be made to draw up?"

"No; that will hardly be necessary. Let them consist of two beams with planks laid crosswise. They need not be more than four feet wide, and the planks can therefore be easily pulled up as the garrison falls back. I have told the tenants that during the winter, when there is but little for their men to do, they can keep them employed on this work, and that I will pay regular wages to them and for the carts used in bringing in the stones."

Guy was very glad that there was something specific to be done that would give him occupation and keep the men employed. Sir Eustace had informed the garrison of the work that would be required of them, and of the ration of wine and extra pay that would be given, and all were well satisfied with the prospect. For the English especially, having no friends outside, found the time hang very heavy on their hands, and their experience during the last siege had taught them that the additional fortifications, of the nature of which they were ignorant, however, would add to their safety.

As soon, therefore, as Sir Eustace had left, Guy commenced operations. A few men only were kept on guard, and the rest went out daily to prepare the stones under the direction of a master mason, who had been brought from Arras by Sir Eustace. Some fifty of the tenants were also employed on the work, and as the winter closed in this number was doubled.

The quarry lay at a distance of half a mile from the castle, and as fast as the stones were squared and roughly dressed they were taken in carts to the spot where they were to be used. Guy had the foundations for the walls dug in the first place, to a depth below that of the bottom of the moats, and filled up with cement and rubble. The trenches were then dug at a distance of five feet from the foot of the walls. With so many hands the work proceeded briskly, and before springtime the three works were all completed, with their bridges and ladders, passages pierced through the castle wall, and stone steps built inside by which those who passed through could either descend into the court yard or mount to the battlements. At the end of September fifteen archers and men-at-arms arrived from England to take the place of those who had desired to return home, and who on their coming marched away to Calais.

From time to time reports were received of the events happening in Paris. Paris had been strongly occupied by the Orleanists, and a proclamation had at once been issued in the name of the king condemning all that had been done in the city, and denouncing by name all the ringleaders of the late tumults, and such of these as were found in Paris were arrested. Another proclamation was then issued enjoining all parties to keep the peace, to refrain from gathering in armed bodies, and to abstain from the use of expressions against each other that might lead to a breach of the peace.

On the 13th of November, the year being 1413, fresh and more stringent orders were issued by the king against any assemblies of men-in-arms, and at the end of this month the Duke of Burgundy sent to the king a letter of complaint and accusation against his enemies. Those surrounding Charles persuaded him to send no answer whatever to what they considered his insolent letter. Some of the Burgundian knights had still remained in Paris, and on the advice of the Dukes of Berri and Orleans and other princes, the queen caused four knights of the suite of the Duke of Aquitaine to be carried away from the Louvre. This so much enraged the duke that he at first intended to sally out and call upon the populace of Paris to aid him to rescue the prisoners. The princes of the blood, however, restrained him from doing this; but although he pretended to be appeased he sent secret letters to the Duke of Burgundy begging him to come to his assistance.

This served as an excuse for Burgundy to gather all his adherents and to march towards Paris, and as he collected the force he sent letters to all the principal towns saying that at the invitation of his son-in-law, the Duke of Aquitaine, and in consequence of the breach of the peace committed by his enemies, he was forced to take up arms to rescue his beloved daughter and the duke from the hands of those who constrained them. Upon the other hand, letters were written in the king's name to the various towns on the line by which Burgundy would advance from Artois, begging them not to open their gates to him.

The Burgundian army advanced and occupied St. Denis, thence the duke sent detachments to the various gates of Paris in hopes that the populace would rise in his favour. However, the citizens remained quiet, and the duke, being unprovided with the engines and machines necessary for a siege, fell back again, placing strong garrisons in Compiègne and Soissons. Then the Orleanists took the offensive, besieged and captured town after town, and revenged the murder of their friends in Paris by wholesale massacres and atrocities of the worst description. The Burgundians in vain attempted to raise an army of sufficient strength to meet that of the king, who himself accompanied the Orleanist forces in the field. The fact that he was present with them had a powerful influence in preventing many lords who would otherwise have done so from joining Burgundy, for although all knew that the king was but a puppet who could be swayed by those who happened to be round him, even the shadow of the royal authority had great weight, and both parties carried on their operations in the king's name, protesting that any decrees hostile to themselves were not the true expression of his opinion, but the work of ambitious and traitorous persons who surrounded him. After occupying Laon, Peronne, and other places, the king's army entered Artois, captured Bapaume, and advanced against Arras, where Sir John of Luxemburg, who commanded a Burgundian garrison, prepared for the siege by sending away the greater part of the women and children, and destroying all the buildings and suburbs outside the walls.

As soon as it was evident that the Orleanist army was marching against Artois, Guy despatched one of the English soldiers to Summerley to inform his lord that if, as it seemed, the Orleanists intended to subdue all the Burgundian towns and fortresses in the province, it was probable that Villeroy would be besieged. The messenger returned with twenty more archers, and brought a letter from Sir Eustace to Guy saying that Dame Margaret had been ill ever since her return from France, and that she was at present in so dangerous a state that he could not leave her.

"I trust," he said, "that as the negotiations for the marriage of the king with the French princess are still going on, you will not be disturbed. The main body of the French army will likely be engaged on more important enterprises, and if you are attacked it will probably be only by strong plundering detachments; these you need not fear. Should you be besieged strongly, hold out as long as you can. I shall be sure to receive news of it from Calais, and will go at once to the king and pray for his protection, and beg him to write to the King of France declaring that, to his knowledge, I have ever been as loyal a vassal of France as of England. Should you find that the pressure upon you is too great, and that the castle is like to be taken, I authorize you to make surrender on condition that all within the castle are permitted to march away free and unmolested whithersoever they will."

# CHAPTER XVIII — KATARINA

As soon as the king's army approached Arras, Guy repeated all the precautions that had before been taken, but as this time there had been long warning, these were carried out more effectually. A considerable number of the cattle and sheep of the tenants were driven to Calais and there sold, the rest, with the horses, were taken into the castle. The crops were hastily got in, for it was near July, and these were thrashed and the grain brought in, with the household furniture and all belongings. A great store of arrows had been long before prepared, and Guy felt confident that he could hold out for a long time. The women and children took up their abode in the castle, and the former were all set to work to make a great number of sacks. A hundred cart-loads of earth were brought in, and this was stored in a corner of the court-yard. The earth was to be employed in filling the sacks, which were to be lowered from the walls so as to form a protection against heavy missiles, should an attempt be made to effect a breach.

GUY WELCOMES THE COUNT OF MONTEPONE AND HIS DAUGHTER
TO VILLEROY.

A few days after the king's army sat down before Arras, the look-out informed Guy that a horseman, together with a lady and two attendants, were riding towards the castle. Wondering who these visitors could be, Guy crossed the drawbridge to the outwork, where a small party were now stationed. As they rode up, he saw, to his surprise and pleasure, that they were the Count of Montepone and his daughter. He ran out to meet them.

"I am delighted to see you, Count, and you also Mistress Katarina. I regret that Sir Eustace and Dame Margaret are not here to receive you properly."

"We were aware that she was absent," the count said as he dismounted, while Guy assisted Katarina from her saddle. "I received a letter three months since; it came by way of Flanders from Sir Eustace, expressing his thanks for what slight services I had rendered to his wife. He told me that they had crossed over to England, and that you were his castellan here. But I thought that ere this he might have returned."

"I heard from him but a few days ago," Guy said. "He is detained in England by the illness of Dame Margaret, or he would have hastened hither on hearing that the French army was moving north. I need scarcely ask how you are, Mistress Katarina, for you have changed much, and if I may say it without offence, for the better."

The girl flushed a little and laughed, and her father said: "It is nigh three months since we left Paris; the country air has done her good. Since we left she has till now been in disguise again, and has ridden as my page, for I could not leave her behind, nor could I in an army, with so many wild and reckless spirits, take her in the dress of a girl."

By this time they had crossed the drawbridge, the servants leading their horses after them.

"My stay must be a short one," the count said as they entered the banqueting-hall, and Guy gave orders for a repast to be served.

"I hoped that you were come to stay for a time, Count; I would do all in my power to make your visit a pleasant one."

The Italian shook his head. "No, I must ride back tonight. I have come here for a double purpose. In the first place I must send Katarina to England; she is almost a woman now, and can no longer wander about with me in times like these. In the second place, I have come to tell you that I think you need have no fear of an attack upon the castle. That news you gave me, which enabled me to save those three Orleanist nobles, has, added to what I had before done in that way, helped me vastly. One of them is a great favourite with Aquitaine, and the latter took me under his special protection; and he and many other great lords, and I may tell you even the queen herself, consult me frequently. Shortly after you left I moved to a larger house, and as there was no longer any need for me to assume the character of a vendor of medicines I abandoned that altogether, and took handsome apartments, with my negro from the booth to open the door, and two other lackeys.

"My knowledge of the stars has enabled me with some success to predict the events that have taken place, and Aquitaine and the queen have both implicit confidence in me and undertake nothing without my advice. The Duke of Orleans, too, has frequently consulted me. I have used my influence to protect this castle. I have told them that success will attend all their efforts, which it was easy enough to foresee, as Burgundy has no army in the field that can oppose them. But I said that I had described a certain point of danger. It was some time before I revealed what this was, and then said that it appeared to me that the evil in some way started from the west of Arras. I would go no further than this for many days, and then said that it arose from a castle held by one who was not altogether French, and that were an attack made upon it evil would arise. I saw that it would lead to a disturbance, I said, in the negotiations for the marriage, and perhaps the arrival of an English army. More than this I said the stars did not tell me.

"Aquitaine made inquiries and soon found that my description applied to Villeroy, and he and the queen have issued strict orders that no plundering party is to come in this direction, and that on no account is the castle to be interfered with, and I shall take care that their intentions in this matter are not changed. I had the royal orders to accompany the army. This I should have done in any case, but of course I professed a certain reluctance, by saying that I had many clients in Paris. However, I received various rich presents, and was therefore prevailed upon to travel with them."

"I thank you most heartily, Count, for, as you saw on crossing the court-yard, I have already called all the vassals in and made preparations to stand a siege. As to your daughter, I will, if you wish it, appoint two of the tenants' daughters as her attendants, and send an elderly woman as her companion, with an escort under Robert Picard,—one of those who were with me in Paris,—and four other men-at-arms to accompany her to Summerley and hand her over to the charge of Dame Margaret, who will, I trust, be in better health than when Sir Eustace wrote to me. It will be a great relief to our lord and lady to know that their presence is not urgently required here. The escort can start to-morrow at daybreak if you wish that they should do so."

The count hesitated, and Guy went on: "I will appoint the woman and the two maids at once. Mistress Katarina can occupy Dame Margaret's chamber, and the woman and the maids can sleep in those adjoining it."

"That will do well," the count said cordially. "We have ridden twenty miles already, and she could hardly go on to-day, while if she starts at daybreak they may reach Calais to-morrow."

"I will give Picard a letter to the governor, asking him in my lord's name to give honourable entertainment to the young lady, who is under Dame Margaret's protection, and to forward her upon her journey to join them by the first vessel sailing to Southampton, or if there be none sailing thither, to send her at once by ship to Dover, whence they can travel by land. One of the four men-at-arms shall be an Englishman, and he can act as her spokesman by the way."

"That will do most excellently," the count said, "and I thank you heartily. As soon as I have finished my meal I must ride for the camp again. I started early this morning in order not to be observed; in the first place because I did not wish my daughter to be seen in her female dress, and in the second because I would not that any should notice my coming in this direction, and indeed we rode for the first mile backwards along the road to Bapaume, and I shall return by the same way."

"What will the end of these troubles be, Count?"

"As I read the stars there will be peace shortly, and indeed it is clear to me that the Duke of Burgundy must by this time see that if the war goes on he will lose all Artois and perhaps Flanders, and that therefore he must make peace, and perhaps keep it until the royal army has marched away and dispersed; after that we may be sure that the crafty duke will not long remain quiet. I have a trusty emissary in Burgundy's household, and as soon as the duke comes to the conclusion that he must beg for peace I shall have intelligence of it, and shall give early news to the queen and to Aquitaine, who would hail it with gladness; for, seeing that the latter's wife is Burgundy's daughter, he does not wish to press him hard, and would gladly see peace concluded."

An hour later the count rode off with his two followers, after taking an affectionate leave of his daughter, and telling her that it would not be long before he joined her—if only for a time—in England. Before he went Guy had chosen the woman who, with her two daughters, was to accompany Katarina, and had installed them in the private apartments.

"What shall we do with ourselves for the day?" he asked the girl, who was, he saw, shy and ill at ease, now that her father had left. "If you are not tired we might take a ride. We have some hawks here, and now that the harvest has been gathered we shall doubtless find sport with the game-birds."

"I am not at all tired," she said eagerly, "and should like it much."

Calling upon Long Tom and another to accompany them, horses were brought up, and they started and remained out until supper-time, bringing home with them some seven or eight partridges that had been killed by the hawks. Guy suggested that perhaps she would prefer to have the meal served in her own apartments and to retire to bed early. She accepted the offer, and at once went to her room, which she did not leave again that evening. Guy, as he ate alone, wondered to himself at the change that some nine or ten months had made in her.

"I suppose she feels strange and lonely," he said to himself. "She was merry enough when we were out hawking; but directly we got back again she seemed quite unlike herself. I suppose it is because I always used to treat her as if she were a boy, and now that she has grown up into a woman she wants to forget that time."

The town of Arras resisted sturdily. The garrison made frequent sorties, took a good many prisoners, and inflicted heavy loss upon the besiegers before these could gather in sufficient numbers to drive them in again, and all assaults were repulsed with loss. The Castle of Belle Moote, near Arras, also repulsed all the efforts of the king's army to take it. Foraging parties of Orleanists committed terrible devastations in the country round, but gained no advantage in their attacks on any fortified place.

On the 29th of August the Duke of Brabant arrived with some deputies from Flanders to negotiate a peace between Burgundy and the king. They were well received, and an armistice was at once arranged. The French troops were suffering severely from disease, and the failure of all their attempts to capture Arras made them ready to agree willingly upon a peace. This was accordingly concluded on the 4th of September, and the next day the royal army marched away.

Three weeks after Katarina had gone to England, Sir Eustace himself, to Guy's great joy, arrived at the castle, bringing with him his esquire and eight men-at-arms, as well as the three serving-women and their escort. As soon as his pennon was seen Guy leapt on a horse that was standing saddled in the court-yard, and rode to meet them. As he came up he checked his horse in surprise, for his father was riding by the side of Sir Eustace. Recovering himself, however, he doffed his cap to his lord.

"Welcome back, my lord!" he said. "I trust that our dear lady is better."

"Much better, Guy. You see I have brought your father over with me."

Guy bent low to his father.

"I am right glad to see you," the latter said, "and to hear such good accounts of you. Dame Margaret and Mistress Agnes were never tired of singing your praises, and in truth I was not weary of hearing them."

"Are you going to make a long stay, father?"

"I shall stay for some little time, Guy. Our lady is going to be her own castellan for the present. And in truth things are so quiet in England that Summerley could well go on without a garrison, so Sir Eustace suggested that I should accompany him hither, where, however, just at present things have also a peaceful aspect. The young countess arrived safely, Guy, and was heartily welcomed, the more so since, as your letter told me, it is to her father that we owe it that we did not have the king's army battering our walls, or, even if they did not try that, devastating the fields and ruining the farmers."

By this time they were at the gate. Long Tom had the garrison drawn up in the court-yard, and they hailed the return of their lord with hearty cheers, while the retainers of Summerley were no less pleased at seeing Sir John Aylmer. "And now, Guy," said Sir Eustace, "I will tell you why I have come hither. It is partly to see after the estate, to hear the complaints of my vassals and to do what I can for them, and in the next place I wanted to see these fortifications that you have raised, and, thirdly, I shall shortly ride to Paris in the train of the Earl of Dorset, the Lord Grey, Admiral of England, some bishops, and many other knights and nobles, amounting in the whole to 600 horse. They go to treat for the marriage of the princess of France with the English king. I had an audience with the king at Winchester as soon as we heard that the royal army was marching towards Artois, and he gave assurance that he would instruct the governor of Calais to furnish what assistance he could should the castle be attacked, and that he himself would at once on hearing of it send a remonstrance to the King of France, urging that I, as a vassal of his as well as of France, had avoided taking any part in the troubles, and had ever borne myself as a loyal vassal of his Majesty.

"He was at Winchester when the young countess arrived, and I rode over to him to tell him that I had news that it was not probable that Villeroy would be attacked. It was then that his Majesty informed me that the Earl of Dorset with a large body of nobles would ere long cross the Channel for the purpose that I have named, and begged me to ride with them. The king, being disengaged at the time, talked with me long, and questioned me as to the former defence of the castle, and how Dame Margaret had fared when, as he had heard, she was obliged to go as a hostage to Paris. I told him all that had befallen her, at which he seemed greatly interested, and bade me present you to him at the first opportunity.

"'He must be a lad after my own heart,' he said, 'and he shall have an opportunity of winning his spurs as soon as may be, which perchance is not so far away as some folks think.'"

Guy thanked Sir Eustace for having so spoken of him to the English king, and asked: "What do you think he meant by those last words, my lord?"

"That I cannot say, Guy; but it may well be that he thinks that this marriage which has been so long talked of may not take place, and that the negotiations have been continued solely for the purpose of keeping him quiet while France was busied with her own troubles. Moreover, I know that the king has been already enlisting men, that he is impatient at having been put off so often with soft words, and that embassy is intended to bring matters to a head; therefore if, as I gathered from some of my friends at his court, he is eager for fighting, it may be that his ambassadors will demand conditions which he is sure beforehand the King of France will not grant. At any rate I shall ride with Dorset to Paris; whatever the sentiments of the Burgundians or Orleanists may be towards me will matter nothing, riding as I shall do in the train of the earl. I am going to take you with me, as well as John Harpen, for I must do as well as others, and have had to lay out a goodly sum in garments fit for the occasion, for the king is bent upon his embassy making a brave show. Your father will be castellan here in my absence. I shall also take with me Long Tom and four of his archers, and five French men-at-arms. I have brought some Lincoln-green cloth to make fresh suits for the archers, and also material for those for the men-at-arms."

Both Sir Eustace and Sir John Aylmer expressed great satisfaction at the manner in which the new outworks had been erected.

"Assuredly it is a strong castle now, Sir Eustace," Sir John said, "and would stand a long siege even by a great army."

"What is all that earth for in the corner, Guy?" Sir Eustace asked as they re-entered the castle after having made a survey of the new works. "I had that brought in, my lord, to fill sacks, of which I had three hundred made, so that if guns and battering machines were brought against us, we might cover the wall at the place they aimed at with sacks hanging closely together, and so break the force of the stones or the cannon balls."

"Excellently well arranged, Guy. You thought, Sir John, that I was somewhat rash to leave the defence solely to the charge of this son of yours, but you see the lad was ready at all points, and I will warrant me that the castle would have held out under him as long a time as if you and I both had been in command of it."

# At Agincourt

It was not until January, the year being 1414, that the Earl of Dorset and a great company arrived at Calais. As they passed not far from the castle they were joined by Sir Eustace and his retinue. The king's wishes had been carried out, and the knights and nobles were so grandly attired and their retinues so handsomely appointed that when they rode into Paris the people were astonished at the splendour of the spectacle. A few days after they reached the capital the king gave a great festival in honour of the visitors, and there was a grand tournament at which the king and all the princes of the blood tilted. The English ambassadors were splendidly entertained, but their proposals were considered inadmissible by the French court, for Henry demanded with Katherine the duchy of Normandy, the county of Pontieu, and the duchy of Aquitaine.

No direct refusal was given, but the king said that he would shortly send over an embassy to discuss the conditions. Many handsome presents were made to all the knights and noblemen, and the embassy returned to England. Sir Eustace left them near Villeroy with his party, and stayed two days at the castle. Sir John Aylmer said that he would prefer that Guy should return home with Sir Eustace and that he himself should remain as castellan, for he thought that there was little doubt that war would soon be declared; he said that he himself was too old to take the field on active service, and preferred greatly that Guy should ride with Sir Eustace. Long Tom made a petition to his lord that he too should go to England for a time.

"If there was any immediate chance of fighting here, my lord," he said, "I would most willingly remain, but seeing that at present all is quiet, I would fain return, were it but for a month; for I have a maid waiting for me, and have, methinks, kept her long enough, and would gladly go home and fetch her over here."

The request was at once granted, and Sir Eustace, his two esquires, and the archer rode to Calais, and crossed with the company of the Earl of Dorset.

For some months Guy remained quietly at Summerley. Agnes, though nearly sixteen, was still but a young girl, while Katarina had grown still more womanly during the last six months. The former always treated him as a brother, but the latter was changeable and capricious. Occasionally she would laugh and chat when the three were alone, as she had done of old in Paris, but more often she would tease and laugh at him, while sometimes she would be shy and silent.

"I cannot make out the young countess, my lady," he said to Dame Margaret when Katarina had been teasing him even more than usual. "She was never like this in Paris, and I know not that I have done aught to offend her that she should so often pick up my words, and berate me for a meaning they never had."

"You see, things have changed since then," Dame Margaret said with a smile; "'tis two years since you were in Paris, and Katarina, although but little older than Agnes, is already a young woman. You were then still under seventeen, now you are nineteen, and in growth and stature well-nigh a man. You can hardly expect her to be the same with you as when she was running about Paris in boy's attire, for then you regarded her rather as a comrade than as a girl. I think, perhaps, it is that she a little resents the fact that you knew her in that guise, and therefore feels all the less at her ease with you. Do not trouble about it, the thing will right itself in time; and besides, you will shortly be going off to the war."

In fact, preparations were being already made for it. A French embassy of nobles and knights, with three hundred and fifty horsemen, had come over, and, after passing through London, had gone to Winchester, and there met the king and his great lords. The Archbishop of Bourges, who was their spokesman, at once set forth that the king could not hand over so large a portion of his kingdom, but that he would give with his daughter large estates in France, together with a great sum in ready money. This offer was refused, and preparations for war went on in both countries. France was, indeed, but in poor condition to defend itself, for the Duke of Aquitaine had seriously angered both parties. He had made a pretext to get the great lords to ride out from Paris, he being with them; but he had secretly returned, and had ordered the gates to be closed, had called the citizens to arms, and had resumed the supreme authority of the realm.

Having done this, he sent his wife, Burgundy's daughter, to a castle at a distance, and surrounding himself with young nobles as reckless and dissipated as himself, led a life of disorder, squandering money on his pleasures, and heavily taxing the city for his wants. The Duke of Burgundy, indignant at the treatment of his daughter, sent an ambassador to demand that she should be taken back, and that all the persons, five hundred in number, who had been exempted from the terms of the treaty, should be allowed to return to Paris. Both requests were refused, and the consequence was that the Duke of Burgundy, with his partisans, returned to his own country in deep anger; he would take no part in the war against the English, although he permitted his vassals to do so.

In July the English levies gathered at Southampton. The king was to have embarked immediately, and a great fleet had been collected for the purpose; but, as he was on the point of sailing, Henry obtained news of a plot against his life on the part of Sir Thomas Grey, Lord Scroop, and Richard, Earl of Cambridge, the king's cousin. As Scroop was in constant attendance upon the king and slept in his room, the conspirators had little doubt that their purpose could be carried out, their intention being to proclaim the Earl of March king, and to summon assistance from Scotland. The three conspirators were tried by a jury and were all found guilty. Grey was beheaded, but his companions claimed to be tried again by their peers. No time was lost in carrying out the trial; all the lords assembled at Southampton were called together, and, after hearing the evidence, at once found the two nobles guilty, and they were immediately beheaded.

Orders were then given for the embarkation. Sir Eustace had brought with him thirty archers and as many men-at-arms, and, as they were waiting on the strand for the boats that were to take them out to the ships to which they had been appointed, the king, who was personally superintending the operations, rode past. Sir Eustace saluted him.

"Is this your following, Sir Eustace?" the king asked.

"It is, my lord king, and would that it were larger. Had we landed at Calais I should have been joined by another fifty stout Englishmen from Villeroy, and should we in our marches pass near it I will draw them to me. Your majesty asked me to present to you my esquire, Guy Aylmer, who, as I had the honour of telling you, showed himself a brave and trusty gentleman, when, during the troubles, he was in Paris with my wife. Step forward, Guy!"

The latter did so, saluted the king, and stood erect in military attitude.

"You have begun well," the king said graciously; "and I hereby request your lord that in the day of battle he will permit you to fight near me, and if you bear yourself as well when fighting for your king as you did when looking after your lady mistress, you shall have your share of honours as well as of blows."

The king then rode on, and Sir Eustace and Guy took their places in a boat where the men had already embarked.

"This is something like, Master Guy," said Long Tom, who was in command of the archers. "It was well indeed that I asked to come home to England when I did, else had I been now mewed up at Villeroy while my lord was fighting the French in the open field. Crecy was the last time an English king commanded an army in battle against France; think you that we shall do as well this time?"

"I trust so, Tom; methinks we ought assuredly not to do worse. It is true that the French have been having more fighting of late than we have, but the nobles are less united now than they were then, and are likely to be just as headstrong and incautious as they were at Crecy. I doubt not that we shall be greatly outnumbered, but numbers go for little unless they are well handled. The Constable d'Albrett is a good soldier, but the nobles, who are his equals in rank, will heed his orders but little when their blood is up and they see us facing them. We may be sure, at any rate, that we shall be well led, for the king has had much experience against the Scotch and Welsh, and has shown himself a good leader as well as a brave fighter. I hope, Tom, that you have by this time come to be well accustomed to your new bow."

"That have I. I have shot fourscore arrows a day with it from the time I reached home, not even omitting my wedding day, and I think that now I make as good shooting with it as I did with my old one. 'Tis a pity we are not going to Calais; if we had been joined by thirty archers there we should have made a brave show, and more than that, they would have done good service, for they are picked men. A few here may be as good, but not many. You see when we last sailed with our lord the times were peaceful, and we were able to gather the best shots for fifty miles round, but now that the king and so many of the nobles are all calling for archers we could not be so particular, and have had to take what we could get; still, I would enlist none who were not fair marksmen."

This conversation took place as they were dropping down Southampton waters. Their destination was known to be Harfleur, which, as it was strongly fortified and garrisoned, was like to offer a sturdy resistance. The fleet was a great one, consisting of from twelve to fourteen hundred sail, which the king had collected from all the ports of England and Ireland, or hired from Holland and Friesland. The army consisted of six thousand five hundred horsemen and twenty-four thousand footmen of all kinds. On the 13th of August the fleet anchored in the mouth of the Seine, three miles from Harfleur. The operation of landing the great army and their horses occupied three days, the French, to the surprise of all, permitting the operation to be carried on without let or hindrance, although the ground was favourable for their attacks, As soon as the landing was effected the army took up its position so as to prevent any supplies from entering the town. They had with them an abundance of machines for battering the walls, and these were speedily planted, and they began their work.

The garrison had been reinforced by four hundred knights and picked men-at-arms, and fought with great determination and valour, making several sorties from the two gates of the town. There were, however, strong bodies of troops always stationed near to guard the engines from such attacks, and the French sorties were not only repulsed, but their knights had much difficulty in winning their way back to the town. The enemy were unable to use their cannon to much effect, for a large supply of gunpowder sent by the French king was, on the day after the English landed, captured on its way into the town. The besiegers lost, however, a good many men from the crossbowmen who manned the walls, although the English archers endeavoured to keep down their shooting by a storm of arrows. The most formidable enemy, however, that the English had to contend with was dysentery, brought on by the damp and unhealthy nature of the ground upon which they were encamped. No less than two thousand men died, and a vastly larger number were so reduced by the malady that they were useless for fighting. The siege, however, was carried on uninterruptedly. The miners who had been brought over drove two galleries under the walls, and the gates were so shattered by stones and cannon-balls that they scarce hung together.

The garrison surrendered after having by the permission of the English king sent a messenger to the King of France, who was at Vernon, to say that unless they were succoured within three days they must surrender, as the town was already at the mercy of the English, and received for answer that no army was as yet gathered that could relieve them.

In addition to the ravages of dysentery the English army had suffered much from want of food. Large bodies of French troops were gathered at Rouen and other places, and when knights and men-at-arms went out to forage, they fell upon them and drove them back. Still a large amount of booty was gathered, together with enough provisions to afford a bare subsistence to the army. A considerable amount of booty was also obtained when Harfleur fell. The greater portion of the inhabitants of the town were forced to leave it, the breaches in the walls were repaired and new gates erected. A portion of the treasure obtained was divided by the king among the troops. The prisoners and the main portion of the booty—which, as Harfleur was the chief port of Normandy, and indeed of all the western part of France, was very great—he sent direct to England, together with the engines of war. The sick and ailing were then embarked on ships, with a considerable fighting force under the Earl of Warwick. They were ordered to touch at Calais, where the fighting-men were to be landed and the sick carried home, and Henry then prepared to march to Calais by land.

# CHAPTER XIX — AGINCOURT

The English king waited some time for an answer to a challenge he had sent to the Duke of Aquitaine to decide their quarrel by single combat; but Aquitaine cared more for pleasure than for fighting, and sent no answer to the cartel. It was open to Henry to have proceeded by sea to Calais, and it was the advice of his counsellors that he should do so; but the king declared that the French should never say that he was afraid to meet them, and that as the country was his by right he would march wherever he pleased across it; and so, after leaving a thousand archers and five hundred men-at-arms under the command of the Duke of Exeter, he set out on the 6th of October on his adventurous journey.

Accounts differ as to the number that started with him, some French historians put it as high as 17,000, but it is certain that it could not have exceeded nine thousand men, of whom two thousand were men-at-arms and the rest archers. Now, while the siege of Harfleur had been going on, the arrangements for the embarkation of the troops and stores carried out, and the town put in a state of defence, troops had been marching from all points of France at the command of the French king to join him at Rouen, so that here and in Picardy two great armies were already assembled, the latter under the command of the constable.

The English force marched by the sea-shore until it arrived at the river Somme. No great resistance was encountered, but large bodies of the enemy's horse hovered near and cut off all stragglers, and rendered it difficult to obtain food, so that sickness again broke out among the troops. On reaching the Somme Henry followed its left bank up, intending to cross at the ford of La Blanche-Tache, across which Edward the Third had carried his army before fighting at Crecy.

The French, as on the previous occasion, held the ford; but they this time had erected defences on each of the banks, and had strong posts driven into the bed of the river. Still ascending along the river bank the English found every bridge broken and every ford fortified, while a great body of troops marched parallel with them on the right bank of the river. At Pont St. Remy, Ponteau de Mer, and several other points they tried in vain to force a passage. Seven days were spent in these attempts; the troops, suffering terrible hardships, were disheartened at their failure to cross the river, and at finding themselves getting farther and farther from the sea. On the morning of the 19th, however, a ford was discovered which had not been staked. The English vanguard at once made a dash across it, repulsed its defenders on the other bank, and the whole army with its baggage, which was of scanty dimensions, swarmed across the river.

Sir Eustace, with his little force, now reduced to half its number, was, as it happened, in front of the army when the ford was discovered, and, followed by his two esquires and ten mounted men-at-arms, dashed into the river, while the archers, slinging their bows behind them, drew their axes and followed. For a short time there was a desperate conflict, but as reinforcements hurried across, the fight became more even and the French speedily gave way. When the king had crossed he thanked Sir Eustace for his prompt action.

"Had you waited to send back for orders," he said, "the French would have come up in such numbers that the ford would not have been won without heavy loss, whereas by dashing across the moment it was discovered, you took the defenders by surprise and enabled us to get over without the loss of a single man."

The constable, disconcerted at finding that all his plans for keeping the English on the left bank of the river were foiled, fell back to St. Pol in Artois. Henry followed, but without haste. His small force was greatly reduced by sickness, while by this time the whole of the royal army had marched round and joined that of the constable. On the day after the passage had been effected three heralds arrived in the English camp to acquaint the king with the resolution of the constable and of the Dukes of Orleans and Brabant to give his army battle before he reached Calais. Henry replied that fear of them would not induce him to move out of his way or to change the order of his march; he intended to go on straight by the road to Calais, and if the French attempted to stop him it would be at their peril; he accordingly continued to advance at the same rate as before.

The constable fell back from St. Pol and took up his post between the villages of Ruissanville and Agincourt, where, having received all the reinforcements he expected, he determined to give battle. On the 24th the English crossed the Ternois at Blangi, and soon afterwards came in sight of the enemy's columns. These fell back as he advanced, and towards evening he halted at the village of Maisoncelles, within half a mile of the enemy's position. Fortunately provisions had been obtained during the day's march; these were cooked and served out, and the English lay down to sleep. The king sent for Sir Eustace.

"You know this ground well, I suppose, Sir Eustace," he said, "for your Castle of Villeroy is not many miles distant?"

"'Tis but six miles away," the knight replied. "It is a good ground to fight on, for facing it are fields, and on either flank of these are large woods, so that there will be little space for the enemy to move."

"That is just what I would have," the king said. "Were they but half as strong as they are I should feel less confident that we should defeat them; their numbers will hinder them, and the deep wet ground will hamper their movements. As for ourselves, I would not have a man more with me if I could; the fewer we are the greater the glory if we conquer, while if we are defeated the less the loss to England. Does your young esquire also know the ground, Sir Eustace?"

"Yes, sire; he has, I know, often ridden here when hawking."

"Then let him go with four of my officers, who are about to reconnoitre the ground and see where we had best fight."

Guy was accordingly called up and started with the officers. He first took them up to the wood on the right of the French division, then they moved across its front at a distance of fifty yards only from the French line. The contrast between it and the English camp was great. In the latter all was quiet. The men after a hearty meal had lain down to sleep, heeding little the wet ground and falling rain, exhausted by their long marching, and in good spirits,—desperate though the odds seemed against them,—that they were next day to meet their foes. In the French camp all was noise and confusion. Each body of troops had come on the ground under its own commander, and shouts, orders, and inquiries sounded from all quarters. Many of the Frenchmen never dismounted all the night, thinking it better to remain on horseback than to lie down on wet ground. Great fires were lighted and the soldiers gathered round these, warming themselves and drinking, and calculating the ransoms to be gained by the capture of the king and the great nobles of England. Knights and men-at-arms rode about in search of their divisions, their horses slipping and floundering in the deep clay.

Passing along the line of the French army Guy and the officers proceeded to the wood on the left, and satisfied themselves that neither there nor on the other flank had any large body of men been posted. They then returned and made their report to the king. Guy wrapped himself in his cloak and lay down and slept until the moon rose at three o'clock, when the whole army awoke and prepared for the day's work. The English king ordered the trumpeters and other musicians who had been brought with the army to play merry tunes, and these during the three hours of darkness cheered the spirits of the men and helped them to resist the depressing influence of the cold night air following upon their sleep on the wet ground. The French, on the other hand, had no manner of musical instruments with their army, and all were fatigued and depressed by their long vigil.

# At Agincourt

The horses had suffered as-much as the men from damp, sleeplessness, and want of forage. There was, however, no want of confidence in the French army—all regarded victory as absolutely certain. As the English had lost by sickness since they left Harfleur fully a thousand men out of the 9,000, and as against these were arrayed at least a hundred thousand—some French historians estimate them at 150,000—comprising most of the chivalry of France, the latter might well regard victory as certain. There were, however, some who were not so confident; among these was the old Duke of Berri, who had fought at Poitiers sixty years before, and remembered how confident the French were on that occasion, and how disastrous was the defeat. His counsel that the English should be allowed to march on unmolested to Calais, had been scouted by the French leaders, but he had so far prevailed that the intention that Charles should place himself at the head of the army was abandoned.

"It would be better," the duke had urged, "to lose the battle than to lose the king and the battle together."

As soon as day broke the English were mustered and formed up, and three masses were celebrated at different points in order that all might hear. When this was done the force was formed up into three central divisions and two wings, but the divisions were placed so close together that they practically formed but one. The whole of the archers were placed in advance of the men-at-arms. Every archer, in addition to his arms, carried a long stake sharpened at both ends, that which was to project above the ground being armed with a sharp tip of iron. When the archers had taken up their positions these stakes were driven obliquely into the ground, each being firmly thrust in with the strength of two or three men. As the archers stood many lines deep, placed in open order and so that each could shoot between the heads of the men in front of him, there were sufficient stakes in front of the line to form a thick and almost impassable *chevaux-de-frise*. The baggage and horses were sent to the rear, near the village of Maisoncelles, under a guard of archers and men-at-arms. When all the arrangements were made, the king rode along the line from rank to rank, saying a few words of encouragement to each group of men. He recounted to them the victories that had been won against odds as great as those they had to encounter, and told them that he had made up his own mind to conquer or die, for that England should never have to pay ransom for him.

The archers he fired especially by reminding them that when the Orleanists had taken Soissons a few months before they had hung up like dogs three hundred English archers belonging to the garrison. He told them that they could expect no mercy, for that, as the French in other sieges had committed horrible atrocities upon their own countrymen and countrywomen, they would assuredly grant no mercy to the English; while the latter on their march had burned no town nor village, and had injured neither man nor woman, so that God would assuredly fight for them against their wicked foes. The king's manner as much as his words aroused the enthusiasm of the soldiers; his expression was calm, confident, and cheerful, he at least evidently felt no doubt of the issue.

The Duke of Berri had most strongly urged on the council that the French should not begin the attack. They had done so at Crecy and Poitiers with disastrous effect, and he urged them to await the assault of the English. The latter, however, had no intention of attacking, for Henry had calculated upon the confusion that would surely arise when the immense French army, crowded up between the two woods, endeavoured to advance. The men were therefore ordered to sit down on the ground, and food and some wine were served, out to them.

The constable was equally determined not to move; the French therefore also sat down, and for some hours the two armies watched each other. The constable had, however, some difficulty in maintaining his resolution. The Duke of Orleans and numbers of the hot-headed young nobles clamoured to be allowed to charge the English. He himself would gladly have waited until joined by large reinforcements under the Duke of Brittany and the Marshal de Loigny, who were both expected to arrive in the course of the day. As an excuse for the delay, rather than from any wish that his overtures should be accepted, he sent heralds to the English camp to offer Henry a free passage if he would restore Harfleur, with all the prisoners that he had made there and on his march, and resign his claims to the throne of France. Henry replied that he maintained the conditions he had laid down by his ambassadors, and that he would accept none others. He had, in fact, no wish to negotiate, for he, too, knew that the French would very shortly be largely reinforced, and that were he to delay his march, even for a day or two, his army would be starved.

Perceiving at last that the constable was determined not to begin the battle, he sent off two detachments from the rear of his army, so that their movements should be concealed from the sight of the French. One of these, composed of archers, was to take post in the wood on the left hand of the French, the other was to move on through the wood, to come down in their rear, and to set on fire some barns and houses there, and so create a panic. He waited until noon, by which time he thought that both detachments would have reached the posts assigned to them, and then gave the orders for the advance. The archers were delighted when their commander, Sir Thomas Erpingham, repeated the order. None of them had put on his armour, and many had thrown off their jerkins so as to have a freer use of their arms either for bow or axe. Each man plucked up his stake, and the whole moved forward in orderly array until within bow-shot of the enemy. Then the archers again stuck their stakes into the ground, and, taking up their position as before, raised a mighty shout as they let fly a volley of arrows into the enemy.

The shout was echoed from the wood on the French left, and the archers there at once plied their bows, and from both flank and front showers of arrows fell among the French. As originally formed up, the latter's van should have been covered by archers and cross-bowmen, but, from the anxiety of the knights and nobles to be first to attack, the footmen had been pushed back to the rear, a position which they were doubtless not sorry to occupy, remembering how at Crecy the cross-bowmen had been trampled down and slain by the French knights, desirous of getting through them to attack the English. Therefore, there stood none between the archers and the French array of knights, and the latter suffered heavily from the rain of arrows. Sir Clugnet de Brabant was the first to take the offensive, and with twelve hundred men-at-arms charged down upon the archers with loud shouts. The horses, however, were stiff and weary from standing so long in order; the deep and slippery ground, and the weight of their heavily-armed riders caused them to stagger and stumble, and the storm of arrows that smote them as soon as they got into motion added to the disorder.

So accurate was the aim of the archers, that most of the arrows struck the knights on their helmets and vizors. Many fell shot through the brain, and so terrible was the rain of arrows that all had to bend down their heads so as to save their faces. Many of the archers, too, shot at the horses; some of these were killed and many wounded, and the latter swerving and turning aside added to the confusion. And when at length Sir Clugnet and the leaders reached the line of stakes in front of the archers, only about a hundred and fifty of the twelve hundred men were behind them.

The horses drew up on reaching the hedge of stakes. Their riders could give them no guidance, for without deigning to move from their order the archers continued to keep up their storm of arrows, which at such close quarters pierced all but the very finest armour, while it was certain death to the knights to raise their heads to get a glance at the situation. The horses, maddened with the pain of the arrows, soon settled the matter. Some turned and rushed off madly, carrying confusion into the ranks of the first division, others galloped off to the right or left, and of the twelve hundred men who charged, three only broke through the line of stakes, and these were instantly killed by the bill-hooks and axes of the archers.

The second line of battle was now in disorder, broken by the fugitive men and horses of Sir Clugnet's party, smitten with the arrows to which they had been exposed as that party melted away, and by those of the English archers in the wood on their flank. The confusion heightened every moment as wounded knights tried to withdraw from the fight, and others from behind struggled to take their places in front. Soon the disorder became terrible. The archers plucked up their stakes and ran forward; the French line recoiled at their approach in order to get into fairer order; and the archers, with loud shouts of victory, slung their bows behind them, dropped the stakes, and with axe and bill-hook rushed at the horsemen. These were too tightly wedged together to use their lances, and as they had retired they had come into newly-ploughed ground, which had been so soaked by the heavy rain that the horses sank in the deep mud to their knees, many almost to their bellies. Into the midst of this helpless crowd of armed men the English archers burst. Embarrassed by their struggling horses, scarcely able to wield their arms in the press, seeing but scantily, and that only in front through the narrow slits of their vizors, the chivalry of France died almost unresistingly.

The Constable of France and many of the highest nobles and most distinguished knights fell, and but few of the first line made their escape: these, passing through the second division, in order to draw up behind, threw this also into some confusion. The Duke de Brabant, who had just arrived on the field, charged down upon the flank of the archers. These met him fearlessly, and he and most of those with him were killed. This fight had, however, given time to the second division to close up their ranks. The archers would have attacked them, but the king caused the signal for them to halt to be sounded, and riding up formed them in order again. The French were unable to take advantage of the moment to try and recover their lost ground, for the horses were knee-deep in the ground, upon which they had all night been trampling, and into which the weight of their own and their riders' armour sunk them deeply.

"Now, my lords," the king said, turning to those around him, "our brave archers have done their share; it is our turn;" and then, as arranged, all dismounted and marched forward against the enemy.

In accordance with his orders, Sir Eustace de Villeroy and Guy were posted close to the king, while John Harpen led the men-at-arms from Summerley. For a time the battle raged fiercely. In the centre fought the king with his nobles and knights; while the archers, who had most of them thrown off their shoes and were able to move lightly over the treacherous ground, threw themselves upon the enemy's flanks, and did dreadful execution there. In the centre, however, the progress of the English was slower. The French knights made the most desperate efforts to attack the king himself, and pressed forward to reach the royal banner. His brother, the Duke of Clarence, was wounded, and would have been killed had not the king himself, with a few of his knights, taken post around him, and kept off the attacks of his foes until he recovered his feet. Almost immediately afterwards a band of eighteen knights, under the banner of the Lord of Croye, who had bound themselves by an oath to take or kill the king, charged down upon him. One of them struck him so heavy a blow on the head with a mace that the king was beaten to his knee, but his knights closed in round him, and every one of his assailants was killed.

The Duke of Alençon next charged down with a strong following; he cut his way to the royal standard, and struck the Duke of York dead with a blow of his battle-axe. Henry sprung forward, but Alençon's weapon again fell, and striking him on the head clipped off a portion of the crown which Henry wore round his helmet. But before the French knight could repeat the stroke Guy Aylmer sprung forward and struck so heavy a blow full on the duke's vizor that he fell from his horse dead. His fall completed the confusion and dismay among the French, and the second division of their army, which had hitherto fought gallantly, now gave way. Many were taken prisoners. The third division, although alone vastly superior in numbers to the English, seeing the destruction of the others, began to draw off. They had moved but a short distance when loud shouts were heard in the English rear. Two or three French knights, with a body of several hundred armed peasants, had suddenly fallen upon the English baggage and horses which had been left at Maisoncelles. Many of the guard had gone off to join in the battle, so that the attack was successful, a portion of the baggage, including the king's own wardrobe, and a great number of horses being captured.

Ignorant of the strength of the attacking party, Henry believed that it was the reinforcements under the Duke of Brittany that had come up. At the same moment the third division of the French, whose leaders were also similarly deceived, halted and faced round. Believing that he was about to be attacked in front and rear by greatly superior forces, Henry gave the order that all prisoners should be killed, and the order was to a great extent executed before the real nature of the attack was discovered and the order countermanded. The third division of the French now continued its retreat, and the battle was over. There remained but to examine the field and see who had fallen.

The king gave at once the name of Agincourt to the battle, as this village possessed a castle, and was therefore the most important of those near which the fight had taken place. Properly the name should have been Azincourt, as this was the French spelling of the village. The loss of the French was terrible, and their chivalry had suffered even more than at Poitiers. Several of the relations of the French king were killed. The Duke of Brabant, the Count de Nevers, the Duke of Bar and his two brothers, the constable, and the Duke of Alençon all perished. No less than a hundred and twenty great lords were killed, and eight thousand nobles, knights, and esquires lost their lives, with some thousands of lower degree, while the Duke of Orleans, the Duke of Bourbon, and many others were taken prisoners.

The accounts of the English loss differ considerably, the highest placing it at sixteen hundred, the lowest at one-fourth of that number. The plunder taken by them in the shape of costly armour, arms, rich garments, and the trappings of horses, was great; but of food there was but little, many of the victors lay down supperless around the village of Maisoncelles.

The knights who had led the peasants to the attack of the baggage-train, instead of joining in the fight, and had thereby caused the unfortunate massacre of so many prisoners, fell into great disgrace among the French for their conduct, and were imprisoned for some years by the Duke of Burgundy.

That evening the English king knighted many esquires and aspirants of noble families, among them Guy Aylmer, who was indeed the first to receive the honour.

"No one fought more bravely than you did, young knight," he said, as Guy rose to his feet after receiving the accolade; "I will see that you have lands to support your new dignity. Twice you were at my side when I was in the greatest danger, and none have won their spurs more fairly."

John Harpen would also have been among those knighted, but he declined the honour, saying that he was not come of gentle blood, and wished for nothing better than to remain his lord's esquire so long as he had strength to follow him in the field.

The next morning the army marched to Calais. The king turned aside with Sir Eustace, and with a strong party rode to Villeroy. Guy had gone on with the men-at-arms at daybreak, and a banquet had been prepared, and twenty cartloads of grain and a hundred bullocks sent off to meet the army on its march.

"'Tis a fine castle, Sir Eustace," the king said as he rode in, "but truly it is perilously situated. If after this I can make good terms with France I will see that the border shall run outside your estates; but if not, methinks that it were best for you to treat with some French noble for its sale, and I will see that you are equally well bestowed in England, for in truth, after fighting for us at Agincourt, you are like to have but little peace here."

"I would gladly do so, my lord king," Sir Eustace replied. "During the last three years it has been a loss rather than a gain to me. I have had to keep a large garrison here; the estate has been wasted, and the houses and barns burned. Had it not been that there was for most of the time a truce between England and France I should have fared worse. And now I may well be attacked as soon as your majesty and the army cross to England."

"You will have a little breathing time," the king said; "they will have enough to do for a while to mourn their losses. I will not leave behind any of your brave fellows who have fought so hard here, but when I arrive at Calais will order two hundred men of the garrison to come over to reinforce you until you can make arrangements to get rid of the castle, if it is not to remain within my territory."

Sir Eustace introduced Sir John Aylmer as the father of the newly-made knight.

"You have a gallant son, Sir John," the king said, "and one who is like to make his way to high distinction. I doubt not that before we have done with the French he will have fresh opportunities of proving his valour."

After the meal was over the king went round the walls.

"'Tis a strong place," he said, "and yet unless aid reached you, you could not resist an army with cannon and machines."

"I have long seen that, your majesty, and have felt that I should have to choose between England and France, for that, when war broke out again, I could not remain a vassal of both countries."

"It shall be my duty to show you that you have not chosen wrongly, Sir Eustace. I cannot promise to maintain you here, for you might be attacked when I have no army with which I could succour you. As soon as I return home and learn which of those who have fallen have left no heirs, and whose lands therefore have come into my gift, I will then make choice of a new estate for you."

The army marched slowly to Calais. It was weakened by sickness and hunger, and every man was borne down by the weight of the booty he carried. On arriving there the king held a council, and it was finally determined to return to England. The force under his command was now but the skeleton of an army. Fresh men and money were required to continue the war, and he accordingly set sail, carrying with him his long train of royal and noble prisoners. The news of the victory created the greatest enthusiasm in England. At Dover the people rushed into the sea and carried the king to shore on their shoulders. At Canterbury and the other towns through which he passed he received an enthusiastic welcome, while his entry into London was a triumph. Every house was decorated, the conduits ran with wine instead of water, and the people were wild with joy and enthusiasm. Great subsidies were granted him by Parliament, and the people in their joy would have submitted to any taxation. However, throughout his reign Henry always showed the greatest moderation; he kept well within constitutional usages, and his pleasant, affable manner secured for him throughout his reign the love and devotion of his subjects.

On his arrival at Calais Guy discovered that among the prisoners was his friend Count Charles d'Estournel.

"I am grieved indeed to see you in this plight," he exclaimed as he met him.

"'Tis unfortunate truly, Aylmer, but it might have been worse; better a prisoner than among the dead at Agincourt," the light-hearted young count said; "but truly it has been an awful business. Who could have dreamt of it? I thought myself that the council were wrong when they refused all the offers of the towns to send bodies of footmen to fight beside us; had they been there, they might have faced those terrible archers of yours, for they at least would have been free to fight when we were all but helpless in that quagmire. I see that you have knightly spurs on, and I congratulate you."

"Now, Count, what can I do to ensure your release at once? Whose prisoner are you?"

"I surrendered to one John Parsons, an esquire, and I shall, of course, as soon as we get to England, send home to raise money for my ransom."

"I know him well," Guy said; "his lord's tent was pitched alongside that of Sir Eustace, before Harfleur, and we saw much of each other, and often rode together on the march. If I gave him my guarantee for your ransom, I doubt not that he will take your pledge, and let you depart at once."

"I should be glad indeed if you would do so, Aylmer."

"At any rate he will take the guarantee of Sir Eustace," Guy said, "which will, I know, be given readily, after the service you rendered to his dame, and it may be that you will have it in your power to do him a service in return." He then told the count of the intention of Sir Eustace to sell the estate, or rather to arrange for its transfer.

"It is held directly from the crown," he said, "but just at present the crown is powerless. Artois is everywhere Burgundian, and it would certainly be greatly to the advantage of Burgundy that it should be held by one of his followers, while it would be to the safety of France that it should be held by a Frenchman, rather than by one who is also a vassal of England."

"I should think that that could be managed," the count said thoughtfully. "I will speak to my father. I am, as you know, his second son, but through my mother, who is a German, I have an estate on the other side of the

Rhine. This I would gladly exchange—that is to say, would part with to some German baron—if I could obtain the fief of Villeroy. I have no doubt that Burgundy would not only consent, but would help, for, as you know by the manner in which your lady was made a hostage, he looked with great jealousy on this frontier fortress, which not only gives a way for the English into Artois, but which would, in the hands of an Orleanist, greatly aid an invasion of the province from Pontoise and the west. And, although the court would just at present object to give the fief to a Burgundian, it is powerless to interfere, and when the troubles are over, the duke would doubtless be able to manage it."

Guy had no difficulty in arranging the matter with D'Estournel's captor, to whom Sir Eustace and he both gave their surety that his ransom should be paid; and, before sailing, Guy had the satisfaction of seeing his friend mount and ride for St. Omar with a pass through the English territory from the governor.

# CHAPTER XX — PENSHURST

After accompanying the king to London Sir Eustace and Guy rode to Summerley, where Long Tom and his companions had already arrived, having marched thither direct from Dover. There were great rejoicings at the castle. Not only the tenants, but people from a long way round came in to join in welcoming home two of the heroes of Agincourt. The archer had already brought news of Guy having been knighted, and he was warmly, congratulated by Dame Margaret and by Agnes, who received him with her usual sisterly affection. Katarina, also, congratulated him, but it was with less warmth of manner. In the evening, how ever, her mood changed, and she said to him:

"Though I do not say much, you know that I am pleased, Sir Guy."

"KATARINA SWEPT A DEEP CURTSEY, AND WENT OFF WITH A
MERRY LAUGH,"

"I am not sure, Countess Katarina—since we are to be ceremonious to
each other—that I do quite know, for since I returned from France last time,
I have seldom understood you; one moment you seem to me just as you

used to be, at another you hold me at a distance, as if I were well-nigh a stranger."

Katarina shrugged her shoulders. "What would you have, Guy? One can't be always in the same humour."

"You are always in the same humour to Dame Margaret and Agnes," he said; "so far as I can see I am the only one whom you delight to tease."

"Now that you are a belted knight, Sir Guy, I shall not presume to tease you any more, but shall treat you with the respect due to your dignity." Then she swept a deep curtsey, and turning, went off with a merry laugh, while Guy looked after her more puzzled than ever.

That evening he received the news that during the absence of Sir Eustace and himself Sir William Bailey, a young knight whose estates lay near, had asked for the hand of Agnes, and that, although Dame Margaret had been unable to give an answer during her lord's absence, Agnes would willingly submit herself to her father's orders to wed Sir William.

Guy remained for some months quietly at Summerley. The Emperor Sigismund had paid a visit to England, and then to Paris, to endeavour to reconcile the two countries. His mediation failed. Henry offered, as a final settlement, to accept the execution, on the part of France, of the treaty of Trepigny. Nothing, however, came of it, for there was no government in France capable of making a binding treaty. In spite of the disgrace and the slaughter of the nobles at Agincourt there was no abatement of the internal dissensions, and the civil war between Burgundy and Armagnac was still raging, the only change in affairs being that the vicious and incapable Duke of Aquitaine had died, and the queen had once again gone over to the Burgundian faction. Count Charles d'Estournel had carried into effect the mission with which he had charged himself. Burgundy had eagerly embraced the opportunity of attaching to his side the castle and estates of Villeroy, and he and the Count d'Estournel between them raised a sum of money which was paid to Sir Eustace for the relinquishment to Burgundy of the fief, which was then bestowed upon Count Charles.

The sum in no way represented what would now be considered the value of the estate, but in those days, when fiefs reverted to the crown or other feudal superior upon the death of an owner without heirs, or were confiscated upon but slight pretence, the money value was far under the real value of the estate. Sir Eustace was well satisfied, however, with the sum paid him. Had his son Henry lived he had intended that the anomalous position of the lord of Villeroy, being also a vassal of England, should have been got rid of by one of his sons becoming its owner, and a vassal of France, while the other would inherit Summerley, and grow up a vassal of

# At Agincourt

England only. Henry's death had put an end to the possibility of this arrangement, and Charlie would now become, at his father's death, Lord of Summerley and of such other English lands as could be obtained with the money paid for the surrender of the fief of Villeroy.

In the first week of July there were great rejoicings at Summerley over the marriage of Agnes with Sir William Bailey. The king had not forgotten his promise to Sir Eustace, and had raised him to the title of Baron Eustace of Summerley, and had presented him with a royal manor near Winchester. Guy was summoned to court to take part in the festivities that were held during the visit of Sigismund, and the king said to him pleasantly one day:

"I have not forgotten you, Sir Guy; but I have had many to reward, and you know importunate suitors, and those who have powerful connections to keep their claims ever in front, obtain an advantage over those who are content to hold themselves in the back-ground."

"I am in all ways contented, your majesty. I have lived all my life in the household at Summerley, and am so much one of my lord's family that I have no desire to quit it. Moreover, my father has just returned from Villeroy with the garrison of the castle, and it is a great pleasure to me to have his society again."

"I thought that some day you would have married Dame Margaret's fair daughter, after acting as their protector in the troubles in Paris, but I hear that she is betrothed to Sir William Bailey."

"Such an idea never entered my mind, your majesty. She was but a child in those days, not so much in years as in thought, and brought up together as we were I have always regarded her rather in the light of a sister."

Guy's quiet stay at Summerley came to an end suddenly. A fortnight after the marriage of Agnes, Harfleur was besieged by the French by land and water, and the Earl of Dorset, its governor, sent to England for aid. The king sent hasty orders to his vassals of Kent, Surrey, and Hampshire, to march with their retainers to Rye, where a fleet was to gather for their conveyance. A body of archers and men-at-arms were also sent thither by the king, and the Duke of Bedford, his brother, appointed to the command of the expedition. Sir Eustace was suffering somewhat from the effects of a fever, the seeds of which he had contracted in France, and he accordingly sent his contingent, thirty archers and as many men-at-arms, under the command of Guy.

"I had hoped that we had done with Harfleur," Long Tom said as they started on their march to the seaport. "I don't mind fighting, that comes in the way of business, but to see men rotting away like sheep with disease is not to my fancy."

"We shall have no fighting on land, Tom," Guy replied, "at least I expect not. When the French see that the garrison is reinforced they will probably give up the siege, though we may have a fight at sea with the French ships that are blockading the town and preventing provisions from reaching the garrison. Doubtless we shall take a good store of food with us, and the French will know well enough that as we had such hard work in capturing the town, they can have no chance whatever of taking it by assault when defended by us."

Guy and his party had a small ship to themselves, with which he was well content, as, being but a newly-made knight, he would, had he been in a large ship, have been under the orders of any others who chanced to be with him; while he was now free to act as he chose. The voyage was favourable, but when the fleet arrived off the mouth of the Seine they found that the work before them was far more serious than they had expected. In addition to their own fleet, which was itself considerably stronger than the English, the besiegers had hired the aid of some great Genoese vessels, and a number of galleys, caravels, and many high-decked ships from Spain. They occupied a strong position off the town, and could be supported by some of the siege batteries. The English fleet lay to at the mouth of the Seine, and at night the captains of the troops on board the various ships were rowed to Bedford's ship, which displayed a light at the mast-head, so that the fleet could all lie in company round her. Here after much discussion a plan for the battle next day was agreed upon. The enterprise would have been a very hazardous one, but, happily, at daybreak the French ships were seen coming out to give battle. Confident in their superior numbers, and anxious to revenge their defeat at Agincourt, the French commanders were eager to reap the whole glory of victory without the assistance of their allies, whose ships remained anchored in the river.

Bedford at once made the signal to attack them, and a desperate fight ensued. Great as was the slaughter in those days in battles on land, it was far greater in sea-fights. Except to knights and nobles, from whom ransom could be obtained, quarter was never given to prisoners either by land or sea, consequently as soon as soldiers in a land battle saw that fortune was going against them they fled. But on sea there was no escape; every man knew that it was either death or victory, and therefore fought with determination and obstinacy to the end. The two first French ships that arrived were speedily captured, but when the rest came up a desperate battle took place. Guy was on the point of ordering his ship to be laid alongside a French craft little larger than his own, when his eye fell upon a great ship carrying the flag of a French admiral, and at once diverting the course of his vessel, he ran alongside her. The archers were on the bow and stern castles of his ship, and as they came within a short distance of the Frenchman, they sent their arrows thick and fast into the crowded mass on her deck. Two grapnels, to each of which were attached twenty feet of chain, were thrown into the shrouds of the French vessel, and Guy shouted to the men-at-arms in the waist to keep the enemy from boarding by holding the vessels apart by thrusting out light spars and using their spears.

The French had a few cross-bowmen on board, but Guy, running up on to the castle at the bow, where Long Tom himself was posted, bade him direct the fire of his men solely against them, and in a very short time the discharge of missiles from the French ship ceased. In vain the French attempted to bring the ships alongside each other by throwing grapnels; the ropes of these were cut directly they fell, and although many of the English spears were hacked in two, others were at once thrust out, and the spars, being inclined so as to meet the hull of the enemy below the water-line, could not be reached by their axes. The wind was light, and there was no great difference in point of sailing. The English sailors were vigilant, and when the Frenchman brailed up his great sail, so as to fall behind, they at once followed his example. At the end of a quarter of an hour the effect of the arrows of the thirty archers was so great that there was much confusion on board the enemy, and Guy thought that, comparatively small as his force was, an attack might be made. So the spars were suddenly drawn in and the chains hauled upon. The archers caught up their axes and joined the men-at-arms, and as the vessels came together they all leapt with a great shout upon the enemy's deck.

The French knights, whose armour had protected them to some extent from the slaughter that the arrows had effected among the soldiers, fought bravely and rallied their men to resistance; but with shouts of "Agincourt!" the men-at-arms and archers, led by Guy,—who now for the first time fought in his knightly armour,—were irresistible. They had boarded at the enemy's stern so as to get all their foes in front of them, and after clearing the stern castle they poured down into the waist and gradually won their way along it. After ten minutes' hard fighting the French admiral and knights were pent up on the fore castle, and defended the ladder by which it was approached so desperately that Guy ordered Tom, with a dozen of the archers, to betake themselves to the English fore castle and to shoot from there, and in a short time the French leaders lowered their swords and surrendered. The French flag at the stern had been hauled down and that of England hoisted as soon as they boarded, and the latter was now run up to the mast-head amid the loud hurrahs of the English.

The moment the French surrendered, Guy called to his men to cease from slaying and to disarm the prisoners, who were still much more numerous than themselves. The common men he told to take to their boats and row away, while the admiral and knights were conducted to the cabin, and a guard placed over them. As soon as this was done Guy looked round; the battle was still raging and many of the French ships had been captured, but others were defending themselves desperately. Twelve of Guy's men had been killed, and several of the others more or less severely wounded, and seeing that his countrymen did not need his assistance, he ordered the decks to be cleared and the dead bodies thrown overboard. In a quarter of an hour, the last French ship had been taken. There was now breathing time for half an hour, during which the Duke of Bedford, whose ship lay not far from Guy's prize, had himself rowed on board.

"All have done well to-day, Sir Guy Aylmer, but assuredly the feat you have performed surpasses any of the others, seeing that you have captured this great ship with one of the smallest in our fleet. Their crew must have been three or four times as strong as yours, which was, as I know, but sixty strong. Has the Count de Valles fallen?"

"No, my lord duke, he is, with six of his knights, a prisoner in the cabin."

"I will see him later," the duke said; "we are now going to attack the Genoese and Spaniards. Is there aught that I can do for you?"

"Some twenty of my men are dead or disabled," Guy said, "and I must leave ten in charge of this prize. I have suffered the French soldiers, after disarming them and the sailors, to leave in their boats, and ten men will therefore be sufficient to hold her. If your grace can spare me thirty men-at-arms I will go on in my own ship to attack the Genoese."

"I will do so," the duke replied. "I will send ten to keep this ship, and twenty to fill the places of those of your men who have fallen. I can spare ten from my own ship and will borrow twenty from such of the others as can best spare them."

In a few minutes the thirty men came on board, with a sub-officer to take charge of the prize. Guy returned with his own men and twenty new-comers to his vessel, and sailed in with the fleet to attack the great ships of the Genoese and Spaniards at their moorings. As they approached they were received with a heavy cannonade from the enemy's ships and shore batteries, but without replying they sailed on and ranged themselves alongside the enemy, their numbers permitting them to lay a vessel on each side of most of the great caravels. Their task was by no means an easy one, for the sides of these ships were fifteen feet above those of the low English vessels, and they were all crowded with men. Nevertheless, the English succeeded in boarding, forcing their way in through port-holes and windows, clambering up the bows by the carved work, or running out on their yards and swinging themselves by ropes on to the enemy's deck, while the cannon plied them with shot close to the water-line.

Most of the ships were taken by boarding, some were sunk with all on board, a few only escaped by cutting their cables and running up the Seine into shallow water. The loss of life on the part of the French and their allies in this brilliant British victory was enormous. With the exception of those on board the few ships which escaped, and the men sent off in the boats by Guy, the whole of the crews of the French, Genoese, and Spaniards, save only the nobles and knights put to ransom, were killed, drowned, or taken prisoners, and during the three weeks that the English fleet remained off Harfleur, the sailors were horrified by the immense number of dead bodies that were carried up and down by the tide. Harfleur was revictualled and put into a state of defence, and the Duke of Bedford then sailed with his fleet to England, having achieved the greatest naval victory that England had ever won save when Edward the Third, with the Black Prince, completely defeated a great Spanish fleet off the coast of Sussex, with a squadron composed of ships vastly inferior both in size and number to those of the Spaniards, which contained fully ten times the number of fighting men carried by the English vessels.

This great naval victory excited unbounded enthusiasm in England. The king gave a great banquet to the Duke of Bedford and his principal officers, and by the duke's orders Guy attended. Before they sat down to the table the duke presented his officers individually to the king. Guy, as the youngest knight, was the last to be introduced.

"The duke has already spoken to me of the right valiant deeds that you accomplished, Sir Guy Aylmer," the king said as he bowed before him, "and that with but a small craft and only sixty men-at-arms and archers you captured the ship of the French admiral, which he estimates must have carried at least three hundred men. We hereby raise you to the rank of knight-banneret, and appoint you to the fief of Penshurst in Hampshire, now vacant by the death without heirs of the good knight Sir Richard Fulk. And we add thereto, as our own gift, the two royal manors of Stoneham and Piverley lying adjacent to it, and we enjoin you to take for your coat-of-arms a great ship. The fief of Penshurst is a sign of our royal approval of your bravery at Harfleur, the two manors are the debt we owe you for your service at Agincourt. We have ordered our chancellor to make out the deeds, and tomorrow you will receive them from him and take the oaths."

Guy knelt and kissed the hand that the king held out to him, and acknowledged the royal gift in fitting words. On the following day, after taking the oaths for his new possessions, he mounted, and the next day rode into Summerley. Here to his surprise he found the Count of Montepone, who had arrived, by way of Calais and Dover, a few days previously. He was suffering from a severe wound, and when Guy entered rose feebly from a chair by the fire, for it was now October and the weather was cold. His daughter was sitting beside him, and Lady Margaret was also in the room. Lord Eustace and Sir John Aylmer had met Guy as he dismounted below.

"So you have gone through another adventure and come out safely," the count said after Guy had greeted him. "Truly you have changed greatly since you left Paris, well-nigh three years ago. It was well that Maître Leroux had the armour made big for you, for I see that it is now none too large. I too, you see, have been at war; but it was one in which there was small honour, though, as you see, with some risk, for it was a private duel forced upon me by one of the Armagnac knights. Up to that time my predictions had wrought me much profit and no harm. I had told Aquitaine and other lords who consulted me that disaster would happen when the French army met the English. That much I read in the stars. And though, when Henry marched north from Harfleur with so small a following, it seemed to me that victory could scarce attend him against the host of France, I went over my calculations many times and could not find that I had made an error. It was owing greatly to my predictions that the duke readily gave way when the great lords persuaded him not to risk his life in the battle.

"Others whom I had warned went to their death, in some cases because they disbelieved me, in others because they preferred death to the dishonour of drawing back. One of the latter, on the eve of the battle, confided to a hot-headed knight in his following that I had foretold his death; and instead of quarrelling with the stars, the fool seemed to think that I had controlled them, and was responsible for his lord's death. So when in Paris some months since, he publicly insulted me, and being an Italian noble as well as an astrologer, I fought him the next day. I killed him, but not before I received a wound that laid me up for months, and from which I have not yet fairly recovered. While lying in Paris I decided upon taking a step that I had for some time been meditating. I could, when Katarina left Paris with your lady, have well gone with her, with ample means to live in comfort and to furnish her with a fortune not unfitted to her rank as my daughter.

"During the past three years the reputation I gained by my success in saving the lives of several persons of rank, increased so rapidly that money has flowed into my coffers beyond all belief. There was scarcely a noble of the king's party who had not consulted me, and since Agincourt the Duke of Aquitaine and many others took no step whatever without coming to me. But I am weary of the everlasting troubles of which I can see no end, and assuredly the aspect of the stars affords no ground for hope that they will terminate for years; therefore, I have determined to leave France, and to practise my art henceforth solely for my own pleasure, I shall open negotiations with friends in Mantua, to see whether, now that twelve years have elapsed since I had to fly, matters cannot be arranged with my enemies; much can often be done when there are plenty of funds wherewith to smooth away difficulties. Still, that is in the future. My first object in coming to England was to see how my daughter was faring, and to enjoy a period of rest and quiet while my wound was healing, which it has begun to do since I came here. I doubted on my journey, which has been wholly performed in a litter, whether I should arrive here alive."

"And now, father," Katarina said, "let us hear what Sir Guy has been doing since he left; we have been all full of impatience since the news came four days ago that the Duke of Bedford had destroyed a great fleet of French, Spanish, and Genoese ships."

"Guy has had his share of fighting, at any rate," Lord Eustace said, as he entered the room while the girl was speaking, "for fifteen of our men have fallen; and, as Long Tom tells me, they had hot work of it, and gained much credit by capturing single-handed a great French ship."

"Yes, we were fortunate," Guy said, "in falling across the ship of the French admiral, Count de Valles. Our men all fought stoutly, and the archers having cleared the way for us and slain many of their crew, we captured them, and I hold the count and five French knights to ransom."

"That will fill your purse rarely, Guy. But let us hear more of this fighting. De Valles's ship must have been a great one, and if you took it with but your own sixty men it must have been a brilliant action."

Guy then gave a full account of the fight, and of the subsequent capture of one of the Spanish carracks with the aid of another English ship.

"If the Duke of Bedford himself came on board," Lord Eustace said, "and sent you some reinforcements, he must have thought highly of the action; indeed he cannot but have done so, or he would not have come personally on board. Did he speak to the king of it?"

"He did, and much more strongly, it seems to me, than the affair warranted, for at the banquet the day before yesterday his majesty was graciously pleased to appoint me a knight-banneret, and to bestow upon me the estates of Penshurst, adding thereto the royal manors of Stoneham and Piverley."

"A right royal gift!" Lord Eustace said, while exclamations of pleasure broke from the others.

"I congratulate you on your new honour, which you have right worthily earned. Sir John, you may well be proud of this son of yours."

"I am so, indeed," Sir John Aylmer said heartily. "I had hoped well of the lad, but had not deemed that he would mount so rapidly. Sir Richard Fulk had a fine estate, and joined now to the two manors it will be as large as those of Summerley, even with its late additions."

"I am very glad," Dame Margaret said, "that the king has apportioned you an estate so near us, for it is scarce fifteen miles to Penshurst, and it will be but a morning ride for you to come hither."

"Methinks, wife," Lord Eustace said with a smile, "we were somewhat hasty in that matter of Sir William Bailey, for had we but waited Agnes might have done better."

"She chose for herself," Dame Margaret replied with an answering smile. "I say not that in my heart I had not hoped at one time that she and Guy might have come together, for I had learnt to love him almost as if he had been my own, and would most gladly have given Agnes to him had it been your wish as well as theirs; but I have seen for some time past that it was not to be, for they were like brother and sister to each other, and neither had any thought of a still closer relation. Had it not been so I should never have favoured Sir William Bailey's suit, though indeed he is a worthy young man, and Agnes is happy with him. You have not been to your castle yet, Guy?" she asked, suddenly changing the subject.

"No, indeed, Lady Margaret, I rode straight here from London, deeming this, as methinks that I shall always deem it, my home."

"We must make up a party to ride over and see it to-morrow," Lord Eustace said. "We will start early, wife, and you and Katarina can ride with us. Charlie will of course go, and Sir John. We could make a horse-litter for the count, if he thinks he could bear the journey.

"Methinks that I had best stay quietly here," the Italian said. "I have had enough of litters for a time, and the shaking might make my wound angry again."

"Nonsense, child!" he broke off as Katarina whispered that she would stay with him; "I need no nursing now; you shall ride with the rest."

Accordingly the next day the party started early. Charlie was in high spirits; he had grown into a sturdy boy, and was delighted at the good fortune that had befallen Guy, whom he had regarded with boundless admiration since the days in Paris. Katarina was in one of her silent moods, and rode close to Lady Margaret. Long Tom, who was greatly rejoiced on hearing of the honours and estates that had been bestowed on Guy, rode with two of his comrades in the rear of the party. Penshurst was a strong castle, though scarcely equal in size to Summerley; it was, however, a more comfortable habitation, having been altered by the late owner's father, who had travelled in Italy, with a view rather to the accommodation of its inmates than its defence, and had been furnished with many articles of luxury rare in England.

"A comfortable abode truly, Guy!" his father said. "It was well enough two hundred years since, when the country was unsettled, for us to pen ourselves up within walls, but there is little need of it now in England, although in France, where factions are constantly fighting against each other, it is well that every man should hold himself secure from attack. But now that cannon are getting to so great a point of perfection, walls are only useful to repel sudden attacks, and soon crumble when cannon can be brought against them. Me thinks the time will come when walls will be given up altogether, especially in England, where the royal power is so strong that nobles can no longer war with each other."

"However, Guy," Lord Eustace said, "'tis as well at present to have walls, and strong ones; and though I say not that this place is as strong as Villeroy, it is yet strong enough to stand a siege."

Guy spent an hour with the steward, who had been in charge of the castle since the death of Sir Richard Fulk, and who had the day before heard from a royal messenger that Sir Guy had been appointed lord of the estates. The new owner learned from him much about the extent of the feu, the number of tenants, the strength that he would be called upon to furnish in case of war, and the terms on which the vassals held their tenure.

"Your force will be well-nigh doubled," the steward said in conclusion, "since you tell me that the manors of Stoneham and Piverley have also fallen to you."

"'Tis a fair country," Guy said as the talk ended, "and one could wish for no better. I shall return to Summerley to-day, but next Monday I will come over here and take possession, and you can bid the tenants, and those also of the two manors, to come hither and meet me at two o'clock."

"Well, daughter," the Count of Montepone said to Katarina as she was sitting by his couch in the evening, "so you think that Penshurst is a comfortable abode?"

"Yes, father, the rooms are brighter and lighter than these and the walls are all hung with arras and furnished far more comfortably."

"Wouldst thou like to be its mistress, child?"

A bright flush of colour flooded the girl's face.

"Dost mean it, father?" she asked in a voice hardly above a whisper.

"Why not, child? You have seen much of this brave young knight, whom, methinks, any maiden might fall in love with. Art thou not more sensible to his merits than was Mistress Agnes?"

"He saved my life, father."

"That did he, child, and at no small risk to his own: Then do I understand that such a marriage would be to your liking?"

"Yes, father," she said frankly, "but I know not that it would be to Sir Guy's."

"That is for me to find out," he said. "I asked Lady Margaret a few days ago what she thought of the young knight's inclinations, and she told me that she thought indeed he had a great liking for you, but that in truth you were so wayward that you gave him but little chance of showing it."

"How could I let him see that I cared for him, father, when I knew not for certain that he thought aught of me, and moreover, I could not guess what your intentions for me might be."

"I should not have sent you where you would often be in his company, Katarina, unless I had thought the matter over deeply. It was easy to foresee that after the service he had rendered you you would think well of him, and that, thrown together as you would be, it was like enough that you should come to love each other. I had cast your horoscope and his and found that you would both be married about the same time, though I could not say that it would be to each other. I saw enough of him during that time in Paris to see that he was not only brave, but prudent and discreet. I saw, too, from his affection to his mistress, that he would be loyal and honest in all he undertook, that it was likely that he would rise to honour, and that above all I could assuredly trust your happiness to him. He was but a youth and you a girl, but he was bordering upon manhood and you upon womanhood. I marked his manner with his lady's daughter and saw that she would be no rival to you. Had it been otherwise I should have yielded to your prayers, and have kept you with me in France. Matters have turned out according to my expectation. I can give you a dowry that any English noble would think an ample one with his bride; and though Guy is now himself well endowed he will doubtless not object to such an addition as may enable him, if need be, to place in the field a following as large as that which many of the great nobles are bound to furnish to their sovereign. I will speak to him on the subject to-morrow, Katarina."

Accordingly, the next morning at breakfast the count told Guy that there was a matter on which he wished to consult him, and the young knight remained behind when the other members of the family left the room to carry out their avocations.

"Hast thought of a mistress for your new castle, Sir Guy?" the count began abruptly.

Guy started at the sudden question, and did not reply at once.

"I have thought of one, Count," he said; "but although, so far, all that you told me long ago in Paris has come true, and fortune has favoured me wonderfully, in this respect she has not been kind, for the lady cares not for me, and I would not take a wife who came not to me willingly."

"How know you that she cares not for you?" the count asked.

"Because I have eyes and ears, Count. She thinks me but a boy, and a somewhat ill-mannered one. She mocks me when I try to talk to her, shuns being left alone with me, and in all ways shows that she has no inclination towards me, but very much the contrary."

"Have you asked her straightforwardly?" the count inquired with a smile.

"No, I should only be laughed at for my pains, and it would take more courage than is required to capture a great French ship for me to put the matter to her."

"I fancy, Sir Guy, that you are not greatly versed in female ways. A woman defends herself like a beleaguered fortress. She makes sorties and attacks, she endeavours to hide her weakness by her bravados, and when she replies most disdainfully to a summons to capitulate, is perhaps on the eve of surrender. To come to the point, then, are you speaking of my daughter?"

"I am, Sir Count," Guy said frankly. "I love her, but she loves me not, and there is an end of it. 'Tis easy to understand that, beautiful as she is, she should not give a thought to me who, at the best, can only claim to be a stout man-at-arms; as for my present promotion, I know that it goes for nothing in her eyes."

"It may be as you say, Sir Guy; but tell me, as a soldier, before you gave up the siege of a fortress and retired would you not summon it to surrender?"

"I should do so," Guy replied with a smile.

"Then it had better be so in this case, Sir Guy. You say that you would willingly marry my daughter. I would as willingly give her to you. The difficulty then lies with the maiden herself, and it is but fair to you both that you should yourself manfully ask her decision in the matter."

He went out of the room, and returned in a minute leading Katarina. "Sir Guy has a question to ask you, daughter," he said; "I pray you to answer him frankly." He then led her to a seat, placed her there and left the room.

Guy felt a greater inclination to escape by another door than he had ever felt to fly in the hour of danger, but after a pause he said:

"I will put the question, Katarina, since your father would have me do it, though I know well enough beforehand what the answer will be. I desire above all things to have you for a wife, and would give you a true and loyal affection were you willing that it should be so, but I feel only too well that you do not think of me as I do of you. Still, as it is your father's wish that I should take your answer from your lips, and as, above all things, I would leave it in your hands without any constraint from him, I ask you whether you love me as one should love another before plighting her faith to him?"

"Why do you say that you know what my answer will be, Guy? Would you have had me show that I was ready to drop like a ripe peach into your mouth before you opened it? Why should I not love you? Did you not save my life? Were you not kind and good to me even in the days when I was more like a boy than a girl? Have you not since with my humours? I will answer your question as frankly as my father bade me." She rose now. "Take my hand, Guy, for it is yours. I love and honour you, and could wish for no better or happier lot than to be your wife. Had you asked me six months ago I should have said the same, save that I could not have given you my hand until I had my father's consent."

During the next month Guy spent most of his time at Penshurst getting everything in readiness for its mistress. Lord Eustace advanced him the monies that he was to receive for the ransoms of Count de Valles and the five knights, and the week before the wedding he went up with the Count of Montepone to London, and under his advice bought many rich hangings and pieces of rare furniture to beautify the private apartments. The count laid out a still larger sum of money on Eastern carpets and other luxuries, as well as on dresses and other matters for his daughter. On jewels he spent nothing, having already, he said, "a sufficient store for the wife of a royal duke."

On his return Guy called upon the king at his palace at Winchester, and Henry declared that he himself would ride to Summerley to be present at the wedding.

# At Agincourt

"You stood by me," he said, "in the day of battle, it is but right that I should stand by you on your wedding-day. Her father will, of course, give her away, and it is right that he should do so, seeing that she is no ward of mine; but I will be your best man. I will bring with me but a small train, for I would not inconvenience the Baron of Summerley and his wife, and I will not sleep at the castle; though I do not say that I will not stay to tread a measure with your fair bride."

Two days later a train of waggons was seen approaching Summerley; they were escorted by a body of men-at-arms with two officers of the king. Lord Eustace, in some surprise, rode out to meet them, and was informed that the king had ordered them to pitch a camp near the castle for himself and his knights, and that he intended to tarry there for the night. As soon as the waggons were unloaded the attendants and men-at-arms set to work, and in a short time the royal tent and six smaller ones were erected and fitted with their furniture. Other tents were put up a short distance away for the grooms and attendants. This greatly relieved Lady Margaret, for she had wondered where she could bestow the king and his knights if, at the last moment, he determined to sleep there.

For the next three days the castle was alive with preparations. Oxen and swine were slaughtered, vast quantities of game, geese, and poultry were brought in, two stags from the royal preserves at Winchester were sent over by the king, and the rivers for miles round were netted for fish. At ten o'clock Guy rode in with fifty mounted men, the tenants of Penshurst, Stoneham, and Piverley, and these and all the tenants of Summerley rode out under Lord Eustace and Guy to meet the king. They had gone but a mile when he and his train rode up. He had with him the Earl of Dorset and five of the nobles who had fought at Agincourt and were all personally acquainted with Guy. The church at Summerley was a large one, but it was crowded as it had never been before. The king and his nobles stood on one side of the altar, while Lord Eustace, his wife, Agnes, and Charlie were on the other. Guy's tenants occupied the front seats, while the rest of the church was filled by the tenants of Summerley, their wives and daughters, and the retainers of the castle, among them Long Tom, with his pretty wife beside him. When everything was in order the Count of Montepone entered the church with his daughter, followed by the six prettiest maidens on the Summerley estate.

"In truth, Sir Guy," the king whispered as the bride and her father came up the aisle, "your taste is as good in love as your arms are strong in war, for my eyes never fell on a fairer maid."

After the ceremony there was a great banquet in the hall, while all the tenants, with their wives and families, sat down to long tables spread in the court-yard. After the meal was over and the tables removed, the king and the party in the banqueting-hall went out on the steps and were received with tremendous cheering. Guy first returned thanks for himself and his bride for the welcome that they had given him, and then, to the delight of the people, the king stepped forward.

"Good people," he said, "among whom there are, I know, some who fought stoutly with us at Agincourt, you do well to shout loudly at the marriage of this brave young knight, who was brought up among you, and who has won by his valour great credit, and our royal favour. Methinks that he has won, also, a prize in his eyes even greater than the honours that we have bestowed upon him, and I doubt not that, should occasion occur, he will win yet higher honours in our service."

A great shout of "God bless the king!" went up from the assembly. Then the party returned to the hall, while casks of wine were broached in the court-yard. As Lord Eustace had sent for a party of musicians from Winchester, first some stately dances were performed in the hall, as many as could find room being allowed to come into it to witness them. The king danced the first measure with Katarina, the Earl of Dorset led out Lady Margaret, and Guy danced with Lady Agnes, while the other nobles found partners among the ladies who had come in from the neighbourhood. After a few dances the party adjourned to the court-yard, where games of various kinds, dancing and feasting were kept up until a late hour, when the king and his companions retired to their tents. At an early hour next morning the king and his retinue rode back to Winchester.

Until he signed the marriage contract before going to the church, Guy was altogether ignorant of the dowry that Katarina was to bring, and was astonished at the very large sum of money, besides the long list of jewels, entered in it.

"She will have as much more at my death," the count said quietly; "there is no one else who has the slightest claim upon me."

Consequently, in the course of the wars with France, Guy was able to put a contingent of men-at-arms and archers, far beyond the force his feudal obligations required, in the field. Long Tom was, at his own request, allowed by his lord to exchange his small holding for a larger one at Penshurst, and always led Guy's archers in the wars.

Sir John Aylmer remained at Summerley, refusing Guy's pressing invitation to take up his abode at Penshurst. "No, lad," he said; "Lord Eustace and I have been friends and companions for many years, and Lady Margaret has been very dear to me from her childhood. Both would miss me sorely did I leave them, the more so as Agnes is now away. Moreover, it is best that you and your fair wife should be together also for a time. 'Tis best in all respects. You are but two hours' easy riding from Summerley, and I shall often be over to see you."

Four years after his marriage the king promoted Guy to the rank of Baron of Penshurst, and about the same time the Count of Montepone, who had been for some months in Italy, finding that his enemies at Mantua were still so strong that he was unable to obtain a reversal of the decree of banishment that had been passed against him, returned to Penshurst.

"I have had more than enough of wandering, and would fain settle down here, Guy, if you will give me a chamber for myself, and one for my instruments. I shall need them but little henceforth, but they have become a part of myself and, though no longer for gain, I love to watch the stars, and to ponder on their lessons; and when you ride to the wars I shall be company for Katarina, who has long been used to my society alone, and I promise you that I will no longer employ her as my messenger."

Once established at Penshurst the count employed much of his time in beautifying the castle, spending money freely in adding to the private apartments, and decorating and furnishing them in the Italian style, until they became the wonder and admiration of all who visited them. In time he took upon himself much of the education of Katarina's children, and throughout a long life Guy never ceased to bless the day when he and Dame Margaret were in danger of their lives at the hands of the White Hoods of Paris.

# The End